The New King

Book Two of the
Chronicles of Athan

by

Thos. Pinney

authorHOUSE®

AuthorHouse™
1663 Liberty Drive, Suite 200
Bloomington, IN 47403
www.authorhouse.com
Phone: 1-800-839-8640

First published by AuthorHouse 10/24/2008

ISBN: 978-1-4389-0269-2 (sc)
ISBN: 978-1-4389-0268-5 (hc)

Printed in the United States of America
Bloomington, Indiana

This book is printed on acid-free paper.

Acknowledgements

This book, perhaps more than most, has been a labor of love. I have had many people encourage me in continuing the story of Athan and his friends. I particularly want to thank my expanded Editorial Review Board: Bil Pinney, Ruth Pinney, Ellen Rayner, and my high proof crew, Glen Rector and Richard Pinney.

I was fortunate to have Sandy Roberts once again provide her wonderful illustrations.

Thanks to you all.

Table of Contents

People

Athan –King of Dassaria, formerly known as Chief Athan the bandit and Captain Athan the Guardsman – Protagonist and Hero

The Bear - formerly King Ratimir, and before that, Ratimir the Bandit – A Bad man and a worse king

Talos – A convenient guide, if a strange one – He knew about the inside of the Hold

Myron – A man who knows even more than his cousin Talos about the countryside

Ixon – A good man with horses and women who need rescuing

Sergeant Tenucer – A long serving member of Athan's band; once from Illyria

Prokopios – A fighting sergeant of long service and considerable loyalty

Linus – Another sergeant; from Rodas' band; a big blonde warrior from the far north

Tenucer – Another member of Athan's band; a quick thinking man of good judgment

Spiros – A man who closed a door and opened his future

Ioannis – A member of Athan's old band; one of his better scouts

Giles – A young man who has a hero

Baruch – Another keeper of the baths, he has neither a talent for it nor a choice about it

Cook & Cook's Wife – Just what they sound; the Hold's cooks. They might be slaves, but who cares?

Titania – A big and big hearted slave who tends her laundry

Adara, Cenobia, Evania, & Kepa – Unfortunate lost women, rescued after a fashion

Tito – The Hold's Blacksmith, of a sort

Celeno – A simple housekeeper, or so it might seem

Alesin & Beryl – her plain, but plainly marriageable daughters and assistants

Iason – The band's first aid specialist

Hypnos – A more capable physician

Aeolus – Not a bad guy for an Illyrian cavalryman

Yure the elder and Xenos – Two of Athan's men, left in Lychmidas to recruit, now needed in the Hold

Sergeant Stamitos - A stalwart leader from Athan's bandit days

Beryl - Stamitos' wife, left for a time with her husband in Lychmidas

Aorastus & Amara; Tracy & Cadis; Pontus & Neysa – The same: couples left behind

Abacus – A man who can count and be counted upon

Hali – A fisherman, a boatman, a leader

Stone – A mason of Dassaria

Needles & Neeta – A man whose name describes his job and his new wife

Adem (aka Amphora) & Ana – A wine merchant from town and his wife

Zotikos – The former and would-be future steward of the Hold

Mouse – The little man who knows things as befits a 'natural sneak'

Balasi, Amycus, & Nomiki – The King's Secretary, Personal Valet, and Shield bearer, respectively

Leotychides – A strange man of contradictions

Zoe – An interesting woman more alive than most, but with problems such as her husband

Bukchos – Zoe's husband and erstwhile caravan guard while he waits for better things

Agalia – A simple working girl - really

Egaria – An acquaintance of Ana

Lux – Zoe's faithful companion

Peder – A cousin of Adem and an unsatisfactory agent

Adara – Once a lost woman, now the fierce wife of Ixon, the Master of Horse

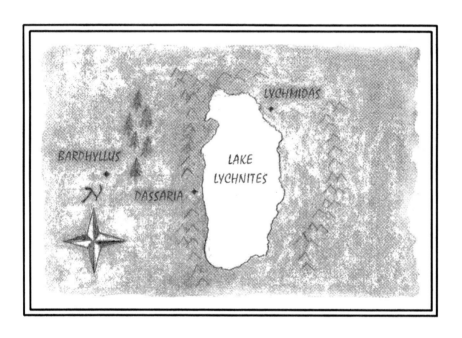

Prolog

The Old King sat at the entrance of a small cave and looked out on a late winter's afternoon wondering about things. Mostly he was wondering just how he had come to be a king in the first place. He had never expected to become a king. He certainly had not been trained for the position; no one could imagine he was qualified to run a kingdom. He had been a hill brigand when he seized his crown. He had been a very successful brigand, but his band consisted of just over two score men, hardly an army. They had not even been trying to conquer a kingdom. They just wanted to take a secure place where they could set up for a while and enjoy the gold they had stolen from the Achaemenid Empire in relative security. Somehow the fortress they had conquered, the Hold, had come with territory attached that made it sort of a kingdom. And since the man who had been in charge of the Hold called himself a king, Athan felt compelled to assume that title as well, and thus Chief Athan became King Athan.

That complete innocence of what was expected of him was probably an advantage, though. It allowed him to try new ideas in his little kingdom. He and his men could start with a clean slate and do things the way that seemed best to them. It had worked, too. Some of those ideas might have been new and untested, but all in all, Athan considered himself to be a pretty good king. Perhaps it was because he had a lot of life experience before he became king, so that his head was not easily turned. Athan was not sure, but he knew he had been over forty years old when he became King of Dassaria. Also King Athan had the advantage of having a long stable reign. How long had be been King? The years tended to run together. It could not have been less than fifty years; a long reign, indeed. As always, he simply did not consider how old he actually was. Such things were not important to him.

Suddenly Athan heard a faint flutter of wings. He caught a glimpse of movement out of the corner of his eye. A raven had just alighted on the evergreen just outside the entrance of his cave. Athan bent down smoothly and picked up a rock, kept to hand for just such situations. With a quick turn he hurled the stone at the raven. It was a good throw; the bird squawked and fell back off the branch. Athan was after it in an instant, springing down and bending to where the bird was flapping on the hard winter ground. Alas, the stone had not made a solid hit. Despite Athan's speed, the raven was able to take to wing and narrowly avoid his grasping hands. Athan skidded on a patch of ice, wheeling his arms frantically to maintain his balance. He almost made it; just as he was coming to a stop, his boot slid off the ice onto the hard ground. Athan sat down with an ignominious thump.

He laughed ruefully and levered himself up, dusting the seat of his voluminous trousers. He took a good look around to make sure no one was watching. There were people in these hills who had already tried to kill him. He dusted some snow out of his thick brown hair where he had brushed against the branches of the tree in his dash after what he had hoped would be his dinner. He was very hungry. He had been very hungry for a long time now. It was too cold to be outside for long without his cloak. He moved rapidly back up to the crevice where he had been spending the long, lonely winter. Athan wished he had someone to talk to; if there were someone to share the time with perhaps he would not be spending so much time thinking about his long, long life. In any case there was not much else to do but think.

Although he had never been arrested, detained, captured, or otherwise held by any human enemy, he was a prisoner. His jailer was invisible; Old Man Winter kept him imprisoned. King Athan of Dassaria could try to leave any time he wanted. But leaving would almost undoubtedly change his current sentence from 'detained until spring arrived' to a life sentence, since his life would be very short if he left his shelter before the snows were gone.

The Old King had suffered the dangerous embarrassment of being ambushed by hill bandits on the outskirts of his own kingdom. He had suffered the loss of at least four of his six companions; the two men at the rear of the little column might or might not have survived. The Old King had spurred his horse out of the killing zone and fled alone up into the hills. The pony he had been riding had been willing enough, carrying him without complaint until she died of the two arrows that had hit her instead of her rider. That left him alone and afoot in a wild and desolate land with enemies behind him and a major winter storm approaching quickly. He had found his current little place of refuge, a snug crevice in the side of a gully, just as the mid-winter storm had finally hit with full fury. It was fortunate that the old man had been able to bring in his clothing, bedding, and what little gear he had into the crevice in the rocks before the storm dumped the heavy snows that had effectively trapped him ever since.

He had brought some provisions into his refuge as well. There had initially been perhaps enough food for ten days. He had long ago consumed those provisions; the oats he had with him for his dead pony had been devoured; even the leather on his saddle had been cut up and boiled as 'saddle soup'. He was not sure just how long he had been in his lair; it could not have been less than two months. Now his reserves of body fat were almost gone. All he could do was wait and conserve the strength he had left.

The old man had done a lot of thinking during his enforced idleness. Mostly he had thought about his long life. He had once been just Athan, son of Medius, conventionally raised and an ordinary soldier in the Epirian Guards. His early aspirations did not envision anything higher than achieving the rank of Sergeant. Then his girlfriend, Erinsys, had disappeared. He and his comrade and mentor Captain Thaddeus had rescued her from a very disreputable house. Not only did that result in Athan marrying Erinsys, it also introduced the two men to Persis, the most influential hetaira in all Epiria. Hetaira, she-companions, knew all the upper-class men; all of the men who could afford her.

Persis knew a good thing when she saw it, and she quickly decided that brave Thaddeus was a very good thing, indeed.

With the help of Thaddeus and the beautiful hetaera, who became Thaddeus' lifelong companion, Athan was able to set his sights higher - he became Captain Athan of the guards. He would have been quite content to remain as a captain for the rest of his life, raising his children with his rather prickly wife, Erinsys, but he suffered a double disaster. First, he was on the losing side of a battle. And he lost that battle when his wife, youngest daughter and only son were in the camp that was overrun by the victorious enemy. His only son, Jason, died defending, and being defended by, their teenaged servant girl, Karen. His wife and youngest daughter had simply disappeared. Athan and a remnant of his command had escaped the carnage and fled to the hills.

That disastrous loss, called Achilles' Debacle after the unfortunate General Achilles who led the Epirian army into the catastrophic defeat, immediately led to the fall of the city of Epiria itself. It was pillaged by the victorious Dorian army which had been treacherously assisted by some other city states in the region of Epirus. For a long time, Athan thought that his two remaining daughters, Persephone and Dionme, who had been left behind in the city with Thaddeus and Persis, had been killed along with his two friends when the city had fallen.

In despair, Athan had taken the survivors of the battle and reformed those remnants into a band of hill brigands that raided the Dorian patrols and caravans. It was one of those raids that changed Athan's life once again. He had dared to attack the caravan of Azziz, the mysterious sorcerer priest. It was said Azziz could not be harmed by any edged weapon. He attacked the strongly defended caravan in large part because he discovered this sorcerer priest had children from Epiria in his camp, and he hoped that perhaps his daughters might be there. It had been a desperate fight, ending only when Athan knocked Azziz in the head with a stout oaken club, breaking his skull. Though he and his men were victorious, Athan had not found his family among the captives. His men took a great deal of plunder from Azziz' caravan that day, including jewels, beautiful dancing girls, rich cloth, and precious metals. Yet there were two things Athan took from dead sorcerer priest's body that he came to realize were of far greater value than all the other booty in Azziz' caravan combined.

Athan fingered the stiff leather vest he wore. It was an unusual item of clothing for that time and place. Athan often wore it under his outer tunic to conceal the fact that he almost always had it on when he left his Hold. Ever since the day he put it on, through all the murderous attacks, skirmishes, and outright battles he had fought, he had never received a cut while he was wearing the vest. He had been thoroughly thumped on several occasions; his arm had been broken by a heavy stroke on his shield; he had cut himself while shaving or peeling a bit of fruit, yet no enemy had drawn his blood while Athan had that red leather vest on. Perhaps it was because, despite having lived a very long and active life, Athan had not really been in all that many fights. Perhaps it was because Athan had always believed in wearing the best armor he could afford, and King Athan of Dassaria could afford the best. Perhaps it was because the vest itself seemed oddly resistant to blades. On two memorable occasions, Athan knew the vest had withstood powerful thrusts from daggers that should have gone right through simple leather. Or, perhaps the vest and its wearer were just lucky. Athan had spent a lot of time wondering about that strange red vest. He was even willing to credit the story that Azziz had put an enchantment on the vest, protecting the one who wore it from edged weapons and arrows. Athan was not sure he believed that; he certainly never relied upon it for supernatural protection. After all, it had not kept Azziz from having his skull caved in. Athan had learned of the vest's reputed powers and that had been the reason carried a long club when he attacked Azziz' caravan. Athan did feel more secure when he was wearing the vest. After all, a man can't be too careful in some things. Athan liked his 'lucky old red vest.'

The other item he had taken from the body of the defeated sorcerer priest was worn around Athan's neck. He took it out and held it up to the thin winter sun. His feelings about it, unlike those for his vest, were mixed. It was a crystal talisman, worn on a thin chain of some strange metal. About the size of his little fingernail, it was cut symmetrically with eight facets; two four sided pyramids base to base. A sturdy-looking clasp at the top of the crystal was made of the same material as the chain.

The crystal did not seem to do anything; it never had, other than making him a bit nauseated the first time he had put it on. There must have been something to the little gem, however. Ever since he began to wear it, Athan had been blessed with unusually good health, but that was not what was so eerie about the talisman. It was hard to tell just how old Athan was just by looking at him. He could have been a hard-used man in his early thirties or a well-preserved one in his late forties. His hair was still brown and thick, his eyes sharp, and he had all his teeth. His teeth were the most unsettling thing. Athan was on his fifth set. It always embarrassed him when he lost his teeth and got a brand new set, like some adolescent.

Like many others in that time and place he did know exactly how old he was, only that he was very old indeed. It was not natural for a man to remain active and hale for so long. Athan was not certain, but he strongly suspected that the crystal he wore around his neck had something to do with this unusual phenomenon. However, his talisman had let him down when he needed it most. At this moment, Athan was not sure if the thing was a blessing or a curse.

Athan had always considered himself an honorable and more or less honest man. It was true that he had been a hill brigand for almost ten years, but there had been extenuating circumstances. And yet he had stolen his four most important possessions. First, Athan had taken the leather vest and crystal amulet from the dead body of a man he had killed. Years later, he had established his wealth by stealing dozens of talents of gold from the tribute the conquered province of Doria intended for the Achaemendian Empire. And finally, King Athan had essentially stolen his kingdom.

At the time it had all seemed so inevitable. He had been persuaded by his lieutenant and closest friend, Simeon, to steal the golden tribute so that they could quit their tenuous lifestyles as hill bandits and retire. Athan had known the risks of the theft of the tribute. He was aware that the Satrap who was responsible for the safe delivery of the treasure would do everything in his considerable power to avenge such a humiliating theft right from under his nose. Or he would die trying. Still, they had successfully purloined the gold and made good their escape, though it had been a close-run thing.

It had also been inevitable that when the Empire invaded Macedonia where the band was living a version of 'the sweet life' they must flee over the mountains into the west. They had not really had a plan; they were simply moving out ahead of the invaders. The men in Athan's band had a pretty good idea that the Empire had not forgotten them. The Satrap who had lost his tribute would certainly be looking for them. So they headed west to put a mountain range between themselves and the Empire, before winter closed the passes.

Rodas, who had replaced Simeon as his new lieutenant, was the one who thought Athan should become a king. He came up with the idea of setting up in a quiet little corner of the hills with Athan promoting himself from Bandit Chieftain to local despot. And it had also seemed just inevitable that, when the men in his band learned of a small bandit kingdom having a succession crisis they should try to take advantage of an unexpected opportunity.

The sad little region called Dassaria had been inflicted with a vicious Robber-King for or a dozen years. His followers lived by brutalizing and extorting money from the people who lived in the town of Dassaria and the surrounding villages, hamlets and independent farmsteads in the region. This Robber-King, who styled himself as King Ratimir but was almost universally referred to as the Bear, resided in a strong little fortress he had built called the Hold. This Hold sat on a hill overlooking the crossroads where the poor town of Dassaria managed to exist.

One of Athan's guides, a man called Talos, had learned that the Bear had been stricken down by a stroke. As was usually the case when a strongman rules, there was no successor. The Bear viewed future successors as present threats; he knew how to deal with threats to his authority. Thus, anyone who might have stepped in to take charge once the Bear became infirm had been already been eliminated. Talos' cousin, Myron, had discovered that the Bear's leading henchman had sent a message to a neighboring kingdom, asking the nearby kingdom of Bardhyllus to send troops to come and help 'stabilize the situation.' The Bear's men were not too popular with the locals, and his men feared that with their leader dead there would be a popular rising against him.

Athan had seen the opportunity at once. The band made the four-day trip from the city of Lychmidas to Dassaria in just two and one-half days. Athan remembered how he had stood alone on a hill the night before they entered Dassaria, wondering if he dared to take his band - men who were his closest comrades -into such a desperate venture. He smiled to himself when he realized that the hill where he had stood that night was not all that far away from where now was taking shelter from the winter weather.

Rodas had gone up to the Hold's gates first with a handful of men to try to talk his way into the Hold; claiming he was the advance for the expected reinforcements from the King of Bardhyllus. He had done it - he had done it brilliantly. The gates were open wide for Athan and the rest of his men. Athan led his entire band right in to attack the garrison. It had been a very good thing that none of them realized just how strong the Hold was, or just how outnumbered they were by the garrison. Athan shivered despite himself. Attacking the Hold with just two score men was beyond merely rash. Perhaps that was why it had been successful; that, and the fact that the Bear's men had not been in a real fight against other soldiers in a long time. They had grown complacent and they had no strong leaders. Before they could organize and arm themselves, Athan and his men had overwhelmed the defenders, killing many and ejecting the rest from the Hold.

The Bear had been the last to go. Even partially paralyzed, he was a formidable man, huge and dominating. Athan had taken the crown off his head and had him put out into the cold rain with the only three people who had remained with him: a sneaky catamite; the henchman who had sent for Buttarian cavalry; and a faithful woman of an indeterminate age and relationship to the deposed king.

'That is how it started', thought Athan. Some kings were born to their station. Some gained their rank by intrigue and manipulation. Athan had simply seized the power base of the existing King, killed or scattered his followers, and threw him out of what had once been his own castle. There had been no coronation, no cheering multitudes, just lots of work to perform.

"It's a good thing I didn't know what a king was supposed to do before I became one, or I would have never taken on the job." Athan spoke aloud. His own voice startled him.

It was getting dark; there was nothing left to see outside. The man who had become King of Dassaria drew back into the sheltering rock. He would drink some water, build up his fire and lay back down for the night. As he did these things his mind went back to those days when he first started learning how to be a king.

It began to rain outside of the entrance to the little cave where he had been holed up all that winter. Athan remembered that it had been a day much like this when he had led his band up to the Hold. It had been autumn, not early spring, but it had been cold, gray and raining just like it was now.

Chapter One – House Keeping

The man once known as Ratimir the Bandit, then King Ratimir, and now just the Bear, was ushered out the front gate of what had an hour before been his home, seat of government, his strong place of refuge, his Hold. He had been undisputed Lord of over a hundred fighting men and dozens of slaves and servants. Now his only companions were one old woman, one worthless catamite, and a single henchman of doubtful ability and dubious loyalty. The big gate closed behind the four miserable people with a soft inexorable thud. A few moments later, the Bear was down to two attendants, as the boy skipped off downhill toward Dassaria. Behind them, men closed and barred the gates of the Hold, leaving them outside in the cold, rainy night. Athan turned and took a deep breath. He had stuffed the bits of golden jewelry he had taken off the former King Ratimir into his purse without thinking, but he had kept what had been the Bear's crown in his left hand. Athan looked down at it. Unlike much of the stuff the Bear had possessed, this piece was simple, a flat gold band a bit wider than his finger. Except for three small prongs that jutted up from the circle it almost looked like an oversized ring. Athan picked off a few strands of coarse black hair left from where he had taken it off the former king's head. It did not look as though it would be big enough to fit around the Bear's massive head. Seemingly by their own volition, his hands took the narrow crown and lifted it to his head. The metal seemed to contract somehow as he put it on. The crown fitted Athan perfectly. For a moment he felt a little silly wearing the thing. It would be poor protection from the rain. On the other hand, his head was already wet. A second, stronger feeling come over him; putting on the crown was the right thing to do. If he was going to be a king he needed to start acting like a king. Athan was not sure how a king was supposed to act, but wearing a crown seemed to be a good start.

There was a pause. Athan looked back into the place he had just taken. Capturing a fortress was a new experience for him. During his years as a hill bandit, he had always taken what he wanted and then gone back into the hills. Now he hesitated, unsure of what to do next.

Athan looked around himself. He was standing in the archway of the front entrance of the Hold. It was cold and wet. There was a smell of horses. The Hold's stables were to the left and right of the arched tunnel that led from the main gates into the central courtyard. He could see men moving around in the courtyard at the open end of the passage. They were running to get out of the rain. That normal activity seemed somehow strange after the frantic activity of the recently won battle. He could feel the fatigue deep in his bones. He had not taken any wounds and was not bleeding, however he was battered and sore.

The handful of men who had come with him to send off the Bear looked at him, waiting for orders. That helped steady him. He might not know how to be a king, but he did know how to lead men. He started walking back toward the courtyard, giving orders as he walked.

Men were assigned to watches in all four bastions; sentries were designated with orders to walk the walls and let themselves be seen. There was a quick muster of the men. All were accounted for, including those who were with Sergeant Prokopios, who was still clearing the south side of the Hold of any remaining knots of resistance. Two of Athan's men were dead and three wounded seriously enough to be out of action. The wounded were being tended on the second level of the north east bastion by Iason, the band's acting medic. Other men were detailed into teams to conduct thorough searches of every room, looking for anyone who remained in hiding. Any members of the garrison so discovered were to be disarmed, secured, and brought to the lower level of the south east bastion, where they would be placed under guard. Ixon was to take inventory and see to the care of, the horses.

There were suddenly cries of 'Fire!' Smoke was coming from a room in the upper level of the north wall. Men were sent to deal with this danger and quickly extinguished the blaze before it could spread. During all this, Prokopios showed up with his little squad and a handful of prisoners. He was assigned to complete the search of the lower level of the north side of the Hold.

Thus began what many of the men would remember as the strangest night of their lives. Many commented that the whole thing seemed more like a dream than reality. There were certainly many very odd things occurring in the Hold that night.

The first odd thing happened as soon as Athan cleared the entrance tunnel and reentered the courtyard. Still giving orders in a rapid-fire sequence, he was stopped by a chubby bald man in a white tunic standing bare headed under the overhang. He was clean shaven with a ruddy complexion. His hands were on his hips and he was clutching a long wooden spoon in his right hand. His attitude was just short of truculent. Athan had been in the thick of the fighting and was literally covered in blood. Athan's sanguinary appearance did not appear to faze the man in the white tunic in the slightest.

"So," he asked Athan, "are you in charge now?"

Astonished, Athan stopped and looked at him. That apparently was confirmation enough for the man. "So, you want me to feed the men now, or what?"

This man, his real name was Aeolus, but he was called 'Cook' by one and all, was not about to let a little thing like the invasion and conquest of the Hold upset his kitchen. Cook had been in the Hold for almost 10 years. Originally he had been a slave, though whoever had once owned him lost track of him. Cook had gradually come to be in charge of all meals in the Hold. He was assisted by his wife, Xipity, who was called 'Cook's Wife' by everyone except Cook himself, who referred to her as 'Wife". Between them they ran the kitchen with a set of iron fists. If the slaves who helped in the kitchen were afraid of Cook (and generally they were) they lived in terror of Cook's Wife. She was actually larger than he was and much more demanding. The two of them provided meals of their choosing on their schedule. The only reason they were allowed such autonomy was that they were very good at what they did. The food was well prepared, wholesome, and always there when they said it would be. But their autonomy (which they both cherished) was dependant on their performance. Cook's Wife was of an age where she knew she was unlikely to ever have children, so her position was correspondingly more important to her. Neither of them could imagine doing anything else but providing food for the men of the Hold's garrison, whoever they might be. So, although they and their kitchen staff had taken shelter when the fighting erupted, as soon as things had calmed down, Cook decided that, since the food was prepared, he had better let the new boss know who was in charge of the kitchen. After a decade under the Bear, he had little fear of whoever might be in charge.

Athan was completely taken aback. The situation had a surreal quality. It was as though an army assaulting the breach in a city wall suddenly had to make way for workers white-washing around the new opening. But at the mention of food he was suddenly ravenous.

"What are we having?" he asked.

Cook shrugged, "Chickpeas, with the kid we slaughtered this morning, olives and maza."

Maza was the flat round bread that was part of almost every evening meal.

More orders came from Athan; men not otherwise assigned were to go eat and then report back for further duties.

"Make sure this man and his staff sample the meal first," Athan told Myron, who was waiting at hand.

Cook looked offended at the implication that he would poison the Hold's conquerors.

"I do not know you yet," Athan explained with a hint of apology.

"Well, we don't normally eat with the men; however we will make an exception under the circumstances. Will your men be coming in by shift?" A nod from Athan, "Well, we will serve for an extra hour then. But do not expect us to feed like this every day."

And grumbling, he shuffled away, calling out to several men and women who stood peeking out from doorways near the kitchen.

Athan and his men stood watching him go in complete astonishment. Athan stopped Myron, who was already heading for his dinner. The man had a bandage over a cut on his forearm. "Did you say there were baths in this place?"

Athan, still accompanied by Giles, the young man who had remained by his side for the worst of the fighting, was directed over toward the middle of the north wall. There, next to the smithy, its door ajar, was a rather nice bath. There were two sides to the bath, Athan went into the smaller. To his surprise and delight he found a tub of warm water with strigils and oils already laid out. A servant appeared from somewhere. He was obviously the attendant and had seen them come into the baths. Smiling and bowing he introduced himself as Baruch. When Athan threw him a sudden glance he cringed.

"Where are you from Baruch?"

"Illyria, my lord; I served a man there who was traveling and, umm, made the brief acquaintance of the Bea… ummm… the King. Ah, sir, is the King still with us?

"No, Baruch, he is gone. I am in charge now. I once knew a man of the same name as you who kept a bathhouse, some years ago."

"This is my first service in a bath, sire, nevertheless, I will do my best to serve you well. This used to be for the Bear himself, but lately Borna has been using it with the old master so sick and all." Baruch bustled about lighting lamps and bringing out warm cloths. "We get the hot water from a tub that is next to the forge on the other side of that wall; very convenient."

Baruch was ordered off to bring a fresh tunic while Athan washed the blood and gore off his body and out of his hair. His whole body ached, especially his ribs, where his vest had stopped a dagger meant for his heart, and his bloody tunic was slashed and torn. For all that, there was not a single scratch on him.

"What is that, sire?" asked Giles, pointing toward the crystal around Athan's neck. Athan had removed the leather bag holding his flint and tinder that normally obscured the talisman.

"Just a luck piece given to me by an old lover," lied Athan, "hand me that strigil."

By the time Athan had scraped his body clean Baruch was back with warm (!) towels and a clean tunic. Leaving his old bloody clothes lying on the floor, Athan donned the new tunic, put on his vest, which showed no damage from resisting strenuous efforts to punch through it, took his cloak, still stiff with dried blood, stepped into his boots, and went out to his waiting dinner and his new responsibilities.

He did not make it across the courtyard before the first of his new responsibilities hit him. It was in the form of Sergeant Linus, of all people, who stood before him looking distinctly odd. Linus was a barbarian, that is, a foreigner, from the far north. He was a big man with light skin and blond hair, now going a bit gray, which he wore long. He shaved his cheeks but left a long set of mustaches. He face was scarred, and tended to go red whenever he was drunk, angry or exerted himself. All this gave him an alien and therefore frightening air. In fact, Athan had found he was a good, conscientious sergeant, phlegmatic and unflappable.

"Sir," he began, "I think you should see this."

Not all the rooms in the Hold had been inspected. Some had merely had a cursory glance by men looking for enemies. One with a thick reinforced door with a lock was without doubt the treasure room. Sergeant Prokopios had put that room off limits until Chief Athan (as Prokopios called him) had time to get to it. Doors barred from the outside had been bypassed in the first sweep because anyone inside those doors could not get out. Now the men were investigating what was behind these doors as well. What Linus and his comrades found behind one of these barred doors troubled them enough that he sought guidance from his old chief Rodas, who immediately sent him to ask the new king.

Athan followed Linus down the north wall to the far end of the Hold, between the northeast bastion and the armory. Two men stood uncertainly in the entrance of a room, standing half in and half out of the ongoing drizzle, as though they could not decide which was worse, the cold rain, or what was inside the room.

Athan pushed them inside and stepped into a small stone-floored space lit by a single lamp, high on the wall. His first thought was that the men were avoiding the smell, for the stench in the room was vile; then he saw the five figures in the room.

The men that Athan had led up to take this fort were hard men. They had seen death, rape, murder; some had committed terrible crimes. But there was something eerie about the unfortunate women, for that was what they were, that unsettled even the toughest trooper. All were more or less wrapped in stinking rags. One was cringing in a corner, two sat rocking wordlessly against the back wall, one was lying motionless in the center of the floor and one was standing with hopeless defiance on the far wall, fury visible on her twisted features even in the dim light.

Athan moved cautiously into the dim stinking space and nudged the covered shape on the floor.

"Yes! She's dead! I told you to quit screwing her! Now she's dead like the others! Like we'll be! Are you going to keep doing it to her now she is dead?"

Athan recoiled not just from the shock of the corpse, or the vile curses that spouted from the mouth of the woman standing against the wall, but from the hatred and rage that projected from her in almost visible waves. The poor wretch huddled in the corner looked up at him in abject terror and tried impossibly to shrink further away. The other two women just continued their rocking, looking at nothing at all.

Recovering himself Athan paused by the door and tried to interrupt the flood of curses from the standing woman. "We have come to rescue you," he started.

"I know you men, you're interested in one thing," the harridan shrieked at him lifting up a flap of cloth that covered her loins and waving it at him, exposing herself. A further fusillade of curses and abuse followed. Athan withdrew in confusion.

"What do you want to do with them?" asked Linus anxiously. The encounter had taken them completely aback. A rush of armed enemies they could handle. Give them a roomful of treasure and they would know just what to do. But when you rescue female captives, there are expectations, and the scene in that stinking space met none of them. These were no grateful maidens eager to reward their rescuers; in that room was misery, madness, and death.

"I think we should get a woman to help," suggested Athan who was also out of his depth in this situation. "Send for Cook's Wife." She was the only woman he had heard was within the Hold, and that report had been second-hand. "Meanwhile get that body out of there and put it in the courtyard."

This reminded him of some of the other things that needed to be done. Linus' men endured a short trip into that den of horror, emerging dragging the dead woman, closely pursued by the Fury who stood in the doorway making vile accusations to the two men carrying out the thin body. They learned that Cook's Wife provided the women with their rations and fresh water twice a day anyway, so Athan enjoined her to try to get across to the former captives that the Hold was under new and kinder management and that they would be free to leave.

Meanwhile Athan had found his lieutenant, Rodas and Sergeant Prokopios eating with some of the men. He issued more orders to them to have some of the prisoners bring the bodies of the defenders out into the courtyard. Any remaining slaves or servants they found inside the hold were to clean up the blood off the floors and walls. Arrangements were discussed and the men were ordered to secure the prisoners in a room under guard after they had finished taking care of the remains of their former comrades. The shifts for men standing watches were reviewed and confirmed. Care of the wounded, both friend and enemy, was established. While they talked, Athan stuffed food in his mouth with the speed of an old campaigner who is more concerned about refueling his body than enjoying a meal. Even so he was aware that the fare, chickpeas with a bit of meat, he was shoveling into his mouth was very good. He heard more shrieks and curses from the northeast corner while this was going on, but he paid them no mind until Cook's Wife returned, shaking her head.

"Mad harpy," she grumbled.

Apparently she had had no better success in getting the message through to the abused women that they had been rescued than the men had. Cook's Wife was unsympathetic, even though she admitted the women had received exceptionally brutal treatment at the hands of the Bear's men. They were the last of a long list of women who had been held in that room over the years, kept for the carnal pleasure of the garrison. In the past, the women had been released from that dreadful service after a month or two. Some had established more or less permanent relationship with a man from the garrison, others were just pushed out of the gate to fend for themselves, and some simply died.

But lately things had gotten worse for the unfortunate souls caught in that hellhole. As discipline slackened, the men became more brazen about carrying off women and bringing them back to the Hold. Adara, the angry one, and Cenobia, the frightened one, had both been captured in raids on passing caravans. Evania was a hostage, exchanged for one of the Bear's people. She was supposedly to be held safe, but when she was raped by one of his men, the Bear decided to simply keep her, sacrificing one of his cousins who had been sent as an equivalent hostage. Kepa, the oldest woman, both in age and time in the room, was brought to the Hold from her farmstead after her husband objected to her rape by a passing group of the Bear's men. Her husband and his brother's family had been murdered in front of her and her young children left behind wailing with no adults to care for them. After a time in the room she had quit noticing anything at all. She was now very thin. Cook's wife thought she would die soon like the one they had just carried out.

"They quit wanting to live," she explained. Then she picked up on the dangerous mood of the men she was addressing and hurried back to her pots and pans.

"We need a better woman to help with this," said Athan, wondering what he could do for those poor wretches. No one was willing to endure Adara's abuse; the very sight of any man seemed to set her off on a screaming frenzy. Orders were passed to find a more suitable ambassadress than Cook's Wife. Most of the women who could be found had been companions of members of the former garrison. These fell into two categories; one group consisted of nasty, abusive slatterns who were quickly expelled out the front gate. Other women who had once been supported by men now dead or driven from the Hold were now urgently on the make for a new man. They were far too busy auditioning with various members of the band seeking the role of one of the victor's 'new woman', to be bothered trying to deal with some crazy women.

After a time, a female candidate was located; Titania was brought forward, a hulking middle aged female slave even larger than Cook's Wife. Titania was the Hold's current laundress. Her age, appearance, and attitude had kept her from being abused, and she had the reputation of being a good-hearted woman. Unfortunately Athan discovered upon talking with her that, though she did appear kind, she was also somewhat stupid; this was not the sensitive and insightful person needed to calm the furious Adara, reassure the terrified Cenobia and bring the other two pitiful women back to something resembling a normal life.

The four unfortunate women were only one of a horde of urgent issues that confronted Athan that night. He was very grateful that Cook had remained on station to feed his troops; at least the problem of feeding his men was resolved. Most of the people who were needed to run such a place had either fled or hidden themselves away.

As his men cleared the detritus of battle and items left behind in subsequent hasty evacuation from the structure, they made finds of varying value. Though Athan's men were supposed to surrender all valuables to a common pool where it could be divided equally among the band at a later time, everyone kept back items that were either valuable, such as money and jewelry, or were especially desirable, such as footgear, armor, weapons, and women. As Athan's men investigated the Hold they found more and more people tucked away. A few were members of the garrison, either hiding for fear of a massacre, or in one case, too drunk to notice the place had fallen. There were noncombatants in the Hold as well, including, of course, women. For every man who discovered a woman who was looking for a new protector to replace the one she had just lost, there was another man who found instead a frightened old woman, or a young stable hand fearing he would be raped or eaten or both.

Though there were a number of people discovered in the Hold, most were mere hangers-on; there had not been a large staff of people to take care such a large structure. This probably explained the run-down appearance of the place. Apparently, a portion of the people who worked in the Hold lived down in the town and walked up to work each morning.

Athan had to know just what it was he and him men had just captured, especially if they intended to be here all winter, and perhaps longer. He set men to inventorying everything from firewood, (there was plenty), weapons (there was more than plenty, including dozens of fine bows and many hundred arrows), food (the larders were full), lamp oil (no one seemed to know), and on and on. Sleeping arrangements needed to be established. Where would the men sleep so they could be found for their watches or if there was an alarm to repel an attack? How would the alarm be given? The treasure room had been identified early. It was the only room with a lock, located immediately next to the sick room on the first level where the Bear had his final lair. Athan put off opening that door until things had settled down, just as he put the Bear's quarters off limits. Best if he explored that foul place himself in the light of day. At least it had finally quit raining, although the wind was still gusty and it had gotten colder.

He had just turned to discuss the status of the livestock with Ixon when they became aware of a disturbance in the back of the courtyard where the garrison's dead were being stacked. The madwoman, Adara, was crouching over one of the corpses lined up in the courtyard. She was waving a knife in the direction of two of his men who were trying to get her away from the bodies. Athan and Ixon walked over, joining several others in approaching the scene. The weirdness of the night was increasing. The woman, looking out from her room, had seen the growing rows of the bodies of her former tormenters had somehow found a knife. She had waited until no one was near the two rows of dead men, and then begun to mutilate their bodies; specifically she had castrated three of the corpses. Now she was working her way down the line and she was not about to let anyone stop her.

Cursing and threatening, she kept her eyes on the two men who tried to dissuade her while she fumbled with the tunic of the next corpse in line. The dead man had not been wearing small clothes; Adara triumphantly grabbed the corpse's male member and hacked it off, then waved it at the men watching her. They all winced and turned away.

"Captain, you've got to stop her," implored one of the men.

It was not clear just to whom Adara was talking, but she kept up an almost continuous stream of invective, interspersed with comments such as 'How do you like that?' 'Missing something, Gojslav?' and 'Won't use that any more, will you!' Her outbursts were punctuated by wild laughter.

"She is mad," said Athan with dismay.

"No," replied Ixon, "I think she is just angry; really, really, angry."

Athan looked at his unofficial 'master of the horse.' The two men looked much the same; Athan a bit taller, Ixon had darker hair, but their build was the same, and ever since their bacchanal days in Pella, Ixon had begun to shave his beard and wear his hair in the same style as Athan. Though Athan was more than ten years older than the new manager of the horses, they looked enough alike to have been brothers.

"I have an idea," he told Athan, "I will be right back. Don't do anything until I return."

Athan took that as a respectful suggestion which he chose to accept. The gods knew he did not have any ideas. So when some of the men approached the woman with the butt ends of their spears intending to bludgeon her, he stopped them.

"What do we do with the rest of the dead'uns?" asked Spiros. "What she is doing just ain't right. Besides, I ain't getting anywhere near her." In the wildly flickering light from the torches and lamps, Adara was the very image of a Fury. Her twisted expression, battered face, and wild hair and tattered attire were all accentuated by the weird setting. Athan felt the hair on the back of his neck rise. Still carefully watching him, she slid over to the next body in line and lifted his tunic. Her expression was watchful and less manic now.

From the corner of his eye Athan saw Ixon returning from his stables in the front of the Hold. Even as he caught sight of him Ixon was slowing to a casual saunter. He caught Athan's eye and made a slight gesture for him to move away. Ixon continued his slow approach to the end of the line of dead men. Adara was finishing her work on the third one from the end of the line. Seeing Ixon she hissed and brandished her bloody knife at him. Corpses do not bleed like living men, but there was blood enough on the knife, her rags, hands, and smeared on her face. Ixon noted that there were tracks of tears in the bloodstains on her face; good.

As Adara crouched over the corpse Ixon casually tossed a metal implement onto the belly of the next man in line. Her eyes followed the movement but snapped back to watch him. All the other watching men had stepped back from the lines of the dead.

"Try that," he told her in a conversational tone. "Be careful, it is very sharp."

"What is it?" she asked her eyes darting again to the object on the dead man's stomach.

"A gelding knife; we use them on fractious horses. It should work a little better."

With a chuckling laugh she moved over and snatched up the curved blade. Then she threatened him with both knives. He stood with his arms crossed watching her, seemingly perfectly relaxed, just a man having a conversation with a woman. Dropping the dagger she had been using she shifted the gelding knife to her right hand and squatting beside the remains of a young man, scarcely more than a boy, and began sawing away.

"Does that help?" asked Ixon. There was nothing beyond a casual question in his voice.

"They made me dirty," she replied keeping her head down. Even though the gelding knife was a sharp tool designed for the purpose, she seemed to be having trouble completing her self-imposed task. "They made me so dirty. I am so dirty. No one will ever love me. I am too dirty." All this delivered in a low tone.

"You know," continued Ixon conversationally, "when I was a little boy my mother found me once playing with my dog. It was a hot day and we found a big soft wallow where the horses had been. When she found us I was so covered in mud and horse dung they say all you could see of me was my eyes and teeth. But she cleaned me up. Boy did she clean me up! I can still remember! The thing is, even when I was as dirty as a boy can be, she still loved me, even though I was dirty."

"They made me dirty inside," Adara mumbled her head down. "It is not where you can wash it off." The comment was still in the low monotone, but Ixon noticed she was now replying to him, not just ranting. So he squatted down and talked quietly with her for a while. She left the bodies alone, though she continued to keep her head down and crouch over the next man in line. Ixon could feel the cold beginning to bite. He could tell she was feeling the cold as well, or at least her body was beginning to shiver.

"How about a nice hot bath?" he suggested, "That way we could start to get you cleaned up." There was a long pause and then she turned her head and looked into his eyes.

"All right."

Ixon stood and moving slowly and carefully approached Athan, who was waiting over by the kitchens. He explained that the women should be bathed and that it might be best if no men were present. So Titania was again summoned to help transport the women from their place of imprisonment down the wall to the baths. Baruch prepared the baths and then was hustled out. Titania took Adara's arm and led her toward the door where they had been imprisoned. Adara baulked at the entrance so Ixon remained outside talking quietly to her while Titania went inside and came out holding a cringing Cenobia. The two women clung to Titania until they disappeared into the baths. Two of the band entered the room and came out carrying Evania and Kepa, who continued to be totally unresponsive.

While the women were being bathed by Titania, Cook's Wife was summoned and directed to provide hot food to them in the baths. She objected. This was a mistake. Cook's Wife was frog-marched over to the kitchen by an angry Rodas who had been watching the proceedings. There Rodas instructed Cook and his wife in proper etiquette and how to respond to orders. For a good-natured man, he could be very persuasive; frighteningly so. An old slave, a woman of almost 50 years named Phila, was found and sent in to help Titania in the baths.

Once the unfortunate women had been cleaned, there was a problem of where to let them sleep. It was out of the question to put them back in their old room; in fact Adara and Cenobia refused to enter any room. Eventually, Ixon came to the rescue again. Talking to the two women who would respond to him, he was able to worm out of them that they liked horses. So he cleared out a stall in the far corner of the stables, next to the donkeys. The friendly animals watched as Titania and Ixon piled on loads of fresh hay, and arranged blankets on top of the hay and then over the women. Phila was prevailed upon to remain with them for the night, calming Adar and Cenobia. Evania and Kepa continued totally unresponsive, though Evania did grip the blanket and pull it up to her chin. As sleeping quarters it left much to be desired; it was cold and drafty, there could be no fire in a stable, there were few lamps, and it smelled like, well, a stable. Still, the donkeys were quiet and kind, the sweet straw was piled high, the blankets were thick, and five women made enough body heat to keep them warm. Best of all for the first time in a long time they had a small measure of security. Soon enough, they were asleep.

While the women were in the bath, Pirro came up to Athan. Pirro had been detailed to help get the prisoners and slaves to bring out the dead to the courtyard. This unpleasant job had been made worse by the episode of the mad woman. Athan gave him new orders.

"Pirro, I saw some carts in the stables." The red head nodded mutely. "Have some men load the bodies onto the carts and push them out the gate."

"Um, Chief, what do we do with them once they are outside the gates?"

"Carry them a ways down and stack them out there. We'll figure out what to do with them tomorrow. I just want them out of the Hold. Keep our dead here. We will have funerals for them as soon as we can arrange something."

"Um, Boss," said Pirro using the familiar expression of a junior addressing a superior. "What do we do about those?" he indicated one of the body parts severed by Adara.

"Use a shovel," said Athan as he walked away.

As a new king, he certainly had to make some strange decisions.

In the fourth hour of the night, Athan called a council of war with his remaining staff. These meetings with his senior officers might have been more properly called staff meetings, but traditionally they were referred to as councils of war, even when the meeting had nothing to do with fighting. In that time and place it was common for men under arms to speak their mind. Athan, like most of his contemporaries, encouraged this frankness, especially in meetings like the one he called at the very beginning of his reign as King of Dassaria. It did not occur to any of them that running a kingdom would be different than running a band of fighting men. This was perhaps fortunate, because they really weren't running a kingdom yet.

There were seven men in that first council. In addition to his second in command, Rodas, Athan's newly designated shield-bearer, Giles, and the two sergeants who had survived the battle, Prokopios, and Linus were in attendance. Athan had also asked the two cousins, Myron and Talos to be there as well. Even though they had not been in either Athan's or Rodas' band, they had participated in recent councils for their local knowledge, and they had both fought bravely in the assault on the Hold. In particular, it had been Talos who noticed that the garrison's armory was still closed; the defender's heavy weapons and armor had been locked up where it was not available to the off-duty fighters inside the fort. Talos had forced his attention on Athan, who had managed to get to the armory with a handful of men and take possession of it before the rest of the garrison could reach it. With the armory in the hands of Athan's men, the enemy garrison had been armed with only a few personal weapons to fight against well armed and armored attackers. That had been decisive.

The men met in a room on the second level on the west wall next to the northwest bastion. A few lamps gave enough light to take in the gloomy scene. Giles, who was staying close to Athan, helped Myron light the rest of the lamps in the space as the men took their places around the table. Talos and Prokopios placed stools around a table they set up in the center of the room. The mood was tense; Talos and Myron were especially on edge.

Talos was immediately put on the defensive by Athan's opening remark to him.

"You almost got us killed today."

Talos squirmed where he sat on a stool but said nothing. It had been Talos who had provided most of the intelligence that had led Athan to attack the citadel of the Dassaria with only forty men.

"Rodas," asked Athan still looking at Talos, "how many men did we kill in the fight, do you think?"

"I don't know, captain, I mean sire; at least a score, probably more, maybe as many as two score."

"And how many prisoners did we take?"

This Rodas was more certain about, "We are holding 14, of those eight are wounded more or less severely. Half of them may die."

"And just how many got away?" It was becoming unsettling for all of them. Athan might have been speaking to Rodas, however he continued to stare directly at Talos who shrank down under that glare. Even Myron, who had not made any input into the estimate of the Hold's garrison, was becoming nervous. He wanted to speak, to explain, to defend his cousin, but wisely held his tongue. That afternoon's events had left him with a deep respect for his new king; respect mingled with not a little fear.

"Hard to say, sire, perhaps two or three score. There were servants and women who got out, and nobody was really counting."

"I think it is safe to say at over two score fighting men got away. Let me add this up: more than a score killed, almost a score captured, and at the very least more than two score that have fled; that makes more than four score warriors inside one of the strongest little forts I have ever seen. So tell me Talos, tell us all, why there were more than twice as many men in here than you told us about?"

Their former guide rubbed his hands on his trousers and felt the bandage that covered the wound he had gotten on his thigh. Then he responded in his typical curt style.

"Dunno. When I was here before I wasn't coming in to spy on the place. I just did my job and kept out of trouble. I stayed down in town, never slept up here. Just stood watch and mustered; and ate sometimes; the food was good. Maybe more men were out patrolling or something when I came inside."

Rodas interrupted, "The prisoners say the garrison has over a hundred men. There used to be a lot more, maybe twice as many, they said a lot of men left over the last few years."

Athan asked Talos another direct question, "Why didn't you tell us about the armory? Why didn't you tell us that the Bear kept most of the heavy weapons secured in a single room? If they had gotten to that gear, we would not have been able to push them out. Then where would we be, hmmm?"

Talos blushed, "I forgot," he mumbled looking at the floor. "Until I saw the door to the armory; then I remembered."

"You forgot," said Athan flatly.

The tension stretched even tighter. After a long moment, Athan unexpectedly smiled and said in a jesting way, "Talos, you might be a good guide, but you are a terrible spy."

Athan's smile became a grin. The tension broke like a fever, the men coming to themselves. Now they all began to laugh, cautiously at first, then uproariously.

Myron could not restrain himself any longer. Speaking for the men who were still laughing with sheer relief he stood and exclaimed, "Sire, it was a great victory! To take a place like this outnumbered more than two to one, surely the gods smiled upon us. It is a victory that will never be forgotten!"

Athan calmed things down with his next pronouncement. "Yes," he said, slowly regaining control of the council, "we must have had some divine support. But we also had surprise on our side. They were completely unprepared for an attack. We will never let that happen to us." The men around the table were now listening closely. "We are going to know what to do in case we are attacked, or have a mutiny, or a fire. We are going to decide what we will do before we are faced with any possible emergency we can think of. If Zeus himself attacks with his mighty thunderbolts, I want our men here to know what to do." He gave them all a long look and continued. "We won because they let Rodas inside the gates, they didn't get into the bastions and secure them when we came in, they didn't get to the armory, and they didn't form up to fight together. Mostly we won because they were not prepared to fight and we were."

Rodas, thinking of the men at the entrance of the fort who talked to him and dithered when they should have been sounding the alarm, nodded to himself. He saw the others nodding as well, remembering how the garrison had not been willing to come to grips with their attackers until it was too late.

"They were fat, and lazy," continued Athan, "and they had become used to just taking what they wanted without resistance. There were no leaders to tell these men what to do or we would all be dead, because take it from me, some of them did remember how to fight. But most of these men were no longer battle-minded." And the men nodded to themselves again.

They had little time to ponder his lessons that night because Athan immediately began discussing plans and setting up the new garrison.

First, they reviewed what they had found. The gear in the armory, especially the armor, had been immediately plundered by the men; most of them were now burdened with heavy gear more appropriate to a hoplite on parade than a brigand, even a former brigand. This did not trouble their leaders since the men would not need to move far, and the extra protection was always welcome. Athan instructed that extra spears, bows and quivers of arrows be left on the top two levels of all four bastions ready for immediate use. One storeroom had extra cloaks and warm weather gear. The woolen cloaks did not interest Athan, he had recently equipped all his men with nearly identical new gray cloaks in the city of Lychmidas. He was interested in a stock of grass woven cloaks found stacked in a corner. Athan remembered grass cloaks like these from his youth. They were lightweight and did an excellent job of shedding rain. Everyone expected rain again that night. Wool cloaks, though warm, became heavy when wet. Grass cloaks on the other hand, were like a little thatch roof, shedding the rain nicely and keeping the clothing under it dry and warm. Athan directed that every man who went on watch be issued a grass cloak to wear over their gray cloaks while walking the ramparts. Athan knew men would tend to avoid getting out of the relative warmth of the bastions, especially in the rain. Giving them the grass rain cloaks told them first, that their leaders were concerned about their welfare and second, that the men were expected to get out there and walk the walls. The men grumbled about having to wear the grass cloaks; they said they made too much noise, and that they were shepherd's clothing, not suitable for a warrior. This was partially true; shepherds often did wear grass cloaks in bad weather. But the cloaks did a good job of keeping a man dry. Despite the complaints, when it started raining that night, the men donned the garments and were grateful for them.

The cloaks were only one of a host of issues the men discussed up in that room. Tenucer was made acting sergeant to replace Sergeant Nikolas, who had been severely wounded in the fighting. They then divided the men into four watch teams, so that a long-term schedule could be established. The numbers of men on watch (four during the day, six at night) their locations, and the duration of watches were all set. They made good decisions or perhaps the decisions were obvious, for the standard guidelines they created that night for sentry duty in the Hold were to stand with few changes for many decades.

It was after midnight before the council finally ended. Rodas and Athan agreed that even with a sergeant of the guard on duty, one of them should also be awake for the rest of the night. Rodas looked at his friend and offered to take the first watch. Athan gratefully agreed. As the men were heading out the door Myron asked a casual question that had long-ranging effects.

"Um, chief…captain…sire," Myron's voice reflected his own respectful confusion, "What do we call you?"

And that simple question required definition of Athan's status, a topic he had been avoiding. Despite being carried away by Rodas' enthusiasm, Athan was not really comfortable declaring himself a king.

But if he was not a king, what was he? There could only be one captain, and Rodas was well suited to that job. A general was strictly a military rank, and Athan intended to rule the surrounding area as more than just an occupying military force. He looked at his men. The men looked back at him, stopped still in their places. This was the real question. Were they merely raiders, leaving the Hold after a successful raid, or were they going to try to stay and build a kingdom? Or steal it, depending on your perspective.

"What do you think?" he temporized, looking at all of them and none of them.

There was an awkward silence. Some men shuffled their feet. They knew what needed to be said, but no one wanted to be the one to say it. How do you proclaim a king? The silence stretched.

'Ah, well', thought Rodas to himself, 'this was my idea. Besides I still think this man will be a good king.'

"I think we call you by your name," said Rodas speaking out loud. He was not sure how to do this but if it was to be done it was best done boldly.

"Hail, King Athan, King of Dassaria!"

"Hail," came the answer from some of the men in the room. Then gathering confidence they repeated it together in unison, and louder, "Hail King Athan of Dassaria! Hail to the King!"

Not knowing what to do next, the men gathered around him and clasped his arms. There were no vows of fealty, however, each man knew that their futures were now bound inextricably with that of this former bandit chieftain. Still unsure of just what they should do, they awkwardly departed. In the end only Giles and Rodas remained. Giles had prepared a pile of cushions on the floor with blankets for his new king to sleep on.

"Well," Rodas grinned at his new King, "you did it."

"We did it," corrected Athan. "Now the real work begins."

"That's why you are king," responded Rodas. "The job is way too much work for me." And still smiling, he left.

Athan watched him out the door. He was unsure of what to do next; his body answered that question with a jaw cracking yawn. He had been up since before dawn, ridden all day, fought a battle, and worked without respite since then. Exhaustion pulled at him. Giles had set up his own place to sleep by the door so that Athan would not be disturbed until it was time for him to go on watch. Athan's first act after being proclaimed king was to lie down and fall instantly into a deep sleep.

And so Athan became a king. He did not know it himself but it was also his forty-second birthday.

There was little rest for the new king. He was not awakened to spell Rodas; instead he was jerked awake by a horrible nightmare. Considering that Athan had been a fighting man for over twenty years he had not really had very many serious fights. He had literally gone years without striking a blow in anger. After all, as a bandit chieftain it was his job to arrange things so that his men did not get killed. Even so, in the aggregate he had seen a fair bit of personal combat. He knew that the invariable consequences of a battle were vivid nightmares. This one had been particularly bad. He had been fighting that little devil he had killed in the fight upstairs; in the dream he could not get his kopis to bite on the man. No matter how he cut at him his blade seemed to bounce off. Making matters worse, the madwoman from the courtyard was somehow there in the room, too. She was standing in a corner waving a bloody knife and laughing manically and screaming 'I'll cut off your willie!'

He awoke sweating, glad to get up from that dream. He splashed water on his face from the pitcher and basin Giles had set up on a stand the night before and cleaned his teeth with a frayed twig. He decided not to try shaving in the dim light of the single lamp and, quietly stepping over a still snoring young Giles, went out to find Rodas.

Rodas was looking very tired and, despite a few protests about a king not having to stand watch, was grateful to head off to find a place to sleep for the few remaining hours of the night. The word of Athan's change in status had obviously spread. As Athan moved around the Hold he could sense unease in some of the men. A few congratulated him. Some others offered weak jokes about being familiar with kings and such. It did not take him long to put the men at ease. He took pains to speak with every man, taking a cup of hot tea with some, putting on a woven grass cloak over his own gray one and walking the walls, inspecting the watch without giving the men the impression that he was trying to catch them out. He did find some sleepy soldiers, but no sleeping ones. Soon he saw Cook and his wife heading into their kitchen. By the time it was just getting light, the smell of fresh baking bread began to fill the southern, downwind, half of the Hold.

Athan walked down the ramp and entered the kitchen. Cook's Wife told him that they did not allow anyone in the kitchen underfoot before the regular breakfast time. Athan ignored her. Cook, with much greater sense, spoke to Athan, answering questions about his helpers, how he decided on the menus, how he drew the required supplies out of the larder, and other technical details. Athan stayed until the first loaves of flat bread came out of the oven. Cook, continuing a series of good decisions, gave half of them to the new king. Athan then walked the circuit of guards again, sharing out loaves of the delicious hot bread with the grateful sentries. Even with the early snack he was one of the first down to the kitchen that morning to eat the regular breakfast of hot spiced tea, apples, bread, and olive oil when breakfast began serving at sunup.

It had been a very strange night as well in the assemblage of shops and houses that was referred to as Dassaria. The previous afternoon, the people who lived there had been interested and disturbed to varying degrees by the large band of mounted men who had arrived in town and, instead of dismounting and getting their animals and themselves out of the weather, had taken only a short time to arrange themselves and ridden straight up to the Hold. Members of the garrison who were off duty down in Dassaria were much more alert to dangerous situations than those who were on watch up in the Hold. Curious eyes watched the Hold. Rumors of a force coming up to reinforce the Bear had been circulating for several days now. Were these the expected men?

It did not take the watchers long to realize something was seriously wrong up on the hill. The Bear's men in town hurried to don whatever armor they had and weapons were taken up. By the time the men in the Hold had realized they were under attack, support in the form of over a dozen members of the garrison was heading up the road that led to the front gate. These men saw the gates being closed and broke into a run, but it was impossible to make much speed up a hill burdened with arms and armor. The gates were closed and barred in their faces. They milled about outside the gate for a bit. Some suggested going down to town, get ropes and ladders, and then scale the walls, but no one knew exactly where ladders could be found. They then decided to see if the back gate was open. As they made their way around the south wall toward the rear of the Hold they encountered a stream of refugees coming the other way. They heard a despairing story: the Hold had fallen. There was a general slaughter going on inside. There were scores of hoplites by the rear gate. The situation was hopeless. Men fleeing a battle always exaggerate the threat and prowess of the enemies that have routed them. Some of the reinforcement from the town did make it around the corner of the bastion, only to find more of their compatriots fleeing out the back gate. Then men in the bastions began shooting arrows at them. It was cold and raining and everyone was running away. After a time the men from the town joined the stream of disheartened men and women who were headed down hill to the town.

There were not taverns as such in Dassaria at that time, but there were houses that served the same functions, providing wine, food, gambling, women, and other entertainments. It was to the common room of such a house where the Bear's pretty young boy-companion headed after leaving his former master at the front gate. He put up a gay façade as he ordered mulled wine and some bread. The foolish young man made a whole series of fatal mistakes. He forgot that in his time as the temporary favorite of the Bear he had made enemies, and his previous protector could no longer shield him from those enemies. He further antagonized those in the house with carefree and cutting remarks as he waited for his food and wine. Then when he paid, he let the men in the room see he had a full purse. When he finally realized that the men in the room were regarding him like dogs watching a cat that has inadvertently entered a kennel, he made a final blunder. Instead of attempting to bluff his way out or leave by a back door, he panicked and attempted to bolt. They let him get outside first in order to spare themselves the trouble of throwing the body outside. It was the first murder of the night. It would not be the last.

There was general uproar in the town. Men tried to figure out just what had happened and who was to blame. Fistfights broke out, and then more serious fighting began as men settled old scores or merely vented their tension on anyone around them. Those who were not actively engaged in combat began drinking heavily. This made a bad situation worse. By the time Borna arrived, minus his former king, it was death for some men to enter certain houses. Borna was fortunate to find himself with a few of his friends, and so lived out the night. The men slept in a stables and at first light rode out on stolen horses, headed south, with no particular destination, just away from where they were. They were joined as the day went on by others of the previous regime who decided that Dassaria had suddenly lost its charm.

As ordered the night before, a mounted ride of seven men headed out of the Hold as soon as it was full light. Pirro was put in charge. He had Myron with him who knew the country a little, and Ioannis who, in addition to being a good scout, was an accomplished signaler. Their orders were to find out what was going on in town without getting trapped in among the buildings. Then they were to head west, climb a hill that offered a view, and keep a watch out for any Illyrian troops that might be coming in response to the request for support allegedly sent by Borna.

When the gate was opened to send the seven riders out, Athan, who was there to see them off and make sure Pirro understood his orders, saw a lone woman making her way up the hill. She stopped briefly by the two carts full of the corpses of the late garrison that had been left by the side of the trail the night before. Two slaves passed out of the gate, each leading a donkey. They would hitch the animals up to the carts and carry the remains to a garbage pit that had been dug down the hill only two days before. It would be converted from garbage pit to unmarked grave, covered over, and a new pit would be dug elsewhere.

The woman came up steadily. The big gates were closed; Athan waited outside next to the small door. Giles, who had joined his new king shortly after dawn, very embarrassed at having overslept, stood next to him in the entrance of the door, also watching the woman.

The woman, a plain matron in her middle years, walked right up to Athan. "Do you know who is in charge in there now?"

"I am," was the calm reply.

Surprised that a leader would also be acting as the doorman, she straightened herself and announced, "I am Celeno, a respectable woman. I help keep this place clean. I presume after the excitement last night it will need cleaning."

In fact Celeno was a servant of long standing. She and her two daughters all worked as cleaners in the Hold. This morning Celeno bade her daughters to lie low until she was certain it was safe for maidens. Celeno desired her daughters to marry well enough to become freewomen, but her two horse-faced daughters unfortunately shared their mother's plain looks. Getting a good husband was going to be a challenge, but Celeno was nothing if not hopeful, and had a secret that might now make a difference.

Athan smiled, moved aside and gestured for her to enter.

Celeno must have been nervous because she hesitated and asked, "Is it safe?"

Athan, still smiling simply said, "Yes."

With a doubtful look she entered the Hold. 'There are many kinds of courage,' Athan thought. And turning to look down at the houses at the bottom of the hill he wondered just what was going on down there.

The morning remained busy but without further alarms until almost noon when a flustered Rodas joined his new king, embarrassed at having slept so long while leaving Athan to deal with the management of the Hold.

"I was fine," lied Athan. He could feel the big soft furry arms of the sleep monster, pulling him toward bed. After a very quick bite to eat, washed down with some well-watered wine, he retired to the place that Giles had prepared for him. He was asleep as soon as he crawled under the covers.

He slept soundly for an hour and a half before the Illyrian cavalry arrived.

The winter storms were definitely weakening. The Old King could hear life returning in the form of rustling and furtive scurrying of small animals. At first he was annoyed by the irritating intrusions, but then he realized that even a mouse could provide a meal. He spent the next several days devising a variety of traps, snares and deadfalls in an attempt to capture some of the little creatures. He was not very successful; however, the activity and mental exercise was good for his morale. On the third day he was suddenly successful, acc umulating no fewer than six small rodents. He was not exactly sure what they were.

Perhaps they were voles, mice, or some other small furry creatures; he did not care. The old man cleaned them with considerable difficulty as the curving bronze blade of his dagger was ill suited for such fine work. In the end he was able to pop the tiny carcasses into his pot, mixed with some promising-looking shrubs and make a thin soup. It was not much but it was far better than nothing.

Chapter Two – Uninvited Guests

ᛗhe scouts had done their job as well as they could. After confirming that there was no obvious effort to attack the Hold going on in the town, the scouts had moved past the houses, taking the road to the south and east. There was a fine bare hill half an hour's ride past the town and the men had gone up to its summit for a good look around. It was from there that they saw first, distant motion, then the appearance of a long line of mounted men, headed their way, coming up from the southwest. With the roads still muddy, there was no dust to give advance notice, so the column was uncomfortably close by the time the scouts could see the composition of the approaching riders. The sun was not visible through the heavy overcast so their signaling mirrors did not work, and it was too far for anyone from the Hold to see the small signal flags they carried. News of the approaching force arrived the way such news had traditionally arrived - carried in person by a hard-riding scout.

Athan was awakened by the alarm that turned out the guard. He stumbled out to the nearby guardroom in the northwest bastion to find Prokopios and several of the other men peering out the arrow slits that overlooked the town.

Seeing Athan, the sergeant stepped back making room and indicating out the opening, "Cavalry coming; probably Illyrian."

Athan saw the last of his scouts on the final leg of the road to the hill, urging their tired little horses up the final incline. Just beyond the houses of the town were horsemen in a long column of twos. The head of the column had already dismounted and even from that distance, he could see men talking and gesturing animatedly. He turned as Rodas and Pirro came into the guard room.

Pirro reported that there were about a hundred men in the column with fewer than a dozen pack animals. If there were more troops coming they were far behind. **If** there were more troops coming.

"I think that is all the Illyrians will send," opined Rodas. "If Myron was right, these men were expecting to be welcomed with open arms."

"If they join forces with the men that escaped from us last night, they will outnumber us by three or four to one," put in Giles. The young man had appointed himself to be Athan's personal aide. Athan did not mind, in fact Giles had made himself very useful. But the older men present did not need to be advised about the odds.

"We could stand odds of five to one in this place," said Rodas dismissively. "Besides those men are cavalry. They do not like to fight on rough ground, they do not like to fight warriors in formation, and they damn sure are not going to try to storm a fortress. And those men we ran off last night will still remember how to run away. No, this lot is not even going to try to get us out of here. Now if they have a few hundred hypastas and hoplites coming along behind with artillery, then we would have something to worry about."

"Council of war," ordered Athan, "here, as soon as you can get the sergeants assembled."

Giles took it upon himself to dash out to summon the remaining sergeants. They were already on the way, so that in a short time Pirro was giving them an expanded version of what was going on outside the Hold. Aside from the rather obvious arrival of an entire troop of cavalry, remarkably little could be seen to indicate that a battle had occurred and power had been transferred from the previous long-standing regime to a new set of completely unknown masters.

"They'll come up here," predicted Rodas. "They will talk to the people down there and then they will come up here to talk. They will have to find out just who and what they are dealing with."

"But they will not come to fight. Not with just a troop of cavalry," put in Tenucer, who had not heard the previous comments on that subject. "They will need to send a big force and it is too late in the season for that. If they come in force, it will not be until the spring."

"How long do you think it will be until they send someone to talk?" asked Giles diffidently, to no one in particular.

"Hard to say," said Rodas. "Probably sooner rather than later."

"I think," here young Giles' voice became a little firmer, "that the King should get ready to receive them."

"Not a bad idea," Rodas agreed. "Cap…umm Sire, I think you should start looking the part of a king if you want to be one. What do we have that can make you look majestic?" Athan was still in the tunic he had slept in; his hair was a mess and his beard a dark stubble. He looked more like a reveler who had been awaked too soon after a particularly rough night.

"We ain't got enough robes and jewels in this place to make the boss look majestic," teased Prokopios with a grin. He had known Athan too long to take him as anything more than his chieftain. Of course, to the old sergeant that was a high status indeed.

Sergeant Tenucer was detailed to see if he could find some appropriate clothing while Giles took his new king down to the baths to clean him up for his first audience.

In less than half an hour, Giles had shaved, combed, and generally brightened a fatigued Athan into a crisper, more alert facsimile of a king. Tenucer was not able to find anything that would suit a king making a formal appearance, but he found a tunic that was at least clean and fit him well enough. The last thing young Giles did was to put the golden diadem taken from the recently departed King Ratimir on Athan's head. The armbands and rings they had taken from the former king were too large for Athan, so Giles put them aside to be resized later. The result, if not exactly regal, did convey the impression of a man of substance who was in charge. Athan did feel much more alert.

It was well that they had moved to prepare Athan right away for he returned to see a small group of riders heading up to the Hold. Athan reviewed in his mind the recommendations his council had just given him as he donned a fresh gray cloak replacing his old, blood-stained one that had been sent down to the laundry. That big laundress, Titania, and her helpers were going to be busy for a while. Athan was sure, however, that she had experience in removing bloodstains.

He, Myron, Talos, Tenucer, and Giles walked through the door into the southeast bastion and up the stairs that led to the fighting platform at the top of walls, joining the men that were already in place. More of his men were above them on top of the west bastions. Athan moved out onto the wall and stood next to an embrasure directly over the gate, watching the mounted party pull up before the gates. There they paused in some confusion. Apparently they did not know how to address this silent fortress. They could see the men on the walls and on top of the bastions. No doubt they had also seen movement behind the arrow slits where the shutters had been opened and men waited. But there was no one to greet them. The council had decided that they could not risk Athan coming out to speak with the men; although a treacherous attack during a parley was not likely, the loss of the new leader would be disastrous. Athan would remain on the walls with the men who possessed the most local knowledge, while Rodas and a strong party would come out to talk directly with any emissary.

Athan let the men below the gates stew for a moment, then, when he saw them preparing to hail the walls, he stepped into an embrasure where they could see him and called out, "Who comes to this place?"

"I am Aeolus of Illyria, captain of the King Bardhyllus' person guard. Who are you?"

It was interesting that this Aeolus identified himself as being from Illyria and not Bardhyllus. The city state of Bardhyllus was part of the loose coalition that made up the region of Illyria of course, but either Aeolus wanted them to believe he represented a larger entity than just a neighboring city or he had a broader world view than most.

"I am Athan, King of Dassaria. What brings you to my hold?"

"Who?" shouted up the confused horseman. "We have business with Ratimir, also called the Bear. Where is he?"

"He is gone. What is your business here?"

"We are here at the request of the ruler of this place. What have you done with him?"

"Are you here to parley?"

More confusion, then, "We are here at the request of lord of this place, one Ratimir, also called the Bear. We would treat with him."

"If you come in peace to this place to parley say so, otherwise begone!"

Aeolus was getting tired of shouting up to the man standing in the embrasure. He did not actually doubt that the man on the wall above him was now in charge; his dress and demeanor indicated that, and Aeolus could just make out a circlet of gold on his head. He was simply unsure of what to do with these radically changed circumstances. The King of Bardhyllus had it in his mind to bring this troubling little fort on his eastern borders under his control, if he could do so without much effort. Now apparently there was going to be some considerable effort involved after all. Aeolus consulted with his political advisor, an older, balding man, related to one of the king's courtiers. This man was supposed to have administered the Bear's fortress if Aeolus and his troopers could take over the Hold from the presumably enfeebled Bear. But men with sharp and active minds are not the ones selected to take over minor forts on the distant fringes of the frontier. The councilor had no useful advice to Aeolus. So the riders just sat on their horses in front of this dominating fortress and under the gaze of a strong- looking leader who stood on the battlements looking impassively down on them. A leader very different than the one they were expecting to find. After a bit Aeolus came to a decision.

"Yes," he called up, "we are here to parley."

At once Athan stepped away from the embrasure and out of sight. On the ground the small door in the gates opened and Rodas and an escort stepped through and onto the flat ground in the front of the gate. He brought exactly the same number of men as Aeolus had, wearing full, fine armor and carrying shields but no spears. They wore swords, but these were sheathed.

Rodas wasted no time but approached Aeolus, who was still mounted, and asked him directly, "State your purpose in bringing your men into King Athan's domain without his leave."

Aeolus was put off by the abrupt change and challenging question. He was no fool and understood that he might be involving his king in a great deal more than what he was interested in. The King of Bardhyllus was no empire builder; he was getting on in years and did not want to fight an unnecessary war for little or no gain. That had been made clear to Aeolus before he left the court. Now he was being challenged on legalistic grounds by some serious fighting men. Things were just falling apart. Aeolus had a number of choices to make on the spot; fortunately he had good sense. He hopped down from his horse and began a dialog with what was clearly the new king's chief lieutenant.

The discussion went on for a while, running in a circle that soon wore itself into a rut.

Aeolus held that he had been invited to Dassaria at the request of the lawful and established ruler.

Rodas would respond that things had changed and now there was a new lawful and established ruler.

Aeolus would reply in various versions that the previous ruler had requested the help of King Bardhyllus, and was therefore under his king's protection.

Rodas would reply in different ways that if they wanted to protect the previous ruler of Dassaria then they should find him and put him under their protection.

What was understood but not spoken was the obvious fact that Aeolus was there to take over the Hold, and Rodas was in effect telling him that if he wanted this place he would have to take it by force.

It was a cold blustery day, and after a while Aeolus decided that further dialog was not only fruitless, but was becoming uncomfortable. No agreement of any kind was made, no common ground found. The horsemen rode down hill to join the rest of their troop, who were taking over whatever structures they could, and pitching tents for the men who could not find billets in a building. There had been objections to the forced occupation and some fighting. After two more of the old garrison died, the rest became disenchanted with their foreign would-be reinforcements. More of the Bear's men began to slip away.

The people who lived in the town were caught in a dilemma. They did not even have a choice between their old master who was bad but familiar and a new master who was unknown - they had to decide between two potential new masters both of whom were equally unknown.

For some the decision was easy. Celeno quickly decided that these new men on the hill who had taken the Hold were not so bad. None of the staff had been mistreated so far and things seemed under control, better organized. Obviously anyone would be better than the monster who had ruled here since the wretched place had been built, and Celeno had a good feeling about this new king. She thought he might make a good one, or at least a much better one. In late afternoon, her work finished, she went to the front gates to return down the hill. She was stopped in the entrance tunnel by the guard.

"Where are you going?" he asked not unkindly.

"Down to my house to bring my daughters up here. There is too much work for me to do alone, and now that those hooligans have come into town it is not safe for respectable girls to remain down there, certainly not unchaperoned."

The sergeant of the guard was called who informed the cleaning woman that his orders were to let no one out. She demanded to speak to his superior officer. She did this with such persistence, sense of moral outrage, and volume that eventually both Rodas and Athan arrived at the gate to see what was the matter.

"We can't let you go," explained Rodas, "it might be unsafe."

"Then it is unsafe for my daughters. They are far too pretty to be left down there alone and unprotected with all those strange foreign soldiers."

This won her points with the men who had drifted into earshot, gathering as people do when there is a chance to listen in on what might become prime gossip. The men were all in favor of bringing up a couple of fair maidens and placing them under their protection.

It was Athan who was blunt enough to finally come to the crux of the matter.

"We do not want you telling them of our numbers." There it was, the heart of the matter: Athan's band was small, perhaps too small to defend the Hold.

"Pffft," said Celeno dismissively. "I am no spy. Besides, that group of fancy horse boys could no more take this place from you than they could fly. In a few days they will get tired of watching this stone pile and leave. Why would I help a bunch of foreigners that are here today but gone tomorrow?"

"If your daughters were threatened, you would tell the men down there whatever they asked," said Athan not without some sympathy.

That simple statement alone swung Celeno over to Athan's side forever. Here was a man who understood a mother's fears; a man who cared about those fears. This was a man she would be glad to serve.

"Tell me what you want me to say," she suggested. "I will say nothing to anyone. If they ask I will tell them what you want me to say. I will tell them you are five score hardened warriors from Macedonia."

"Go, then," yielded Athan. "If anyone asks you, tell them you do not know how many we are or where we came from but that we are at least four score."

"If I bring back my daughters may we stay here unmolested?"

"You may," smiled Athan, "so long as you obey the rules of the Hold. But you may not find it so easy to return. I think they will want to stop anyone from coming back up here just as we wanted to stop you from going down there."

Celeno smiled, "I will not come back up the road," she said, "I know the way to the back gate. I will come there," here she hesitated, thinking, "we will knock on the back gate like this: 'knock, knock, knock' when the moon first comes up tonight. Is that acceptable?"

Rodas answered for his king, a bit more harshly than Athan would have, "Come alone, old woman. Know that we do not treat treachery lightly."

"I will bring my daughters," she sniffed and stepped through the small door set into the gates.

As Celeno made her way down the road, a solitary figure, she could feel eyes upon her from ahead and behind. Three fourths of the way down to the town she turned aside to a small collection of shrubs. She had stopped there many times on her daily trips up and down the hill. She told anyone who asked that she was stopping to relieve herself. There was another reason. It was not easy being a witch. In that little concealed place she had built a simple shrine, nothing that would mean anything to someone who did not know what they were looking for. It was there Celeno would sometimes do her little magics. Not all of them were little. She had cursed four men in her time, burying small lead curse tablets called katadesmoi with the proper prayers and incantations. Each time she had eventually brought ruin down upon her victim. Celeno's last target had been strong, too strong she feared for her magic to destroy, but even though it took almost two years it had finally worked, first destroying his strength, now bringing him down all together. She was thinking of the Bear, wondering where he might be when she pushed into the nook and came face to face with him, crouched down and waiting for her.

She was too terrified to even scream. She stood there paralyzed in horror looking at the man who had tormented them all for so long. Then her heart, that had seemingly stopped, began pounding in her chest so hard it was painful. The man once called the Bear was crouched on his haunches, back against a thick shrub, his head bowed, keeping absolutely still. He did not move. No living man could remain that still. Ratimir had been left here in the night by his companions. She thought it likely that he had directed them off to one side for a rest, perhaps he had been too heavy to get up again, but in any event they had left him there. And there he remained. From the position of the body Celeno thought he had probably sat there, still alive, for some time. She stood staring at the figure of the man who had inspired such fear in her and everyone she knew. She could not help wondering what he had thought about as he waited alone in the dark for death to come. Was he afraid? Did he regret the violence and evil he had done? Probably not, she decided.

A shudder went through Celeno. There were times when the power of her own magic frightened even her. "You didn't know about the power of my curse did you?" she told the corpse. "It brought you down and then brought you here to die." Then she turned and walked out of the little cul-de-sac and returned back to her home.

That night just as a narrow moon came above the hills, a single figure approached the rear gate of the Hold and knocked three times.

"Who goes?" asked a voice from within as the little peephole in the back door was slid open.

"It is Celeno, of course," she replied tartly. "I have come back just as I said I would. I have brought my three daughters and a few of the others from below."

"Have them come forward," said the voice, as torches were thrown from the slits in the bastions, throwing an uncertain light around the entrance. Six additional figures stepped up into the light. They all were carrying bags over their shoulders but none of them looked in the least threatening. The back gate did not have a smaller sally port like the front, and had only one door; this was cracked open and a man in the entrance urged them inside, "Quickly, quickly!"

When the last of the seven had reentered, the gate was slammed behind them and instantly barred. Celeno and her companions were surrounded by nearly a score of men fully armed and armored. 'Quite a reception for an old woman and her friends and family' she thought to herself. She had lived a long time with men who could kill her at any time without the slightest consequence, so she kept a respectful tongue in her head. In addition to her daughters, she had brought in a middle aged couple, servants who worked in the Hold, and two of her friends, two women of her age, one a widow the other a spinster. Celeno offered all their services to Rodas as his men began standing down from the alert. Interest in the woman's daughters had quickly diminished when the men had a good look at them. Even in poor light Celeno's offspring were clearly no prizes. Celeno was unconcerned; she was sure that her daughters would make good wives for someone in this place. As to attracting husbands, well, she had love potions to take care of that. All in good time.

Even though there was a foreign force just outside the walls, life (and work) within the Hold continued. In addition to the seven extra workers who slipped in during the night, there were the members of the staff who had remained in the Hold, such as Cook and his wife, and the women who transferred their loyalty from members of the old garrison to the new arrivals. This work force was immediately put to work. Even the soldiers' new trulls were given things to do (much to their dismay) under the direction of Celeno, who had appointed herself the new head of the cleaning staff. With the staff working steadily, the routine chores such as preparing meals, tending the privies, caring for and cleaning up after the horses, and doing laundry continued much as they always had. New jobs such as clearing away the debris of battle, setting up the rooms to better suit the new members of the garrison and carefully searching the Hold were also accomplished.

The most important investigation was the survey of the treasure room. There was only one key in the Hold, just as there was only one lock, and it was easy to find. The key was in the room next to the treasury where the Bear had lived in his final days. This key was typical for that place and time - a slightly curved piece of wood, wide as a man's finger, thick as two fingers, and about as long as a man's hand. At one end were set three wooden pins, each about the same dimensions as a child's little finger. The key was pushed into a slot near the edge of the brass-bound door to the treasury with the pins up. They matched up and fitted into holes cut into the metal bar in the inside of the door. When the pins were aligned with the holes in the bar the end of the key was depressed which lifted the pins up on the inside bar. Once these locking pins were lifted, the bar could be pushed aside with the slide that protruded from the door. It took a bit of fiddling to open the door with the key the first time they tried it; there was a trick to getting the feel of it. When they finally lifted the internal bar and swung the door aside on the afternoon of their first full day in the Hold they were not disappointed.

Athan, Giles, Rodas, Talos, and Prokopios were the only ones to enter the room, although there was a ring of intensely interested men gathered around, kept back a respectful distance by the big sergeant's growled warnings. Taking a lamp, four men entered, with Prokopios peering in from the door, keeping an eye on the men who waited to hear what was inside. At first glimpse it was unimpressive. There were some rich hangings in a corner, dusty now, and a series of chests of varying sizes. The chests were eagerly opened; those with seals were opened first. Some of them were almost empty; others contained cups and jewelry of uncertain quality. All had at least something of value and there were a goodly number of chests. One small heavy chest contained something that was familiar to Rodas and Athan - eight quarter talent bars of gold, source unknown. It was difficult to be certain, but the men estimated that the items in the room were worth at least a dozen talents, probably more. Taking out one chest which was almost filled with silver coins to deal with immediate needs, Athan resealed the other chests and locked the door of the treasury behind him.

He turned back and saw a ring of eager onlookers craning forward to see what riches might be inside. Athan handed the chest to Giles and with a significant look at his companions, gestured them out into the light.

"Well, boys," he said, "it looks like payday tonight." There were small cheers and overall indications of satisfaction, but there were still eager looks on the faces. Athan well knew these were men who were used to literally taking the money and running. He had to impress on them that this time they were staying put, and so he continued, "And a good many paydays to come. We will have a snug winter here. Don't worry about those horse boys down there. They won't bother us."

Then Athan made arrangements for paying the men. Rodas was chosen to determine the pay for each man, because he had experience doing so when he had his own little band. Further, he had a well-deserved reputation for honesty and fair dealing. Yure, the younger, had somehow become the defacto paymaster, perhaps because he could count, so he distributed the coins; Linus provided security. Linus was probably the best warrior in Athan's army and with his size and exotic appearance he was the man others were least likely to challenge.

Athan also had to take care of a much grimmer duty: funerals for his men. In addition to Toxeus, another man of Rodas' old band had been killed in the fighting. Of the wounded, one of the men, who had either been hit on the head or tumbled down some stairs or possibly both, woke up on the second morning. Aside from a dull headache he seemed fine, although the last thing he remembered was when the band had entered the town. It took him a while to be persuaded that the fight was over and won. He never did remember how he came to wind up at the bottom of the stairs leading up to the northeast bastion. The other wounds, a broken arm, numerous cuts, and uncounted bruises all healed under the ministrations of the band's healer Iason, aided by the Hold's own practicing physician, a slave called Hypos. In fact, most of the healed men gave the credit to the older Hypos. His thin graying hair, slightly bent and spare frame gave him a birdlike appearance. He was kindly to all and possessed a solid understanding of healing, especially wounds and inflicted trauma.

But nothing he or Iason did could help poor sergeant Nikolas. The wound in his thigh was deep and long. He lost a great deal of blood from it and never really recovered. Although the blood loss itself did not kill him, the shock weakened him so much that his body was unable to resist the infection that quickly turned his wound red, then black. Within a day he was delirious and he was gone the next. Now Athan had to dispose of three of his own. Although in the cold weather the corpses would keep, it was upsetting to the men to have the bodies remaining around.

On the night Nikolas died the three men were laid out for their *prothesis* or ritual mourning. The female servants of the Hold had washed and prepared the bodies, closing their wounds, arranging their hair and dressing them in clean tunics with one of the new gray cloaks around each man as a shroud. Garlands of celery were put around their brows and a coin into their mouths to pay the ferryman. During the night their comrades came into the room where the bodies lay and sang improvised laments called *goos* that praised their courage and manly qualities. They were each individually praised by their comrades, with old anecdotes shared about them while waiting for inspiration for a new verse of the *goos*.

The morning after the *prothesis,* an honor guard carried the three heroes in a solemn procession, accompanied by flute and drum music out the back gate to a pyre built by the slaves halfway down the spine of the ridge. In addition to firewood, furniture crushed in the fighting was stacked along with some of the vanquished garrison's flammable possessions. Oil was poured on the pyre from a fine white porcelain lekythos and the pyre was set alight. Most of the inhabitants of the Hold came out to observe, excepting the cooks who were preparing the funeral feast and the guards in the bastions who kept a sharp eye out for anyone who might come up the hill to interrupt the proceedings. Some of the men remained until the fire had died down, then, using the same lekythos, this time filled with a mixture of water and wine, doused the fire and collected the ashes into a single urn. They carried them to a short trench dug on the south side of the ridgeline. It was a fine place with a good view of the hills to the south and a clean breeze blowing over it.

"We will erect a suitable stele of marble here," promised Athan referring to a memorial tablet which served as a grave marker.

"Not a bad place," agreed Rodas. "I wouldn't mind being here myself someday." Then realizing the looks he was getting quickly added, "A long, long time from now."

The funeral feast that followed was combined with a ceremony of thanks to the gods. Although neither Athan nor Rodas were religious, some of their men were, so Athan presided over a sacrifice of two of the chickens that scratched out a living in the courtyard of the Hold. Following these solemn rites the Hold then enjoyed a feast. The funeral feast featured the greater part of an ox which had been cooking since the night before as well as a wide variety of dried fruits, some of the remaining vegetables and fresh bread. They did not have proper funeral games, of course, but there were wrestling matches and the inside of the hold was large enough for races, from one wall to the other and back (Giles won) and a javelin throwing competition (won by Linus). The day released much of the residual tension that remained following their conquest.

The people of the Hold began to establish a routine. By the end of that day all the available women who chose to remain had more or less finalized their relationships with their new men. Some of these pairings seemed to change with the phases of the moon, but many, if not most, became more or less permanent; some lasted for decades. The celebrations eventually were brought to an end by a fresh onset of cold rain. Soon after the rain began the sentinels reported Aeolus, the Illyrian captain, and his retinue was coming back up the hill for another parley.

This time Rodas did not make him wait outside the gate, instead offering Aeolus and his advisor safe conduct allowing them to pass the gates and wait in the arched entrance tunnel between the stables. The advisor was visibly grateful to get out of the rain. Any view to the courtyard beyond was somewhat blocked by a dozen large men with shields and spears guarding against treachery. Should any men be seen approaching the Hold, they could easily eject the small embassy and reclose the gate.

Also, this time Athan was there sitting ostentatiously in a chair set back from Rodas. He was a presence there; wearing a fine linen tunic without the wide trousers he normally wore to cover his legs. His hair was freshly (if somewhat hastily) arranged, and he wore expensive-looking sandals. His diadem was upon his head and he wore his kopis by his side. Most importantly, Athan was doing a very good job of maintaining a kingly expression.

More cordial this meeting might be, but the results were exactly the same as the first meeting. Aeolus really did not have anything to offer and was dealing from a position of weakness. Both parties knew this. Still, Aeolus was reluctant to return to his king empty handed. So figuratively speaking he was pushing on a door he knew to be barred because he couldn't think of anything else to do at the moment; perhaps something would happen to change the status quo. And just when it appeared the meeting was coming to an end something did.

Athan entered into the negotiations for the first time, "I assume your king will expect the same payments in tribute as he received under the old regime."

Aeolus controlled his features reasonably well, but the advisor's confusion was evident. Aeolus, Athan and Rodas all suspected the same thing; Ratimir had never paid a single copper of tribute to any man in his life. This was the way Rodas and Athan had decided on to open a new negotiating ploy. What Athan had just said in effect was: 'I know you cannot take my Hold right now, but you might come back with an army and take everything. How much do I have to pay you to keep this from happening?'

Aeolus thought madly. He was not absolutely certain that there hadn't been a tribute of some kind in place. Most kings trumpeted the fact they were receiving tribute from client kingdoms; it made them appear more powerful. But not all payments received were brought to the attention of the king himself. Powerful men around the throne had good reason to keep some payments brought into the kingdom as private matters. The concept of embezzlement was far from new. Aeolus was in treacherous waters here. If he agreed upon an amount for tribute he would be savagely second-guessed by those who remained safely at home. The fact was that agreeing to accept tribute would imply a legal relationship between the two kingdoms. This did not trouble Aeolus much. A king could arbitrarily alter a treaty at any time if it was causing him difficulties. Kings had taken tribute many times just before invading their so-called client states. No, the only issue was would this little kingdom of Dassaria be worth the cost of its conquest?

Tribute would generate less income, but it was easy, immediate, and had no associated costs. Also tribute would come in every year; sacking a kingdom only yielded results once. Most importantly of all, an invasion was expensive and was not certain of success.

"Let us return tomorrow and give you our answer," Aeolus prevaricated.

"No," cut in the new king, still remaining seated, "this a poor country. We can not afford to pay you more than 1,000 drachmae each fall.

This offer changed everything. The question was no longer 'if', the question suddenly became 'how much?'

The temptation was just too great for the political advisor. "We expect 2,000 in the spring, the same in the fall," the older Illyrian demanded.

Negotiations now assumed the same character of a buyer and seller in the village market. The men all knew and understood this form of bargaining. As Athan had hoped, the Illyrians fell easily into something with which they were familiar. Wine and cheese were brought. The Illyrian escorts squatted by the open doorway while Athan's men leaned in to listen to the offers and counteroffers which, in the nature of things, began to come together. Threats to break off the negotiations were made, departures feigned, and alternatives presented and rejected. Rodas was working on the amount he was demanding the Illyrians pay for their stay in the town when the gong which marked the changing of the watch was heard. The sun was about to set and the rain had settled in again, giving every sign that it would continue for a long while. Athan, who had taken no further part in the negotiations, abruptly stood. Everyone else in the narrow tunnel did so as well, even the Illyrian guards, and there was silence.

"Go back to your king and tell him that King Athan of Dassaria sends his respectful greetings. Tell him that if he will keep us under his protection we will prevent any enemies from attacking his kingdom from our lands. Tell him we will also undertake to clear the roads and hills of the bandits that now trouble him. Ask if he will send men to negotiate trading rights and routes between our lands. If he will accede to these requests, I will provide him with tribute of 1500 drachmae to be presented to him in his capital on the winter solstice. I will have it delivered in gold, a full quarter talent. These are my terms. They will not change. Carry them back to your king within ten days or we will consider you an invading force."

With that Athan stepped past a guard who was standing in the small doorway midway down the right side of the tunnel and was gone. Rodas bowed as he departed. So did the Illyrian advisor. Aeolus caught himself beginning a bow and stopped just in time.

'This one acts as a king at least,' Aeolus thought admiringly. He made his farewells and headed down the hill through the rain. The advisor was chatting excitedly about the negotiations. Aeolus scarcely heard him; his mind was full of the possibilities that had unexpectedly opened before him. A chance to improve trade and make the hills safer was a wonderful opportunity. He also understood the value of an alliance to secure the northwest flank of the kingdom. Both men knew that beyond the actual value of the tribute, the king would absolutely love to have a bar of gold presented to him in front of his whole court at the solstice festivities. This would be his first (and only) client state and his prestige would be greatly enhanced. Most of all Aeolus knew his king wanted everyone to see him being presented with shiny gold. That would be why he would accept the offer. Even so, it might be possible to do better. The negotiations had broken off abruptly it was true, but perhaps they were not absolutely terminated. Ten days was a long time. The small group of men made their way down through the cold rain to the houses where warmth and hot food awaited them.

Back up the hill Rodas and Athan conferred quietly in a corner of the stables. They could hear Ixon talking quietly to Adara and though they could not make out what either was saying, her answers were curt and sharp. Near them, Cenobia could be heard gently weeping. Ixon had not been able to persuade them to move from the stables into a proper room. He now seemed to be spending a lot of time talking to the unfortunate women, especially Adara. Celeno, the big cleaning lady, also seemed to take an interest in them. Athan put them from his mind; the women were a problem that could wait.

"Do you think they will go for it?" asked Rodas. "That Aeolus seemed to be the right sort."

"I think they will think on it. While they do, I have to take care of a few things. How do you feel about handling things in here for a few days?"

The offer took Rodas aback. "Why, are you going somewhere?"

"Yes, but only for about ten days or so. I will be taking Giles and Myron with me. We need more men and money if we are going to hold this place and I know where I can get some of each."

The Old King knew that spring would be coming soon down in the lower elevations, but up here he was not certain how much longer it would take for the warm days to reduce the drifts of snow that held him up in the mountains. He was grateful that when he had begun this ordeal he had actually had a bit of fat around his middle. That was long gone now. The old king knew that despite his vanished fat reserves it would be a while yet before he actually starved to death. He decided that his best strategy was to continue to conserve his strength and wait for better weather. The trip back was going to be difficult and dangerous.

He recalled then how, a king only a few days, he had left his brand new kingdom and undertaken another perilous voyage.

Chapter Three – There and Back Again

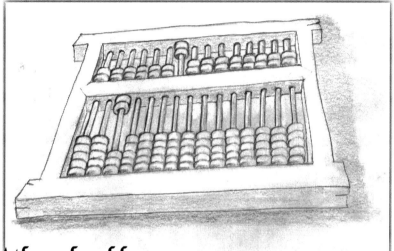

Athan had begun thinking about the future even as he dealt with the enormous list of things that had to be done immediately after the fall of the Hold. Although after the first night, neither he nor Rodas stood sentinel duty, Athan still spent a large part of the next few nights walking the ramparts. Giles would accompany him until Athan sent him to bed, telling him that one of them had to be fresh, and that Giles would need to be alert while Athan slept, implying that Giles would somehow be guarding him. Athan hardly needed guarding from his own men. The battle and its aftermath had cemented his status with them. There are few things to bind men to a leader more tightly than following him into a successful battle. And this little fight had been spectacularly successful. They had routed a numerically superior enemy and taken their fort from them. They had taken a rich haul, and they were the masters of a comfortable and secure fortress. They had suffered few losses. And every man was talking of Athan's heroics during the battle. In fact Athan had only personally killed one man and wounded two others but he had been in the thick of the fight, and somehow his accomplishments were magnified in the eyes of his men.

His people were certainly happy to be here. To a man they wanted to stay right where they were until the spring. Some of the men had already found women, and there was every expectation that there were plenty more down in the town. There was an enemy present to keep things interesting, but not such a strong one as to provoke anxiety. The food was excellent, the quarters comfortable, routines were established, and the work load reasonable. Best of all, the men considered themselves to be rich. Even if they did not fully share in the wealth they had captured, they all knew there was plenty of money being held in the treasury, and they had all been paid a bonus. Just knowing there was more money in reserve gave the men a warm feeling; for the first time in their lives they could look forward to a secure income. In short, Athan's stock with the men had never been higher.

On the other hand, things could change. The situation was still dynamic. Many an honest man had been tempted by money and power. Although the treasury held a great deal of money, there was a great deal more back in the counting house in Lychmidas, the result of their theft of a portion of the tribute to the Empire from the Dorian city-states. He had left half a dozen men behind in Lychmidas in part because they had their wives traveling with the band, and Athan had not wanted to expose the women to the dangers of his assault on the Hold. Athan also wanted to keep a presence in Lychmidas just so the merchants in the counting houses did not forget who owned the goods he had stored there. One of his senior sergeants, Yure the Elder, was in charge of the little detachment. Athan had instructed him to begin recruiting more men to join the band. Of course, now that Athan was a king, he did not have a band any longer; it was the Dassarian army now. Athan grinned at the conceit. With luck Yure would be able to find a dozen men or so and thus bring the garrison's strength up to three score men.

Athan knew that in the long term he could not defend this Hold, strong as it was, with two or even three score men. In order to manage things, he would need at least a hundred men and probably more. That took time and money. The money was available; time was the critical element. He needed time to recruit men he could trust and train. Winter was not a bad time to find men who were looking for work, but collecting them was a painstaking job. Then there was the problem of getting the men and money into the Hold. All of these worries occupied Athan to the point of distraction.

They were not overly concerned about an attack from the Illyrians down in the town, but the horsemen had set up a sort of loose blockade of the Hold. It was a casual siege, since the Illyrians were aware that the Hold was well provisioned. Though horsemen might not be able to capture a fort or even defeat a formation of hoplites in the field, they were very good against small groups of men in the open and thus were able to cut off communications between the Hold and the rest of the world. Each morning since their arrival, a small detachment of riders would ascend the same big hill behind the town that Pirro had used to spy them coming. This hill had a commanding view of the Hold and the roads leading south and east. Another pair of riders would ride out to another prominent hill to the north that gave good sight lines covering the road that Athan and his men had used to approach the Hold from the north. Finally a group of perhaps a dozen more remained at the foot of the hill below the Hold, where they could keep a close watch on the main entrance to the Hold.

These lookouts would man their respective positions from as soon as it was light enough to see, remaining there until just before dusk. Not only would it be difficult to leave the Hold without being detected, trying to get reinforcements into the Hold would be all but impossible. Athan had no doubt that any additional men he attempted to bring into the Hold would be cut to pieces by the main body of the Illyrian horsemen, who would have been alerted by their sentinels. They would be particularly effective against a newly formed, untrained group of men burdened with a supply train of goods, and gold. He would have to wait until the Illyrian horsemen left. It was doubtful the horsemen could remain in the town for too much longer; supplies would become a problem. Still, Athan needed to get more men into place soon, so he could begin the long job of integrating them into a significant fighting force. And now that he had a secure place to keep it, he wanted the bulk of his gold under his personal control. He knew he needed to act quickly while his prestige was at its peak and before gold began to work its insidious evil spell. Gold, especially unsecured gold, could corrupt any man. That included both the merchants back in Lychmidas and the men here in the Hold. That very summer he had seen Jonathan, a friend and confidant of many years, lose his reason to gold fever. Athan wanted to get all his gold into that treasure room and out of sight of everyone else but himself as soon as he could.

The best answer to Athan's problem seemed to be to somehow bring Yure the Elder's little detachment and any additional men he had recruited back to the Hold along with the Satrap's stolen gold. He could wait to decide just how to get significant reinforcements for the garrison after the Illyrians left. What he had to decide right now was how he was going to fetch his two dozen talents of gold from Lychmidas back to the Hold, or more specifically who would go to get it. After considerable thought he confirmed what had he had believed from the start; it had to be either Rodas or himself. He would not trust this assignment to anyone else. So he would have to trust Rodas, but what to trust him with? Should he send Rodas to collect two dozen talents of gold or leave him in charge of an entire fortress? This was the choice that kept him up most of the night walking the battlements.

In the end, Athan's choice was obvious. It was far more difficult to make off with a stone fortress than a couple dozen talents of gold. Athan would have to be the one to bring the gold back to the Hold. Once he decided he was to take the journey it was as though a great weight had lifted off him. He was helped by Theron, the hunter. The scout had mentioned to Athan that he had noticed the mounted scouts did not depart their camp until it was full light, and left their posts before dusk, so that they could arrive back to the safety of their camp before it was dark. This made it difficult to ambush them, but it also meant that there was about a half hour of light in the morning and evening when the posts were vacant.

Athan called a council of war and presented his plan to Rodas, Myron, and the sergeants. The plan was for three men, Athan, Giles, and Myron, to slip out the back of the Hold and make their way from the Hold using a track Myron claimed went around the hills between the lake and the Hold. They would follow it until they cut across the north-south road that led back to Lychmidas. Unfortunately, according to Myron, the trail wound around and traversed some very rough terrain, so it would take them perhaps half a day to reach the point where they could strike the road again. Much worse, they would enter the road less than half a parasang from the north hill where watchers were posted. They would be in full sight of the watchers for over a parasang until they could get over the next low pass to the north and be out of their sight.

The plan for departing unobserved was simple. They would leave from the back gate, which could not be observed from town, and make their way east toward the lake. Then, using Myron's track, go around and almost up to the point where they would be visible to the northern set of sentinels. They would stop there, staying just out of sight, observing the sentries, until they either saw them leave, or if they could not see the sentinels, at least until the evening. Then the men would use the last of the day to make it down the slope, strike the road, and move north until they were out of sight of the sentry hill. From there they would travel back to Lychmidas the same way they had come. Once in Lychmidas they would meet up with Yure and his five men and any others he had recruited. Then they would collect the gold and baggage and return. There was a very spirited debate about bringing along the four women attached to members of the band. Some thought the trip too dangerous to risk the women. Others thought it was too dangerous to leave them in Lychmidas alone. The same argument was made about the gold. Some wanted to bring the entire amount, others only a portion.

Athan finally stopped discussion by stating that he would decide what was to be done after he arrived in Lychmidas. The specifics would be decided on the spot. What did need to be worked out before their departure were arrangements for their return. It was not practical to use the same back trails they employed on the way out. A few active men could follow a goat track. A dozen or more of people with pack animals carrying a heavy load of gold could not. There was also the very real risk of being discovered, cut off, and cut down. Instead Athan proposed a bold alternative. As before, they would stop just below a rise that kept them out of sight from the view of north sentinel hill. Once the watchers were judged to have left for the day, the caravan would move up the road and stop just below the final crest on the road that led down to the town. There the caravan would camp just out of sight of the town. The men would try to signal the Hold with hooded lanterns. If that failed they would signal flashing the rays of the rising sun to the Hold. The men in the Hold would reply using the double mirror reflection technique backed up with flags or failing that, smoke signals. Once the arriving party had confirmed the Hold was ready they would come over the hill and down the road. At a point less than a third of the way to the town a small path led straight across the hill toward the Hold. They would cut off on that trail and start to move as fast as possible, heading in a direct line for the back gate. At the same time, every man who could be spared from guarding the walls would sortie out the back gate and form a double line of hoplites a little way down the ridge. From that position they could threaten any attempt of Illyrian cavalry to interfere with the caravan making its way up the side of the ridge. Athan was under no illusions that the Illyrians would be slow to react, but it would take them some time to mount up and get organized. Further, they would have a longer way to go than the caravan to reach the Hold. Once the returning party had reached the top of the ridge the hoplites could retire behind them. The rear gate would slam shut and Captain Aeolus would know that the Hold had been reinforced.

Of course no one liked the plan; nevertheless, Athan prevailed upon them. The only changes he allowed were an agreement to take Theron the Hunter with them, so their party would be four not three, and to leave out the back gate before the guard on the north sentinel hill was manned. They were not sure if watchers on the northern hill could see the back gate and they did not want to risk any chance of discovery.

The rain that had begun the evening before had continued all night and lasted off and on until noon the next day. The Illyrians sent a delegation in the afternoon; this time Athan did not attend the negotiations. Rodas would not budge a finger's width from the position stated by King Athan the previous day: a quarter talent per year in gold, alliances, trade agreements to be negotiated later. After an hour they left, frustrated. Athan made sure they caught a glimpse of him walking on the battlements as they left.

Other problems were beginning to resolve themselves. Of the 14 prisoners taken when the Hold fell, five of the eight wounded men had died. No prothesis for them, just a wrapping in a cheap cloth shroud. Their only ekphora was the trip down the hill on the back of a squeaking slops wagon with the only mourners the slaves who regretted the extra work. There was no dignified ceremony for their bodies; they were merely thrown into one of the garbage pits. The covering of a mound of dirt was the only stele they would have. It was usually thus for fighting men who violated the most important tenant of their profession: never die in a losing cause.

One minor exception to this rule was made for Ratimir. There was a hubbub when the Bear's body was finally discovered by the people in the town. It was not until the scavengers began to attend to his remains that his former subjects became aware of where he was. The men on the hill could see groups of men and woman coming up to see him, a macabre version of a prothesis. After a time a cart rolled up the hill and several men levered the body into the cart and carried it the rest of the way down the hill.

That night a bonfire was observed on the outskirts of town which the men in the Hold correctly deduced was the funeral pyre of the man once known as King Ratimir, the Bear. What they did not know was from that day forward, even more of the former supporters of the Bear began to slip away from the town; human bits of flotsam that had lost their moorings.

Part of that flotsam included the eleven surviving prisoners. After considerable debate among Athan's council and the band as a whole, four were left to remain chained in a little stone cell, four of them were pushed out the front gate and told to leave the area, and three were taken provisionally into the garrison as new recruits. The men were all young, and newly brought into the Bear's service. The sergeants were confident that with careful supervision and 'positive leadership' they would become trustworthy members of the band. In any event, the sergeants were correct and the men soon became useful members of the garrison.

The following morning, just as the sky began to lighten, the four companions who would be making the trip back to Lychmidas mustered in the stables. The four men made brief farewells to the garrison and walked their horses out the back gate. The sky was covered by a high layer of herringbone clouds that looked as cold as the ground below. They had taken the eight horses that Ixon considered to be in the best condition, so that each man had a fresh remount. They were traveling light. The men carried swords and javelins but no spears, cuirasses but no shields, hats but no helmets.

Athan was carrying one new item, found when they cleaned out the Bear's previous quarters. These included the stinking rooms on the ground level near the southeast bastion where the Bear spent his final days and also the spaces located on the second level directly above the sick room where he had lived before his infirmity. This larger and cleaner set of rooms on the southeast corner held most of the Bear's finer possessions. Some had been pilfered by the time Athan and Rodas had a chance to inspect the apartments, but there was still much of value. Athan gave some of the jewelry and carvings to his men, and the rest were carried down to be stored in the treasury for eventual sale. One item, however, caught the new king's fancy.

It was an unusual dagger. The weapon was a large gaudy thing, with a long ivory hilt, big enough to fit even the Bear's enormous fist. The cross guards had been gilded, though the gilt had begun to wear away from the iron in places. Two crystalline stones of unknown origin had been inserted into the end of each of these guards, and a large milky gem set into the pommel. Gold wire was crosshatched over the hilt so that when it was in its sheath it looked more like an ornament than a weapon. The blade itself had been painted white; Athan had never seen a white blade before. He could see where some of the paint or whitewash used on the blade had been scraped away by use. Gaudy it might be, but the heavy black-iron blade underneath the paint was all business. It was as long as Athan's foot, with a thick, heavy blade. The tip was unusual as well. Instead of coming to a typical point it abruptly ended at a 45 degree angle. The relatively broad tip had been sharpened so that it had a chisel-like quality. Athan understood that such points were very effective at punching through armor. In fact, the more he examined the odd weapon, the more he became convinced it was a cut down (or perhaps broken) short sword, converted to a dagger. This did not bother Athan. It balanced well and the blade had a powerful feel to it. From the men who had previously served King Ratimir they learned it was indeed the former king's personal dagger. It even had a name: Bear's Claw.

The sheath for this weapon was of embossed leather also decorated with gilt. It was also unusual also because the loops to attach it to a belt were above the top of the hilt, causing the weapon to be worn lower than usual.

Athan strapped the dagger to his belt and found that the weapon reached almost exactly from the point of his hip to his knee. He tied the tip of the sheath around his leg just above his knee with a bit of leather thong. Worn so, lying flat along his right leg, it did not get in his way. After a time he could even forget he was wearing it. Athan still preferred his big old kopis for serious fighting, but this dagger would be lethal for close-in work, and being lighter and handier, could be worn where a sword would be out of place. It was against his leg as he rode out that morning.

Athan knew he was taking an entire series of gambles. They would have to evade the Illyrian cavalry, of course, both coming and going. And he would have to trust Rodas with the Hold and all it contained. Ten of the men in the remaining garrison had previously been in Rodas' band and were especially devoted to him. That was a quarter of the entire strength of the garrison. Even after three months of serving with Athan as Chief, they still demonstrated loyalty to their old chief. That gave Rodas considerable influence with the garrison; the opportunity might tempt any man.

The travelers wore the usual baggy wool trousers and gray cloaks but at Athan's insistence they also each brought one of the despised grass cloaks. The spare horses carried only a minimum of supplies and equipment, though they did carry some firewood which was unusual.

Once out the back gate they turned immediately to their left and led their horses carefully down the north side of the ridge, since the far end was too steep for safe descent. Once at the foot of the ridge the men mounted and headed off to the east with the ridgeline looming up to their immediate right and the far northern hills off to their left; the sun was just beginning to light the tops of the highest elevations. By the time it was full light they had made their way along a low twisting trail and were well out of sight of both the Hold and any possible watching enemy.

"Where does this trail lead?" asked Athan to Myron. "I know you said a side trail bends around to the north; why is this path here?"

"I think it goes all the way to the lake," replied Myron. "I heard that fishermen used to sell fish to the Hold. Not for a while, though."

"We have time, let's go see."

They passed by the fork that led up into the hills to the north and continued downhill to where the lake glinted in the near distance. Athan estimated it was not much more than a parasang or so, all downhill. The trail ended at a small cove formed by a short point of land that jutted into the lake. There was a cold breeze that set the waters of the lake moving and sparkling in the early morning sunshine that broke through the high clouds. Athan thought that this would be a pretty place in the spring and summer when the foliage filled in; there were trees here near the shore of the lake, both deciduous and evergreen. There was no sound except the sound of the gentle breeze in the pines and the lapping of the lake. They were well before their time so Athan called an early rest. The men started a fire for a brew up of herb tea and let the horses graze and drink from the lake. Although it was cold, they were sheltered from what wind there was, and in the sunlight it was actually pleasant.

Athan walked down to the lake and then out onto the point of land. Myron followed him. They had a good view of the lake. A distant peninsula was faintly visible jutting out into the lake to the north, but to the east all that could be seen were the tops of the mountains on the other side of the lake. The far shoreline itself was invisible from here.

"You say that fishermen used to bring their catches in here?" Athan asked Myron while musing that this place seemed like a long way from anywhere.

"Once," confirmed the merchant, pointing to an open place in the undergrowth that appeared to be a muddy beach. "Only, the Bear's men started taking their catches without paying for them. After that happened once or twice, the fishermen started taking their catches to markets that gave a better price." This last was delivered dryly.

"Where?" wondered Athan aloud. He had been to sea before and had a great respect for large bodies of water. Compared to the salt sea, this broad expanse of fresh water seemed hostile and alien.

"Many of them live in Lychmidas," answered Myron. "It is just on the other side of the lake."

"We will have to ride all the way around it," said Athan thinking of the long hard days in the saddle before him.

Both men had the same idea at the same time. They looked at one another.

"They don't go across the lake in the winter," said Myron, "it is too dangerous. This lake can turn nasty in a hurry. Winds come swirling down the mountains and the waves get very big, very fast."

"Too bad," said Athan. There was pause. "I think I want to have a better look around." And shedding his new cuirass and sword belt, he approached a tall pine that had apparently been struck by lightning and now stood dead white on the short peninsula. Removing the leather belt around his tunic he swung it around the trunk of the dead tree, grabbed an end of the strap in each hand and twisted the ends over the backs of his hands. There was just enough length for him to lean back slightly. He then hitched the belt up the bole of the tree and bracing himself against the belt, began to work his way up the tree. This went fine until he came to the first major stub where the first branch of the tree had been, about two body lengths up. While he was negotiating this hazard Giles and Thereon noticed him and came over to watch, Giles with concern, his older comrades with amusement. It did not help that Athan was clumsy in getting past this first branch.

All three of his companions then began to offer advice ranging from the practical, 'pull yourself up on the next higher branch,' to the humorous, 'very graceful, just like an old bear looking for honey' to the concerned, 'sire, please come down, let me go up.'

This last was from Giles. It was good advice as Giles was younger, lighter, and more agile. And of course, Athan ignored it all, though he did start to climb up using the dead branches. Inevitably one did not hold his weight and broke suddenly, causing Athan to have to frantically grab the trunk of the tree. This event caused a new round of advice following the same pattern as before. Athan climbed up to another set of branch stubs where he could catch his breath. He was now about four or five times his height and had a clear view of the lake. He thought he could make out the shore on the far eastern side. He guessed it was about five parasangs or so to the other side. It was so close! Then Athan noticed the way his tree was moving in the wind. Unlike the other pines that bent supplely in the breeze, this one made a stiff rocking motion. Athan abruptly decided he had seen enough and headed down.

Ignoring the questions of the others Athan walked down to the end of the point, and stood there looking out on the lake. Turning abruptly he asked "How did the fishermen find this place?"

Myron could only shrug and say "They just knew the way. Fishermen have ways of knowing things," this with a mysterious air.

Athan remembered riding in the Satrap's boats the previous summer, and how the shore tended to look different from the water. Perhaps the fishermen could find this place, but then again perhaps not. Maybe it would be possible to cross the lake in boats, perhaps not. In any event, he wanted to be able to find this place again. He would need to mark it. "Giles," he said, "go get one of those ground cloths from the packs and bring it here. And fetch some of the rope, too."

"Sire," began Myron cautiously, "are you thinking about coming back by boat?'

Athan just looked at him.

"Umm," began Myron again, "sire, that would be much more dangerous than trying to get past those horse boys in town. We can just wait; they will leave pretty soon. What is your hurry?"

Athan did not tell him what was in his mind. It was not just the fear of treachery; he was worried about what would happen to if he were not there to oversee things. He trusted the men he had left behind, but he was afraid they would do something stupid. No, not something stupid; that they would either not take appropriate action or do something that would commit him to a course he did not want to take. Athan recalled his boyhood when he and his friends would play a game; they would bend and tie a flexible willow switch into a hoop. Then using sticks they would roll it along the ground. Athan vividly remembered how it was important to keep the hoop rolling; how it was easy to maneuver the hoop with frequent gentle stokes with their sticks, when it was kept moving briskly and how hard it could be when the hoop slowed and began to wobble. Right now he felt his little kingdom was a hoop that was not moving very fast. He was afraid that soon it would begin to wobble. He could not explain the urgent need he felt to get his treasure all into a nice safe place, surrounded by men he trusted. But it was a real pressure to him, as real as that which drove a springtime bird to urgently build a nest. Every part of Athan wanted to collect his men and money and get back to the Hold just as fast as he possibly could. Only then could he relax.

He did not share any of these feelings. Instead Athan moved to the dead pine, the others following him. When Giles returned, Athan directed him to wrap the ground cloth and rope around his shoulders and climb up the pine. "Get up above these low bushes," said Athan gesturing to the brush that lined the shore. "I want you to tie off that cloth like a flag. I want to be able to find this place from the water." He saw Giles' uncomprehending look so he explained further. "Boats used to come here. It is close to the Hold. I want them to see where to put in by boat."

His young aide still did not see the point of putting a ground cloth on a tree as some sort of flag, but he obediently started climbing up the dead tree. Here on the ground Athan could see the tree's uneasy motion and he worried about the whole tree falling under Giles' weight. He was not the only one.

"I wonder how long this thing is going to stand?" commented Thereon.

"Good point," agreed Athan, "go get another of the ground cloths and some more rope."

"I am too big to be climbing trees," said the scout dubiously.

"Nobody is asking you to," shot back Athan. "Now hurry up and get me that cloth."

While young Giles completed his ascent and attached his makeshift oversized banner to the trunk of the dead pine, the other three tied off another cloth to some of the bushes at the water's edge. Stepping out to the very end of the point, Athan looked back at their handiwork. Giles was almost all the way down the tree now; the heavy cloth lay listlessly against the trunk. It did make a noticeable mark against the white trunk. The other cloth was lower and not as obvious, but if you got closer it clearly marked the place where it seemed other boats had once landed. He took some time to look at the shoreline from this slight protuberance and tried to imagine how the shore would look from a boat further out. He asked Myron to do the same.

"You are not really thinking of coming back here in boats, are you?" asked Myron, alarmed. "I told you the fishermen don't cross the lake this time of year. It is far too dangerous."

Thereon, who had not heard of the fishing boats crossing the lake before this, looked alarmed. Athan only smiled.

"Good work, Giles," he called to the young man as he completed his descent. "Now, we need to get packed up and on our way."

The transformation in Athan was dramatic. The trip down to the lake had been almost leisurely. Athan had even commented that they should not even approach the cut down to the road until the sentinels had departed just to be sure they were not seen. Now, it seemed he had changed his mind. He had them pressing forward up and down the trails, fretting when Myron lost his way once, and scarcely letting them catch their breath in all too infrequent breaks. Everyone was relieved when Thereon was able to come back down from peering over the crest of a hill and report that the road was in sight below them. Only then did Athan allow the men to unsaddle, feed and water the horses. Even so, they rested for only about an hour before Athan had them up again and ready to ride, even though it was well before sunset. He and Thereon lay on their bellies at the crest watching the men on the north sentinel hill, waiting for them to depart. Their tension was heightened by the fact that it was difficult to see the watchers at that distance, though they themselves would be seen at once if they tried to ride down the open slope. Finally they saw movement on the hill as men mounted their ponies and began returning to the town for the night. Athan did not waste any further time, and the four men and their eight ponies were over the top and headed down toward the road almost at once. They headed north as soon as they hit the road, moving at a steady canter until they made it over the crest of the hill that separated them from the sight line of the hill. They continued on at a ground-eating pace until it was fully dark, when Athan allowed another rest. They built a small fire using the firewood they had been carrying, and had a hot meal while the horses ate. Athan did not assign men any watches, nor did he allow them to fully unload their small packs. The high clouds had dissipated during the day, and now it was a clear cold night with the hard bright stars of winter. A partial moon made an appearance.

Thereon, who had been with Athan for years, recognized the restlessness in his leader and knew what that meant. He had already started to repack what little gear he had out when Athan mentioned that it was a fine night for a little ride. They continued, cold and tired, down the dark road, often walking the horses so that they did not lose the way. It was after midnight before Athan finally relented and let the men stop for the night. In an unprecedented move, Athan did not set a guard, but allowed all four to sleep at the same time. They slept in pairs sharing the two remaining ground cloths and body heat, wrapped in their cloaks, blankets, and covered with the grass cloaks.

"First one to awaken after it gets light, wake up the rest of us," was the only set of night orders he gave.

It was hard to roll out of the relative warmth of their covers the next morning. After the long ride the night before, Athan was almost patient in allowing the men to build a fire, brew up some hot tea, and roast a bit of meat to go with the bread and dried fruit. They later realized this was because Athan wanted them to be able to continue without further delays. Myron had told Athan it was four day's travel between Dassaria and Lychmidas. This was true for merchants. Athan's band had done it in three, coming down to attack the Hold. But even a hard riding group cannot hold the same pace as four men, especially if the four have lightly loaded remounts. Athan kept them moving rapidly all through that long day. Well before dusk they came in sight of the corner of the lake where the north road joined the east-west road that skirted the top of the lake. Even then he kept them going until he saw the camp fires of a group of travelers on the road ahead of them. They were able to arrive at the caravan's camp just before dark and gain permission to camp within their lines. They were fortunate that some of the men in the camp knew Myron well enough to vouch for them. Once again, the four were able to sleep the night through without guards, sharing the protection of the caravan.

By now it was clear that Athan was determined to make it to Lychmidas the next day; even so they were astonished at the pace at which he drove them in the morning. Not even when fleeing the Satrap's men after stealing the Empire's gold had he driven his companions so hard. They were able to make it into the town shortly after noon. Athan sent Myron to discover where the men who owned the fishing boats might be found and Thereon to round up Yure and his men while he and Giles made a trip to the counting house to check on his treasure.

The men in the counting house were very surprised to see him back, especially so soon. Athan found that it would be necessary for him to return in an hour in order to be granted a proper audience. Since there would be a delay, the two men went to the house where they had left Yure and his men just over ten days before. Neither Yure nor Thereon were there, so Athan decided he would wait there in the house until it was time for his interview with the counting house. His irritation at the delays was increased when he found he could not get a meal in the house. Giles was sent off with blistering instructions to get them some food. Athan sat in the common room near a fire, tired, hungry and frustrated at the way his plan was already coming apart. He had seen the clouds building to the north. If he was going to cross the lake by boat it would have to be tomorrow, or he would be forced to wait until the next set of winter storms passed by.

He sat there stewing, ready and eager to chew someone's head off, when two of his men, Pontus and Aorastus, walked in with their wives. Surprise was mutual. At once the women hurried off to bring him some wine and provisions from their rooms. His men gave him good news on the recruiting front: Yure had contracted with no fewer than twelve men, most of them experienced. There were others interested as well, and he was sure that at least a score could be persuaded to join them by the end of winter. Pontus had bought some fish from the locals and confirmed that there were several stout fishing boats down by the water and they had been out recently, but not caught any fish in several days. Athan hoped that might mean they would be more amenable to taking his party across the water.

The women returned with bread, cheese, olives and wine and made a fuss over him. Another of the men left behind, Sergeant Stamitos, joined them and got the good news about the successful conquest. There is nothing to sooth an ill temper like food and wine, praise from your men, and admiration of women. By the time Myron, Giles, Thereon, and Yure all arrived (almost at the same time) Athan was beginning to feel positively expansive. He had the great pleasure of telling them to wait there while he and Giles left to meet with the men in the counting house. He would go from there to meet with the boatmen at a location near the lake; Myron would wait there for him. Then the three would return to the house for a council of war. Yure and his men were to assemble all the potential new recruits for an inspection at that time.

At first, the meeting with the men who were holding his goods went satisfactorily. He asked to convert some gold into drachmae and then set a time when he would return with guards to recover his property. From their demeanor Athan began to suspect that the men here had realized that his holdings were considerably more valuable than they had first realized. They may have even realized he had left not just supplies, but a great deal of gold with them.

"We have a modest proposal for you, sir, that you might find interesting," said one of the older men, who was apparently in charge. "Abacus, present your ideas to the captain."

A young man who had been sitting quietly against the wall stood. He was from Magara; a distant relation of one of the partners. He was taller than most, gangly, clean shaven, with a long nose that reminded most people of a beak. Although young, perhaps in his early twenties, his dark hair was already thinning. He bore himself with gravity and the self confidence that in a young man can be taken for arrogance or self importance. In the case of Abacus, these descriptions could be considered accurate, along with pompous, condescending, and brilliant. Abacus' real name was Aesculus but he preferred the sobriquet, since he used the counting tool with such skill. He was clutching an abacus to his chest as he approached Athan, trying to hide his nervousness; because he was still young he was doing a poor job of it. Nevertheless he made his proposal clearly and captured Athan's attention. In that time and place the idea of paying interest on loans was novel, nor was that exactly what Abacus was suggesting here. The young man proposed that Athan leave an amount of gold with Abacus' employers, which they would invest in land and trade and then pay Athan an agreed-upon portion of the proceeds, all on a regular basis.

"How will I know how profitable the ventures are?" smiled Athan. "And what will happen to my money if the enterprises are lost?"

It was an obvious question. There was no standard for accounting. Each merchant and business had their own system, some rudimentary and vague, others sophisticated and accurate, but none of them were open and available for inspection by anything like an auditor. That was why most businesses were based on family ties or long-term relationships cultivated over years. Abacus had the answers for this stranger who was said to have a great deal of gold. He, Abacus, would provide guarantees in writing of the amount to be repaid regardless of the success of the ventures. Here Abacus brought forth a parchment document already completed.

"Will you trust me to read it or would you prefer to bring in your own reader?" Abacus asked unctuously. Even the three other merchants in the room were offended by this youngster's supercilious attitude toward an older (and apparently much richer) man.

"I'll read it myself," growled Athan snatching it over to his side of the table. Abacus' obvious discomfiture brought smiles to the faces of the three merchants.

Athan for his part did not reveal how difficult it was for him to read the document. He had not read anything lately and at no time would he have been called a man of letters. He did make out the offer of a hostage as part of the agreement to insure the funds would be redeemed.

"Interesting," observed Athan after a suitable pause, "perhaps I will invest some of my wealth with you. I will tell you the amount I chose to invest, if any, when I return to collect my goods. I expect to return in the next hour or so. Please have it ready."

"There will be a slight delay in retrieving your goods," smiled one of the merchants insincerely, "please return in two days. We may have your possessions ready by then."

Athan felt a powerful surge of anger. Part of him distantly noted that perhaps he, himself was not completely immune from gold fever. 'These men seem to think they possess my gold,' thought Athan angrily. 'They think they can keep it when they want and give it to me whenever they want.'

Athan's voice hardened, "I will return in one hour to recover my property."

"I am sorry but we will be closed then. Come back in two days."

Athan felt the thick swelling of anger in his throat. 'They are the ones sick with gold fever,' thought Athan. 'They think that since they have my gold in their house they can keep it from me. Soon they will start making up lies to me and each other about how my gold is really their gold. I will **not** let these soft merchants take away my gold.'

"I am coming for my goods with my men."

"Rest assured it is safe here. Our guards are alert and the walls are thick."

"So were the walls of the Hold."

The merchant gave him a puzzled look.

"The Hold is the place where King Ratimir once held sway. It is ours now, and the territory around it."

The merchant smiled with his mouth and said "As you say." He very much doubted that this mercenary could have even gotten to the Bear's Hold and returned in the short time they had been gone, much less taken it away from that ferocious warrior and his men. It showed on the faces of the men.

Athan was now well and truly angry. He wanted to smash this smug merchant's face. He also knew that any sign of weakness would result in further delays in delivery of his gold. Athan had gone to way too much trouble stealing that gold to have some miserable merchant think he could have any of it. His inner rage must have translated to the other men in the room; the tension suddenly became almost palpable. The counting house's two guards had their hands on the hilts of their swords. Giles, too had his hand on his sword and looked ready to sell his life for his leader. Athan's face was a thundercloud, his fury directed not only at the merchants but at himself for neglecting to bring proof of his conquest such as the golden diadem or one of the Bear's rings. Then he remembered that he did have something of the Bear's.

"As this says!" said Athan dramatically and with a sudden move, he drew King Ratimir's dagger out and plunged it deep into the soft wood of the table.

The move almost started a fight. The two guards and Giles drew their swords. The merchant had started at Athan's gesture but quickly regained his self-possession. He started to repeat his 'as you say' comment; fortunately he thought better of it. His two fellow merchants were pale as milk; Abacus was thoroughly rattled.

After a moment, a very tense moment, the chief merchant shrugged and said: "Ajax, go get Philleus and bring him here. He did say he worked for this King Ratimir didn't he?"

The guard Ajax was not happy at leaving his boss in such dangerous company however, he nodded and departed. He was gone for what seemed to be a long time to the men in the conference room where not a single word was spoken, but it was probably less than a tenth part of an hour. Giles and the other guard had lowered the points of their blades; they did not, however, resheath them. At last, Ajax returned with another man wearing what looked to be a hastily donned sword. Athan saw movement outside the door and knew that the merchant's entire guard had been turned out and was waiting outside the door. Yet he was now calm and relaxed. If it came to a fight he was ready. Between the dagger in the table and the kopis at his side he was confident that none of these miserable worms would leave the room alive no matter how many men waited outside.

"Ah, Philleus," said the merchant with a false smile and even more false bonhomie, "do you recognize that dagger stuck into my table there?"

Pilleus was not the sharpest blade in the smithy. He looked carefully at the dagger, turning his head this way and that like a puzzled puppy. After a moment he pronounced "It is the Bear's Claw, umm that is umm, King Ratimir's dagger. I have seen it several times. Once when he took it out he," here poor Philleus realized this might not be the proper time and place for the story he was about to relate and he stopped abruptly. Gathering himself he continued on more formally. "There cannot be two weapons like that, sir. It is a true sign. This man must be a messenger from him." Then he stood tall, a man who had figured things out and done his duty.

There was a pregnant pause as an entirely new set of relationships were recognized and reconsidered. Then Athan said with calm finality, explaining something as though to a simpleton (which was in this case more or less true).

"It is not the Bear's Claw anymore, Philleus. He is dead. I am the King of Dassaria now. My men live in his fortress. All his possessions are now mine." Then turning slightly to the merchant he continued in the same exact tone. "I will consider this man's proposal," here he gestured to Abacus whose earlier conduct now seemed by comparison exemplary, "and return in two hours with some of my men. I expect to have my goods, all my goods, ready to be taken away." There was another pause. Relentlessly Athan continued, "Should the items I left with you not be available, I will have to consider you and your people to be no better than thieves." The last line was given with a long steady look at the head merchant.

The leading merchant was no weakling. He had a long history of successful dealing with dangerous men; he had almost a score of men in the house guard, and was a man of considerable influence in the town. Even so under that steady gaze, he finally and fully understood that this stranger who was looking at him had in fact, seemingly without effort somehow swept away the Bear, the most threatening menace in the entire region. The merchant's nerve broke. He had enough self-control to murmur, "As you wish" in a polite if quiet voice; his body was suddenly bathed in sweat which to his intense embarrassment ran down his face.

There was a stiff and formal departure; Athan and Giles, both of them angry and tense pushed their way past the guards and departed. It took all of Athan's self discipline to restrain himself from shouting threats and imprecations to the merchants and their posturing guards. Instead, he put out a soothing hand on Giles to restrain him from similar comments. They walked out of sight before losing control. First Athan, then Giles stopped and loudly vented their pent-up feelings, shouting curses and threats to the blank wall of an alley. Both wanted desperately to lash out, to fight and hurt those arrogant greedy men who had tried to steal their gold. Athan knew it would be counterproductive to do any of the things they were threatening to do. After a few moments of release he hugged his companion fiercely and praised him for his courage and restraint. It was perhaps the happiest moment of Giles' life. Neither man was aware that back at the counting house similar expressions of rage, mixed in this case with shock and dismay, were being exacted. After a time the group consensus there became that somehow it was all the fault of the outsider Abacus.

Athan's meeting with the fishermen was almost as frustrating. He was fortunate that Myron had been able to identify the leading boatman and arrange a meeting.

"It was not all that unusual to find fishermen in port right now," repeated Myron, "They don't go out on the lake much this time of year."

The two men had discussed strategies for persuading the men to take them across the lake. Myron had mixed feelings when he discovered that Athan only intended to take some of his men with him in the boats, leaving Myron behind to return with the rest of the men and horses.

"I don't want to leave the horses, and there is no way to get that many animals in the boats. I just want to bring over some of the baggage and the women, so if you do have to fight your way into the Hold you won't be burdened with them."

Myron did not reveal his thoughts on the idea of fighting his way past an entire troop of cavalry to get into the Hold again. Perhaps he was considering the other option, riding across a big, deep, scary lake with winter coming on.

Just before they entered the shed near the beach where the boats were drawn up Athan stopped and looked to the north. "We will have to go tomorrow. If we delay beyond that it will probably be better to go back the long way."

Myron looked to the darkening north sky then to the lake. This time of year it was normal for cold fronts to move through the area bringing either snow or cold rain and always winds, sometimes very strong winds that could last for days. It would not do to be out in the middle of that body of water when such weather came through. From the appearance of the northern sky such a storm from was starting to build up; perhaps it would arrive tomorrow or the next day, once it did, the lake would be closed to them for at least three or four days. If they were going to try to dash back to the Hold by crossing the lake, it indeed needed to be soon.

Myron did the talking with Hali, the leader of a group of the fishermen. Hali had an idea that Myron and the two men with him wanted to go somewhere; he did not expect to hear that they wanted to cross the lake. At first he simply refused, but he did not leave the table. Instead they talked of the weather, Hali obviously understood the region's climate; as a waterman, his life depended on knowing the local conditions. In its own way the lake was even more dangerous than the sea. What usually killed boats was the shore, not the waves, and on a lake the shore was almost always nearby. What usually killed men were cold and exhaustion and the lake waters were cold, cold, cold. Worst of all, on a lake conditions could change suddenly, catching a boat that had been lured out too far in pursuit of a good catch and sweeping it helplessly away from safety to smash on a rocky lee shore. Hali thought the storm would not come on the morrow; he was confident it was likely two days away. So he listened and weighed his options. After a time he decided in his own mind that the risks were too great. The men wanted to hire five boats, and he did not want to risk so many men. He might be willing to tempt fate himself, but risking so many boats and men was too much of a gamble. Hali was a polite man. He did not want to offend the strangers, especially since they were obviously dangerous men. So he put them off by simply setting his price impossibly high.

"Five boats are out of the question. Even four boats will need eight men to row them. It will be very dangerous. It will take a day there and a day back, and with this weather coming I do not think it can be done. But we will be willing to try for you. Our fee is four thousand drachmae." This outrageous offer was uttered with bland sincerity.

"Perhaps you did not understand our request," countered Myron, "we wanted only to hire five boats for a short journey, not purchase them." It was an almost standard answer to an initial offer, in this case it was actually close to the true price of the boats.

"I could not get five boats even for five thousand," answered Hali. "We have only four boats that we can make ready. The small boats are all put away to avoid the terrible storms that will soon return. So, for such a dangerous journey at such a dangerous time of year, one thousand per boat is our fee," and Hali smiled.

"I will pay fifty drachmae per boat and one hundred to you personally for choosing the crews and arranging the trip. We can leave as soon as you say," said Athan, entering the negotiations for the first time.

Hali showed nothing; he was suddenly tempted. Three hundred drachmae was a lot of money. He could work a whole season and not earn a hundred drachmae. "You say your need is great," he countered, "perhaps I could find seven other fools who would be willing to risk their lives, but they would not do it for less than five hundred per boat. And I will need five hundred as well."

From that point on they made progress. Several times Hali withdrew from the bargaining to consult with others. Once he spoke with his wife. It seemed they were discussing the merits of the risk against the prospect of significant personal gain. Myron, Athan, and Giles could not be sure if Hali's wife was against the dangerous venture or in favor of a chance for an unexpected windfall. As the deal came closer to finalization Hali became increasingly nervous. He stepped out and began talking to some of the other watermen who had gathered around as new of the discussion had spread. Not only was Hali concerned about the actual trip, now he felt pressure to put the venture together. He owned two boats himself, and would have to convince the owners of two other boats to accompany his two over the lake. He would also need men experienced enough to be able to make such a daunting trip but who were also hungry enough to be willing to try.

The shadows were long when Myron and Hali came to an agreement. Using an odd gesture both spat on their hands and gripped each others elbows then kissed each other's cheeks. Hali had contracted to have four boats carry eight men and four women and their baggage, not to exceed the weight of eight additional people; a total weight of about 20 medimnos. This caused eyebrows to be raised. When asked as to the volume of the baggage Athan blandly informed him it would be dense, 'armor, swords, and some iron for our smith.' The boats could bear this weight, but there was concern and grumbling from the boatmen with vague statements about jettisoning excess weight if the wind came up. For his part, Athan would pay one hundred drachmae per boat and an additional hundred and twenty to Hali for leading the expedition. Hali would be responsible for apportioning the money to the men who would take them over. The first hundred was to be paid before departure, the rest to be guaranteed by the merchants of the counting house. Hali could accompany them to the house in an hour to receive confirmation that the money would be delivered to the fishermen on their return. Hali was local and well known to the merchants of the counting house. A public commitment to them would be honored. As was common in these cases, Athan would tell Hali a codeword once they arrived at their destination. That word would let the merchants know that the fishermen had fulfilled their end of the bargain and could pay the men off in good conscience. They agreed to depart from the boatman's shed that night when the moon set; this would be just over an hour before dawn.

It was now almost sunset, and Athan hurried back to the house where his new recruits were to muster. He was behind his time and walking quickly when he rounded the corner of the house. What he saw caused him to stop so suddenly that Giles, hurrying close behind, bumped into him. Yure, a canny old campaigner, had posted lookouts and when he was told of Athan's approach he had quickly formed the men into ranks facing the corner of the building. Two files of seven men were lined up, standing tall with shields and spears grounded with Sergeant Yure out in front. At his signal they raised their spears and as one man clashed them against their shields with a shout of 'Hail!'.

Athan was pleased, of course. He had asked Yure to see if he could recruit a few more men to supplement the others he had left behind, but this was more than he hoped for. His pleasure increased as he walked along the lines of men, listening to Yure's comments and speaking with each man in turn; most were experienced men of arms, whether with a city guard or an army. Some, using oblique phrases, implied that they had been with various bandit bands in the hills. Yure seemed to have chosen well. There were only three young men who admitted their inexperience frankly; probably Yure had coached them in advance on how to reply. Two of the men caused Athan a bit of unease. These two seemed a little too hard, a bit too anxious to get in on a chance for booty. But they seemed to be tough fighting men, and right now that was what Athan needed.

By the time Athan finished his hasty inspection, dusk was turning into night. Giles was sent ahead to the counting house to inform them that, though Athan was late, he was coming. Athan then held a brief council of war with Yure. Unusually, he did so in front of the men. He did not want there to be any misunderstandings about what he wanted.

"We will be going together to pick up some of our wages for the next season." Athan began in a penetrating voice. "I will go in with Giles and Myron. I do not expect any trouble, but be ready; there are robbers around who may try to steal our wages." This got the growl he expected. "There may even be some thieves inside the counting house itself. So Thereon will stay near the entrance and make sure it is safe inside. If he signals you Yure, bring the boys in. Remember, we don't want any unfortunate accidents. So, keep the men in formation ready to repel and attack from the outside or to respond to an ambush set up inside."

This was enough for Yure to understand that Athan was not certain he could get the gold out and they might have to go in and take it by force. They might also be menaced by the city's guard called to support the men in the counting house. Athan reviewed potential lines of withdrawal and rally points were identified.

Athan finished with a plain declaration to the men. "I do not expect trouble tonight, but we must be ready. And I want us to look sharp. They have to understand what kind of men we are." And with that they moved out toward the counting house, one file on one side of the road, one on the other. Next to Athan strode Yure and Myron, these three walking right down the middle of the road.

They arrived at the counting house to find Giles and another man waiting nervously outside. Yure stopped the two columns of men, while Athan and Myron continued on to where Giles stood.

At a nod from Athan, Giles indicated that all inside was ready. A look at the other man rewarded Athan with a confirming nod. Still tense, they entered the counting house. As agreed, Thereon followed them and waited behind just inside the entrance, as the others went into another room. There beaming, offering welcoming embraces, cups of wine, and trays of delicacies, were three merchants. One had been in the previous confrontation that afternoon; the other two were new. At first Athan feared he was being softened up for a more subtle refusal. He was quickly reassured as the merchant's questions were all about deliveries of goods - what portion of his possessions would he like provided, where would he want them delivered, and when? Two questions had already been decided; he would take the gold from there immediately. How much gold should he take? Ever since he had left the boatmen he had been calculating weights. He could bring along enough baggage to equal the weight of eight men. To Athan's mind, that meant between a score and twenty-two talents of gold. He no longer trusted the men at counting house. He estimated that he could probably get more into the boats, but how much more? Impulsively he made a decision.

"I intend to take advantage of your man Abacus' suggested investment. Where is that young man?" he asked.

Athan later found that his earlier encounter had sparked off a long-simmering conflict within the counting house. After Athan departed following the confrontation, a long contentious and argumentative meeting was held. Eventually the old patriarch of the house was appealed to as final arbiter. His ruling was simple. Their business was based on trust. Even strangers should be treated honestly and with respect. The merchant who had attempted to squeeze Athan was disgraced.

Abacus had suffered by association and was waiting for what he assumed would be his dismissal. He was an unusually self-confident young man, but even his cast iron certainty in his own merits was badly shaken. He was angry and frustrated. It was all so unfair! He had not had anything to do with that idiot's plan to try to gain control of the incredible wealth dropped into their laps by this strange bandit. Oh, for a chance to manage some real sums of money! Now he would be sent back south with no money, no reference, no prospects. If they would just give him a chance! It was at this low point in his life that he was summoned back to where the new conference was being held. He was afraid he was to be publicly humiliated and told to depart. He was to be surprised.

"I have read this young man's proposal," said Athan without preamble. "Does this plan have the support of your house?"

By that time the men in the counting house were ready to do whatever it took to get out of the situation they were in. They were aware that this man who had apparently conquered the kingdom of the greatly feared King Ratimir in one single day had almost a score of trained warriors just outside the gates of the counting house, and undoubtedly could bring even more if necessary.

'Yes,' they said with feigned enthusiasm, 'how much would he care to invest?'

"I would like to invest four and one half talents of gold as detailed in this document. I intend to remove the remainder of my goods at once."

Smiles and relief all around; Athan's investment of that sum would almost double the wealth available in the counting house for investments.

"As to the terms," continued Athan, "it calls for a representative to remain with me to personally assure the terms are maintained." Tension returned to the room. No one cared to use the term 'hostage' but that was what this person was. Athan continued, with barely a pause, "I would like to have this young person Abacus to be that man. Would you mind? I do need someone to help me oversee my finances."

Total quiet met this astonishing request. Athan was not asking for one of the merchant's sons or nephews, instead he was willing to take this troublesome distant relation from Megara off their hands. This was most acceptable. For his part, Abacus was first stunned, then suffused with joy. No maiden, meeting an arranged husband for the first time and finding him unexpectedly kind and handsome, was ever so thrilled. No bee trapped inside a house until, suddenly, a door is opened and the bee is free to fly out into the sun and waiting fields of clover ever felt such a release. All of Abacus' dreams were suddenly made real. He would be in charge of the fortunes of a kingdom, and apparently a very rich kingdom! He would be the one responsible for making it grow! He would be able to track and manage every single drachma! It was the happiest moment of his life. A terrible fear suddenly overcame him. What if the merchants would not let him leave the counting house? A look at their satisfied faces immediately put him at ease.

As if in a dream he heard himself saying, "I am willing to do that service, sir".

And so it was done. The meeting ended with great satisfaction for all parties; the men of the counting house had turned around a potentially damaging situation and created a new and lucrative account. At the same time they had conveniently rid themselves of an annoying member of the counting house, actually putting him to good use somewhere else. Athan was satisfied as his men helped load four score gold bars onto waiting animals, each bar taken from its leather enclosure and carefully checked for signs of adulteration or shaving. While this activity was going on in the walled courtyard, the boatman Hali was brought into one of the outer rooms and the details of his bargain with Athan was explained to the beaming merchants. They gave Hali tokens that could be redeemed for four hundred drachmas, the extra hundred twenty having already been given to Hali. Before the men parted, Athan personally requested of the merchants that if Hali did not return by the spring, the money should be given to the boatmen's families. This was a generous offer and appeared to please Hali.

Hali departed and Yure came in to tell Athan that his goods were loaded and ready for transport to their destination. Final details were completed: the required code words were shared with the merchants, money was provided out of his balance, tokens provided detailing the wealth remaining in their care and finally, with Abacus joining them, his meager possessions carried on his back, the band took its leave.

The band had more or less taken possession of the house where Yure and his group had been staying. Fortunately it adjoined a large stable and manger so that the men were able to get in out of the weather. Hot meals were provided in the kitchen, bonfires lighted safely away from the stables, and watches were set. The leather bags that held the gold were stacked neatly in a stall, guarded by two men, surrounded by the sleeping places of the rest of the band. The gold was kept in twenty heavy packs, made to order during their time of indolence back in Pella. Four quarter talent bars were fitted into leather pouches, two on each side of a wide strap of heavy leather that could be slung over a horse or a man's shoulders. The pouches were covered by flaps that were sealed, though Athan (from personal experience) did not place too much faith in seals alone. Each pack represented one talent, weighing about a medimnos; a heavy load, but manageable by one man. All that night three outside guards and two men inside were themselves watched by first Yure, then Thereon, who acted as sergeants of the guard.

For his part, once Athan had been fed all he wanted was to go to a local bath to clean himself up after the work and worry of the past three days and then to retire for a good night's sleep in the security of the house. Before he retired for the evening he held a council of war with the men who would be riding around the lake to the Hold. First, he reviewed the plan to get past the Illyrian horsemen at the Hold. Thereon and Myron would be traveling with these men. Yure was to take the eight horses Athan had brought around and supplement them by buying more locally as available, until each man in the band had an animal to ride. He was to limit baggage as much as practical, keeping the number of pack animals down to a minimum. He might hire some locals to accompany them to their first camp to carry extra grain and provisions for the first day. Yure did not need to hurry. He could delay his departure if the weather was too inclement, using the time to hire additional men if he considered them suitable. In particular, Yure was to ensure men and horses were fresh before starting their final dash to the Hold. Athan would look for him every morning starting on the fifth day from today.

Athan then turned his attention to the plan for the party that would be crossing the lake in boats. They would cross the lake, cache the gold near the shore, then walk up to the back side of the Hold and get some men from the garrison to come back with animals to retrieve the gold. Nothing to it.

Finally, leaving word that everyone was to be awakened when the bottom of the moon was two fingers above the top of the western hills, he went to his bed. He was asleep almost instantly.

Winter was almost done. There were days when the Old King could wander outside his crevice where he slept. He did not leave the little draw where he had his refuge. He found he ran out of energy after just a few score of steps. The old man did take time to set some more deadfalls for small rodents (or anything else he could catch) farther out from his cave. He was somewhat hindered by the fact he had nothing to use for bait. Still, it gave him something to do besides lay in his bed and watch the fire. He was very aware that a mouse or two every few days would not be enough food to keep him from starving to death. It was a slow race between the coming of spring and starvation.

Chapter Four – Over the Water

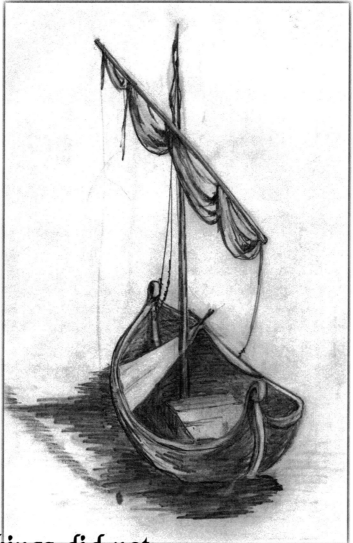

Things did not go well from the moment Athan was awakened, or rather was not awakened. For whatever reason, the watch failed to awaken the departing party until the moon had almost completely set in the west. Cursing, he threw on his tunic and pulled on his boots, leaving his blankets and other gear behind. Stopping only to splash a little water on his face he bolted out of the hut with a ripping set of orders to turn out the entire force, and get the passengers and treasure bags down to the beach right now.

Leaving an embarrassed (and therefore savage) Yure behind to keep things moving Athan and Giles trotted down toward the scheduled rendezvous, buckling on their swords as they went. Athan stopped to tie the lanyard of his dagger above his knee, then put on his vest over his tunic and swirled his gray cape around his body as he hurried down the hill toward the rendezvous. Just before he reached the shed, he stopped and collected himself. Then, walking calmly, he approached a fire where a group of men had clustered in the morning chill. It was still and damp and Athan was grateful when, after a mumbled greeting from Hali, he was offered a bowl of steaming fish stew and a piece of bread.

"You're late," accused the leader of the boatmen.

"I am sorry," apologized Athan, "my people are sometimes hard to get moving in the morning."

"I am used to such," replied Hali generously, "so I set the time early enough for you to have some breakfast before we leave to keep up your strength. Of course, now your people will miss it."

Perhaps the people coming behind heard this small threat, or more likely Yure was verbally setting their behinds on fire, because people began streaming down from the house to the campfire. They did not come in a calm ordered group as Athan had wished, but instead arrived breathless and half-dressed. They began gulping down the offered bowls of stew greedily, making a commotion and disturbing the tranquility that had surrounded the men who had been waiting around the fire. Critical items (at least critical to those who wanted them) had been forgotten and men rushed up the hill to recover them, then dashed back. Athan had hoped for a calm, quiet departure, and this was anything but. One of the young wives, Neysa, took one whiff of the aromatic fish stew put it down and rushed over to a small bush were she emptied the contents of her stomach. This was greeted with general jeers from the boat men, who made comments such as 'not even in the boat and she's puking her guts out,' and 'going to be fine feeding for the fishes on this trip.' Then making matters worse, another of the young wives did not even get close to the stew pot before she, too withdrew, swallowing hard with a hand over her belly.

Athan was fuming. He began to berate the men for taking up with women who were so delicate that they could not even begin a simple ride across a lake. As he was warming to his subject, Athan was brought up short by Stamitos' woman, Beryl. She was the oldest of the women and had taken the role of shop steward for all matters distaff.

"They are with child, lord," she told him with some asperity. "Surely you know that women in that state are prone to illness in the mornings. And here they are about to cross that dark bit of water that looks like the very Styx itself." She gestured toward the direction of the unseen lake, "Then they were awakened suddenly and dragged out of bed. It is enough to make anyone bring up their dinner."

Athan was now caught. He did not really want to leave the women behind. For one thing, he was not sure if the men would leave their women, and he needed the men with him. On the other hand, he did not want to expose expectant mothers to the dangers out there on the dark water that they would soon be crossing. Added to that, he did not relish the prospect of having to cross the lake with two women vomiting over the side of the boat or worse, inside it. He felt like he was going to explode from frustration.

He was rescued from his conundrum when Hali and his men abruptly got up and moved downhill toward the unseen boats pulled up on the beach. Athan saw that a torchlight procession coming down from the stables where the gold had been kept the night before. Yure had every available man up and armed surrounding the four horses and six donkeys that were carrying the 'baggage' to be carried over the lake. While they approached, Hali and his men prepared the four boats for departure. Athan watched as the men lifted the boats one by one and positioned them over wooden rollers then pushed them over the shingle into the water.

The boats made an interesting contrast to the much larger ones Athan had ridden the summer before. They were planked boats, each board having been carefully fitted smoothly into the next and tightly caulked. Athan estimated two of the boats were about eleven cubits in length and four in their beam. The other two were a bit smaller. The boats all had a high prow with the same type of eyes painted on the bow as every other boat Athan had ever seen. There were three thwarts where oarsmen could sit, with pairs of dowels coming up to act as oarlocks.

The bow and stern both had a short covered deck where it would be possible for another person to sit. Each boat had a thick keel consisting of what appeared to be a single solid piece of timber. This part of the boat had to be strong since, not only were all the ribs attached to it, but when the boat was hauled in and out of the water this sturdy member had to take the brunt of that friction. Athan saw that there was no sign of anything that looked like a mast or other gear for hoisting a sail. There were five oars alongside the thwarts and little else. This boat was propelled by oars and oars only.

Hali was going to be in the largest boat. As soon as the boats were floating on the dark lake, Hali beckoned to Athan to begin the loading. It took longer than Athan liked to get the line of animals down to the water's edge, then offload the leather packs (which were wrapped in sacking in a feeble attempt at disguise) from the horses and carried out through frigid knee deep water to dump in the bottom of the boats. Hali and his men were immediately interested in the weighty cargo being put into their boats. As soon as the first of the heavy packs hit the bottom of the boat, Hali shouted at the men to be careful not to stave in the boat's planks. A fisherman stood in each of the boats as the leather packs were handed in and stowed them carefully in the bottoms of the boats, gradually moving the boats into deeper water as they settled with the weight.

"This is more baggage than you said," complained Hali to Athan. "What is in those bags?"

"Weapons, armor, some iron for our smith, as I told you," Athan replied blandly unbuckling his sword and placing it carefully in the boat. His big dagger remained on his thigh.

Hali grunted to indicate he knew he was being lied to but he was unwilling to press the issue. Athan decided this was a good time to give him his advance. The fisherman took the purse and handed it to a stout woman who had to be his wife; she tucked it carefully away. The passengers were bringing few possessions, and the boatmen only a few loaves of bread for provisions.

They would number twelve. Four men and their women would come, of course. Athan and his new accountant, Abacus, would make the journey partly because Athan did not know what else to do with his new employee; he seemed eager to remain with the treasure, and he certainly could not be expected to help fight his way into the Hold. Giles' friend Xenos, who had been left behind in Lychmidas, would come with them partly because he felt he had been unfairly left behind the first time and partly because Athan wanted another fighting man with him in the boats. Athan had divided the party into four parts, one for each of the boats: Stamitos & his woman Beryl would ride with Aorastus in the first boat, Pontus & his young wife Neysa with the new accountant Abacus in the second, Tracy & his new woman Cadis would ride with Xenos in the third and smallest boat as those two men were the smallest in the party; Giles and Aorastus' wife Amara would ride with Athan in the largest boat. The two larger boats would carry six loads of gold so that the two smaller boats only had to carry four of the heavy bags.

Athan had left the house so quickly that he was only wearing his winter tunic and cloak, leaving his trousers off, as he often did when he was not riding. Now, in the cold morning he wished he had remembered them.

The women were put in the bows of their boats while the other male passengers were seated side by side on the middle thwart. The fishermen said their goodbyes, and then with help from others remaining on the beach, pushed the boats out into the lake.

The boatmen began to pull steadily out into the lake. It was cold and very quiet except for the rhythmic thump, thump, thump sound of the oars. As they pulled away from the shoreline Athan saw a lamp, shielded from the wind by a glass globe, being hoisted up to a platform some distance back from the water perhaps a dozen cubits off the ground. Then another lamp moved to a second point and was also raised up, but this time apparently on a pole closer to water and lower to the ground. Once the two lamps were set, the other lamps were either extinguished or were carried off with their owners to bed. The boats immediately shifted their courses until the four boats were proceeding out onto the lake in a single line. Looking back, Athan now saw the two lights; the lower light was directly below the upper light. Suddenly he knew how the fishermen could hold a straight course out on a pitch black lake: they lined up the range lights; so long as the lower and upper lights remained aligned the boats knew they were on course. Thinking back,

Athan now remembered seeing a tall platform on a hill some distance back from the beach and a number of poles set into the earth, just back from the water's edge. They boatmen could put one light in the upper platform and then hoist a lamp in the proper lower pole to give boats their bearings to any desired course out onto the lake

Athan spoke to the back of Hali, who was setting the stroke as the stern oar of the lead boat. "So what I heard was true; you used to cross over to sell fish to Dassaria."

Hali continued to ply his oars, his broad back giving away nothing. Athan could see a faint lightening in the east. Finally the boatman said, "There are things to do other than sell fish; especially to sell fish to men who do not pay. It is a long walk up to that place." Athan assumed he meant the distance from the lake to the Hold. "There used to be people we knew that lived over there on the shore part of the year. Some say there are a few good places to fish on that side."

Athan knew that fishermen guarded such spots jealously. He made a comment on the importance of freshness when eating fish.

The big man responded, "After a time the people who lived in that place on the shore over there left. Maybe somebody up on that hill did not like them. Anyway, not many people live over on that side of the lake now. Now you, a rich man, you might be able to set up some friends on the lake. They could supply you with fresh fish in good weather, in the right season," he continued making it plain this was NOT the right season. "They could carry things back and forth. There are no pirates or bandits on the lake. It might be a useful thing to have friends on this lake."

The two men talked casually back and forth in this vein for a while. Hali was making the initial overtures in the long delicate process of building a mutually beneficial relationship. Athan was interested, but before any real deal was settled upon the two men stopped talking and looked back to the east with increasing dismay.

"Ooohh, it is so beautiful," they heard one of the women in the boats behind them say. In fact it was a passing lovely sunrise; the eastern sky was becoming bright with pinks and red tints on the high cirrus clouds visible against the high pale blue sky. Lower down, the looming cumulous clouds were going from a fluffy pale light tinting at their tops shading darker and darker all the way down to their bases which remained hidden in the last of the night. Athan could not remember seeing a more spectacular sunrise. He also knew what a red sky in the morning meant. The boatmen knew, too; there was soft, intense swearing among them. It was still very still; the lake had a deep calm, the water seeming heavy and solid with only the ripples from the boats disturbing the flat surface. Suddenly the light shifted and the lake waters reflected the red sky.

"We are floating on blood!" exclaimed another woman.

Athan knew he needed to nip any panic in the bud. "No," he said in a carrying voice, "not blood. I know blood. This is much pinker with too much orange in it. It is like we are flying in the clouds."

This was not quite true, but it was certainly a more charming simile. The still lake water was reflecting the pink and red tints of the sunrise, giving the lake an otherworldly aspect with only the boats and their wakes spoiling the perfection. The shore behind them appeared to be a long way back, with the lanterns now merely dim sparks on the dark shoreline. Athan turned and looked over his shoulder, and was relieved to find that the shoreline ahead of them was visible in the distance just below the mountains that rose above the lake.

Hali called out to the other boats, shipped his oars, and taking the extra oar, used it as a rudder to swing the boat to starboard to let the other boats come up alongside. There was a very brief conference between the boatmen. Bad weather was coming and it was obvious the boats could not cross the lake and return home before the storm arrived. The conference ended when Athan pointedly remarked that if they returned he would have to have his advance back. Perhaps Hali did not want to loose his big payday, or maybe he was more afraid of asking his wife for the money back than he was of the coming storm.

All he said was, "We probably couldn't get back home before it hits anyway. I don't fancy pulling into the wind for the rest of the day just to lose our fee." And he slid his oars back out their tholes and began to pull strongly. Looking back over his shoulder to check his position, he altered course a bit to starboard. Then he called out to the following boats something that sounded like 'echelon line astern to port' or some such esoteric phase that was unintelligible to the landsmen. The other boatmen seemed to understand him though, and the boats fell in behind him, slightly off the next boat's port quarter so that each boat had clear water ahead of it.

"How long do we have before the wind starts picking up?" asked Athan.

"Hard to say; at least you will be able to see it coming," responded Hali.

"Do we have an hour?"

"Yes, probably more. It will probably wait until we get right in the middle."

"Do you mind if I spell your man on the bow oars until it gets here? He might need his strength later on."

The two boatmen greeted this offer with amusement, but after some good-natured chaffing, the man behind Athan shipped his oars while Hali kept his stroke and the forward oarsman and Athan changed positions.

This exchange went unnoticed by the other boats because while it was happening one of the women cried out that there was water in the bottom of her boat. This provided a diversion from a number of sources. Responses ranged from the amused to the irritated. She was assured in several different ways that all boats leaked, where did she think she was, was she afraid she would melt away, why didn't she stop bothering them and start bailing? Her naïve comment turned out to be very useful, as it gave the people in the boats something to do other than look back at the developing storm that was coming down fast from the northeast; some began using the bailers in the bottoms of the boats while others saw to storing the goods in the bottoms of the boats more securely.

Athan was grateful that his people had their eyes in their boats, because he quickly found out that pulling a single oar on a ship was a lot different from rowing a small boat with two oars. But after a few embarrassing uncoordinated strokes he began to get the feel of it and, following the movements of Hali, who was pulling smoothly in the stern of the boat, he soon gained the rhythm of the thing. By the time he was noticed, his strokes were matching the other boatmen's. Once the change in oarsman was noticed it brought much amusement in the other boats. The sun was up now and there was a steady breeze from the north northwest, not blowing strongly yet, though there were occasional gusts that promised much more wind and soon. There was movement in the other boats as some of Athan's men began to try their hand at rowing. Giles, always eager to imitate anything Athan did, tried his hand, replacing Athan at the oars. His efforts at rowing were so unsuccessful that to his intense embarrassment, after a few moments, he was relegated to bailing while Athan resumed the stroke. Few of the fighting men lasted at the oars for more than a quarter hour. Although they were tough and fit, they found that rowing a boat used different muscles than they were accustomed to using and their hands, hard though they might be, were not hard in the right places. The new money man, Abacus, made no effort to row, huddling silent, nervous, and clearly out his element. The others in his boat ignored him, which suited everyone. Only Athan was able to maintain his stroke for most of the next hour. He had remembered an old trick from his brief time at sea and had put two wide loops of leather in his purse the previous night. Before he took up his oars he had looped one end of the leather over the back of his wrist and ran the strip of leather along his palm and looped again over his middle finger. It was not exactly a glove but it helped. Athan pulled long enough so that even Hali got an unexpected break. He gave his place to his fellow fisherman and sat on the center thwart resuming his conversation with Athan who continued to pull steadily. Athan did not mind rowing; the work was keeping him warm. Hali seemed to enjoy the turnabout as well.

"Usually one of us will row while the other rests," he confided, "having our passengers row keeps us moving a little faster and is much more amusing."

And the mood of the people in the three boats had indeed lightened as they made fun of the landsmen's efforts to row over the next hour. Slowly, as the wind began to strengthen and the chop began to increase the boats became harder to manage

"Best let us take over again, sir," Hali told Athan, shifting back to his seat and gesturing to his man to resume the bow oar. "It doesn't take long for it to kick up, does it?"

Athan was amazed to see how fast the weather had changed. One moment the boats were gliding over a still pink surface, the next a rippling lake, now suddenly a cold wind was beginning to push hard and the lake was showing whitecaps. The boats began to rock uncertainly and a bit of spray started coming over the gunnels. Athan could hear

Neysa in the boat farthest back, who was not only pregnant but also very young, begin to cry. Giles was bailing and Athan now had nothing else to do except look at the other boats. He noticed Aorastus' wife, Amara sitting quietly in the bow of their boat, watching the water.

"You don't seem worried," said Athan hoping that she would provide a good example to the other women.

Amara shrugged and responded, "I have had three sons and two husbands. All are gone. What more can happen? Besides, I have heard that drowning is not so bad." Athan just looked at her. She continued, "My boys all got sick and died. So did my first husband. And when my last son died my second husband left." Then, that set of tragedies explained matter of factly; she turned and went back to watching the water.

Athan winced. Although Amara was no girl, she was pretty enough. Some of the men had wondered what she saw in Aorastus who, though a good man, was past his prime, was neither learned nor charming, and was far too battered by life to be considered handsome. There he had his answer. Amara was a woman who had quit. Aorastus had been there, so he would do. She would drift along until she was dead, for right now, as far as she was concerned her life was already over.

One thing was in their favor; as the storm grew, the wind was on their starboard quarter and it was pushing them right along.

"Why don't you put up sails," asked Athan to Hali who continued to work the oars steadily.

A sudden gust struck the boat from the beam causing it to suddenly heel to port for a moment before it settled back. A chorus of shrieks from the two younger women in the boats astern told Athan that the gust had affected their boats as well.

"That is why," grunted Hali as he strained to keep the boat on course. "Wind is always moving around on the lake; it comes from anywhere and it can come on strongly. Besides, sails and masts and such get in the way when you are trying to fish. I can get anywhere I want with two oars and these two arms."

The wind grew stronger, and even though the sun must have been getting higher in the sky, the clouds kept it out of view. The day did not warm. Now most of the passengers were more than merely chilled.

Athan wished again he had his trousers on, and that he had brought one of the grass cloaks they had worn on the ride over. He wished he had brought a thick wool blanket. He wished he had dry stockings, or at least did not have to sit with his feet in the cold water rolling around in the bottom of the boat. Instead, he had to sit, chilled to the bone on a hard wooden bench with a cold wind blowing up his tunic.

He could tell that they were well across the lake; the hump of land he had glimpsed to the north of their landing place four days ago was now visible in the distance fine off their starboard bow. Athan noticed that Hali was looking back over his shoulder more and more often, obviously scanning for a familiar landmark. It dawned on Athan that Hali might not know just where the little beach they needed to land was located. Athan remembered how dangerous the sailors considered a lee shore; when the wind blows from the water toward a dangerous shoreline. With this wind pushing them toward land, it would not be easy to row up and down looking for the right place to land.

Athan twisted in his seat and faced forward. Now he could see the land clearly, and it was coming up fast. He would have been delighted to have seen the end of this miserable trip, had he known just where the land they were coming up to was. It all looked very different from the water. He saw no sign of a dead white pine with a ground cloth flapping from it. He saw no dead trees at all.

"Do you know what you are looking for?" Athan asked Hali who he caught looking back toward the upcoming shore.

"Not exactly," confessed the boatman. I tried to head up to weather so we can run down along the shore, but with this wind, who knows?"

Athan turned back to resume his watch of the shore. He noticed Amara sitting listlessly in the bow. "Hey," he called to her. "Help me look for our landing place. It is a big white pine tree, dead, with a big ground cloth attached to it like a flag."

She roused herself and began scanning the shore. They were now only a few bowshots off the land. Hali pulled the boat around to port and began to row parallel to the shore. The wind instead of coming off their starboard quarter gusting astern was now pushing on their port quarter, gusting occasionally on their beam. Even rowing parallel to the land they were inexorably being pushed down on the shore where waves were now breaking.

"I don't want to have to pull up and down the shore in all this wind if I can help it," Athan heard Hali say, "if you see anywhere that looks reasonable, let me know."

Not long after he said those words, Amara spoke. "How about that place, she said. "It looks like it might give some shelter." Then she spoke again, "Is that the flag thing you said to look for? Over there on that bush."

Athan peered just ahead of their beam where she was pointing. It took him a moment to recognize the ground cloth they had secured to the bush. There was no sign of the big white pine, but now that he had his bearings, the little peninsula was also visible.

"There!" he shouted loud enough that the people in the other boats heard him even over the wind and waves. "Right there! See that little bit of land sticking out into the lake? There is a place to pull out there just to the side of it."

Hali immediately cranked the boat around and headed in to shore, followed by the other three boats. The little mud beach was not big enough for all four boats to come in to land at same time. Fortunately, once they got behind in the lee of the little spit of land, the wind, though still strong, eased, and the waves, so rough out on the lake, dropped significantly. Hali shouted some commands to the other boats, and then headed his boat in to the landing. They grounded abruptly. Giles and Athan leapt into the cold water so fast they tangled up with the oars of the forward boatman. Grabbing the gunnels they heaved the boat up and onto the shore. Amara jumped clumsily ashore, getting wet to her knees then unexpectedly laughed as she set foot on dry land. The men hastily hauled the leather bags out of the bottom of the boat and pulled it even higher up out of the way.

Hali, now convinced of the suitability of the site, gestured to one of the other boats holding just off shore. The boat came in pulling hard against the wind. Athan and Giles helped beach that boat. Neysa, miserable in the bows, had to be helped out. The men heaved the bags out of the bottom of the boat and shoved it back out into the lake. Freed of the load the boat maneuvered easily.

"We can pull your boats ashore here, and you can ride out the storm in my fort," offered Athan.

"No, it is too small and unprotected for all of us. It would be too crowded with all four boats in here at once. Besides, this wind is not that bad," replied Hali, looking up at the sky, "There is still much of the day left. I know a place up to the north where we can all spend the night in greater comfort and security. I will be home by tomorrow."

"Thank you," Athan said with heartfelt sincerity, and told him the codeword that would release his payment. "Here is a little something extra for your trouble," and reaching inside his tunic for his purse he took a handful of coins, he had no idea how many, and thrust them into the boatman's hands.

By now the second boat had pushed off and rowed clear as the third began making its approach, with the fourth close behind.

Athan gripped Hali in the warrior's handshake, each man gripping the other's forearm. Athan spoke over the rising wind. "Thank you, Hali, I actually enjoyed the trip. Perhaps we will meet again."

It was a bedraggled little group that stood just above the edge of the lake watching the four boats, now riding much higher in the water, head north, pulling slowly against the wind. The first order of business was to cache the twenty bags of gold they had unloaded. A good place was right at hand; a long white pine had fallen near the end of the peninsula. It had a familiar appearance. Athan and Giles shared a look. No wonder they had not been able to see it from the water. And they had both been up in that tree only three days before. It would have been a nasty fall. The men placed the bags holding the gold along the bole of the fallen tree and then covered it as best they could with dirt and debris. Some of the party peeked out from the undergrowth to make sure the boats did not observe what they were doing. There was some concern the fishermen might return to rob the cache. It had been impossible to keep them from figuring out that those bags held treasure, a lot of treasure. The boatmen were no threat to Athan's band; they were outnumbered and had only their belt knives as weapons, but they might decide to return and pilfer what they could not rob. One glance at lake convinced Athan and his people that the boatmen had other things on their mind out there on the lake; the boats were now scarcely visible through the wind and water, for a cold misty rain had begun to fall.

The little band had little other baggage and no food at all, so as soon as the gold was secured, they were ready to depart. Athan directed that the two ground cloths he had left to mark the site be brought with them. They were draped around the women, who were having a hard time of things. Amara was bearing up well. On the other hand Neysa was still crying softly, and Beryl and Cadis were shivering. There was no thought of stopping to try to warm up. It was late afternoon and Athan wanted to get into proper shelter before dark. After all, it was only a bit more than a parasang.

A parasang in that time and place was far from an exact measure. A single healthy man on level ground could cover that distance in an hour if he were fresh. In this case they were a group of men and women, if you include a fifteen year old girl, pregnant with her first child, as a woman. Though they were lightly burdened, they were far from fresh, and the path was uphill all the way. They soon had another worry. Athan had noticed horse sign at the landing site. That was expected; they had been there only three days before. Then the men began noticing fresher signs, and of more than just eight horses. They could only have been left by Illyrian cavalry patrols. If they encountered one of these patrols, they were doomed. Even a few of riders could delay them while messengers dashed back for reinforcements. There could be no hope of a successful defense with neither spears nor shields. The men did not have bows, javelins, or even a sling. Their only hope was to avoid contact. Should they be discovered, Athan told the group to disperse and head uphill to the steepest point they could find, and then run for the fort as fast as they could. It was not a desirable option.

Athan put one of the men well out ahead as a scout. That entailed further delays, with the weather getting continually worse. 'At least' thought Athan, 'they are less likely to have patrols out this far in weather like this.'

Dusk was coming on before they came to what Athan believed was the far eastern end of the ridge that the Hold sat upon. Everyone was very tired, and the women were approaching exhaustion. They had been dragging themselves up a faint slippery path with wet clothes in a slow steady freezing drizzle all afternoon. Neysa, the youngest and most vulnerable, was on the point of collapse. He husband, Pontus, alternated between yelling at her to be quiet and trying to comfort her. The group, which had become spread out, coalesced at the foot of the hill.

"We are almost home, now," Athan encouraged them. "We just have to climb this hill and then walk a short distance to the back gate. We will be in time for a nice hot dinner."

No one spoke, no one moved. Athan began to climb the hill, the others following. At this point it was a steep ascent. It was necessary to bend over and use their hands to climb, grabbing clumps of earth or tufts of grass. Just before Athan got to the top he motioned for the others who were laboring up behind him to stop. They were all out of breath and glad to comply. Athan lay out on the ground and eased his head over the top, afraid he would see a detachment of horsemen between himself and the back gate. Instead all he saw was the rain-swept top of a ridge, inclining gently down to the Hold's back gate. Looking back downhill he saw eleven upturned faces looking at him anxiously.

"It's clear," he called back, "come on up, dinner is waiting." He lay on the ground, catching his breath as his people came by him in small groups. He gave Neysa a hand up as the party passed by him and headed for the back gate. When the last one had passed him he turned and looked at the group now hurrying toward the gate. He counted to make sure they were all there; then he got to his feet managing a slow trot after them, glad that he did not have to climb any more hills that night.

Perhaps the watch in the back bastion was not as alert as it might have been, but it was alert enough. Before they reached the gate a figure was seen on the battlements over the gate. There was motion partially glimpsed as figures ran past arrow slits in the bastions. Athan's group clustered by the back gate; Giles was the only one with the presence of mind to call for the gate to be opened.

"Who goes there?" asked the man looking down at them from the walls.

"Athan, King of Dassaria," shouted Athan striding up to the gate. "Now open the damn gate, we are hungry."

There was some brief discussion of passwords; Athan put an end to that when he recognized a voice. "Are you going to keep me out of my own house, Niomiki?" he shouted. "Don't tell me you don't know my name like Thereon did."

That did it. The gate opened and they rushed in past the guards, which Athan noted with pleasure were properly armed with shield and spears in case of a ruse. Once the last of the party was through, Athan nodded to Niomiki, who closed and barred the gate with alacrity.

They were deluged with questions. 'Why had they come back?' 'Had they been ambushed?' 'Where did he find the others?' No one could quite grasp that their new King had made it all the way to Lychmidas and returned in just four days. Rodas, hearing the news of Athan's return, came hustling back from the front of the Hold with all these questions and more.

"First let us get dry and fed," interrupted Athan steering his tired little group to the left toward the mess hall. Once there he got them to sit at a couple of tables and dragooned a meal from Cook, even though it was an hour before the scheduled evening seating. Cook brought them hot tea and fresh-baked round maza folded over and stuffed with cheese; it was a simple meal but delicious. A stew was being prepared and they were all promised portions as soon as it was ready. Celeno, assuming the role more of a matriarch than a cleaning woman, took charge of the women. They were spirited away, returning in less than a quarter hour wearing fresh, dry clothes.

"Where are the women to stay, Sire?" Celeno asked Athan with only a brief hesitation before using the title. "All the good rooms are more or less occupied. They cannot stay in one of the barracks rooms. Do you want me to put them in the stables with the other four?"

"What other four?" asked Athan, confused.

"The ones Ixon rescued," she replied. "They are staying in a stall in the corner of the stables. Adara says they feel safer there. Ixon takes care of them and keeps them safe."

Whether the last was Adara's opinion or Celeno's was not clear.

Before Athan could even draw a breath to speak, Celeno resumed her comments. "I think you should reserve the rooms for the married men. It is not right to have wives, even pallake, staying in an open room with those other soldiers. And while you are rearranging who is in what rooms, you really need to set aside some other rooms for the women. My daughters and I are simply packed into that tiny room next to the privies with Titania and Phila. Now that we have more women, we need a better place."

Celeno then announced that the baths would only be open to women for the next hour. The women, carrying pots of hot tea and fresh maza with them, departed, moving under the eaves around the perimeter of the Hold, picking up Celeno's daughters as they passed their rooms, then disappearing into the stables, apparently to collect the four lost women. Athan finally grasped the fact that the four unfortunate women were still apparently where Ixon had taken them the night Athan had captured the Hold.

It took more doing than expected to get dry clothes for the new men. It was easy for Athan and Giles. They had clothes waiting for them in their room. But the others had no spare clothes and nowhere to stay. Athan decided that he needed to have a man in charge of the Hold's spaces, a majordomo, to handle details like this. For now he decided to turn the problem over to Prokopios. Then he thought of another chore that needed to be done.

He turned to Giles, who was eating as only a hungry young man can.

"Giles, companion of my heart," Athan said looking at the tired young aide. "There is more to do this night. Can you lead some men back to where we stashed the gold?"

"Of course, sire," said Giles wiping his mouth. "Right away."

"I would not have you go down alone, for I know you have done much already this day. Go put on dry clothes. Take Xenos with you. Go up and put on the warmest clothes you can find; let Xenos use my other winter tunic and some trousers. Come back here as soon as you can get ready."

The two men headed up to Athan's room, both of them stuffing a maza into their mouths as they went. The wind suddenly gusted savagely, pushing stinging frozen rain ahead of it.

May Poseidon protect those at sea," said Xenos feelingly, thinking of the men who had ferried them across the lake.

"Amen," agreed Giles.

It was much later before the men of the hold learned the fate of the eight fishermen who had carried them over the lake at such peril.

At first, the four boats, freed of their loads, made good headway against the wind. Hali kept them relatively close to land, despite the gusts that sometimes backed around to the west and pushed them perilously close to that dangerous shore. Hali had planned to use the lee of the big headland that jutted into the lake a few of parasangs north to give his men a break from the wind, then carry on around it a few more parasangs to the northwest corner of the lake where he knew of a hamlet with a few little dwellings where they could shelter for the night or even longer. He had stayed there before. But it took both men in each boat pulling hard to make progress against the wind that was steadily increasing and inevitably they grew tired. By the time they neared the big headland they all almost exhausted and the wind had grown so strong that even the lee of the hilly headland did not give them the break from the headwind they needed. Worst of all, they had not been able to hold their earlier pace. Now it was getting dark. Being out on the lake after dark in this weather was more than merely dangerous.

Hali knew that they had to find a place to get off the water and out of the cold. He had never landed on this headland before; even so, he was able to find a likely place on the leeward side of the peninsula where the boats could run in and beach. The men drove the boats ashore and pulled them up with stiff legs. Hali knew that cold made men stupid before it made them dead, so he thought very carefully before deciding what to do. The men had sat down either on the ground or on the gunnels of the boats, all turned with their backs to the wind and thus to him. This angered him and he used that anger to drive his men to action. He got them moving, hauling the boats further up to a fortunate grassy area. There, he had them turn the two biggest boats over side by side a little less than a boat length apart. The high prow meant the boats rocked over to one side, leaving a gap a man could crawl under. Hali stopped one of the men who started to do just that.

"Not yet," he roared. "Get this boat up." And he had them maneuver the next boat to the windward side of the other two boats and placed it crosswise on its side leaning against the other two boats so that the formed a U with the open side facing down wind. Then they lifted the smallest boat up and placed it on top of the two big boats nested against the crosswise boat. Now they had an enclosure that you could sit under that gave real shelter from the winds and some from the rain. Still he would not let them rest. He drove the men to collect dead wood, leaves and bunches of grass. They argued that the material was soaked. They reminded him they had no means of making fire in this wet. They asked him if he had any food left, even though everyone knew the last food had been eaten hours before.

It was while they were collecting this material during one of the intermittent intervals between the icy rain showers that they smelled smoke. The men followed the welcome odor over the closest hill. Here was the greatest stroke of luck of all! A shepherd was sheltering his flock in a little hollow just inland from them. His dogs' barking brought him out of his hut, stick in one hand, knife in the other. Things were tense when he refused them charity. They withdrew from him. Some of the boatmen were ready to attack him and take his food and shelter, but murder was not something these men were eager to do. Besides that the shepherd looked to be the doughty sort and he had three fierce dogs. The fishermen had only their belt knives. It would not be a battle without cost, and as tired as they were they might even lose.

It was when Hali went to touch his knife for reassurance that his hand brushed against the purse he had on his belt. He felt the coins Athan had impulsively thrust upon him as they were leaving. Hali smiled. There are times when a man can feel his luck change, and just like that, Hali knew everything was going to be just fine.

"Perhaps you misunderstand our intent," he said smiling as he approached the shepherd again, this time alone. He ignored the dogs snarling at him. Hali had a good feeling; it was like this sometimes when he was fishing and every set of the nets would come back filled. "I would like to buy one of your flock and perhaps a bit of food for the night." And he held up coins to show his sincerity.

After more discussion, the shepherd reluctantly agreed to part with an old ewe for only four or five times her market value. He also sold them some of his bread and cheese, perhaps enough for each of Hali's men to have a few mouthfuls, for only six or seven times what the shepherd had paid for it. The shepherd was feeling so good about his deals he then threw in a bonus worth more to the chilled fishermen than the sheep and food combined. He came out of his hut with a chipped stone dish lined with moss and covered with a thick leaf. Inside was a live coal. He even threw in a double handful of dry kindling.

All the way back to their makeshift shelter the men fretted about keeping the coal alive in the driving rain. When they returned, the debate intensified as to the best way to start a fire. There were several false starts, but the ember survived and strengthened. Men blew on the coal to strengthen it, and blew on grass and leaves to try to dry them. Finally, between the kindling and some shavings scraped from the gunnels of one of the boats they got a proper fire started, burning brightly enough to dry out the other damp fuel the men had available. Then it was built into a fine warming blaze that scorched the gunnels of their boat shelter. The men didn't care; for the first time since before dawn they were really warm. Then the poor ewe, which had stood tethered watching the men build the fire, was dragged down to the lake and butchered. Her fleece, uncured as it was, made a fine bed for Hali that night. The mutton, roasted on sticks thrust into the fire, though tough and gamey, filled the bellies of the men. Then they banked the fire and brought it further under the shelter of the boats. Finally they curled up in their cloaks, or blankets for those still too poor to afford cloaks, and huddling together, spent the night dozing and listening to the rain pounding off the hulls of their boats.

The next day the weather was no better, and the men spent the day eating the tough mutton, dashing out to collect firewood to be (at least partially) dried under the boats, tending to the fire and telling stories. A trip to the shepherd's hut revealed that he had decided eight fishermen made too many neighbors and despite the weather, had moved his flock to a more secure location. On the second morning in their camp they ate the last of the mutton as a rather unappetizing breakfast. By midmorning Hali decided that it might still be rough but the wind had eased, the rain had stopped, and it would be safe enough to proceed.

They made the little hamlet he had hoped to reach that first day long before dark. There some more of the money Athan had given Hali guaranteed them all a good meal and a place in one of the huts. The next morning, the boatmen revived, and pleased with themselves, left at first light and, with light winds and clearing skies, pulled easily home where they were met with a joyous reception. Neither Hali nor Athan were ever sure just how much money passed between them on that headland, but there was still enough remaining to fund a genuine feast that night as the fishing community celebrated the men who had dared to cross the lake in winter and had survived.

Athan gave Rodas a full briefing about what had transpired over the last four days. The stocky redhead was aghast.

"You mean you just left all our gold down there by the lake? Unguarded?"

"That is why we have to get men down there tonight to bring it in. Giles and Xenos can lead the party down there. Who do you have to go with them?"

Shortly after full dark, fourteen men and four donkeys slipped out the back gate and down the trail that led toward the lake. They were all wearing body armor under their grass cloaks and carried not only swords but shields and spears as well. In retrospect, carrying all those weapons turned out to be a mistake. Athan and Rodas watched them disappear into the gloom from the top of the wall. Then a fresh rain squall came down from the north and the two men dashed into a bastion for shelter.

"One hour down to the lake, say half an hour to load up, and an hour and a half back. They should be back an hour or two hour before midnight" said Athan confidently. "Wake me when they get back."

But they did not get back when Athan expected. Instead, he was awakened by Tenucer after a much longer sleep than he had expected.

"Sir, Rodas sent me. It is past midnight and the men are not back from the lake. He wants to send some men to go look for him."

"Tell him I'll come," said Athan feigning an alertness he did not feel. He splashed water on his face, ran his fingers through his hair, and made himself as presentable as possible. Rodas was waiting on the northeast bastion, looking out into the darkness along the ridgeline.

Rodas was undoubtedly worried.

"I am having Prokopios get a dozen of the boys together," he said without preamble. "I think they are just lost. I can't believe anybody could beat Linus and his men in a fight. Not at night. Not with them ready. They are probably just lost."

They were still getting the rescue party ready when there was a commotion at the front gate. At once Athan redeployed the men around him toward the front gate to repel a possible attack. But it was not an attack at all. It was a very irritated Linus, leading his men and three of the four donkeys he had left with almost six hours before. Two men were limping, leaning on their comrades for support; eight, including

Linus, were carrying the leather pouches over their shoulders, each pouch holding a medimnos worth of gold.

"What happened?" Rodas asked Linus as the men straggled in. Athan was content to let Rodas ask the questions; Rodas and Linus had been together for years and were close.

"Everything," he said letting a fortune in gold drop to the flagstones in the entrance tunnel without even looking down. Athan saw Xenos limping on what appeared to be a twisted ankle. Giles was helping him, his handsome young face pinched and pale in the light of the torches.

"Are you unhurt?" Athan asked Giles putting a kindly concern in his voice.

Giles only nodded. He was not far from tears.

"You two head up to the room if you can negotiate the stairs. It is warm there. I will have someone bring up food and wine. Will your ankle need tending, Xenos?"

Xenos only shook his head.

"Well then, I am glad you were able to successfully retrieve our gold. Up you go."

The two passed him and turned to head up to Athan's room.

"We got lost," began Linus, "no, wait; we lost that damn donkey first. Not a half hour out and it slipped on the trail and fell. Broke its leg and screamed something awful until we put it down. And when it fell it kicked Vissios so we had to put him on one of the donkeys. We probably should have put him down, too," this as Vissios hobbled by. He made an effort at a grin for his old sergeant but he was clearly hurting. The men led him off to Iason for tending. Athan was aware that the leather sacks of gold were being moved back towards the treasury room under the supervision of Prokopios and his men. Abacus was up and flitting back and forth between each load of the gold, checking and counting each one in preparation for securing them in the treasury.

"Then we got lost," said Linus. How do you get lost on a simple downhill track I do not know, but we did it. Finally, we heard the lake and made our way down to it; apparently that was not the right place. I mean, really! Can you imagine? Yes, it was dark and raining, but they had only left it that afternoon. Eventually somebody stumbled over the dead tree. Then we had to get the packs on the donkeys. That was a performance worthy of an autumn fair. If anyone could have seen anything in the darkness it would have been a rare sight. Then the donkeys decided they would not carry more than four medimnos on their backs. Put that fifth bag on them and they just sat down. Then we counted the bags and found there were only eighteen. We nearly had a brawl with people accusing each other of all sorts of things such as not having enough sense to know how many were down here in the first place. Finally I ran my hand all the way along the length of the tree and found not two but three bags! So we counted them all again. It turned out they had been miscounted the first time. Now we had all 20; time to go home. Understand that while all this was going on it was raining and blowing hard. I hope your fishermen friends got home."

Linus continued his tale, "So we had no choice but to carry the extra eight bags the donkeys wouldn't carry up the hill. Of course we got lost. Again. We were lucky because we heard the wolves feeding."

"Wolves," said Athan and Rodas at the same time.

"Wolves," Linus confirmed, "they had found the donkey's carcass and a big pack was sharing it out. We had to make sure they understood that we did not mean to interrupt their meal. Let me tell you, it is a very uncomfortable thing, walking along a hill in the dark with a pack of wolves eating and snarling just down slope of you. It makes you place your feet carefully. But not carefully enough because your boy, Xenos, twisted his ankle a little ways past that. So we had two men to carry, eight men loaded down with that damn gold, wind, rain, pitch black darkness, one of our guides hurt and one pretty much useless. We walked almost all the way to the road before we saw the light inside the northwest bastion. That put us too close to the town. Can you imagine us walking right into the Illyrian camp? 'Here is your tribute, in advance, sir. About eighty year's worth.' Well we scrambled out to the road that comes up to our front gate pretty fast. Then we had to persuade them to let us in. You know the rest."

"Thank you, sergeant. You have done well," said Athan warmly.

"Just doing my job, sir," responded the big blonde man, obviously glad to be done with this night's work.

"Let's see if we can get you dry," Rodas was all solicitude. Looking around he called out to wake Cook up and feed the men.

"I think most of us would just like to go to bed," said Linus wearily.

In the end it was over an hour before the treasure was secured, the extra guards stood down, and the Hold settled down into its normal routine.

Athan and Rodas wound up sitting together in the mess hall only a few hours before dawn. There was a fire there and they had found some wine to mull. Despite his earlier nap, Athan was tired right down to his bones.

"Quite a day," observed Rodas, "this morning I had the weight of the world on my shoulders. The same day you left the horse boys down there," he continued gesturing in the general direction of Dassaria where the Illyrian cavalry was still billeted, "started running patrols. They sent one all the way around the back of the ridge. We were afraid they might have found you."

"We moved out pretty briskly after I decided to try to come back over the lake. We did not see any sign of them."

"Well," continued Rodas, "we figured if they had caught you we would have heard about it. Anyway, they got pretty aggressive about patrolling. The second day after you left they made a mistake. I guess they saw your tracks going out the back gate. Maybe they thought they should put a cork in the bottle. So they positioned a detachment of a dozen horsemen at the far western end of the ridge."

"They didn't!" exclaimed Athan, "in broad daylight? What were they thinking?"

"Well, we know what they were thinking when a score of phalangists in formation came boiling out the back gate just as they were taking their noon meal. They couldn't flank us and they couldn't fight us and it turned out they couldn't even run away."

"I climbed that hill," confirmed Athan, "I know how steep it is."

"Four of them made it down, two broke their horses' legs and their own necks trying to go down that slope, three died trying to fight us and the other three surrendered," smiled Rodas.

"Where are they now?" asked Athan.

"Oh, I sent them back with Aeolus after our daily conference." There was a wicked pause, "I gave them back naked as the day they were born. I figured we needed the horses and could sell the gear. Aeolus was not pleased with them. You should have seen them running down that hill, still naked."

The two men chuckled over the joke and paused to sip their wine.

"I think Aeolus knew you were gone. He kept asking to speak with you. We believe that they are waiting for a messenger to return from Buttrotiuria to see if their king accepts your offer."

"What do you think they will do if he rejects it?" Athan queried.

"I don't think it matters," said Rodas candidly. "Now that you are back there is nothing they can do."

"I only brought back four additional men and some gold," scoffed Athan.

"No," protested Rodas, "you brought back six more fighting men and yourself; most of all yourself. It was not the same without you. You give the men confidence. I tell you honestly, I was very glad to see you back so soon. I was not sure I could hold this place together if you did not come back. I did not think I wanted to be a king; now I **know** I don't want to be a king. It is easy to make decisions when you know that there is someone who can correct you if what you do is wrong. But when you are the only one," here Rodas stopped to try to collect his thoughts. "Don't misunderstand me, I like being in charge, being able to make decisions, I just like having a backup when so much is involved. I enjoyed being a chieftain, only with a small band, you know, just us men. But when there is so much on the line, this place, all the people, the money, it was too much. I do not think I was ever as glad to see anyone in my life as I was to see you, especially when you showed up five days early."

'I believe him,' thought Athan. 'I was right to come back quickly, but for the wrong reason. Rodas did not want to usurp me, he needed me. Here is a man I can trust. He is one who will never plot to steal my kingdom from me.'

Athan sighed deeply and spoke from his heart. "Well, I am glad to get home," he said using that term for the first time in reference to the Hold.

And with that Athan stood and embraced his friend. Then he walked slowly up to his room. He would have to check on young Giles and Xenos before he could rest, and tomorrow would certainly be a busy day.

As he sat eating another 'mouse meal' the Old King's thoughts went back again to those days so long ago. He had not thought about that crossing of the lake in many years. What did they refer to that trip as? Ah, yes, 'coming over the water'. Neysa had been a mere teenager then with no children at all yet. How many did she finally have? The old man could not remember, but he did know that she had many and outlived two husbands. The last time he had seen her it had been a formal visit at the request of her family. They were celebrating the old girl's long life and the presentation of her most recent grandson with a big rural feast. Thais had come with him.

Neysa seemed a crone, withered and almost used up from the hard life so many people lived in that time and place. Her mind was still sharp enough though, and she took an active interest in everything around her. Like many older people, she enjoyed reminiscing about the old days. She had been perhaps the last person alive who could remember when the Old King had come to power. She had sat, talking with her daughter, a woman who was herself well into her middle years, about how she had crossed the lake as a girl.

"I was carrying your eldest sister at the time," she explained to her daughter, who had apparently heard versions of this story many times before. "I was sick as a dog and so frightened. I remember I thought the lake was the color of blood. The King was in the lead boat and he told me it was just the clouds and to look how pretty it was. And it was! It was all pink and rosy. I was so young then, just fifteen, and it was the first time I had ever been on a boat. I never got in one again, I'll tell you." There was a pause. "You made us do it."

Here Neysa looked right at the Old King, who was standing nearby listening, waiting indulgently for her to wind down so he could pay her his compliments and leave. Neysa's tone became almost accusatory and she addressed the King directly. "You came in the afternoon and made us cross the lake before dawn the next day. You told Pontus it wasn't safe for us to go by land. You looked just like you do today. You haven't changed a bit. Why haven't you gotten older like the rest of us?"

The people who heard the old woman suddenly became tense. There were things you did not talk about around the Old King. Things like why he did not appear to age.

The Old King smiled a smile he did not feel and leaned in to kiss the old woman on her forehead. "Why you haven't changed either, Neysa. You are just a beautiful as you were when I first saw you." His attempt at gallantry fell flat. He excused himself from the gathering and they left as soon as they could politely do so.

"Beloved," she had asked him that night, "did you really cross the lake with that old woman when she was a girl?"

That question led to a long discussion that turned into an argument that turned into a passionate reconciliation, all in one night.

The old man recoiled from that memory as though it was a suddenly discovered snake. He was not ready to think about Thais again; not yet.

Chapter Five – Domestication

And, in fact, having Athan back did seem to make a difference to the Hold. Somehow the Illyrians seemed to sense that change. Aeolus had come up every day Athan was gone, demanding to see the "so-called king", becoming quite insistent. But on the day after Athan returned Aeolus remained in town. Perhaps it was the weather, which remained nasty, that accounted for his absence. But Rodas and Athan both felt he knew that Athan had left the Hold and had now returned.

"Mouse's work," suggested Celeno darkly. No one in Athan's band seemed to know just what that meant.

The bad weather did not lessen the workload on the new king. Athan was personally besieged with requests either to overturn or confirm decisions made by someone else in his absence or make decisions that had been pending. Too many of these were minor or even inconsequential. Fortunately, Athan had capable people in his band. Even more fortunately, he knew to trust them.

Most of the problems centered around the newness of everything. There was nothing in place to tell people that if Prokopios told them to vacate a room and let someone else move in, they could not get his decision overruled. There was no precedent for Ixon to commandeer three servants to care for the horses. No one could tell Celeno that she was not in charge of all cleaning servants. Athan had to weigh in and resolve these and many other issues in the first few full days of his reign. Most of them were sorted out with common sense and the good will of the people involved.

Three of the room assignments made during this time had far-reaching effects. In his absence, Rodas had occupied the room Athan and Giles had been using. Located next to the northwest bastion, it was comfortable and handy to the main gates. That made it very desirable to a man who had to be able to respond to events at all hours. Rodas found the location to be just as convenient for the man in charge of the Hold as Athan had. In actuality, Athan had not really made the two adjoining rooms his as such. In the short time he had been in the Hold, his presence in those rooms had been more in the nature of camping out, rather than settling down. So Rodas stayed in his rooms in the bastion closest to the front gate.

Abacus settled into his rooms at once. When Abacus had finished supervising loading the gold into the treasury that first night it was late. As soon the gold had been locked up and the key given to Rodas for safekeeping, Abacus moved into the closest room he could find to 'his' treasure, which just happened to be the Bear's old sick rooms. The fact that they was far better appointed than any other rooms on the ground floor and were in a prime location did not faze him in the slightest; to his mind he deserved it. Although Celeno made a half-hearted effort to eject him, no one else cared, least of all Athan. So there he stayed, and put down not merely roots, but deep, mighty, tap roots.

Celeno had assumed that the new king would like to stay in the old king's former rooms on the upper level. She and her daughters had labored mightily to clean and air out not only the sick rooms on the first floor next to the treasury (perhaps this was why she resented the newcomer Abacus moving in there), but also King Ratimir's apartments located above them as well.

Athan and Giles spent their first night back sharing the room with Rodas. In the morning they found that their gear had been moved by order of Prokopios to the Bear's old set of apartments on the second level in the opposite corner of the Hold.

"The old lady told me to do it," explained the Prokopios, who was now the acting unofficial majordomo.

He was referring of course to Celeno, who had been bustling about the Hold for the last few days trying to mold it into the kind of place she thought it should be. The big sergeant had established an uneasy working relationship with the woman. They were of an age, were both practical people and saw things much the same way. What made Prokopios uneasy was that he was afraid the homely old cleaning lady had designs on him. He was right.

King Ratimir's old rooms on the second level were by far the nicest in the building. Not even the neglect of the past months had ruined the furnishings, and with Celeno and her daughter's work (aided by others she bullied into helping) the three upstairs rooms were ready for occupancy. There was a receiving room where visitors entered the apartments. This room was the only one that opened onto the corridor. A sitting room or office was next in line, with a sleeping area in the final room. It actually had a raised bed; it was far and away the nicest place to sleep Athan had ever had for his own use. Giles set up a pallet for himself behind a screen in the receiving room and kept his belongings there. Anyone who wanted access to the King had to pass by him. Of course, that was just the way Giles wanted it.

By the third morning after his return, things had settled down again, as had the weather. Perhaps the Illyrians had been waiting for the weather to change, for Aeolus and his advisor presented themselves at the gate just before midmorning and requested a 'final conference'.

The sentries had reported unusual activity among the Illyrians in town all morning, so their appearance was not unexpected. This time Athan and Rodas met the Illyrians and made them welcome with tea and bread in the entrance corridor. Chairs and a table had been set up to enhance the sense of increased hospitality.

After the normal courtesies, Aeolus began the discussion by inquiring how Athan had enjoyed his voyage.

Athan smiled and avoided answering the question directly. Clearly Aeolus wanted them to think he had very good intelligence about the goings on within the Hold.

"We are returning to the King this morning," the advisor stated formally. His announcement as a surprise as King Bardhyllus' advisor had seldom spoken during the previous meetings. Athan and Rodas guessed his little pronouncement had been decided before the Illyrian party rode up to the conference.

"So this is a leave-taking then," said Rodas, addressing Aeolus.

The advisor continued on, ignoring Rodas' comment, confirming that he had a speech to give and intended to give it. "We expect your tokens of fealty to be delivered to King Bardhyllus, along with the tribute, in his capital of Bardhyllus at the midwinter celebration."

"One gold bar with the value of a quarter talent?" asked Rodas to confirm the arrangements.

The advisor looked over at Aeolus. Aeolus shrugged and simply said, "Yes."

There was not much else left to discuss after that, so with a few further comments the Illyrians rose to leave.

Athan spoke then his first substantive words of the conference, "When you next come into my domains, be fewer in number and come with an arranged safe conduct." Athan did not specifically say that troops of Illyrian cavalry would in the future be attacked as an invading force; there was no doubt, however that was what he was implying. It was a statement of his implied sovereignty over the land he had taken.

His pronouncement was received in silence. The two men collected their escorts and left the Hold. An hour later the column of Illyrian horsemen rode out of Dassaria, returning the way they had come.

Almost as soon as they were out of sight, seven scouts rode out of the Hold after them, maintaining a prudent distance to monitor their departure. Once the following patrol was past the town, three of them broke off and headed up the watch hill. They carried flags and mirrors and were prepared to signal back to the Hold if any unexpected threats materialized. Another pair of riders left the Hold and turned north to meet Yure's party, which should now be coming in from Lychmidas. These men were to update Yure and his recruits on new and improved situation in Dassaria.

Once these scouting groups were in place and able to provide advance warning, a much larger group of men wearing armor and carrying shields and spears walked out of the front gate of the Hold, down the hill toward the town. The soldiers could see movement down below in the town as they approached. Shutters and doors were closed and locked. There was considerable anxiety on the part of the inhabitants as to what would happen when the new masters of the Hold entered the town. The Illyrians had not behaved too badly during their stay in town and so had made a number of alliances (if not to say friendships) with the townspeople. Since the foreign troops departed so abruptly any locals who might have wanted to evacuate had no chance to leave with their goods, and so they waited with trepidation for their new rulers to come down to begin their new rule.

The people of Dassaria had lived under the rule of a brutal tyrant for so long that they had no illusions about their new ruler being benign. What kept most of them from fleeing frantically into the hills as soon as they learned the Illyrians were leaving was that there were consistent reports that things were not so bad up on the hill; that the new men were not mistreating the people who remained in the Hold. These reports, combined with hope and simple inertia kept most of the people in their houses. Simple prudence kept their doors and windows closed and barred and many went into their prepared hiding places.

Athan led a score of his warriors down the hill, cautiously looking around and walking all the way around the outskirts of the little town. After verifying that there were no enemies lurking about outside the town, the soldiers began to investigate the insides of the dwellings. This might have led to touchy situations except that the new King had one major advantage. Athan had brought a noncombatant down with him: Celeno. She might not be the most respected or well-liked person in the town but she was well known and perhaps a little feared as well. At each dwelling she called upon the master of the house to come out and greet his new lord. Athan greeted the first man to open his door, a tailor called 'Needle', and courteously explained that he, Athan, was the new King of Dassaria, and invited the man and his people to stay in town under Athan's protection. He further informed the astonished Needle that though he was invited to remain, he was also free to leave with all his possessions at any time.

All this had been worked out the night before in a rather contentious council in the Hold. Prokopios and Linus in particular had thought it ridiculous for Athan to personally introduce himself to the people in the town. Athan had overruled them. He knew there would be a great deal of suspicion in the minds of the town's people. If he could put a face on the new occupiers of the Hold, he was much less likely to have problems down in town. And so he went from house to house, assuaging fears and putting minds, if not at ease, at least in a reduced state of fear. Things got easier after the man of one of the houses, Stone, so called because he was a mason and claimed to have been born in a quarry, refused to come out.

Celeno began abusing him as a coward in a carrying voice, telling him to send his women out to meet the king if he was afraid. Laughter was heard in some of the other buildings; partly at the embarrassment of Stone and in part because the inhabitants were beginning to realize that this was not an attack. Stone came out shamefacedly and prepared to be beaten, arrested, or worse. He had worked for the Bear, making repairs on the Hold; he had once had friends in the garrison and was not best pleased to see them leave. Yet even he was greeted respectfully.

All at once, the people began to come out of their houses and greet their new master. Relations were further improved when Athan returned to the Hold and Cook, along with Rodas and Abacus, came down the hill to make purchases of food and wine. The goods were not really necessary; initiating the flow of commerce was. The highlight of the day came when Rodas negotiated purchase of a bullock, paid for in cash on the spot by Abacus. Then, sweetest of all, the entire village was invited to a feast set for the front of the Hold in three days time.

Athan returned to the Hold to deal with the other problems facing him, now reduced to a mere myriad. In the long run, this workload turned out to be a blessing in disguise. Athan did not shirk from work, but there were just too many things going on for him to take care of everything. So, by necessity he began to delegate specific jobs to individuals based on what he thought they could do. Some of these were easy decisions to make.

From the first, Abacus wanted to manage the finances of the nascent kingdom. He had set up tables with writing tablets and his abacus in his new apartment, for there were in fact two spaces in his area, making it technically an apartment. Beside the large and well appointed room where Athan had found the Bear, there was a small space located against the wall of the treasury room where Abacus set up a pallet and placed his few personal belongings. Abacus had requested (actually informed) Athan that he required parchment and ink to record the financial ledgers. He had been keen to show Athan his own personal system of accounting for money, which involved making two entries for each transaction. This seemed like twice the work to Athan, however, he merely nodded politely at the gawky youth who was so enthusiastic about a subject that Athan found profoundly tedious.

Finally, he cut the young man's explanations off and informed him he would be responsible for payment of all bills presented. Further, Athan charged him to be prudent with the kingdom's funds and to discharge his duties honestly. He was to treat the moneys and valuables of this kingdom as though they were his own family's goods. He must never misuse, misspend, or allow the misuse of the kingdom's money. And most importantly he must never use his position for personal gain. Abacus' face did more than light up, it positively glowed. He solemnly placed his hand over his heart and pledged to the gods word for word to follow these tenets.

And Abacus meant every word; for the rest of his life he never once knowingly violated these basic rules. And by so doing he caused Athan and himself literally decades of irritation, frustration, and conflict.

Neither man was aware of that then. Each was happy, Abacus because he had the responsibility he craved, Athan because he had one less thing to worry about.

One of the most pressing concerns for Athan was management of the people within the Hold itself. Everyone seemed to be jockeying for new and better rooms. No one was quite sure if they could remain in the rooms they had claimed. It was causing uncertainty, uneasiness, and conflict. For the time being, Athan had assigned Sergeant Prokopios as acting majordomo. He was a competent man and had sorted out most of the immediate problems; still, he was not happy doing the job. Athan considered who he had that he could assign these onerous duties. Only a senior man would have the authority to settle disputes without every one of them being referred to Rodas or Athan. Of his remaining sergeants, Linus had the force of will, but he was not well suited to this sort of routine work. Besides, Athan already had another job in mind for the big blonde northerner that was perfect for him. Yure the Elder could manage people, but he was a military man through and through and Athan wanted him to take over the retraining and integration of the new men he would soon be adding to his force. Besides, Yure had not arrived at the Hold yet and might not arrive for days. The other sergeants were too new to be jumped up to such a prestigious position. That left either Rodas or some outsider. Rodas was almost as busy as Athan and acting as a majordomo was beneath his position.

While he was pondering this particular problem Giles knocked and announced a new petitioner, a man called Zotikos. A man then stepped forward and knelt on the carpets of Athan's office.

"Sire," he began in a respectful voice, "I have come to ask for mercy."

'Good start,' thought Athan, 'I wonder what he did?'

"It is true I once served the old king, Ratimir," the man informed Athan without being asked. "I was not one of his fighting men. I did serve him to the best of my ability. I know he was a bad man, yet he was my lord, and he always treated me fairly. I ask your forgiveness for having once served such an evil man. It is said you are as merciful as you are wise."

Athan could smell flattery as easily as he could barnyard manure. On the other hand, if this man had survived working for the Bear he had to have some pretty finely honed survival instincts. Perhaps this was how you did business under the old regime.

"What did you do for him?" asked Athan a bit more roughly than he intended.

"I served him in this place, lord," responded the man. His head remained down and his comments were seemingly addressed to the floor. "I was responsible for the operations of the building, sire. I arranged things and made sure that the Hold ran smoothly."

"You were the majordomo!" exclaimed Athan excitedly. Here was a lucky break indeed. He was just pondering how to fill this position.

"I prefer the title 'House Steward'," said the man smoothly for the first time looking directly at Athan. There was a trace of a smile on his face. "I served as steward for four years here. I think it is true that I know this place better than anyone else."

He stood and Athan got a good look at him for the first time. He was distinctly ordinary; a bearded man of average size and build. He was of full middle age with a slight paunch about his middle. The man, now off his knees and on his feet, looked confident and capable.

"Will you serve me faithfully and prudently," began Athan in a version of the oath he had laid upon Abacus, "treating all members of my household honestly and with respect. And will you promise to not use your position to personally enrich yourself?"

"Sire, I so pledge upon my honor," intoned the man with his hand over his heart.

As he spoke Zotikos was consciously and deliberately lying. And for the rest of his life he consistently and flagrantly violated these basic rules whenever he thought he could avoid either detection or punishment. And by so doing he gave Athan a great deal of satisfaction. You just never know about these things.

One of the housing problems that required urgent attention was the situation in the stables. The four unfortunate rescued women were still living in a stall. Ixon had more or less moved into an adjacent stall to be near them. He claimed it was to be near the horses and so he could better manage the stables. Ixon was the defacto Horse Master and so the stables located on either side of the entrance were under his control now. He had a nice little herd of animals to manage and extra helpers to assist in feeding and cleaning the stalls. Even during the time the Illyrian horsemen blockaded the Hold, forcing Ixon to keep his animals inside, he was able to muck out the stalls and have men carry the residue outside the walls to compost heaps. Although Ixon had made sure the animals were walked in the courtyard that took little of his time.

With little else to do, Ixon spent hours talking to the women; actually just to Adara and Cenobia, since Evania spoke seldom and Kepa not at all. Still, they seemed to be getting better. They now went willingly with Titania, the big laundress, to the baths. She even talked of having them come help her in the laundry. For Ixon's part, once the Illyrian cavalry departed, his workload tripled. He had to provide horses to support patrols and see about getting the rest of his the animals properly exercised. The women, especially Adara, missed his attention and fretted. Kepa stopped eating again, not that she had ever done more than occasionally accept a mouthful when coaxed like an apathetic toddler.

Celeno provided unexpected relief. Once she was sure the foreign cavalrymen were gone, she headed down to the village for consultations and preparations. She was gone all day. The next day she stayed in the Hold only long enough to ensure her daughters and the rest of the cleaning staff had their instructions and had started on the day's work before she presented herself at the stables to collect 'those four poor girls'. She was accompanied by Titania, which was fortunate, since none of the four women were eager to leave their surroundings. Between Celeno's persistence and the big laundress' reassurances they were able to persuade them to leave the Hold and go down into a small house that Celeno had prepared on the outskirts of town.

Once inside Celeno revealed herself to them as a witch. She informed the women that they were to undergo a purification ritual which was to cleanse them of the evil spirits that still clung to them. This startling news was greeted with dismay by Adara, guarded acceptance by Cenobia, and apathy by Evania and Kepa.

What exactly went on in that house over the next 28 days was never revealed to the men. Celeno was assisted by Titania and two of Celeno's apprentices. The four women being purified were never seen to leave the house during the daylight hours and interested bystanders were thoroughly discouraged from inquiring about the goings on in the house by one of the females that took turns guarding the house. Even Ixon was turned away when he came inquiring about Adara.

During this time, Celeno spent a considerable amount of her time and energy down in the village devoting herself to saving three souls. It was only three because, just two days after moving down to the purification house (as it was called during this time) Kepa just quit living. She had never fully recovered from her catatonia, though she did speak one last time shortly before she died. She was heard to say "Thank you," in a soft voice to no one in particular. When Celeno heard the words she was very encouraged and so was even more affected when the woman simply quit breathing.

Celeno had considerably more success with her other lost souls. After the rites were completed Evania lived in town with a family until winter passed, and then was returned to her own family. Always a quiet girl, she had become even more withdrawn. Still, after her return home she was able to interact more or less successfully within her family. It was later reported that she was passed off as a widow and married to an older widower. Apparently she had a successful marriage since nothing else was heard of her. That is often the way; happy or contented people make for poor gossip.

Cenobia seemed to make a complete recovery and gave little obvious indication of the effects of her ordeal, though it left her with one significant change to her personality. She was now unwilling or unable to reject the advances of any man. Since she was young and pretty, this made her very popular, but she was also the source of some spectacular fights. After a time she became a successful prostitute, eventually moving on to a larger city in the south.

Adara, the angry one, came out of the house after the purification rituals were completed and looked around her. She had plenty of time while waiting in the house to think about the future. She had few prospects. Her husband and family were dead, killed in the caravan raid when she had been captured. She had distant relations who would probably take her in if she could find a way to get to them, but then what? She had no real expectation of a marriage. She had little to look forward to other than working at someone else's looms or tending another woman's children. It would be little better than being a slave. Adara's anger had burned out many days before, leaving her feeling spent and empty.

She had one and only one hope, and she was terrified about reaching out for it. When your only hope is something you truly long for, taking steps to find out if your wish might be actually granted can be a daunting thing. Finally, she began to walk, seemingly without direction, letting her steps lead her where they would.

Adara's steps took her to the foot of the S curved road that led to the stone fortress on the top of the hill. She stood outside the gates for a long time, ignoring the people who spoke to her, just staring with longing and dread at the Hold. That stone pile held the worst memories she could imagine, things she would spend the rest of her life trying not to remember. But it also held her best, her only, hope for happiness. As she stood there in the winter twilight she could feel the cold beginning to seep into her. If she did not do something soon she would have to follow Celeno back to the room they would let her use in Celeno's cottage in town. Then she heard a horse neigh high and piercing, almost a scream, and the gates of the Hold were pushed open wide. Seven horses with men on their backs came pelting out of the gate, riding fast, just for fun, slowing as they cleared the Hold. Adara recognized the horses from her time in the stable. Suddenly she realized she was walking, seemingly without volition, up the hill to the Hold. She wrapped her shawl over her head and looked at the ground as she climbed up the road.

Shadows were getting long, when the man at the gate let her into the Hold. She entered the barns through the small door on the right side of the tunnel. Breathing in the stable air, feeling the life presence of the horses was deeply comforting. Adara had helped her father out with the livestock when she was a girl. She had always loved horses. Was that what brought her back; just a love of animals?" Livestock had been one of the things she had talked to Ixon about when she had lived here in a horse stall with three other women. She looked around the stalls. The day's work was done and no one was in this side of the stables. Adara walked out toward the courtyard, intending to cross the front of the courtyard tunnel and look in the north side stables. As she came out and prepared to cross the arched entryway she came to a stop, halted by a nauseating memory. She remembered vividly the first time she had come through that entrance; bound, half naked, already beaten and raped, knowing her father, husband and uncle were dead. She remembered being half dragged to that terrible room, hearing the whistles and calls of the men who moved over toward her, and waiting for their…. Adara cut that memory off with a conscious effort of will. That was past. What had been done to her, what she had done, were all past, cleansed away and forgiven. She took a deep breath and crossed in front of the entrance and turned into the other half of the stables.

At first she thought this side of the stables was empty as well. Then she caught a flash of movement against one of the back stalls. Once again Adara found herself walking without thinking. She walked up to the man who had been checking the wooden slats of one of the now empty stalls. He stopped and watched her come. At the last moment she lost her nerve and veered abruptly into another stall. Sensing her nervousness Ixon entered the adjacent stall and leaned against the slats as he had during those first days after, after....

"Hello," he said, "are you finished with your rites?"

'Of course, you dolt,' she thought, 'why else do you think I am here?' Instead of speaking these words she looked down at the floor of the stall and only nodded.

A silence stretched between them.

"We have a bit more room with all the horses out working," Ixon tried again. Always before he could get her to talk to him. Her replies were sometimes bitter and often angry, but she would react to him. Now she peeked up at him and then looked down at the ground.

"I see," was all she said still looking down. All the conversations she had imagined with this man, all the planned speeches, all the ways this meeting had played out in her mind were of no value to her now. This man who had rescued her, who had cared for her, who might still care for her, who represented the only chance she had for a real life was right there, and she was so terrified she couldn't think of a thing to say.

The silence grew longer.

"So, what did you do to get purified?" he asked leaning with his arms crossed on top the upper plank of the stall.

Adara looked at him and realized he was trying to put her at ease. 'Had that been why he was so kind to her? Just to put her at ease?' she wondered for the hundredth time. Or was there something else, 'was he attracted to me? Why?'

"I can't tell you," she replied. "They are secrets."

"Oh."

'Well,' she thought, 'that killed that conversational gambit.' Desperately she thought of something to say to him, anything to keep him from moving away. She had made him uncomfortable. He was getting ready to leave. She knew that. She always could seem to tell what he was thinking.

"It was mostly just purification things," Adara moved to the same top plank, a little farther down from Ixon and put her hand on the railing. "Mostly Cenobia just wanted to make sure she had purged all the demons and evil spirits."

He looked at her with a question.

"She made sure we had our monthly courses," explained Adara and for some reason blushed hotly right to her hairline. "And other things," she continued lamely, "woman things, secret woman things." It sounded weak and lame to both of them.

'What did they do to her down in that house?' wondered Ixon to himself. 'This is not the fiery woman I knew. Did they break her spirit?'

"Oh," he said again.

And then she realized that he was nervous, too. This greatly heartened her; maybe this mattered to him, too. She moved over to stand closer to him facing him over the railing.

"In fact," she told him with some force, looking directly at him with some of her old feistiness, "I am assured that I am virtually a virgin again."

"Oh," he said, this time puzzled and a bit off balance, but with a trace of a smile.

There was a silence again, but completely different this time. The two looked at each other and began communicating without speaking.

"Well?" said Adara challengingly. What they both understood this single word to mean was: 'here I am, almost a virgin again, offering to myself to you. Do you want me?'

"I could use some help with the horses," Ixon said. What they both understood in the invisible connection that seemed to have somehow linked them was, 'Yes, I want you. I missed having you around. I find all other women to be bland and uninteresting. I think we should get married and live as one.'

"Where would I stay?" she responded meaning, 'Yes, if you mean it, I will marry you. I never want to be apart from you. But don't expect it to be easy.'

"I moved over there," he indicated a door on the north wall just past the bastion. It used to be a tack room; I moved that stuff out. It still smells of leather." And what he meant was, 'That will be where we will live. If you will have me.'

"All right, but don't get any ideas." And he knew she meant that although she was better, it would still be a while before she was really healed, especially when it came to marital relations. He still had some work to do there.

"Where is all your stuff?" this delivered in a chaffing tone, as though he was afraid she would completely fill their little room with clothing and feminine possessions.

For an answer she lifted her arms and spread them glancing down at her simple woolen shawl, chiton and sandals, a gesture that indicated all she possessed was the borrowed clothing she was wearing.

"Some dowry," he grumbled good-naturedly. And that confirmed to each of them that they had indeed been truly sharing one another's thoughts. And together they burst into loud delighted laughter. Coming around the stall he took her hand and led her still laughing, to her new home.

On the third day after the departure of the Illyrian cavalry, ten men rode out of the Hold following the same route the Illyrians had taken. These were men on a mission. They had to reach the city of Bardhyllus by the winter solstice. They had five days to get there, time enough for a small body of horsemen if they did not dawdle. Rodas and Athan had selected Linus, the big blonde northerner, to head the mission. Linus had been with Rodas for years and was a solid leader of men. Although somewhat lacking in common sense in battle (being a bit overbold when his blood was up) he was intelligent, physically imposing, and had the innate sense of showmanship that the job required. He was going to deliver tribute to a monarch. Since Theron was from this part of the world, he and Myron would be guiding the party. Eustathios, the biggest man in the entire band, would also be coming along. The overall outline of the plan was simplicity itself - they would ride until they came to an Illyrian outpost. Talos and two of the men would wait out of sight near that place for a sign or signal in case anything went wrong. Linus would lead the other seven into Illyria and formally present a bar of gold as tribute to the king from his new vassal state of Dassaria.

The little party made good time, only getting lost once, and arrived at the capital city of Bardhyllus the day before the festivities. They arrived with an escort/guide of a dozen Illyrian troopers. There had been a bit of trouble at the first town that considered itself part of Illyria proper. Normally people passed from kingdom to kingdom without much ado, however a party of armed men attracted considerably more interest, especially when they come to the main gate of a small walled town and demand to speak to the garrison commander. It all worked out in the end, and the three men Linus had left behind to see how the party was treated saw them depart peacefully with their escorts, after signaling to them that all was well.

Linus was able to persuade the commander of the escort to allow them to delay their entrance into Bardhyllus proper until the morning of the solstice feast. This gave the men a chance to stay in a house in the suburbs where their Illyrian escorts were well known. The two groups had come to a relatively comfortable relationship on the ride down as fellow travelers often do, especially when they share a common avocation. Relations were improved further when Linus (spending Athan's allowance for the trip generously) funded an excellent little party including good food, fine wine, practiced musicians and even more practiced women.

The next morning the Dassarian delegation received word that they would be received at the King's residence at sunset. This suited everyone as they were all a bit rocky from the previous evening's little bacchanal. Linus took the time to make sure his men were bathed and properly attired. He intended to make a good impression. He did. His men were dressed in the showiest armor available in the Bear's considerable armory. Even Myron, who was no warrior, looked splendid. In addition to polished bronze breastplates and crested helms, they all wore matching greaves on their shins. All but two of the men wore the gray cloaks of Athan's band. Linus and Eustathios wore bearskins over their shoulders. Not surprisingly, King Ratimir had a number of bearskins in his ensemble; only Linus and Eustathios were big enough to wear them without looking ridiculous. Linus' bear skin had to be altered a bit to keep it off the ground. Eustathios was a very big man, but even he was unable to completely fill out the Bear's old attire; this made a deep impression on the big warrior. He shrugged the heavy skin around to better fit his broad shoulders.

"How did Athan, I mean the King, beat him?" he wondered aloud to Linus as they checked one another's appearance. Most of the men had been otherwise engaged when Athan had his confrontation with the Bear; there had been lurid rumors of a great fight.

"I guess the old Bear was sick. I heard it said that the boss took him with his bare hands. Bear hands, get it." Linus' joke got a bigger laugh than it warranted; the men were a little nervous. No one was quite sure what kind of a reception they would receive. It was not unheard of for emissaries to be murdered. If they were set upon here, there would be no chance of surviving. If that happened here, the men were determined that if they were to die by treachery they would die well and take as many of the bastards with them as they could.

The seven men and their escorts made a fine show as they rode slowly into Bardhyllus. The men knew that far from being a single kingdom, Illyria was more like a confederation of tribes, cities, and small kingdoms. Men might call themselves subjects of this kingdom or members of that tribe but they often just referred to themselves loosely as Illyrians to outsiders. Although Bardhyllus was not an especially large or imposing city it did have a protecting wall and was one of the major cities in Illyria. There was a brief ceremony at the gate with formal challenges and responses. Linus noted they seemed to be taking a roundabout way up to what passed as a palace. People came out into the streets to watch them pass. Linus realized that this winding route was deliberate, a way for the King of Bardhyllus to display his might. Vassals were coming to pay him homage. Besides, people like to see a parade, even a small one.

"Look sharp, lads," the big man growled at his little company.

And the others seemed to understand, for they rode proudly, side by side. Everyone noticed how the visitors looked much better than their escort. This was a source of pride to the Dassarians and of irritation to their Illyrian escorts.

They arrived at the Hall of the King, a relatively modest two-story dwelling which, though serving the role of a palace, really did not deserve the title. There the emissaries dismounted and approached the entrance. As expected they were asked to disarm. Linus made a fuss about this. He was armed with shield and an enormous ax with a haft as long as his arm. None of the men carried the normal short swords that were so useful in actual fighting; instead they carried big, and in Eustathios' case enormous, swords. There were protestations and negotiations, some ritual, some real. Finally Linus gave way and put his shield aside and surrendered his ax and long dagger. He would be allowed to enter the king's presence with only one retainer, Eustathios of course. The big man would be allowed to keep his staff, a long thick pole that came up to his ear, topped with an ornate heavy crest. The rest of the men would stay with the weapons in the anteroom.

Before he was brought into the King's presence, a number of well-dressed men had questions of Linus about the tribute to be provided. 'Where was the gold?' There was pressure to give it to various self-important courtiers and councilors who would then deliver it to the King for him. Such was Linus' imposing appearance and force of personality that no one was able to prevent him from executing his mission of delivering the gold personally. Athan, Rodas and Myron had talked with him for hours on what to expect, what to do, and what not to do. He had to deliver the gold with impressive ceremony directly to the King and deliver his message to the entire court. The display was considered vital. Linus had also been prepared for a wide number of potential proposals, deals, and temptations that would probably be offered him. He was honored that his old chieftain and comrade Rodas and this new king, Athan, trusted him to carry out this important mission. When, after all the delays, he was finally announced and called before the King he was ready; and he was magnificent.

Although Linus still did not know what his reception would be he was prepared. If things went wrong he was ready to end his life in that hall. They had taken his ax and dagger from him but they did not remove the links of chain around his waist attached with a heavy iron fastener. That heavy fastener on the end of a whirling chain could be used with lethal effect. And there were knives in each of his high topped boots. When he first stepped into the hall Linus, took a long appraising look at the men who filled the hall. He decided that if things went wrong between his knives and chain and Eustathios' staff (which would make a fine weapon) the two could probably make it outside to the others. If he could get to his ax and shield there would be a fine slaughter.

Every person has a 'best day'. In a long line of accomplishment it may be hard to single out one time that was more significant than another, but most people do have a 'shining moment'. An athlete may have an outstanding race, a dancer the perfect dance presented to an appreciative audience, a warrior a victory in battle, a bride her wedding, an artisan might recall recognition for quality work, a mother the birth of her healthy and perfect child; upon deep reflection most people can recall a greatest single day. Linus had such a moment when he came before the Illyrian court and he knew it at the time. Handsome, exotic, and swelled with pride he drew every eye. He dominated the room with his sheer presence. Then he gave a booming speech addressing the King of Bardhyllus directly, also pitching his presentation to the rest of the assembly. The room was filled with important men there to witness their king's reception of this new client. Well, that and to share in the feast that followed.

Linus spoke slowly, and carefully, for he knew he had an accent that could be difficult to understand. He formally acknowledged that his liege the King of Dassaria would support King Bardhyllus. His king would ally himself to Bardhyllus, (meaning both the King and his kingdom) defending the western borders against any threat. Further, King Athan would clear the hills to the west of the bandits and brigands that had so troubled trade and commerce in the past. Finally, as token of his respect for the mighty King Bardhyllus, King Athan of Dassaria would present to him each solstice the sum of 1500 drachmae, a quarter talent of gold, in acknowledgement of his fealty. The crowd ate it up; it was a fine dramatic speech, just the sort of entertainment they liked, even better than singers and dancers. The assemblage leaned forward to see where this gold was. Was there a chest of coins somewhere? How would the tribute be delivered? In answer Linus quietly reached under his bronze breastplate and from a leather pouch sewn into his tunic he withdrew the gold and suddenly, dramatically held up the gold bar with flourish. To most of the watchers it seemed as though he had manifested the bar from mid air. Linus took two long steps to the foot of the ornate chair where the King was sitting (it really didn't qualify as a throne any more than the hall qualified as a palace) and dropped the gold bar at his feet with a thump, going to one knee at the same time.

"Hail, King Bardhyllus!" he cried, head bowed.

It was great theater. The King was absolutely thrilled. The crowd cheered and also shouted out "Hail". The King of Bardhyllus smiled and nodded and accepted the accolades. Then with a gracious gesture he offered this strange barbarian a seat on one of the couches near him. Poor Eustathios still stood in the middle of the hall holding his staff now looking confused; confused but still impressive with his mighty frame wrapped in a bearskin. Linus instinctively knew that if he left him out there he would soon stop looking impressive and would become ridiculous. It was safe now. Linus made a gesture to the big man; Eustathios who had been watching Linus much like a hunting hound watching his master gratefully nodded and withdrew, joining the others just outside.

Linus became the center of attention. Serving girls rushed to bring him delicacies and cups of wine. Men asked of his native land. He had to be careful not to upstage the King. A quick glance assured the big northern hero that even the old King seemed interested. Linus had barely had a chance to whet his considerable appetite before the questions turned to his new king: what kind of man was he? Where was he from? What were his intentions? How did he capture the Hold? Did he really kill the Bear in single combat? This last question came from King Bardhyllus himself.

Perhaps it was the two cups of unwatered wine, perhaps the relief of a job well done, or perhaps it was the secret ambition of a natural actor suddenly given the stage. Linus suddenly stood up and was 'on'.

"You ask about the fall of the Hold and the death of Ratimir the Bear?" he announced to the hall. A sudden complete hush fell on the gathering. Guards put their hands on the hilts of their weapons. Linus stepped back into the center of the hall. "It is a great story, a mighty epic. I will tell you." Hands were removed from the hilts and the crowd leaned forward.

In that time and place options for entertainment were limited. There was singing and dancing, but most commonly people told stories. Everyone told stories, some were better than others and there was a constant demand for new stories, especially about dramatic and exciting events. Some of these were presented by professional bards as sung or chanted poems, others more plainly in common vernacular. A good storyteller could actually make a good living just telling stories for a fee. And Linus was a very good storyteller. His comrades who had heard him tell stories said that Linus could make seining for minnows in a stream seem like harpooning whales in the Hellespont. This time Linus had a story to tell worthy of his skills.

Now he began to tell the tale, and tell it in full as he had reviewed it in his head in the days since he had unexpectedly found himself alive and part of a tiny band of men that had captured a mighty fortress. He did not simply recite poetry; instead he unconsciously began to follow the ancient cadences of a skald: simple, terse lines ornamented with similes and metaphors. No one there had heard such a style before and the novelty of it had an almost hypnotic effect on his listeners. So vividly did he tell his tale that the audience felt they were there, watching the events. They groaned to hear of the injustices and cruelties of the brutal Bear; cheered when Athan ringingly promised to rid the people of this monster, gasped when they heard of the strength and power of the Bear. When Linus described the ride into the mouth of the mighty fortress, the listeners leaned forward and gripped one another. The story Linus told was more or less true, at least in the broad elements. Like all good artists he did not let facts get in the way of a good narrative. So it was that in Linus' story, the garrison was larger and prepared for the battle, the combats were fiercer, the deaths of heroes more dramatic and the ultimate victory more complete. Chief among the heroes he chronicled was King Athan, who slew the Bear's invincible champion by striking off his head. The hall recalled in shock when Linus described how the enemy's severed head rolled over and attempted to bite Athan. And of course Linus included his own mighty exploits in the battle. (Here he did not need to exaggerate; Linus had personally killed six men in the fight, three in the early desperate struggle in the bastions where he speared two men above him 'like a fish reaching up from the water to gig the fisherman.')

When he spoke of the battle line advancing down the length of the hold against the remnants of the Bear's men, those listening Illyrian warriors in the hall who had been in a shield wall became completely caught up in the tale. Linus began to sing the chant they had sung as they crossed the yard and those warriors, who all knew it, began to sing with him. When it came to the part where Athan's men clashed their spears against their shields he stamped his feet and clapped his hands. Some of those in the hall stamped with him. Linus and his male audience continued to sing. When it came to that point in the song again, all the men stamped with him and the guards in the room clashed their own spears against their shields. On the final chorus every man in the room stamped, clapped, or clashed in unison, Thump! **Thump! THUMP**! Women and children screamed, for by now, drawn by the performance, the hall was packed with women and youngsters peering in the windows and literally hanging from the open rafters.

"AND THEN," roared Linus to regain control of his audience. The hall went absolutely still. "They ran like rabbits," he concluded with a smile and a nonchalant shrug. The hall erupted in cheers. He captured a mug of wine from a spellbound serving girl and took a long pull. And at that moment Linus went from being an expert storyteller to a master. He knew with a sure instinct that one climax can serve to make the real climax even grander.

"And that was when the Monster awoke at last!" The buzz in the room died down as they realized there was more. As an encore Linus gave them a dramatically enhanced version of the fall of the Bear. Linus showed them his bear skin, assuring them that it had been far too small for the Bear to wear. Many of the heroes fell to the Bear's mighty blows. He had Eustathios stand and move around the hall. Eustathios was a hand taller than any other man in the room, yet they could see the edge of the bearskin touched the floor. Women shuddered. Mighty warriors looked worried. Linus recounted an entirely fictional and highly entertaining battle between Athan and the Bear with Athan not even drawing his sword but instead wrestling with the beast, ending when Athan lifted the Bear over his head and threw him to the earth, breaking his back and forcing him to yield. Wild cheers again resounded in the hall. Then, winding down his tale Linus recounted how Athan had granted his fallen foe mercy, and how the beaten Bear had limped out of his former den and out into the night.

Linus stopped talking. His tale had taken over an hour. There was complete silence as the crowded room waited for his next words, completely spellbound.

"And that is how it happened," he concluded in a matter-of-fact voice, and he went back to his couch snatching another cup of wine as he went. A low murmuring began in the room growing in volume as everyone began praising the performance. Men and women lined up to complement the big blonde soldier who reclined on his couch in satisfaction with a cup of wine in his fist, starry-eyed serving girls waiting by the head of the couch to provide him with delicacies or refill his cup.

Linus was a mighty warrior but he never did better service for his king and comrades than he did that night by telling a story. He was well rewarded for that service that very night. The King insisted that Athan's men sleep in rooms within his hall that night, though poor Linus was so popular with the serving girls (and perhaps other women, too) he later claimed he had not a wink of sleep that whole night. When asked if he would deliver the tribute the next year he laughed and said he would because he would like to visit all his children there. Though he was to tell many stories in his life he never told one better than he did that night; certainly no one who heard the epic told that night ever forgot it. The story was repeated with changes and variations for many decades until it no longer bore the faintest resemblance to the original and eventually faded into other heroic legends.

Linus was not the only one who attended a great feast that winter. Athan was as good as his word. The same day that he dispatched his emissary to Bardhyllus he sent men down to the town to make purchases and arrange contracts for his promised feast. Though several different men were assigned to go on these errands, Abacus was always in attendance. The young treasurer made certain everyone understood that he and only he was authorized to actually pay the King's money for contracts. It did not take long for various aggrieved parties to begin to complain to first Rodas, then to Athan. Abacus was driving brutally hard bargains, using all his leverage to wring not just every drachma but every little copper bit he could from each of his deals. After a few days of this Athan had to call his treasurer and explain something to him.

"There is more to doing business than simply getting the best possible deal," he explained to his sulky accountant. The two men were standing on top of the wall where Athan had been called to look at damage to some of the masonry on the south wall near the Southwest bastion. "We live here. We must do business with these people, I hope to do business with them for years. If you ruin them with sharp business practices, who will we do business with then? It's like fertilizing your fields with salt."

Abacus was highly intelligent and an innovative thinker, but he was young, inexperienced, and overconfident. "If you let these men take advantage of you, sire, they will not respect you. They will cheat you at every opportunity."

Athan thought for a moment, stopping his angry retort to his tall young steward. Athan did not know much about managing a kingdom's money; he did know about managing a band of men. Athan had brought this youngster back to the Hold because he believed the kid might be able to help him manage his finances. And although Athan was intrigued by money, he simply did not have the time to give it the attention it deserved. Athan knew that he had to trust his subordinates and let them do their jobs. On the other hand he also knew that he had to keep them from making mistakes.

"Tell, me," asked Athan taking his new treasurer by the elbow and walking along the wall widdershins, back along the south wall toward the east. "How much do I have in the treasury?"

"Thirty and one half talents in gold bars, four talents in a variety of specie and jewelry and other various objects of value that I estimate at a value of not less than another six talents. Plus, there is another four talents back in Lychmidas as well," Athan's steward promptly answered.

"That much, eh," said Athan dryly.

"Yes, sir, that does not, of course, include the quarter talent we sent as tribute to Illyria."

"No," responded, Athan continuing to use a dry tone whose import Abacus still did not grasp. "There is quite a view from here, isn't there?" Athan's abrupt change of subject confused the younger man. There was a brief cessation as they walked through the door of the southeast bastion and out the other side to cross the short stretch of west wall then through the northeast bastion and out onto the north wall.

"I think that now it is safe to say," continued Athan, "that everything you can see from up here is mine, now. Well, at least all the people who live where we can see."

"Yes, sire," said a somewhat mystified Abacus. Only the evening before he had been advising Athan and Rodas of the potentials for taxation of the area they now controlled.

"That means I have a responsibility to those people."

Abacus did now know how to reply to that.

"That means that from this time on," Athan abruptly stopped and took Abacus by the arm. The steward was suddenly very aware that he was standing next to an open embrasure above an uncomfortably long drop. "From today, until you are no longer in my service you will provide fair and just contracts with my people. That means everyone in my domain. I do not expect you to be taken advantage of, but I want equitable deals. There was an old saying I once heard a merchant use: 'every buyer deserves a bargain and every seller should be able to make a profit.' We live here. I expect to live here for a long time. These people are your neighbors and my subjects. I do not want them exploited. I am rich enough for now. Do you understand?"

"Yes, sire," Abacus had gone pale. He was not sure if he was humiliated, angry, or afraid. He did not trust himself to speak more with the strong emotions running through him.

"Good," smiled Athan, turning to continue his transit of the walls. "Please bring me a slate this morning listing all of the contracts you have made so far. Also, I will require a regular allowance. I do not care to have to come to you for every small thing I need. Let's see, I want 100, no better make it 200 drachmae a month, payable on the new moon. And since I consider myself in arrears, please bring me two month's pay when you bring me the tablets this morning."

"Yes, sire," Abacus said as they passed through the door of the northwest bastion.

"Well, then," said Athan stopping by the stairs that led down to the courtyard. "You had best get to it." Both men were aware that there were ears that could overhear their conversation in the bastion. "And keep up the good work!"

Later that day, Athan and Giles made a casual walk down to the village to see how preparations for the feast were going. And Athan just happened to drop by the men that had made disadvantageous deals with his financial steward. In each case he thanked the man for their generosity for allowing the youngster to 'win' the negotiation. He gave each man some additional money, bringing the payment of the deal up to normal standards. Athan then thanked them again for their kindness in assisting his young assistant in making contracts, and that in the future, they need not be quite so very kind. The message was received with smiles.

Cook and his wife did a considerable amount of complaining about preparing another feast so soon after the funeral feast. "There won't be any oxen left by the spring at this rate," Cook grumbled. Of course, deep down, Cook was gratified at the attention and excitement. There had been feasts for the Bear, but they had been tense little things. When the host can have you killed on a whim, it rather spoils the atmosphere. This affair, on the other hand was to be an open feast to celebrate the beginning of a new reign. Almost everyone was feeling optimistic about the future. There were still problems, of course, but now they were nice problems like, where are we going to have the celebration, and what shall we wear?

At first, the thought was to have the feast in town. Upon reflection, the threat of bad weather and the size of the event precluded using any of the houses down there, so it was decided the event would be held in the main courtyard of the Hold. There were disadvantages to this of course; security would dictate that some of the men would have to stand guard and not partake in the feasting. More significantly, the Hold still had a sinister reputation. The continuing good behavior of the new garrison and reassurances from servants and workers who went up and down the hill helped assuage these fears. Also on the positive side of attending the banquet was the list of comestibles being ordered and prepared. Cook made sure everyone knew the menu: an ox, a sheep, a wild boar, and a goat all roasted whole. There would be other dishes as well, requiring two more sheep and another goat. And there would be fresh bread, cheeses, pastries, and every delicacy that Cook and Cook's Wife had ever wanted to make, for Athan had given them a virtually unlimited budget. Abacus had complained; Athan reassured him it would be just this once. Cook was sure he would never again have a chance to spend 1000 drachmae on a meal (the budget was not really unlimited) and he went all out. Even cooks know they get only one 'best day'.

The day of the feast was cloudy and cold, but it was not raining. Well before noon people began cautiously going up to the Hold, sometimes finding excuses to return to the town to reassure the others that it appeared safe, and that it in fact looked very promising. By the midafternoon when feasting began inside the courtyard, almost everyone had relaxed and began to enjoy themselves. Children ran laughing around the tables that had been set up in courtyard, which was lighted and warmed by torches and open cooking fires roasting meat. It remained cold and gray; on the other hand, the rain held off and the walls shielded the feasters from what little breeze there was. Banners had been hung from some of the windows and the fort had been brightened up as much as practical. If there were no professional singers or dancers no one minded; they sang their own old folk songs that everyone knew, and as the evening went on and the wine flowed there was dancing as well. Of course, everyone was there mostly to eat, and the food offered was spectacular. The presentation of four different types of animals cooking over open fires all at once let everyone know this was a special occasion. No one present had ever seen such a display; it would be long before they saw the like again. The roasted animals were wonderful, but most of the feasters thought the very best dishes were Cook's special delicacies such as tender chopped meat wrapped in grape leaves or the poached fish. Even the chickpeas, flavored with exotic spices, were memorable.

The children all remembered the specialties made by Cooks Wife: desserts. She had a variety of flavored almonds, dried fruit that had been somehow been gently steamed back to life then honeyed to perfection, and baked apples with cinnamon. Best of all were her pastries. There was one dish in particular that became very popular in the region. Sheets of dough were rolled to almost translucent thinness and then placed layer upon layer with wonderful things inside - spices, nuts, and above all honey. Children had to be driven away from the table so that adults could have a sample. A sort of competition developed between feasters who were determined to eat every scrap, and cooks who are equally determined to have food left over. In the end the cooks won. The garrison continued to work on the remnants for two days.

There were some that did not get to relax during the feast.

First, Cook and his helpers had to work hard to make the feast successful. Most of them had been preparing food for days and some had been up all day and all night. During the feast they had to serve the food and try to make sure everyone had a chance to appreciate their labors.

Second, the men unfortunate enough to draw guard duty that day had to remain literally above the festivities. Lookouts remained on the hills until full dark to look for any enemies that might seek to take advantage of the festivities and attack the Hold. Once it was dark, though, they were able to return and join the feasting. The normal complement of six sentinels was expanded during the feast to control the arrivals and respond to any possible contingencies. Once things settled down and the gates were secured, these were replaced by other men who, though they did get to eat first, were allowed little wine. Most unfortunate of all were the men who had to be able to stand an alert watch in the middle of the night after a heavy meal.

Finally, Athan could not bring himself to relax that night. He had ultimate responsibility for the quality of the food, for the security of the Hold, and he had to play a role that was still new to him, that of King and Lord of the Hold. He was not sure if he should withdraw and stand aloof like an oligarch or mingle with the people as he would have were he still a bandit chieftain. He did his best to strike a middle ground. The tension in trying to do so, resulted in giving him acute indigestion. After the feast he spent much of the rest of the night walking the walls inadvertently convincing the guards he was trying to catch them sleeping. Eventually Rodas solved the problem in a practical way. He hired the best prostitute in town; she was able to persuade the King to come down off the wall and go to his chambers. She viewed the whole thing as a professional challenge. Though it took her almost an hour she eventually she got Athan off to bed where, with hot teas, massages, and kind, loving ministrations she eventually eased his tension, resolved his heartburn, and got him to sleep.

The feast was a huge success. It did much to sweeten relations with the people in the town. During the dining Athan and Rodas periodically stood to announce new business contracts. Stone the mason was awarded a contract to build a stone shelter on the west lookout mountain, the beginning for a lifetime of work for him and his sons after him. There were agreements to repair clothing, provide additional food and wine to the Hold, stabling and fodder for horses, and construction of new furnishings to replace those damaged either by time or in the fighting. Abacus looked pained at the expenses being incurred but held his peace. The new majordomo Zotikos, on the other hand, seemed very pleased at the new business and opportunity to undertake much needed repairs and renovations to the old Hold. Zotikos had been a strong advocate for starting maintenance work at once, since basic repairs had been deferred during the long illness of the 'previous occupant', as the majordomo discretely put it. He and Abacus had clashed repeatedly on the subject of the need to spend money. Zotikos prevailed in most of these disputes. He seemed to know everyone in town and vice versa and once Athan had reined in Abacus' parsimony, deals began to flow much more rapidly.

On the evening of the eighth day after Athan's dramatic return across the lake, two riders were reported coming in by the north watch station. Rodas had directed that watchers would remain on that northern hill in the future. His men built a shelter for their horses, erected tents, and set up two oversized flags that could be seen from the Hold. They were ordered to report anyone or anything seen approaching from the north. The two oncoming riders were met by one of the watchers who rode down to greet them. There was a brief discussion before he gave a wave to his comrade on the hill who sent a fresh signal to the hold, which translated as "Riders, many, friendly, approaching north." Rodas quickly dispatched a seven-man patrol out to meet them.

It was well they were prepared for the arrival of friendly riders, because the group that rode over the north pass a quarter hour later was somewhat larger than expected; almost two score men, some mounted, others on foot. The watchers on the Hold were soon able to make out Yure the Elder in the lead, and so the gates were opened for the newcomers, who arrived just before sunset. Of course, Rodas had the entire garrison alert, and a full score of men armed and waiting out of sight near the gate. This did nothing to ruin the warm reception the new arrivals received.

Thereon and Myron were astonished at the changes they found. They had left a somewhat battered fortress besieged by a strong hostile force of cavalry who were camped in and apparently being supported by the residents of an equally hostile town. Now, there was no sign of the enemy, and it was obvious at a glance that the town was not only no longer hostile, but welcoming. The remains of the feast had been cleared away and the Hold was still semi-decorated. The general good will that the celebration had engendered remained. The Hold was clean, signs of repair were in evidence, and most of all there was a busy sense of well being around the place.

"I've brought you a few extra men," explained the old sergeant when greeted by his old chieftain now the new King. "Word got out you had some money. That does wonders for recruitment. I had to turn some away. Glad you made it over the lake. They were a little concerned for a while back there in Lychmidas. On the way here we saw the four boats that brought you across out on the lake headed home so we figured you had made it. Sorry for the delay. I thought the weather was too bad for travel. We used the time to train the new recruits a little better."

"I'll bet you did," said Rojas, speaking what was in Athan's mind. The two were delighted with the extra men. They looked to be a promising lot. This brought the garrison up to close to a hundred men. That was enough for Athan to run patrols and still have enough people to safely garrison the Hold against any reasonable threat.

"Well, done," Athan confirmed. "Have them stable the horses with Ixon. He may have to put some in the courtyard for the night. He can send the extras down to the stables in town tomorrow. The men can get a hot meal over there. Theron, introduce them to Cook. Talk to Zotikos about billeting your men. We will have a council in two hours in my offices. We can discuss your men in detail and set up the new watches. Then we can start planning for training."

As Yure set about getting his men and animals down and settled for the night, Athan began reviewing in his head a new host of problems he would have to solve. It never seemed to end.

It was an almost warm day, a real harbinger of spring that almost got the Old King killed. It was clear, sunny and moist; the kind of day that turns snow banks into gentle irrigation projects. The old man had drunk his morning tea. That was all he had left to consume that morning so it would have to do for breakfast. He left his little lair and decided to simply sit in the sun and think of nothing at all. Just uphill from the cave's entrance was an old stump that was broken off about knee high. The old man took his gray wool blanket and sat down gratefully on the rough stool. The sun was out and he faced it with his eyes closed and dozed, his head lolling comfortably to one side. 'Isn't this what old men are supposed to do?' he thought as he nodded off, 'sleep in the spring sunshine?" It was one of the only times in his life he had ever referred to himself as an 'old man'.

When he heard the horse neigh he opened his eyes without shifting his position. There, at the entrance of his gully, a long bow shot away, was a horseman looking right at him. The Old King sat frozen in place like a rabbit staring at a fox. The instinct served him well. After a moment the old man could tell from rider's posture that the horseman had not yet noticed him. He did not recognize the horseman, but he knew he was no friend. In fact, he was willing to bet his life that the man on the horse below him was an enemy. If he had not been in the ambush that had killed his comrades and forced him up here, this man was almost certainly a brigand. He wore no armor and carried no shield. He did carry a lance and had what appeared to be an ax on his saddle. The Old King considered his position. He was unarmed, and even if he got to the entrance of his little hiding place the horseman could ride up and use that lance to poke him out of his hole with little risk. Undoubtedly he was not alone, and the old man knew he was in no condition to take on even one, much less several enemies. He would die in that little crevice either by a spear thrust, or arrows, or maybe they would just set his little dead tree he used to block the entrance on fire and burn him out.

Why didn't the rider see him? Then the old man considered how hard it must be to spot him. He was remaining absolutely still. He was wrapped in a gray blanket that was the same color as most of the other boulders that littered this little gully. The blanket also obscured his form; he looked more like a lump than a person. His long beard that had come in gray, further helped to break up his outline. The fire in his hiding place was low, making no smoke, and what wind there was blew any smell of it up the hill away from the watcher below.

Suddenly the brigand gripped the horse more tightly with his knees and partially turned his mount to face more down slope. He called out words the Old King did not make out. There was an answering call from below and to the left. The man finished turning his mount and without a glance back, turned and headed down the hill the same way that the Old King had come what seemed so long ago. There was something in the horseman's posture that seemed to indicate he had come up as far as he intended to come and was returning to a camp, back the way he had come. The Old King had passed his unexpected inspection.

He sat on his stump until he was sure that the man had truly gone. Then, suddenly feeling the cold he moved quietly and quickly back to the shelter of the tree near the entrance. When he was sure he remained unobserved he reentered his hiding place. If bandits were moving, spring was almost here. He would have to move out as soon as the weather permitted.

Chapter Six–Justice

After the arrival of Yure the Elder with his contingent, things in Dassaria seemed to slow down. It was inevitable; events had been moving at breakneck speed in the little kingdom since Athan's forty men had ridden into town. Athan and his men had been under an enormous strain since they first received word that the Archimedean Empire had invaded Macedonia that fall when they were back in Pella. Had it only been a few months? And in a larger sense, things had been moving fast for Athan ever since he had let Simeon persuade him to steal the Satrap's gold. Since they had taken that tribute, it seemed as though he had been like a squirrel in a forest fire, leaping from one tree to another, just ahead of the flames. He and his people welcomed a chance to catch their breath. There had been a break when they had settled into the compound in Pella, after they had stolen the Satrap' gold. This was different; this time the men were less frantically engaged in seeking pleasure and more interested in settling down. It was just as well, for winter closed in with snow and storms. It was bad enough that Linus and his men had some difficulty in returning through the mountains from their embassy to Bardhyllus.

With so many horses and ponies now in their possession, it was necessary to stable some of them in the town. Inevitably some of the men, especially those with women, began to seek billets there as well. Athan was aware of tension caused by housing men both in the Hold and in town, but he put it down to the normal strains of settling into a new place. He also noticed there were issues with the bargains being struck with the people in Dassaria. Those could be typical problems as well; Athan had little experience with that sort of thing. Still he could feel that things were not quite right though there was nothing he could put his finger on, and so he let matters proceed.

There was certainly enough to keep him busy. Now with winter here, the men wondered why they should continue to keep sentinels up on the watch hills. Athan liked having an early warning of anyone approaching his Hold. On the other hand he was reluctant to leave men up there all winter; it got awfully cold up there on a windy hill in a tent. The men also complained that often they could not see anything in the frequent rain, snow, and fog. That was what eventually caused Athan to give in and stand down the watches on the hills. Stone and his men had a contract to build a shelter/watchtower on the hill to the west of town, but construction on that structure would not even begin until spring. Athan vowed he would make sure the structures built on the watch hills would be comfortable enough to allow his men to spend the night up there even in the coldest weather.

Always one to look for a way to turn a difficulty into an advantage, Athan took the opportunity of having his men all together in one place to start formal training. Provided it was not raining, the courtyard allowed for excellent practice both for the exercise of individual arms and, most importantly, for group training. Rodas reminded him that they were no longer fighting as brigands; he now had an army. Athan took the point and ordered that the men organize into sections and begin training them as proper hypastas. Fortunately Yure the Elder had served with a city guard and actually enjoyed 'whipping the men into some sort of fighting force' as he put it. Yure, Rodas, and Athan had nightly meetings reviewing the past day's training and planning for the morrow.

The heart of any local army had always been the phalangists, standing shoulder to shoulder, four or more ranks deep with their heavy round shields overlapping and spears bristling ahead of the line. Nothing could resist such a formation. The men who made up these formations were militia, citizen-soldiers who provided their own equipment (no small cost) and were expected to train together periodically; it was considered a civic duty. Unfortunately, Dassaria had no wealthy upper class of citizens that could afford to arm themselves to serve as militia. Worse, there were not that many men of fighting age in the town at all. There were fewer than a hundred fighting men in the garrison and that would scarcely make a decent single line, much less four or eight ranks of soldiers. Though most of Athan's men were well-equipped, they were primarily equipped as hypastas, not phalangists. Some of the new recruits brought in by Yure had little equipment of any sort. This problem of just how to train the men to fight led to some fine discussions among the experienced hoplites. They had to try to find out if and how they could change from being mercenaries and vagabond hill fighters to men organized to defend a realm. Under King Ratimir, it had been a simpler problem. His band operated like bandits, moving swiftly, and fighting in irregular order relying on individual fighting skills to overwhelm weaker opponents. They felt no obligation to protect the people of the kingdom. If faced by a superior force, Ratimir's men retreated. They could always return to the Hold; it required much less military skill to defend a fortress. But in fact, no one took the trouble to attack the walls of the Hold because Dassaria was too distant, the terrain too difficult, and the people too poor. It had simply not been worth the trouble to invade them.

Athan had a different problem. He had been listening to Abacus and Zotikos. For once the two men had the same advice. Athan would have to tax his new subjects. The two had radically different ideas on methods of tax collection but they both felt that the people in the area could provide a continuing source of wealth. Athan had also been listening to Rodas who was all in favor of 'civilizing' the kingdom. To Rodas that meant a proper city state with a wall, oligarchs, magistrates, and a real army to keep the people safe. Unfortunately, Rodas was not sure how to do all this.

At the most elemental level, before he built up his forces, Athan had to decide just how he wanted to use his fighting men. Should they be a light force, specializing in collecting taxes and hunting bandits? Should they be a mirror of the city states with powerful bands of phalangists? Or should he stand pat and leave things just as they were? He had enough men to defend the Hold and enough money to pay them. He had an alliance with the nearest credible threat. He could finally relax and enjoy life. Of course, it was not that simple or straightforward; Athan found himself frequently discussing the direction of this new kingdom with many of his men in what were the equivalents of the campfire meetings he had held as a bandit chief. These men were not shy about expressing their ideas concerning what they should do and how they should do it.

It was in one of these meetings about this problem that two ideas began to grow. No one was exactly sure just who first came up with the ideas though Prokopios was the first to really express it fully. The first idea was simple; use more hypastas and peltasts with only a single or double rank of phalangists making up the front ranks with the more lightly armored hypastas behind them making up the rear ranks. That way there would be a large force of well trained and mobile men who could chase bandits, collect taxes, enforce laws, yet who would also be able to stand in the line and be useful in a real battle. This was not a fresh idea; the problem was how to get enough trained and equipped men in the absence of a good-sized city and without hiring a large body of fighting men whose salaries would empty even Athan's large treasury.

The second new (to them) idea was to conscript men to serve Athan for a time then allow them return to their homes. There were a number of interesting advantages to this system. Adding some locals to the garrison would give them enough men to patrol the kingdom and guard the Hold. After their service ended, they could be recalled if needed, and provide a reliable, trained reserve of militia. Their equipment could be stored in the armory; if Dassaria was invaded the former conscripts could be quickly recalled and incorporated into the army. There was another acknowledged value to this; Athan's men all understood how shared military service bonded young men. The young men who had completed their service would almost certainly be left with a sense of loyalty to Dassaria. Finally, while the conscripts were spending their time in the army they would be defacto hostages for their family's behavior.

There were some problems with this plan. For example, how could you keep track of who had had not been conscripted and who already served? Abacus thought he could come up with a system to create and maintain the record.

"Men are easier to account for than money," he said confidently, "they are larger. And no one is trying to steal them; except for some of the village maidens, of course." That was the level of Abacus' attempts at humor. Abacus was in good spirits during this time. He was working harder than anyone, even Athan, but he loved what he was doing and was convinced his work was important. Things were going well. He was sure he could develop a system for tracking the men who were conscripted within a matter of days. As is often the case when a young man tackles a new problem that he really doesn't understand, Abacus was wildly optimistic in his estimate.

The other major problem was how to provide equipment for an expanded army.

The men soon discovered they had an unexpected limitation. Despite the seemingly huge armory of weapons that the Bear and his men had collected over the years, there were shortages. Not all of it was suitable for their needs. Some items were in bad repair, some things, such as the big ax appropriated by Linus, were of limited value for a regular formation, and some of the weapons were ceremonial pieces, better suited for display than to battle. They had plenty of spears, enough swords, and even enough greaves of varying quality. But the two most critical items for a heavy infantryman, hoplons and helmets, were in relatively short supply. They found that there were only about two score of the heavy round hoplons suitable for phalangists and only about a dozen proper helmets. Exacerbating the problem, these two things were not only the most important pieces, they were also the most expensive and most difficult to construct.

They found out another problem when they went to the Hold's resident blacksmith to see about making new equipment locally. Athan was glad to find the blacksmith used a real name and did not identify himself, by his job title, like so many others in this region. Unfortunately,

Tito was not much of a blacksmith. He did not like to work with iron at all. He was much more familiar with bronze and the other softer alloys. It was quickly clear he would not be able to construct the sophisticated phalangist helmets with their complex curves and Y shaped eyepieces. Swords would also be beyond him. He was capable of making bronze spear and arrowheads, but he was not confident in his skill beyond using forms made of simple strips of bronze.

It was Tito himself, embarrassed by his lack of skill, who came up with an innovative and effective solution for making acceptable helmets. Instead of trying to build a helmet by molding sheets of bronze, he worked with simple strips of bronze perhaps two fingers wide and less than half the thickness of a man's little finger. First, Tito made a mold for the helmet. Usually he simply took a man's own pilleus and made a form by wrapping it in thick sheets of wet leather with linen on top of it. He let the form dry until it was stiff. Then he removed the pilleus from under the form and returned the hat to the owner no worse for wear. He placed the new form on his anvil and bent a wide bronze bar around the brim attaching the circle with a rivet at the back. Now he had a leather and linen hat with a horizontal strip of metal that rode just above the ears. Next Tito took two other bronze strips and attached them vertically to the crown, one on either side of the form's peak, after which he added one more piece going front to back, over the peak of the helmet. Where the crosspieces passed over one another, Tito attached them together with a simple rivet. Finally he attached the crosspieces to the crown by heating them and pounding the strips to the crown adding rivets as he did so.

A blow by an enemy to the top of such a helmet would be stopped by the three crosspieces and a blow given to the side of the head was protected by the horizontal crown piece. To cover the gaps between the bronze strips, Tito added a covering of thick, stiff leather over the top of the metal framework giving it the characteristic forward tipped conical appearance of the pilleus. He molded the leather while it was damp and tying it to the bronze framework with leather strips so that it dried tightly to the frame. This leather was lacquered, which helped keep it water resistant and added another bit of protection. Likewise, a lining of either heavy linen or leather was attached to the inside of the metal framework. A leather chin strap completed the helmet. This helmet would protect against stones, arrows fired from a distance, and would deflect many slashing blows. Later improvements were made such as dangling nose and cheek pieces of leather or bronze and wider chin straps. Tito's helmets were relatively inexpensive and within his capability to construct. Even though each one was custom fitted for its owner, Tito or his apprentice could make one of the helmets in less than a day. Best of all, the helmet was relatively comfortable; it could fit right over a man's own pilleus, giving him even more padding from knocks on the head. These helmets were distinctive and in time, like the gray cloaks, became a readily identifiable item of Dassarian units.

While all this was being worked out, training with the existing soldiers continued. The men were divided into four sections. Yure took the newly hired recruits and, leavened with a few experienced men, began to teach them how to fight in a formation; how to advance (that was easy) how to retreat (this was much harder than it looked) and how to change formations. The other sections took turns acting as opponents using padded staves as spears and rattan swords. Even wearing armor these blunt weapons took a toll in bruises, cuts, and even occasional broken arms. As two of the sections practiced in the yard, another would stand guard duty, and, weather permitting, portions of another would ride out to investigate the local area. Whenever possible, Athan accompanied these patrols. He wanted to get a better feel for the surrounding land. He took time to pay visits to villages and homesteads in the area. At first, the inhabitants greeted him and his men nervously. Athan did his best to reassure the locals as to the good intentions of himself and his men. He carefully noted things in the places he visited. People typically hid their valuables and put their women away when armed men came calling. Of course, Athan was looking for young men of military age he could return and conscript later. Men like these were often in evidence when strangers come by. Athan always tried to buy food from and eat with these people. By springtime, between the peaceful visits of his patrols and the good reports that came out from Dassaria, the people in the immediate area, if not exactly friendly, were no longer hostile to their new overlords. Athan carefully noted on tablets everything he had seen on his visits. He shared this information with

Abacus and most especially Rodas as they held long talks about how best to proceed when the weather turned.

The passage of time did not diminish the tensions among the staff inside the hold as Athan had expected. In fact things got worse. Athan knew that his majordomo and treasurer hated each other. This was to be expected. Their duties put them in constant conflict, and their personalities were very different. Neither was a likable man; Zotikos was of the old regime, oily, of doubtful sincerity, and somehow gave the impression of smirking behind your back. Abacus was young, rude, and overly conscientious. For every complaint Athan heard about Zotikos, he heard two about Abacus. Yet it was the older man than made Athan uneasy, though he was not sure why.

A month and a half after capturing the Hold a charge against Zotikos came to Athan's ears that troubled him deeply. He was first approached by Rodas. Athan could tell at once his second-in-command was bothered by something.

"Ixon needs to talk to you," he told Athan quietly.

"Have him come, then," Athan replied. He was busy preparing to ride out with a patrol but something about Rodas' manner told him this was important.

"I would prefer it to be a discreet meeting," Rodas said in a private voice.

This got Athan's full attention. Never before had his friend said something to him quite like that. "Should I see him now?"

For some reason that reply seemed to reassure Rodas, "No," he responded. "After you get back Ixon will be in the stables to oversee putting the horses away. You know how he is. You should be able to get a quiet word with him then."

Athan nodded. And all that day while riding out to see a small farm south and west, not too far from the lake, he wondered what Ixon needed to talk to him about. There had been too many fights in the garrison in the last few days. Not just fights between men in the training yard; that was to be expected when men had their blood up. There had been too many fights in the barracks the evenings, especially late at night. Rodas had stopped the serving of wine after the third hour of the night in an effort to quell the unrest, but this measure seemed to have no effect. Then there was the issue of the man who fell off the wall. He was heard groaning at the foot of the south wall by a patrolling sentinel or he probably would have died of exposure in the night. The man's name was Leksi, one of the three taken in from the Bear's service. There had been nothing to indicate he was doing anything suspicious. What was troubling was that he seemed to have more injuries beyond his broken leg than were consistent with a fall from that height. Leksi said that it was an accident, he had climbed the ramp in the night for a breath of fresh air (in winter?) before retiring, and when he went to look over the edge he slipped on a piece of ice and fell over. Athan and Rodas both thought he was lying, but neither could come up with a better explanation of what might be the cause, so they let it go. Now all the worries and uncertainties of the past few days came back to distract Athan all through the short little patrol he took that day.

It was snowing that evening when they returned and the wind was picking up. Athan's patrol was eager to be back to their rooms to get warm and so did not linger in the stables. Ixon did linger, watching his workers get the horses into stalls and provide them with food and water.

Glancing over at Athan he shrugged and said, "A cold day for a ride, sire. Would you like some mulled wine in my room?"

They left the stables and cut over to the little room next to the bastion, beneath Rodas' larger series of suites. There was no fireplace in the room; just a lamp burning beneath a small pot that smelled of spiced wine. There was a table, three chairs, a tattered chest, an even more battered cupboard that might be acting as a wardrobe and two beds in the back corner, head to head, perpendicular to each other. And there was his woman, Adara, sitting stirring the pot of wine and staring at Athan with a strange expression on her face. When they entered she hesitated for a moment before rising and making a sketchy gesture of welcome. She poured two cups of wine without speaking.

Athan watched her with some curiosity. In a small community like the Hold, Ixon and Adara had generated a considerable amount of interest, if not to say gossip. Most of the men could not understand why he had taken so much trouble with her. She was not unattractive, neither was she a great beauty. They were staying in his room, but they were not sleeping together. And she had been one of the garrison's whores for a month or more; every man in the old garrison must have had her. And then there was that thing she did to the bodies the night the Hold fell; this gave most of the men the shivers. They wondered why Ixon put up with her. Some of the women wondered the same thing and decided that Ixon was crazy. Other women thought he was the best man in the entire Hold. The general view came to be that he was treating her like one of his injured horses. Ixon was famous for being able to bring animals that were injured or had been mistreated and restoring them to health.

"He probably expects to ride that filly someday," opined Pirro over a cup. "I hope she is not too worn out to be worth the trouble."

Athan was not sure himself why Ixon and Adara were together. He suspected it was because Ixon thought it was the right thing to do and she still needed him. In the back of his mind he suspected the two had come to enjoy one another's company in a completely different way, now that they were spending so much time together.

The two men sat at the table with the wine; Adara moved to the back of the room and sat on her bed. She looked rather pointedly at nothing at all. Her back was stiff, her posture tense. 'What was going on here?' thought Athan.

The men spoke of the day's ride. They had not spent half an hour in the farmstead before, to the evident relief of everyone Athan decided the weather was closing in. It had, and the last hour of their return had been ridden into the teeth of a cold blustery wind.

This conversation was somewhat perfunctory and was very obviously to prepare for the real topic of discussion. Athan was chilled, tired, and hungry and had a great deal of work to catch up on since he had been out of the Hold all day. So after a few comments he came right to the point.

"Rodas says you have something important for me," he said bluntly.

Ixon who had been trying to find a way to broach the subject was relieved to have a way to start the discussion. "It is about that majordomo fellow Zotikis," he confessed. "I know he is in your service now, and I know you are aware he worked for the Bear."

Athan shrugged and indicated he should go on.

"The thing is, this Zotikis, he is the one who decided to rape Evania." Seeing Athan's puzzled expression he explained, "She was the one who was exchanged as a hostage with one of those hill tribes. Ratimir sent his cousin, one that he couldn't get married off, in exchange for Evania as a token of goodwill. Anyway, Zotikis decided he fancied Evania so he broke in to her room and raped her. When the Bear heard about it Zotikis told him that they could always send her back and tell them she had just fallen in love with his handsome majordomo and seduced him. That made the Bear laugh. Then Zotikis convinced the Bear that giving up his cousin would let the tribes know how ruthless he could be and besides it would save the price of a dowry. Really all he wanted to do was keep on raping Evania; which he did. Finally when he tired of her he brought her down to the woman's room and threw her in, telling her she would now have more friends to pleasure."

"He is evil, that one," said Adara from her corner. He doesn't like to screw, he likes to hurt. Power is what excites him."

Both men were silent after that. The intensity and coarseness of the speech were unsettling.

Athan pondered what this meant. Rape was a serious charge in that time and place. It could result in a blood feud. Where was this girl's family? Where was the accuser herself? Athan believed the charge, it seemed to fit what he had been able to discover about Zotikis' character. However, he was not willing to condemn a man or even discharge him on the testimony of a single hearsay witness, no matter how credible. He told Ixon that he would investigate the matter. Both knew what that meant. There would need to be more evidence presented before Athan would take action. There were others in the Hold who had served the Bear. What would they think?

"He cheats," said Adara still in her corner looking at the wall. Then she turned and looked at him. "He cheated the Bear, he will cheat you. That is what he does." Adara turned back giving the stone wall a properly stony look.

The two men looked at one anther, neither knowing what to say. 'I don't know if this meeting will help her recovery or be a setback' thought Athan. To Ixon he said, "I will look into that. If he is stealing from me I will find out."

"Then ask Celeno," suggested Ixon in a low voice as he let him out, "she knows everything that goes on."

"You need to meet the Mouse," Celeno advised him the next morning when he contrived to speak with her in private. "What I hear is nothing compared to what he knows. I will have him speak with you." Then looking around she confided another secret before leaving. "That demon is doing more that just cheating you. He is a bad one." And touching the side of her big hooked nose with her forefinger with a knowing glance she scurried away leaving Athan a bit confused as to just who this bad demon was, Zotikis or Mouse, whoever he was.

He found out that evening. He had just been getting ready to go down to the evening meal when Giles announced a man had brought some slates up from Abacus. Sighing, he looked out at the man standing at the door to his office and immediately knew he was looking at the Mouse.

Men took names for a variety or reasons. Athan had noticed that in this part of the world they sometimes took names that they thought gave them prestige, such as the Bear or The Badger. Names like that were not always accepted. Athan knew one of his new recruits had tried to pass himself off as Ox. Despite his thick neck and shoulders, the men would have none of it; he was too new and inexperienced. Some men, in this region took the name of what they did or worked with. There was Abacus, Stone, Needle, and a carpenter called Chips down in Dassaria. But once in a while a man earned a name that fit him so perfectly that no other moniker would do. This was such a man, with just such a name.

Mouse was a small man both in size and stature. He had brown hair, not russet and wavy like Athan's, but brown and straight, worn like a dark wooden bowl around his head. Though his cheeks were bare, he did have a small beard around his mouth covering his weak, receding chin. He had a prominent nose with visible nose hairs protruding from his nostrils. His bright eyes were wide set and a brown color that matched his hair almost exactly. Wide ears stuck out through the bowl of his hair. His narrow shoulders were hunched, his posture poor. He was wearing a common brown (of course) wool tunic with brown leggings for the cold and plain sandals. He stood with both hands in front of him, clutching a slate. Athan could not decide on his age but he was clearly an adult. At first, Athan thought the man was assuming this odd posture as a way of announcing who he was; in time he realized that

146

this first impression was a true one. The man was not trying to imitate a rodent; he was just naturally, well, mouse-like.

"Celeno said I should talk to you," the mouse-man said.

Athan almost laughed at that voice. It was too much, a small, squeaky voice. The Mouse, indeed!

"Come in and close the door," Athan instructed him. He saw the surprised face of Giles as the little man closed the door. Athan had never closed the door of his office with a stranger before. Briefly Athan considered the possibility that this man was an assassin.

Another look at him and Athan could definitely tell this was not a man of violence.

"So," he said, "they say you know things. Tell me about myself."

It was a simple test for Athan to verify. Let him prove how much he actually knew. And Athan wanted to know just how much this strange fellow could reveal about his new King.

The little man looked at a couch. Athan gestured at him to sit. The Mouse sat down delicately on the edge of the couch and placed the slate next to him. Then bringing his hands together over his sternum in a characteristic gesture he began to speak in his high voice, keeping his voice low and confidential.

"I think your name is Athan, son of Medius. You are probably originally from Epiria." Athan was startled, so surprised, that he let the little spy go on. "I believe you were in the guard there and lost your family in a battle called Achilles' Debacle. It is likely you were chieftain of a band that fought and killed a great sorcerer called Azziz a while back. You stole the tribute from the Dorian cities destined for the Achaemendian Empire. You took this fortress with only two score followers. You wear a magic amulet around your neck that gives you unknown powers. Some men say you are much older that you look. You are very rich. Right now in your treasury you have thirty and one half talents in gold bars, four talents in a variety of specie, and jewelry and other various objects that are estimated at not less than another six talents. Plus, there is another four talents back in Lychmidas as well. This is less, of course, the cost of the recent feast which was just over 1000 drachmas."

Athan had lived a long and eventful life to that point; he would live for many eventful years thereafter. Never, not once, was he more completely astonished than he was at that moment.

"How," he gabbled, and instinctively reached for the Bear's Claw, the dagger he wore on his right hip.

The Mouse looked nervous but resolute; he explained. "I heard your name from one of the men in your old band," he began in the same small precise voice. "Then I heard the red headed one, I think his name is Pirro, telling some stories he had heard about you when he was in your band. I also heard a bard sing 'Beltos' Epic' once. I really liked it. There was a part in there about a dashing bandit called Athan." He flashed an unexpected smile. "Then the bard sang another called the 'Song of Athan'. When I heard what your name was I thought you might be the same man, especially when I heard your all your men talking about how long you had been around. Baruch has seen you in the baths and says you never take off your amulet. You can get a lot from him. People talk in the baths. Everybody knows about how you stole the tribute." He shrugged and continued, "The rest I just picked up here and there."

"Like when Abacus answered my question about how much was in the treasury."

The Mouse grinned. Suddenly the little man knew, just knew, he and this new King were going to get along. Mouse was suddenly confident enough to speak plainly and openly. "Yes, sir."

"Where were you?" asked Athan, still amazed at the knowledge this man possessed. It crossed his mind that this knowledge was dangerous to him, but immediately he recognized that the information this little Mouse might get in the future could be immensely valuable.

"I was just on the wall, sir. I hang around and listen."

"Tell me about yourself, oh, Mouse. Tell me about Mouse, as you told me about myself."

Mouse gathered himself again and began speaking in the same quiet precise way. "Mouse is my real name, at least the only one I have ever had. I am much younger than my other brothers and sisters; most of them were out of the house before I came to surprise my parents. I was sickly as a child and my mother always fussed over me. She still does. I live with her in town. My father died and left us an inheritance; I help out by doing things for people."

"People like Celeno," interrupted Athan.

"Yes," confirmed Mouse, "I find out things for people, well for certain people. She's a witch you know."

"Who?" asked Athan briefly confused by the abrupt switch, "oh, you mean Celeno. Yes, I had heard she might be."

"Well, she is. A real witch with real power; she can put curses on people. She cursed the Bear. It took over a year before the Bear got sick. That is not the only time, she has cursed someone. She said the Bear took so long because he was the strongest person she ever cursed. She gave me two charms after I helped her. One makes me inconspicuous."

"You mean invisible," asked an intrigued Athan.

"No sir, when I invoke it, people just seem not to notice me as much."

Athan thought how much Mouse would blend into the scenery even without the aid of magic charms. "And the other charm?"

"It helps me understand people better, I mean, when they talk. You know how sometimes you can't understand what people are saying. Well, when I activate the charm the right way it is a lot easier for me to make out what they are trying to say. It's great! I use it sometimes when I am talking to my wife. It helps a lot."

"You're married?!" Athan continued to be astounded by this creature.

"Well, sort of," Mouse said evasively. We have a kind of understanding, like."

"Tell me about Zotikis," Athan prompted getting back to the subject at hand.

Mouse smiled, "How much do you pay?"

Athan thought for a moment. "I will pay you as much as one of my men; paid at the same time, on the day of the new moon."

Mouse looked doubtful. Athan decided he needed this man and what he knew to be available to him.

"That is just for the exclusive right to your services. You will work only for me. I will pay you more for each report you provide, depending on its value." Athan thought for a moment and added, "Provided it is true."

"Sir," and here Mouse tried to draw himself up to look dignified, "my business depends on my honesty. If I ever give information that I know to be wrong I am out of business…finito. My reputation is my fortune."

"Damn well better be," growled Athan intimidating Mouse for the first time. "And, if you are not sure about something, you better tell me."

"I did, sir," protested Mouse. "I always do. I always will."

Athan thought about what Mouse had told him about himself. He now recalled that Mouse, when made his report, had sometimes said 'I think' 'you are probably' and 'likely'. On the things Mouse was more sure of there were no such modifiers. As to the man's so-called magic charms, Athan was skeptical. This man had obviously been in the Hold quite a bit. Athan was an observant man yet he could not remember seeing him before; or had he? Perhaps he had seen a small brown man going about his business here and there.

"Well, then," Athan said yielding the point, "tell me about my majordomo, Zotikis."

"He is a crook," said Mouse promptly, using a word that meant a man who was venal and corrupt. "He is very good at worming his way into power. That is what he likes, being over people. Once he has a position he trades things for money or favors and he keeps on building his power. The old Bear never did figure out what was happening. Zotikis stole him blind. If you wanted a room, or a better watch, or a girl, or anything, you paid Zotikis. If you didn't pay his price you paid for it in another way; maybe you got assigned bad jobs, or night watches, or nasty duties, or thrown off the wall."

Athan stiffened to full attention. "Did he throw Leksi off the wall?"

Mouse shrugged, "I don't think he did; probably he had someone do it for him. He did that a couple of times when the Bear was here."

"Who would do that for him?" asked Athan seriously. This was far worse than he had thought. 'You better be able to prove this, little man,' thought Athan grimly.

And in the same precise way he had described Athan's life Mouse told Athan about Zotikis. How he had been in his fine house down in the town when Athan took the Hold. How as soon as Athan had taken over Zotikis had immediately begun to suborn people in the Hold. His grasp was still tenuous, but it was growing. If you wanted a good room, either in the hold or in town, you had to do something for Zotikis. The tavern houses and prostitutes in town were under his control. Already he had three of the servants who worked in the Hold doing his bidding as well as two of the local men who had joined the band. Zotikis had strong influence on two more of the men Yure had brought in. One man from Athan's original band that had taken the Hold was helping Zotikis out in a small but growing way. There was a quiet rumor that Zotikis had approached one of the three men from the Bear's garrison who had been released and taken into Athan's service and when the man, Leksi by name, had objected, he was beaten and thrown off the wall to die.

"That is the way he sometimes does things. People may not even know they are doing what Zotikis wants. They just go along with some other tough guys. Sometimes he frightens people into doing what he wants. Sometimes he gets people to do a thing they are ashamed of and that binds them to him." There was a pause and Mouse answered Athan's unspoken question. "Like when you throw a comrade off a wall or steal from a friend. Also Zotikis liked to play games. He would make women, and men too, 'play his flute' in front of others." Athan had a sudden suspicion why the Mouse disliked his majordomo so much. "There is a problem with his methods, however," continued Mouse regaining his typical reporting style. "For people to be afraid of you, they have to know what you can do to them. And you know how people who fear someone usually hate them as well. Also he sometimes makes mistakes. He threatened Celeno. Just three days ago he suggested that he might find a place for her daughters in one of his houses; one with bad light so their customers would not notice how ugly they were. I have never understood why people taunt their enemies. Anyway, I think she put out a katadesmoi on him."

Athan shivered despite himself. He did not like magic. He had heard of these cursing tablets before and had doubted their power. Perhaps this Celeno's katadesmoi were actually effective; frighteningly so. He held up his hand to stop his little spy.

Taking us a fresh slate he took a deep breath and asked Mouse to repeat the specifics of the accusations against his majordomo including those involved in this alleged conspiracy.

A half hour later Giles saw the plain little man slip out the door and into the outer corridor. He craned his neck to make sure his king was all right. He saw Athan sitting at his table examining a slate in each hand looking worried.

Without looking up Athan spoke to Giles. "Is there anyone out there waiting?"

"No, sire," Giles assured him.

"Then listen. I do not want others to know that I talk with that man who just left. You are never to speak of him with anyone except me. His name is Mouse, and we will never speak that name when anyone else can hear. You can refer to him as a 'certain man' if you need to talk about him where others can hear. If he asks to see me, let him. He is our private spy, and I want to keep him private, just between the three of us. Do you understand?"

"Yes, sire."

"Thank you. Can you bring me up some food? I have some work to do before the Council of War this evening. 'Council of War'," Athan mused, "we have to give our meetings with my sergeants a different name. Let me know if you have a better idea for one." At the end of this speech Athan finally looked up from the two tablets and smiled. "Thank you," he said in dismissal.

"Yes, sire," It was not the first time Athan had asked for food to be brought to him. Earlier in their relationship Athan had sometimes simply forgotten to eat; Giles, who deeply loved his king, felt it was his duty to care for him and so had trained his lord to ask for food to be brought to him when he was hungry. The affair with the small man Athan called Mouse fascinated him. The sort of intrigue that was going on was just what Giles thought a king should be doing. There was exciting work afoot. Of course, first Giles had to go fetch his king some food; that was part of his responsibilities. 'Do the small and the large with equal attention' his father had always said.

Athan sat in his office looking at his notes. Mouse had repeated the details of the conspiracy almost word for word. Athan was later to find out that his new spy was almost perfect for the role of informer. In addition to his inconspicuous demeanor, Mouse had keen eyes, sharp hearing, and an incredible memory. Beyond this he seemed able to gain people's confidence, and he was an excellent listener. In time, he would establish a regular network of people who kept him informed on what was happening. He honed his already fine instincts about what people were planning until he was sometimes aware of plots before they had even been finalized.

Before Mouse left that first meeting Athan had him promise two things. First, he was not to share what he knew or learned about Athan with anyone else. Second, he asked Mouse, 'not to do anything that will make me have to kill you.'

Mouse had smiled and willingly agreed. But in the end, he only kept one of those promises.

Athan had considered and reconsidered his options by the time Rodas and the sergeants came in for the council of war. The first order of business was for Athan to announce that they would refer to these get-togethers in the future as the military council, since they were not actually at war and hoped to avoid one for the foreseeable future. This brought the expected smiles. They discussed the events of the day and progress of the training. A storm was expected that night; clouds were visible rolling in and they all predicted precipitation the next day, so training was cancelled for the morrow. These men knew Athan well enough by now so that they knew that there was something on his mind.

He looked around the room at the men that filled it: there was Rodas his second-in-command, and Giles his shield bearer and aide, who stood in the doorway. He had five sergeants, Linus, Prokopios who had been with him for years, old Yure, who had been with him even longer, Stamitos and Tenucer who had been with Athan off and on all through his years as a brigand. Stamitos, who was the older man, had his own section. Tenucer was seconding Linus with his section. Soon, thought Athan we will have to create another section. Either that or take some of the men from Yure's group and distribute them around to the others. That would be for another day.

Athan had been considering what to do ever since he realized he had a major problem with his majordomo. He knew that as a despot he could simply kill the man out of hand. That would solve the problem; it would also create several more. Athan was unsure about the justice of the thing. He did not want to start arresting people without some sort of process in place. That sort of thing made folks nervous and uncertain.

As to the accusations, well, he had a charge of rape; of course, most of the people in the Bear's service were guilty of that. He had a claim of embezzlement. Athan suspected this was not uncommon. Indeed, people in positions of authority were almost expected to siphon off some money. There was the implication of blackmail and extortion. These were more serious. They challenged Athan's authority. There were other charges, though it hardly mattered. There was no system of incarceration to speak of in that time or place. In general there were two penalties for felonies: exile or death. Yes, there were four unfortunates left from the Bear's garrison still chained in that room where the captive women had once been kept, but they were not being kept in jail as such. It was just that they were too dangerous to exile, and Athan didn't really have any specific reason to kill them. If Zotikis had done all the things that Mouse said he had, the punishment of exile would not fit his crimes.

"Men, we have a problem," Athan said after the routine issues had been decided. "Guard the door, Giles," Athan said. Giles moved to the door in the reception room so he could look up and down the corridor for any eavesdroppers. The men in the room were glad to finally have what ever had been bothering the King out in the open. Athan outlined the accusations against Zotikis. First, that he had raped a lawfully constituted hostage who had been promised safety. This did not cause much excitement. That he had extorted bribes from the servants for easier jobs. Still he got little reaction. That he had extorted money and other favors in exchange for room assignments. That got more response. The men knew that secret bribes undermined their authority. And finally Athan told them there was evidence that he had suborned some of the men in the Hold to intimidate others and extort protection money from them. That got a serious set of growls from some of the dangerous men in the room. Finally, Athan told them that Zotikis had approached him yesterday with a plan to turn the four prisoners over to his custody. Zotikis had claimed the men could be used to perform heavy labor under his supervision. That was news to most of them but they understood the implications immediately; it would give the majordomo more men who could enforce his will upon the other members of the Hold. This could be a direct challenge to Athan's authority and therefore to their own.

He got the expected recommendations from his sergeants; they wanted to have a chat with Zotikis while he bled to death. Athan stopped that cold.

"No man, no matter who it is, will get summary judgment from me," he announced. There was grumbling about that but Athan knew that later on they would think upon that and be glad of it. "Just because he has been accused does not mean he is guilty. I want more evidence, more proof." He looked around. They knew he had an idea on how do get this proof. Athan did. "Rodas, I want you to get to the bottom of this and soon. If these charges are real, this Zotikis is a real threat. If not, he deserves to have his name cleared. You name any man you need to assist you. Find out the truth about these charges and report back to me, no matter what the hour. And I repeat, be careful. Now you are dismissed."

Athan had characteristically delegated the job to the right man. Rodas was fair right down to his core. He also liked people, had a good understanding of human nature, and enjoyed puzzles. This particular puzzle did not take long to unravel. Rodas took Linus and Yure up to his room and came up with a plan. It was simple and effective. They brought in the people who had been named as Zotikis' accomplices and started asking questions beginning with the youngest and least involved. It did not take torture. Under the looming presences of the two sergeants and intimated by Rodas' authority (for he could be a very formidable personality) they quickly found out that the accusations were not only true, they were understated. After the third man was called in, Rodas had Prokopios come in to guard the men who had already been interrogated. After the fourth man had broken, Rodas went to visit Leksi who was still in the care of Hypnos the healer.

Rodas sat by the man's bed and awakened him. The young soldier stirred surprised at the appearance of the Hold's second officer. Rodas looked the man in the eye and spoke in a low clear voice.

"Who threw you off the wall?"

At first the boy denied anything of the sort had happened. Then, as Rodas revealed how much he had learned, the boy began to shake. Then he cracked like an egg, abruptly and wetly. Weeping he told all. How he had been told to come to the south wall, how he had been told the old ways were coming back. That he could be part of the in crowd;

be with the right sort. That he would get rich and ride out on a horse with gold in his purse or stay here and be a senior sergeant with women for him any time he wanted just like before. He had protested he was being watched, that it was too dangerous. They had insisted. He decided he did not want to be part of the venture. Then he remembered being struck from behind and awaking up at the bottom of the wall. He knew who had done this to him. They were the same two local men who had been named by Mouse.

That pretty much wrapped up the investigation. It had all the sophistication of a schoolmaster determining which boy had stolen some apples, still it was undeniably effective. They now had assault and attempted murder to add to the charges.

Rodas was sure enough of his investigation that he immediately went to Athan and presented his case. He asked permission to arrest the two local guards who resided in the Hold. These were apparently Zotikis' muscle within the Hold and had been with him from the first. Once they were in custody Rodas intended to take a few lads down to Zotikis' house and make general arrests of anyone there. Athan granted permission, cautioning Rodas to bring a strong force with him when he went to arrest Zotikis.

"Remember, that is his home. It will be guarded, and he may have some bolt holes and hiding places. Hit it hard and fast before they can react." Athan smiled, and added, "Use it as a training exercise."

Prokopios and Linus were sent to arrest the two men in the Hold. They brought along Pirro, Xenos, ropes and stout staves. It was well they did so. Even though it was now late, the men they sought were not in their sleeping quarters. They found one playing dice and talking to several other men in a confiding way. He looked alarmed when they arrived and tried to bluff his way out. The arresting party had not noticed the other suspect in a corner and even though no one had asked about him, he attempted to bolt from the common room. When Xenos tried to block him the suspect slashed at him with his dagger then tried to escape out the door. He was clubbed down as he fled. The two were bound and bundled up to Rodas. The other men in the room were detained, separated and individually questioned. These two, unlike all the other suspects questioned so far, were uncooperative to the point of defiance. Rodas had them chained and thrown into the room where the four men captured when the Hold fell were still secured. These four men had not done anything beyond being taken in the initial fighting, but it was the general judgment that they were far too dangerous to simply release. Now there were six hard cases in the makeshift jail cell, with half a dozen other men detained separately elsewhere in the Hold. An extra guard was assigned to keep a watch on the jail, just to be safe.

By this time, even though it was the sixth hour and the middle of the night, almost everyone was awake. The gate guard would not let anyone leave at that hour, and Athan had directed the sergeant of the guard on duty, Tenucer, to place another man on the rear gate to ensure no one went down to spread the news of what was happening up on the hill.

Realizing that everyone was more or less awake anyway, Athan decided to issue a midnight alert and called a general stand to. It made noise, but Athan figured no one down in the village would deduce what was going on up on the hill or why. After the men had been armed and had manned their assigned ready response stations in the bastions, on the walls, and in the courtyard, a stand down was ordered. Athan then called for a general muster for the garrison in courtyard. This was novel and created quite a buzz. The garrison had only had a night alert once before, and it had been announced in advance. When this alert was initially called, many of the men thought the Hold was actually being attacked. As an exercise it was very successful; it revealed many flaws in their planning to resist a surprise attack at night.

Once the men were in formation, Athan climbed up the ugly stone cistern in the center of the courtyard to address them. A ladder had been kept there as it provided instructors a good viewpoint to oversee training in the courtyard. Now it acted as a pulpit. Athan stood in the cold night wind and in an equally cold voice made some plain statements about the poor performance in the night attack drill. He promised the men that they could expect more such drills and directed the sergeants to attend him after the men were dismissed. Then he addressed what was already being rumored among the men. Even the men on watch in the bastions leaned in to hear.

"Men," Athan began with a carrying voice, "there were some traitors amongst us." That got their attention. Athan explained that there were all kinds of treason. There were small treasons and big treasons. There were big treasons against him as King, and small treasons against them as soldiers; for example they should not have to pay extra money for better rooms and better duty. Most of them now knew where this was going.

"One brave man refused to be corrupted, and he nearly paid with his life."

They all knew who that was. The men hadn't been sure Leksi had been attacked, however, and certainly not that he had been attacked for refusing to play along with the majordomo's boys. Athan went on to warn them about the dangers of barrack room deals, listening to strangers who were not one of their comrades. He told them to avoid secret deals and listen to their sergeants.

After this exhortation Athan told Rodas to dismiss all the sections with the exception of Linus' men. "They have some more work to do tonight."

The place was really abuzz after this. Everyone was talking; even the servants were up getting the latest news. It was necessary to move Linus' men down to the back gate to get some quiet. There, with the entire section standing around them Linus, Rodas, and Athan developed a plan of action. The men were more or less already armored, so after the plan was firmed up they were dispersed to modify their equipment as directed. A rather large group of spectators formed around the men as the plan was developed. Athan had to stop at one point and have Giles move them back and to tell the men to stay off the walls and out of sight.

It was about the eighth hour of the night, still four hours or more from dawn, and cold as Hades itself by the time the men reassembled at the rear gate of the Hold, ready for action. It was a good group. Just less than a score, the heart of the section was Rodas' old band. There was a good mix of old veterans and eager young men, each wanting to look good in front of the others. They were armored and wore helmets. All carried shields and swords; about a third also carried spears. The rest were burdened with unlighted torches, lighted dark lamps with the black metal doors shut, lengths of rope for captives, and a large log supported by two lengths of rope. Linus called it his master key, since it would open any door no matter how well locked. They assembled before the rear door of the Hold, each man knowing his assignment, each fully equipped and prepared. They were ready and eager. They were hoplites, the best fighting men in the world, and they knew it.

Rodas led them silently out the back gate, each man wrapped in his gray cloak. In the dim light Athan thought they looked like a silent gray mist flowing out the rear gate. Last of all went Giles. Athan longed to go with them; he knew could not justify it. Linus would lead the assault on the house of Zotikis; Rodas was there in the capacity of Magistrate, and Giles as Athan's personal representative. Athan, in violation of his own prohibition, climbed to the north wall to see what he could. He knew that the men would make their way down the side of the slope to the bottom of the ridge where the Hold stood. There they would reassemble and move around the ridge to the edge of town as a tight unit. The house of Zotikis stood separate from other houses on the north side of the town of Dassaria facing south toward the rest of the town. Once the raiders could see the house, the section would split into three units. The largest group under Linus would carry the log to the main door. The other two groups, one directed by Tenucer, the other consisting of Rodas and Giles with one other man would move to opposite back corners. That way they could see anyone attempting to leave either from the side or rear of the building. When Linus was ready he would light the torches from the dark lanterns, open the front door, using the battering ram if necessary, enter the building and arrest anyone inside. That would probably include some slaves, servants, cooks, prostitutes and perhaps a few sleepy customers. Everyone was to be collected and moved up to the Hold. A detachment of men would remain to secure the house until it could be searched.

Up on the wall Athan tried to see any sign of his men working their way down the hill. There was only a gentle breeze was from the northwest, but even with that in his favor he heard only a few faint noises and no spoken voices. He thought he might have detected someone speaking in the distance; then he decided it was probably his imagination. It was a dark night and little could be seen. As he walked along the wall looking down for any sign of his raiding party Athan abruptly missed Giles. He had come to rely on his company. Suddenly, he realized that here he was, alone on a wall on the very night he was trying to crush a budding conspiracy against him. If they had overlooked one of the villains, the man might be out looking for revenge. It would not be hard to guess where the new king had gone. Athan was aware that he had not brought his kopis with him or even one of the short swords they kept in his office. He was very grateful for the length of the Bear's Claw along his right thigh. The dagger might be ugly, but it was a sturdy weapon. He drew the big blade out and held it in his right hand for comfort.

Just after these thoughts had run through his mind, Athan heard the scrap of footgear ahead of him on the parapet. Athan dimly made out an approaching figure. He could see the man had his sword out.

"Who goes?" he called out nervously.

"It's me, sir, Pirro," came back a relieved voice.

Athan relaxed slightly. He had known Pirro so long and so well that he knew Pirro would never conspire against him.

"I have the watch," the little red head said coming up to Athan, "and I thought I saw someone on the wall. I knew you said to keep the walls clear so I came to see."

"Sorry, sir," said Pirro noticing Athan's look and hurriedly sheathing his sword. "You can't be too careful."

"No," agreed Athan putting up his own dagger. "Let's go watch the action."

The two men moved to the top of the northwest bastion. The men were allowed to keep a brazier going on top of the bastion. There was a tendency for men to huddle around a fire instead of looking out into the night if a fire was allowed inside the bastion. So the men had a choice, they could stay up on top next to a glowing charcoal fire, or they could get out of the wind and weather inside the unheated bastion. Typically the decision was heavily influenced by the weather. On rainy or windy nights no one stayed outside. With the overcast, the night was very dark. If you looked in the right spot it was possible to imagine faint lights where perhaps a forgotten lamp or comforting candle for a child still burned. The two men stood wrapped in their cloaks with their backs to the warmth talking quietly about the old times.

Pirro was recalling a particularly wild party he had attended in Pella when the men saw a torch suddenly flare into life. Then there was another light at the front of what had to be Zotikis' house. The torches moved rapidly around lighting others around the house. They could hear a faint thud and shouts from below. Athan had asked them to shout out that they were the King's men as they entered. There was no concept of warrants or unreasonable search or seizure, Athan just wanted to let the residents know who was coming for them. They could hear some faint shouts and see the torches moving about around the outside of the building. Then the there were lights inside the building. They heard a man screaming in agony. The screams suddenly cut off. In less than a tenth part of an hour the whole inside of the house was lighted by lamps and candles. Some object appeared to flame up briefly inside the house; it was quickly extinguished. The two men watched from the battlements in the cold for what seemed to be a long time. Then a party of lights started moving up from Zotikis' house toward the Hold. A few minutes later a runner arrived at the front gates with the news: the raid had been a success.

Giles and Rodas told Athan the story in the warmth of the King's quarters just as the sky was lightening in the east. It had gone as well as any operation Rodas had ever experienced. They had a bit of difficulty in getting down the hill but once there had assembled with only an occasional brief flash of a dark lantern to guide the stragglers. Once everyone had joined, they had moved out like a line of blind beggars, shuffling along in close contact, the log intended as a battering ram lived up to its name, battering against their shins all the way in a most annoying fashion. Tenucer had been put in the lead, and he had done a splendid job of navigating them to the target house in pitch-black darkness. Of course afterwards the men could not help teasing him about his route which they claimed included every bush and pothole possible between the Hold and Zotikis' place.

Once they could see the house things went very smoothly. The men split into their assigned groups with little fuss. Rodas and his two companions were expecting a long wait in the cold before things started, but Linus wasted no time. They had hardly had time to get on station before the first torch came around the corner and they heard the ram hit the door. Rodas had been hoping the door might merely have a latch or be unlocked altogether, unfortunately, Zotikis was a suspicious man. It took four stout hoplites five heavy blows with a log to spring the bolts and allow the hoplites to pour in. Once inside it went reasonably well with the men meeting little resistance. The only casualty in the whole operation happened outside. Perhaps because there were fewer men on the corner where Giles and Rodas were waiting that was the place where Zotikis chose to make his break. He leapt out of a second story window, cloak flapping, a cloth bag in hand. He landed, crouched and attempted to dash away. Giles, who was carrying a spear, used the butt end to trip the majordomo. He then followed up with a few well placed kicks to the head and back. The other trooper with them joined in the fun. What they did not see was Zotikis' companion, a man who managed the house and served as a bouncer and whore's protector, leap out the window behind them. Seeing his master being attacked the thug drew his knife and went for Giles who had his back turned. Rodas was there; unfortunately he was carrying a torch, not a shield or spear. Without giving the matter the slightest thought he whipped out his sword and stabbed the man before he could do Giles any harm.

"I think I have forgotten how to fight," confessed a shamefaced Rodas recounting the story. It was not a very good blow." Instead of thrusting into the man's chest for a quick, lethal strike, he pushed the tip too low, cutting across the man's abdomen and almost disemboweling him. The man began screaming then howling whether from the pain or the certainty of his own death no one could say. Rodas was unsettled by the noise and swung his sword down on the neck of the man who was by then kneeling on the frozen earth holding his intestines in both hands. One benefit of the sloppy killing was that all resistance, scattered as it was, stopped instantly when the people inside heard the screaming.

"Rodas saved my life," stated Giles.

"I don't think so," countered Rodas. "You had your cuirass, and he just had a knife, you were already turning around."

"Have it your way," replied Giles looking Rodas in the face, "but thank you."

"Glad to help," said a smiling Rodas.

The raid netted eight people and a corpse. Four of the people were prostitutes. One of them claimed to be Zotikis' wife until she realized which way the wind was blowing. Then she decided she was only an acquaintance, and a recent acquaintance at that. Two of the men were local men, domestic staff, who were questioned and released. One young skinny man with a cleft palate was sort of a thug in training. He was held for a time before being exiled.

The last person was, of course, Zotikis. He was initially cowed, then puffed himself up and became imperious. When he was brought before the King, he became fawning and subservient. He had explanations for everything. Of course, if a man wanted something special, he arranged it. What good was money if you could not use it to buy things for yourself? No, he did not know anything about extorting money from people in the Hold. He did know those men, but he knew nothing about stealing money. Had he not managed the Hold efficiently? Athan was not sure if he should kill him out of hand or let the man go. Instead he decided to do what he had intended from the beginning; he let Rodas sit in judgment of the case.

Rodas made the long room directly above the stables on the second level his seat of justice. The case began after everyone was fed breakfast. It was midday before Rodas finished hearing all the defendants. He did not call any witnesses. The idea of confronting one's accusers was not a requirement. Rodas did visit privately with Ixon and Adara to hear the woman's accusations. Based upon the testimony of Leksi he had heard the night before and actions of the two men accused of attacking Leksi when they were arrested, Rodas decreed the two men guilty. He sentenced them to death. The three servants and two men who had come with Yure from Lychmidas and were implicated in Zotikis' schemes were exiled. They were given three days to depart the area; not a kind thing in winter. Three other men were found to have been peripherally involved and were fined a portion of their pay, given extra duties for a month, and a stern admonition to mind their behavior in the future. In his own mind Rodas decided the majordomo's plots had been growing fast, and they had been lucky to nip it in the bud.

Finally, after lunch and a short nap, for Rodas had no sleep to speak of the previous night, the case of Zotikis was heard. He was brought out of the jail room chained and linked with the other four of the Bear's men who had been taken when the Hold fell. Zotikis knew he was in a tight place, but he was confident. There was little linking him to the intrigues inside the Hold. He was almost certain he would be discharged and probably would be exiled. That did not trouble him; he had tired of Dassaria in any event. It was time to take his money and go south.

The significance of his attachment to the other four prisoners did not dawn on him at first. Zotikis was confused when, instead of addressing him, Rodas instead spoke to each of the four hardened toughs (for they could not really be called warriors) in turn about things they had done under King Ratimir! It made no sense to Zotikis. His fellow prisoners were somewhat bemused by the events as well. Most were surly and uncommunicative. One was defiant. None admitted to anything at all.

Then the Magistrate came to Zotikis, the last man in line. The new Magistrate sat on a chair placed upon a dais and did not ask him a single question about taking money from people in the Hold. Instead he asked if he had served under King Ratimir! Zotikis began a long discussion of his service as one of the Hold's servants.

Rodas cut him off. "That means yes." And before the astonished Zotikis could respond the new magistrate asked him another question that made no sense to him at all. "Did you know a woman named Evania?"

Zotikis gaped at him. "Who?"

"Evania, a hostage exchanged for a female cousin of the late King Ratimir."

Recognition dawned on Zotikis' face. He almost smiled, "Oh, her. Yes." The Magistrate said nothing. Zotikis felt a bead of sweat run down the side of his face despite the fact that the room was quite cool. What was this all about? "She seduced me, poor child. I have that effect on women." It was meant as a joke. No one in the room so much as smiled.

"What was her fate?"

"Oh," Zotikis said stumbling on his words a bit, "the attraction passed. She took up with other men. Many other men." He smiled with his mouth trying to look around the room now aware of the hostility of the people in the room.

"How did she end up in that room with the other women that were available, how was it put, for common usage?"

"She was a whore. That is where the whores stayed in the Hold."

"And did you visit those whores?" Rodas tone was neutral. Zotikis felt like the Magistrate was driving toward something but for the life of him he could not see what it was.

"Sometimes," the prisoner shrugged.

"How about that woman there in the back of the room?"

Surprised, Zotikis turned his manacled hands in front of him to see Adara in the back standing in directly in front of Ixon who seemed to be supporting her somehow.

"Remember," cautioned Rodas, "lying to a magistrate is a serious charge."

Again Zotikis shrugged. "I suppose so. We all used the whores from time to time."

Changing his voice for the dispassionately precise tone he had been using to a penetrating one, Rodas called across the room. "Adara have you ever been a prostitute?"

"NO", she said clearly and defiantly.

"I believe you," said Rodas resuming his previous tone. "And I also believe that this Evania was never a prostitute either. I believe she was a lawful hostage who was under the protection of then King Ratimir. Therefore, Zotikis, I find you guilty of rape. I hereby sentence you to death. I also sentence your fellow prisoners to death."

"What for?" shouted one, surprised not at the sentence that they had all long expected, but in the manner in which it was pronounced.

"You worked for the Bear for a long time," explained Rodas to him almost conversationally. "We all know you did many things to deserve death."

The man shrugged, accepting the verdict.

"Yeah? We all did stuff; it was our job. So why are you giving us the chop?" objected one of the older condemned men.

"Because you're just a bunch of assholes, that's why."

And with that the Chief Magistrate of Dassaria got up and left the room. As he left he saw Adara weeping softly into Ixon's shoulder.

The executions were carried out that evening. Servants had begun digging a grave for the two men condemned earlier in the day; when they found there would be seven executions not two they simply widened the hole. About an hour before sunset the prisoners were led out the front gate, each with a guard on either side, down to the north side of the hill. The hole had been prepared near the foot of the slope, next to where a garbage pit had been. The condemned men were in chains and now also had ropes pining their arms to their side. They were followed by Sergeants Prokopios, Yure, and Linus. Rodas, who had just been awakened from another nap and was somewhat grumpy, followed behind the sergeants along with Athan and Giles. Ixon and Adara brought up the rear. Others watched from the walls of Hold and a few people from town gathered at a distance.

Yure had a stout club over his shoulder, about a long as a man's arm with a good thick barrel wrapped with three wide bronze bands at its head. The prisoners were made to kneel in front of the trench. Yure stepped up behind the man at the end of the line and brought the club around in an arc into the back of kneeling man's head. There was a 'thunk' and the man dropped. Yure passed the club to Linus who killed the next man in line. The three sergeants continued in turn, each dispatching two of the condemned men until only Zotikis was left. He was sobbing openly, blubbering at the unfairness of it all. He did not notice that the sergeants had stepped aside and handed the bloody instrument of execution to Ixon. At the last, Zotikis' nerve broke and he tried to get to his feet, perhaps in a hopeless effort to run to what had once been his house, so plainly visible from this place of execution. Ixon stepped forward with a mighty swing.

Athan had seen many men die but he had never seen a man have his brains literally knocked out before. Ixon dropped the club to the ground and went up to where Adara waited. He put his arm around her and led her up to the Hold.

The servants waited for them to go, then took the ropes and chains off the bodies, (no sense in wasting them) slid the corpses into the trench, and covered them up with dirt.

A thorough search of Zotikis' old house revealed half a talent of coins in small denominations. This Athan had shared between the men who had conducted the raid. A few of the various valuables such as carpets and hangings were brought in to enhance Athan's rooms. A more thorough search uncovered some additional quantities of gold, silver, and jewels that Abácus valued at not less than a talent; that money went into the treasury. Rodas was given Zotikis' old house to use as a residence and a House of Justice. There was always the rumor that after Rodas moved in there he found even more hidden treasure that he kept for himself. But then that might have just been wishful thinking.

People in the Hold noticed in the next few days that the position of the beds in Ixon's little room had changed. They were no longer head to head at right angles; they were joined, side by side. The two were married in the spring.

Rodas was a natural magistrate, the Old King reflected. He was looking out from his little cave at a typically dreary day. After his experience with the rider, the old man was much more careful about showing himself. He began considering what he would need to take with him when he left. There was not much.

During his time in the crevice he had done little except sleep, think, and mostly remember. There was a lot to remember. He had been king for such a long time that people tended to forget things were not always as settled as that they were these days. And when things are unsettled they are not safe. It certainly had not been safe for anyone during that first spring of his reign.

Chapter Seven – Hopes and Fears

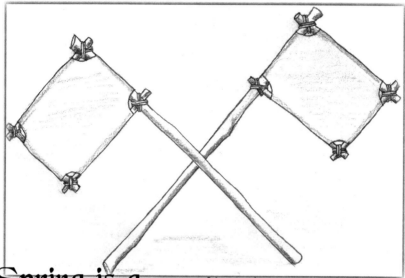

Spring is a season of hope, but it can sometimes be a cruel hope. Fresh tender crops just coming up out of the ground can be destroyed in a sudden frost. New lambs are sometimes snatched by wolves. Jobs that promised a good wage can be suddenly canceled. Prospects that seemed so promising can be abruptly dashed.

It felt that way to the residents of Dassaria that first spring of Athan's rule. There was a promise of plenty of work from the Hold. People were feeling more and more confident in the future as they came to know the new people in the garrison. Not that there wasn't suspicion and grumbling from some, especially those who had lived long under the rule of the Bear. In these people's minds, change, any change, was usually bad. Most of these had taken a 'wait and see' attitude. This was prudent since there was nothing else they could do.

And when the spring rains came, melting the snow and softening the land the hope for a good year seemed reasonable. It had not been an especially hard winter. Many things began to become settled. Dassaria had a real Magistrate for the first time since, well, ever. Instead of a tribal leader or the resident strong man resolving disputes based on family relations, bribes, or the self interest of the judge himself, now there was a court in place that was allegedly impartial. He entertained there for members of the little community. Newcomers were sometimes invited to share meals in the household so that they could meet and be met by the Magistrate. One day this habit of meeting new people would have an unexpected and unintended result that changed Rodas' life.

These entertainments were often modest affairs, just a chance to sit and share a meal with the Magistrate and members of his house staff. His staff consisted of some of his old band, including Stamitos and his new wife, Alesin, Celeno's youngest daughter. No one quite understood just why Stamitos suddenly became enamored of such a plain girl so quickly after the death of his woman, Beryl. He only met her when she offered him some cakes and tea one evening. Shortly after consuming Alesin's offering he began to show a great interest in her. The interest intensified to love and quickly ended in marriage. Even odder, Celeno's other daughter, Adara, had a similar whirlwind courtship and was now married to Iason, once the band's healer. The men were a bit defensive about their choices of brides, touting their cleanliness and fine cooking. They were also confident in their wives' faithfulness. Other men commented out of their hearing that this was more a confidence in the good taste of other men than anything else, for both girls inherited their mother's strong hooked nose and coarse complexion. Yet the marriages turned out to be very successful. The two sisters made good wives, caring for their men, providing them with healthy children, and a tranquil home life.

Alesin and Stamitos began their married life in Rodas' new house, Alesin cooking and cleaning and Stamitos providing security and picking up heavy things as necessary. Like most of the former members of the band, now referred to as the new garrison, they settled in comfortably. There were a number of members of the new garrison living in town by spring. Ixon, now called Master of the Horse, and Adara had taken up residence after their marriage in a house next to the largest stables in town where the garrison's extra horses were kept. Even the Hold's ample stables could not lodge all the animals they had accumulated. Ixon and two stable boys minded the horses 'in town', first thing in the morning, then Ixon would go up to the Hold to check on how his assistants 'up on the hill' were doing with the horses in his other stables. It was a pleasant domestic existence, and he and his wife were quite content.

In addition to his title of Provost, the job of Majordomo had devolved back to Sergeant Prokopios. He quickly found it was much easier if he let Celeno advise him on matters within the Hold. Prokopios remained uneasy around the woman and refused to take any food or drink from her hand. He had heard the rumors of Celeno's powers and had seen what had happened to Stamitos and Ixon. He did appreciate how much she helped him, making intelligent recommendations for housing, and smoothing feathers when there were complaints, but there were limits to his gratitude! Of course, as everyone settled in, watch standing became routine, and as more men moved into residences outside the Hold things were bound to become easier. With the passage of time, Prokopios and Celeno acted as a team more and more often.

Even King Athan, usually referred to by his subjects outside of the Hold as the 'New King', was able to settle into a rhythm. He had a more or less regular contract with Delbine, the prostitute Rodas had engaged for him on the night of the feast. Giles hated her almost as much as he did Abacus; however, he also knew she was good for the king, and so tolerated her. They worked out a standing retainer for her services which Athan paid out of his 'allowance'.

Delbine had decided to focus on this new king and devoted herself to him exclusively. If she was a bit older than most women in her profession, she was still very attractive. A very feminine person, she provided things Athan had forgotten he needed. These needs consisted of much more than sex; she brought him his food (when Giles would let her), and shared meals with him, poured his wine, gave him massages, provided a discreet and patient ear, and a most import of all, a calming presence to a harassed and overworked man who found himself trying to do too much. Although she visited him almost daily (and nightly) she continued to live in her own house in Dassaria.

Yure the Elder continued his duties training the men. At first, Athan was not used to the idea of having only one sergeant acting as the single point of training. In his past experience, he had been accustomed to new men being trained by the men in their section; with so many new recruits, however, he finally agreed it was better to have a single place where all the new men could be trained. He and Yure would talk almost every night about the men and how the training was coming. Yure was almost as old as Athan, a solid veteran. He had come to that time in his life when he was more comfortable teaching than doing. Yure had, like Athan, been a sergeant of a guard for a city state and like Athan did not willingly discuss his departure from that post. He knew his business, which was fighting as a hoplite, and he was a good teacher. The Military Council had decided to organize the garrison into five sections, four regular sections of troops to guard the kingdom and one permanent training section. Yure would have a few assistants and focus on training new men for later allocation to other sections. The Council decided to conscript a number of the young men in the town and nearby farmsteads. Of course this was a closely held secret since most subjects of conscription could be expected to have the great good sense to try to avoid being taken from their homes. Athan stressed repeatedly that the time of service should not interfere with peak farming time; that the time to service in his garrison would last less than two years, and the men would be paid a wage while in service.

The last promise of more expense never failed to agitate Abacus. He appreciated the fact that his lord knew how to read because it let him show Athan just how expenses were outrunning income. He would meet with his king and his advisors almost every day. Rodas and Prokopios were the most common victims who were caught and required to sit in on the difficult meetings. The meeting of the steward/treasurer of the Kingdom of Dassaria and its King followed a standard pattern. They would start with Abacus laying out the current bills and expenses, (somehow almost always more than Athan had expected) the estimated upcoming expenses, (which somehow Athan always underestimated) and the available funds to meet these just debts. Then Abacus would give them a gloomy estimation of how long it would take before the treasury would be empty. Although Athan was very wealthy, even all the golden talents he had laid away would not last for more than two or three years; any kingdom has a ferocious set of fixed operating expenses. In later years Athan would be glad of this harsh lesson he had from his treasurer, but in those early days he was irritated to distraction by the daily arguments, for that was the next regular part of the meetings. Athan would sneer and bluster; Abacus would fall back on the inevitability of the truth of his calculations.

The arguments had certain stock phrases that tended to appear:

"Why is it so expensive?"

"You told me to pay 'fair' prices."

"That is too much!"

"Do you intend to simply confiscate these things my Lord?" This was guaranteed to get Athan tight jawed.

"Just pay the bills!"

"We cannot continue to use our reserves. Even a deep well can run dry." That was an especially favorite reference to the diminishment of the reserve funds.

"Where did the money go?"

"I welcome a review by any competent auditor." This would be offered in a deeply offended tone.

There were a number of variations on this theme; after every meeting, Athan's neck and shoulders were tight with tension. And every time his king yelled at him, Abacus left with a sense of martyred self-satisfaction. He felt that no one appreciated him or valued his critical work. To their credit, neither man shirked these difficult meetings. Abacus continued to give his master what he considered to be honest advice, and Athan continued to (usually) follow this advice.

The primary beneficiaries of the steady outflowing of money from Athan's treasury were the people of Dassaria. The men of the new garrison had money to spend, and they spent it in town. The artisans had work and a steady cash flow. The few traders out this time of year had safe trips and made good profits.

The word of this prosperity began to spread. Merchants considered making trips to the area, or at least to pass through and see if the reports the roads were now safe once again were true. And people all around the area who were dissatisfied with their current positions began to think about relocating to the vicinity of Dassaria, looking to improve their sagging fortunes.

It also happened that the word of the fall of the Bear and of the wealth contained within the small fortress with its handful of defenders rippled out to the rest of the world. The Saga of Linus told and retold in and around Illyria emphasized the small number of men that captured the Hold. Another source of rumor ripples came from the west where stories of gold, lots of gold, spread from the counting houses of Lychmidas and fishermen of Lake Lychnites. And other rumors from further west hinted at the loss of a great treasure of gold by the mighty Achaemendian Empire. All over the region men who had served King Ratimir confirmed and even exaggerated the great riches the Bear had maintained in that little fort. Around dozens of campfires hungry fighting men talked about this immense horde, just waiting for a few brave men to take it.

'Those other fellows did it,' these hill bandits said to one another, 'why can't we?' In the hills to the north, south and east bands of masterless men and desperados of every type dreamed and planned and, as the spring warmed, began to coalesce into a fearsome force.

It was well that Stone and his men had started work on the two watch towers on fine winter days. They had completed the initial work on the western hill, now called Watch Hill by almost everyone, and were working on the tower on the northern hill that overlooked the road that Athan and his band had first used. This hill was lower than Watch Hill, but had a good view of the road that led around Lake Lychnites and back to Lychmidas. Watch Hill was now manned by at least two men day and night. The northern hill, which was being called North Watch, was only partially completed though it too, now had sentinels watching the northern road. There were plans to construct a third tower, on a hill that overlooked the south road; this post was already being referred to as South Watch.

Even though North Watch was still incomplete it was common for patrols in the area to camp there. Though it was less than an hour's easy ride from there to the Hold, it was useful as a first step in a patrol that might last five days. One wall was completed, and the men had built a lean-to against it to shield themselves from the weather. It also gave an excellent view of the surrounding countryside.

That was why a patrol of four men under command of Thereon the hunter, were making themselves comfortable up on the hill late up one spring afternoon. Thereon intended to ride north the following morning and see what they could see all the way to where the road turned west toward Lychmidas, and then explore the small trails that led up into hills as they made their way back to the south. They had orders to locate settlements, talk to travelers, and generally see what they could learn. Thereon expected to be back on this hill in three or four days depending on what he discovered. What he was about to discover, however, was coming to him.

"Hello," said Lethe, one of Thereon's new scouts who was looking north toward the pass, "what's this?"

Thereon stepped over to Lethe and stood beside him. There, just past the crest of the low northern pass was a lone rider pushing his horse hard. As they watched they could see the horse stumble. Thereon was a hunter and had been a successful bandit for years. He could sense trouble.

"Here, you", he called to Meletios, another of the new men, "let's saddle up and see who is coming."

Thereon said nothing else, but the speed with which he saddled his horse disquieted the men.

"Have you made a signal to the Hold?" Thereon asked Jason brusquely.

Although he had been with Athan's band for almost a year, Jason was still not very good at signals. He avoided sending or reading them if he could. There was no avoiding it now. Seeing Jason had not even thought of signaling back to their base, Thereon gave him a hard look and simple instructions.

"Try mirrors while the sun is still high enough. Lethe, use those oversized flags over there. Send this signal: Upsilon Mu 2 – 1 Iota 1. Do you know the sequence to make that code?" Jason gulped and said nothing. Thereon told him the sequence of flashes, then demonstrated the proper position to semaphore the same message to Lethe.

As soon as they started signaling the message, 'unknown horseman, one, approaching, am investigating,' Thereon literally leapt upon his pony and with Meletios right behind him, yanked his mount around and headed down the hill. He abruptly pulled up and shouted one further command up to his now concerned men. 'Keep a watch on the road. If anything happens to us, signal the Hold."

As he pounded down the south side of the hill toward the road Thereon hoped that they knew what signal to send if that happened. As they rode toward the bottom of the hill he was relieved to see the sentinels positioned in the north bastion of the Hold begin to flash back to the hill. At least they were paying attention over there. Thereon could not say just why he was so agitated at the sight of one rider riding over the road; he just felt his instincts screaming at him. One rider was unusual on the road, a rider pushing his horse hard was also not normal. He could not say why it alarmed him so much. He worried that he was over reacting. On the other hand, what had he really done? He had sent a very simple signal to the Hold and gone down to investigate a suspicious rider. That is what scouts did. If he backed his signals up by sending them by semaphore and mirror, the gods themselves were aware that his men needed practice.

Still, he was very relieved when he finally caught sight of the rider. He recognized him; it was Talos, that ridiculous guide that had been with them that winter and led them here to Dassaria. The fellow might be odd, but he was the right sort. He had fought alongside them when the captured the Hold. He and his cousin Myron had been gone for ten days or so. They had been guiding a small group of traders and their packhorses of goods to Lychmidas. Then Thereon's relief disappeared as he saw his acquaintance first check at their appearance, then come on with renewed speed. Even in the cool air his horse was lathered and stumbling with exhaustion. Something was wrong.

Thereon could see that Talos recognized him. They pulled up together, Talos breathing hard, his pony wheezing and trembling, head down. Thereon sat waiting on his pony, expecting to hear Talos tell a tale of bandits, ambush on the trail, and murder. Instead the man gasped out something that at first did not seem so urgent at all.

"In Lychmidas," Talos said in his strange staccato way, "we, Myron and I, heard stories. Men talking about attacking the Hold. Lots of recruiting going on. Some of the Bear's old men. Decided to tell the King. On the way back ran into a band of brigands. Almost caught us. Myron and the others ran back to Lychmidas. I came ahead to warn you. They are on the march, hundreds of them. Lots of bandits, old friends of Ratimir, men from Lychmidas."

This was alarming news indeed! "How far behind you are they?" asked Thereon.

"Not far," gasped Talos. "In sight from that pass," he pointed back up the hill he had just crested.

It was as though a huge alarm began to gong inside Thereon's head. An army was just over the next hill coming to attack them. He realized he was breathing hard. With an effort he stopped to think. For a shocked moment no one spoke, no one moved. Then Thereon's brain reengaged and he barked out a quick set of orders.

"Meletios, get off that horse. Give him to Talos. Talos, ride to the Hold and tell the Chief." In his agitation he referred to Athan by his old title when he was a bandit leader. "Go!"

As the two men scrambled to change mounts Thereon continued his instructions. "Meletios, walk that animal to the Hold. Walk him mind you! If you get on him now he will drop dead. We will come down and pick you up after I signal this back." Talos was already riding toward the Hold on his new mount. "They will be expecting you!" he shouted to the man's back. Then yanking his pony's head around, he headed up the hill as fast as the little animal could go. The sun was nearing the hills in the west. There was not much time.

Thereon was grimly glad to see the two men he had left on the hill had been watching and had drawn the correct conclusions from his actions. They had already broken their little camp and were standing there beside their saddled horses. They did not get a chance to ask him the questions that they were eager to ask for he started questioning them even as he pulled up.

"Did the mirrors work?" It took Lethe a moment to indicate assent. "Good," continued Thereon cutting off their questions again. "Where is it?" Lethe handed him the large bronze mirror. "Jason, watch the north pass and tell me what you see."

"What do I look for?" asked Jason as he turned to climb the short distance to the top of the hill where he had an unobstructed view of the north road.

"An army," Thereon replied briefly. The two men goggled at him as Thereon peered though the hole in the center of the mirror holding his palm in front of the mirror to confirm his aim. "Get moving!" he shouted at Jason. "You, Lethe, get those flags waving!"

"What do I send?" the youngster asked him as he scrambled for the black and white panels. Jason hurried up to the lookout point.

"Epsilon Zeta – 1 – 1 – 99," replied Thereon as he began flashing the rays of the setting sun toward the northern bastion of the Hold.

"Enemy in sight – approaching; from the north; many, many," said Ioannis reading the flashes.

"What does that mean?" asked the young man next to him who had called him when the first signals from the hill were seen.

"It means that a whole lot of bad men are coming down on us from the north," responded the former bandit flashing a response back to the hill. "What are those flags saying?"

"Looks like the same message," responded the other signaler on the tower.

"Well, I guess I better tell the Chief," said Ioannis laconically. "That rider will be here pretty soon. I bet he will have more to tell us." And with a final flash to the hill Ioannis disappeared down the stairs.

"Who is the Chief?" asked the youngster.

"Ioannis and the King go way back," said the other. The implication that their new king had once answered to a title associated with a bandit leader was both unspoken and clear. The two men thought about that as they watched for more signals and maybe an avenging army coming down the road from the north.

"That was Ioannis," said a satisfied Thereon. "You can stop waving those things. He got the message."

Lethe quit positioning the black and white cloth squares. Some men preferred the mobility, speed and longer range of the mirrors. Others liked the greater ease and reliability of the flags. They felt that the mirrors were too dependent on the sun being out and in a good position. Though the system of signaling was new here in Dassaria, to the men who had been in Athan's band of brigands, signaling was almost second nature.

Thereon, satisfied his warning had been received walked over to join Jason, Lethe trailing behind. The three men looked to the north at an empty road.

"How did you know that was Ioannis back the Hold?" asked Lethe.

"You get to know the way a man flashes," replied Thereon. None of the men took their eyes off the distant horizon. "He will get the message to the Chief. The Chief will know what to do."

His two companions heard the reference to the title 'Chief'. They turned their heads and gave one another a look.

Ioannis emerged from the bastion and headed across the courtyard toward Athan's apartments at a purposeful trot. The first man he saw was Prokopios who had the watch. He somehow had sensed something was up and he was prowling around. One look at Ioannis and he started asking questions.

Ioannis cut him off, "Where is the Chief?" That caused ears to prick up among those in the know around the stables.

"What's up?" asked the now fully alert sergeant of the guard.

"Thereon just sent a signal: maybe lots of enemies coming down fast from the north."

"How many?" queried Prokopios.

"Signal said 99."

"Oh crap!" exclaimed the sergeant using the word for excrement.

"Is the Chief in his quarters?"

"See Giles over there by the kitchen. He'll know. Do you think we ought to turn out the guard?"

"I don't know. There is a rider coming this way fast; Thereon talked to him before he sent the signal. He probably has all the details." With that final bit of information, he hurried off to speak with Giles whom he could see on the other side of the courtyard.

Prokopios called his second and told him to get the rest of the section up and mustered with weapons at the gate. He then headed up the northwest bastion to see what he could see.

Behind him there was a flurry of activity. The man on duty at the back gate, who had idly turned from looking out at the same boring scene behind the Hold, watched with interest the animated exchange between Prokopios and Ioannis. He could see a ripple of activity behind the men spreading out as men spoke to one another each hurrying away after imparting the news. 'Almost like ripples in a pond,' the guard thought. He saw the Master of Horse who had been chatting with his stable hand a moment before suddenly take a pony and, stopping only long enough to hastily put a bridle on the animal, swing up and head out the front gates at a brisk trot. 'Something is up for sure,' the man concluded.

Ixon rode down the hill to his new house at a full gallop. Adara saw him coming and met him at the door of their house with alarm in her eyes. They had been in the house for less than a month, and Adara was still edgy about the change.

"You need to move up to the Hold," he told her without preamble. "Get your things together. We may be up there for a while."

He did not tell her why. She already had a very good idea. Her defenses collapsed. Tears instantly flooded her eyes. "Do we have to?" she asked in a voice that choked despite attempts to sound brave and resolute.

Ixon was wise in managing horses and women, still, tears unsettled him. He stopped what he was about to say and instead made the words a real question instead of the harsh rhetorical one he had started to blurt out. "Would you rather go into the hills?" She did not reply. He slid off the little pony which, excited after his sudden run, stamped and bucked. Ixon calmed him and secured the reins to a small post. He then calmed his wife. "Sweetness, they say there might be raiders coming. I want you safe. It is probably just a bunch of bandits chasing some travelers; I just want to be careful. You will be safer in the Hold. Will you go there and wait for me?"

Adara was a tough woman, but suddenly she was hanging on to herself by the merest thread. She could feel the hysteria batting about like a moth in the corners of her mind. She looked at her husband. The tears that filled her eyes made them seem enormous. Her lower lip was trembling. In a small voice she asked, "Will you come with me?"

Ixon was torn. He did not want to have to stop doing what he knew was urgent just to escort his wife up to the Hold. Once there, he knew she would need settling down and reassurance and he did not have the time, not if raiders were coming down on them. "I have to get the horses out of the stables and up to the Hold where they are safe. We can't have raiders stealing our horses, now can we?" The last bit he said in sort of forced jollying tone.

She looked at him in despair; there was also panic back there in her eyes. Then Ixon had an idea. "Would you like to help me? You are good with horses."

"Yes," she agreed instantly, clutching at the chance to stay near to Ixon in this time of crisis. "Let me get my shawl."

In a short time Ixon and Adara were at the stables, only to find the stable hands there before them, preparing to move the horses. Word was spreading fast.

Athan had not had a good day. He was having trouble getting the system for mounted patrols set up. His councilors also disagreed about the best way to establish and collect taxes. Yure was discouraged at the progress of training and concerned about properly equipping the proposed conscripts. Cook came up to complain about the quality of the stores they had started to receive from the area farmers. Then the King had to endure a second meeting with Abacus about the estimated requirements for funds due in the next month, which did not include any provision for new weapons. He had a dull headache and no appetite at all. He decided to lie down before going to try to eat something. He heard voices, Giles trying to protect Athan's chance to relax for a bit. Bless that boy! Then he recognized the insistent voices had an urgent tone. He swung his feet down to the floor and into his sandals. As he laced them up, he could not help thinking that Rodas had made a better choice of jobs.

When he opened the door to his office he saw Giles halfway across the office coming to wake him. Athan knew this must be serious. "What is it?" he asked.

"Urgent message from the North Watch, sire. They are reporting many hostiles in sight and closing."

"It is Thereon, sir," chimed in Ioannis who was close on Giles' heels. "He confirmed 99."

Athan completely forgot about his headache, money, mealy wheat, and everything else. Grapping his sword belt and dagger from off his table, he charged out of his quarters and headed for the southeast bastion steps that lead up to the top of the wall.

"Come on," was all he said. The two men followed.

Once up top of the wall, Athan emerged from the bastion and trotted over the east wall, through the northeast bastion and along the north wall, looking to the north. Athan was not a man to run, but he was definitely hurrying along the catwalk of the north wall in full sight of the men who were waiting for the evening meal. Every man stopped asking questions and heads turned to watch the King moving fast to the northwest tower. Just then they heard the call summoning the on-duty watch to assemble at the gate with weapons. You could not have scattered the group of men standing in front of the kitchens any faster if you had dumped a basket of vipers amongst them. The alarm was not a general call to arms; however the garrison acted as though it was. Men raced to the closest armory (for there were two smaller sites now as well as the main one) and began donning armor, strapping on swords and snatching spears. Without orders the men began to assemble in their designated rally points with much yelling and shouted questions.

When Athan got to the northwest bastion he raced up the stairs to the signaling point on the top of the bastion, taking the steps two a time. Looking out into the long flat light thrown by the low angle of the sun, the scene was strangely peaceful. He saw a lone rider approaching the Hold directly; one rider and another man farther back walking along, leading his horse. There was no invading army in sight. Athan was at first puzzled, then angry. That passed quickly; it was a good exercise for the men. If he punished his men for being wrong in their reports he would not get many reports. Now if it were due to foolishness or stupidity that would be different, but in no case would the punishments be more than a reprimand.

Giles asked the question, "Didn't the signal say 'many enemies in sight? Where are they?"

"The signals are not specific as to whether they are reporting what is seen or what has been reported," responded Athan peering down at the rider who was pushing his horse hard. "You know Ioannis, we should come up with a modifier about that. Hmmm, I think that rider is Talos. What do you think?"

The three other men on the top of the bastion shifted their gaze to scrutinize the man fast approaching the gate.

"Yes, sire," agreed Giles, "I think it is."

"That Talos is a good 'un," grunted Ioannis. "I bet he talked to Thereon. That is where the reports of the enemies come from."

"Well, let's go see. Come on Giles. Ioannis, stay here. If we get anymore signals send your man down and let us know." Leaving a disappointed Ioannis to remain on the top of the bastion, the king and his shield bearer headed down the stairs.

So it was when Talos pulled his new and freshly wearied horse up to the gates of the Hold, he found a small reception committee waiting for him outside the walls that included the King and most of his sergeants. Rodas could be seen hurrying up from his house in town toward the gathering. The men were waiting just out of earshot of the garrison who watched from the top of the walls and clustered at the entrance. Linus had discouraged those who would have followed the King and his companions outside the gates.

"Welcome, Talos," said King Athan. "I see you come in haste. What news?"

Talos slid clumsily from his horse and to Athan's surprise made a salute to him. "Sire," he gulped, "I have bad news. There are many bandits coming. They almost caught me. Myron and the others turned back. The hills are alive with men. I think they are coming here."

It took time to pull a full story out of him. Talos was not a trained scout and every man there remembered his previous efforts at providing intelligence had been woefully lacking. Even so, before he had finished his first few sentences Athan had nodded to Prokopios who waved at the gate. In a few moments, seven riders pushed out the gates and galloped north. The men in the patrol had already been briefed to contact Thereon and then investigate north.

"Make contact if possible, but that does not mean fighting," Prokopios had warned them. "Find out what you can and then head back. It will be dark soon, so be careful. Don't get ambushed. Send a rider straight back here when you are done. If you don't see anyone, stay up on North Watch tonight and patrol out at first light. Tell Thereon to stay up there and send signals at least once an hour. If you do run into a strong force, have everyone retire back here."

Simple orders: Investigate. See if the bogey men were out there. Don't let them get you.

While the patrol dashed out with the setting sun just on the horizon, Talos continued his story; how Lychmidas had been a hotbed of rumors and recruiters; how they had even been approached and been asked to join as mercenaries for the upcoming attack; how they had decided to return to the Hold. Only four of the eleven who had gone out to Lychmidas decided to return to Dassaria: Myron, and two men from Illyria who wanted to get home. They all were mounted and carried no goods with them. They had no problems the first day, though they noticed there were only a few local travelers on the road and none coming in from the west at all. On the second day they had made the turn and headed south along the road to Dassaria. They traveled cautiously; one man would ride ahead, the other three some distance back so they could not all be scooped up by a sudden ambush. Talos had been the leading rider, the point man, when a group of armed men came marching down on foot from a trail leading down from the hills to their right. They were even with the other three men and a little behind Talos. As soon as they saw Myron and the other two, the strangers began running to cut them off. The three riders had turned their horses and headed back the way they had come. Talos hesitated and lost his chance to follow them.

"The bandits would have been too close. Besides, there might have been as many behind as ahead. I thought you would want to know about this. I thought it might be worth something to you."

Talos made no other comment about his self interest in telling the rest of his tale. It should have taken him an easy two days from where he had seen the armed band; instead it had taken three hard days. He had often been forced to leave the trail at the sight of bands of armed men. He had made cold camps and traveled at night, staying off the road. Late this morning he decided that he was ahead of the enemy so had resumed travel during the daylight hours. He had been seen and chased over hills and through gullies. Finally he recognized the pass that led down to Dassaria. He had chanced a dash down the road and over the hill. It had worked. He had not been pursued, though he felt as though he had been observed.

The last signal from the flags up on North Watch, just as dusk fell indicated. 'Friendly, horsemen, south, all well'. That was interpreted to mean that Pirro and his patrol had arrived and that nothing had been seen of this vague enemy to the north. When Meletios arrived walking Talos' jaded pony, he immediately asked to rejoin his patrol.

"In the morning," he was told. "You can ride up there in the morning."

The Hold had already begun to fill up. People in Dassaria had heard the alarming news. They had seen the extra horses being led up to the

Hold. The Magistrate had gone up there as well. In general, people knew what to do when raiders came down on them: run and/or hide. There were those that thought the best plan was to live and let live, close up their dwellings and wait for the strangers to go away. Some thought the best plan was to take their most precious possessions and headed for places in the hills. The surrounding countryside was rugged, so there were many places where a family could find cover. Some would go into special hiding places they had prepared in and around their homes for just such times. Some, especially those who worked in the Hold, thought that this new King would allow them to take refuge in his stronghold, and so all that evening and into the night there was a steady stream of people pushing carts, leading sheep and goats, and carrying possessions up the hill and into the Hold. At first there was confusion among the garrison about what to do with these townspeople. Normally, the gates were closed at sunset, and with the Hold on high alert, the men on watch thought this would be tightly enforced. After a brief consultation with Rodas, Athan directed Prokopios to leave the gates open with a strong guard set just outside the gate and in the courtyard.

Within a quarter hour a new problem surfaced; where were all these people going to stay? Assignment of quarters was normally Prokopios' responsibility, so he was relieved of his sergeant of the guard duties and put to work finding places for all these people. Within an hour Rodas had to become involved. Although only a fraction of the people living in town had decided to heed the warnings of a strong raiding party close by, those who came still filled every available room in the Hold. Worse, their livestock needed to kept somewhere, and the stables were already overfilled. The garrison was not sure which was worse, being threatened by an invading army or overrun by refugees. Still, things were sorted out and by the third hour of darkness no further refugees came up the hill. The gates were shut. The watch was doubled. People settled down, and everyone within the walls passed an uneasy night.

Rodas was sleeping on a pallet in Athan's outer office. He was astonished to discover that Athan had retired by the fourth hour and stayed in his sleeping chamber all night. Rodas and Giles had been delegated to deal with the inevitable issues and alarms in the night, so both men had sleep in the nature of a dotted line. Athan, well rested, was up before dawn, telling the two tired men who peered blearily up at him to get some sleep. In the cold gray light of dawn the hasty alarm of the night before seemed like an overreaction. Some of the townspeople already wanted the gates opened so they could return home. Athan told them the gates would be opened soon, and they could return home but they would have to leave all that they had brought into the Hold here until he was certain things were safe. He reminded them if enemies were found they might not have time to get back if they were burdened with their goods.

The gates of the Hold were thrown open, and a formation of a dozen armored hoplites poured out, ready for any hidden enemies that might be lurking to surprise the first people to come out into the cold gray dawn. There was no one in the shadows, no one visible at all. At the all clear from the men on the ground, a mounted patrol trotted out and then began cantering out to see what was going on in the north. Athan moved from the gate tunnel and climbed the stairs of the North West bastion to join the dozen or so men who had decided to come up and see the first signals from North Watch. The men made way for him as he shouldered his way to the signaler; it was Ioannis again.

"Anything?" asked Athan quietly.

"No, sir," responded Ioannis in the same tone, not taking his eyes off the dark hill to the north. "We should figure out some way to signal at night. Maybe use fires or lamps somehow."

"Yeah, I know," replied Athan, "we just haven't gotten around to it."

The two men stood side by side, both looking north, and talking not like king and common soldier but like two old comrades—which they were. Both were aware that they were in part responsible for the alarm last night which had turned out to be unnecessary. And though Ioannis was only doing his job, and Athan had only done what was prudent under the circumstances, they both had that uncomfortable feeling of being considered an alarmist. Athan remembered when he had been guardsman. There was an old fellow from the south who used to haunt the public areas with cries of "The End is Coming!" predicting that the world would soon be swept away by an angry god. Poseidon was the one he most often mentioned. One day he was gone, no one knew were. Of course, Athan suddenly remembered, only a few years after the prophet's disappearance the end did come for Epiria.

There was suddenly detectable movement in the shadows on the hill. Then as sometimes happens as the sun rises, suddenly what had been gray and dim became clearly visible. The flags on North Watch were moving. Their signal was the most common one, the one sent every morning: 'All clear'.

Athan felt a sinking in the pit of his stomach and a dull anger at Talos. He had said it once before, "Talos, you are a terrible spy.' Now he had been made a fool of by the man; a very obvious fool. He would need to stand down from this ridiculous alert. Next time the men might not respond so well; the people in town certainly would not.

"Sorry, Chief," muttered Ioannis quietly, "I should have checked out the signal before I called you."

Athan realized the signaler thought this was his own fault, not Athan's. He had only been doing what he was supposed to do. Suddenly, it dawned on Athan that this was exactly what he himself had done as leader of the Hold. He had a credible report of an enemy coming down on them, and he had reacted as though it were true. Well, now he would have to have a meeting to review what went right and what did not. A ray of sunlight illuminated the top of the northern hills. The mounted patrol that had left the Hold could be seen, some of them moving up toward the men at North Watch, the rest continuing up the road toward the pass. Athan could identify the gray pony Meletios had loaned to Talos the night before in this group. The young soldier had obviously recovered his pony and was riding out with the patrol. It promised to be a fine morning, warm and wet with a possibility of some thunderstorms later.

"I am going to get some breakfast, Ioannis," he told the signaler, "We will stand down after the patrol gets a chance to look over the pass."

Therefore Athan was down eating some bread and cheese with a sleepy Giles and was not up on the bastion watching the patrol as it came up to the crest of the northern pass. He did not see, as Ioannis did, the sudden swirl as the patrol yanked their ponies, first up, then around and began racing down the hill with scores of strange horsemen right behind them in hot pursuit. He did not see the repeat of the 'enemy in sight' frantically waved from North Watch before they, too, took flight. But Athan did hear the alarm gong ringing and a moment later the alarm horn being sounded as well. He headed to the bastion in a hurry, Giles at his heels. He made his best speed and managed to reach the wall just in time to watch poor Meletios on his gray pony being overtaken and speared off her back by the pursuers.

The bandit army that Talos had promised had arrived.

It had been raining off and on almost continuously for the two days. The combination of rain and warming temperatures caused the drifts of snow to melt leaving everything wet and muddy. This had an unexpected and welcome side effect. The old man was going down to drink and refill his water at the little stream around the corner of the ridge one afternoon when he noticed the vultures. The Old King had always kept a sharp look-out on these forays; the memory of the rider at the mouth of his gully was still sharp. Now, however, when he saw the low-circling birds he decided to investigate. On the other side of the little draw where he had taken shelter, not three bowshots uphill from where he got his water, was an assemblage of birds pecking at something in a snow bank.

He understood what it must be at once - meat. Leaning on the stout stick he had been using as a staff, he hurried as best he could in a hobbling gait up and over to the source of the bird's interest.

Chapter Eight – Holding On

Athan stood on top of the bastion and watched the spreading force of between two score and half a hundred mounted brigands, chasing his patrol down the hill. He could see the handful of men that had been up on North Watch heading down the west side of the hill trying to avoid direct pursuit.

"Make a signal to Watch Hill," said Athan calmly, "Enemy in Sight North."

He continued to watch the pursuit. "Well," he continued calmly to Ioannis, "it looks like Talos was right after all."

"Sir," came a puzzled question from the signaler who had turned to the west, "Watch Hill is already signaling."

Ioannis and Athan glanced at the flags moving up on the western watch post. Athan turned back to watch the pursuit below and began thinking of his response. There were not as many as Talos thought, although there were plenty enough. If he took two sections he could easily drive them off. Perhaps two sections and another section mounted to exploit the flight of the raiders. That would still leave him just enough men to garrison the Hold. He was formulating the orders when he heard Ionnis curse.

"Those idiots have screwed up the signal,' Ionnis cried in anger. "They are signaling Epsilon Zeta Gamma – 1 – 4 – 99: enemy in sight, infantry, approaching, from the west, many. They got the direction wrong. And they say they are approaching on foot not horsemen. Who is that up there?"

Athan glanced up to see a mirror begin to flash from the top. Being to the west of the Hold, it was well positioned to send back the rising sun.

"The signal is being repeated," confirmed Ionnis in a puzzled tone. "Hmmm… that looks like Enea's hand. He wouldn't make a mistake like that." There was a pause before Ionnis spoke again. "Boss," here the old brigand addressed his King using a word that was more commonly applied from a workman to his foreman, "I think we got troubles coming up the road from Illyria, too." The men were so tense that only the young signaler even noticed the familiar way Ionnis addressed the King.

Athan pulled away from his plan to trap the raiders and put them to flight.

"What?"

"Enea up on Watch Hill says there a lot of enemies coming up the road from Illyria; men on foot. Do you think it is an Illyrian army?"

Athan told the Ionnis he doubted it and not to speculate. Then he turned and hurried down the stairs calling for a quick council at the front gate. Somehow everyone down there already seemed to be full of the news that Bardhyllus had broken its treaty and was invading. Or, perhaps it was some other group coming from Illyria. Men looked nervously at one another, and there was a lot of whispering and avoidance of Athan's gaze.

He found his sergeants trying to muster their men on their stations. These assignments had been in place since the first night in the Hold but they had been just updated in the 'military council' a few nights before. Athan gestured to Prokopios, whose men were still arming themselves, and Rodas to join him in the entrance tunnel. A guard was peering out the observation hole in the closed gates.

"Anybody close by?" asked Athan needlessly.

"Umm, no sir, I mean sire," said the guard, a new man, who leapt back as he recognized the King.

"Let's go outside for a look," Athan told his two companions. Stepping through the small sally port set in the closed gates, the men took a few steps to a vantage where they could see the chaos below. And chaos it was. The enemy horsemen remained in close pursuit of the Athan's men, keeping the patrol from turning aside to head for the safety of the Hold. The two groups of horsemen charging down the northern hill had covered the distance that normally took almost an hour to climb in less than half that time. Even as they watched the men racing past Dassaria, the strange horsemen began to pull up and started riding around inside the streets of the town. Some began entering buildings; others pursued a handful of wretches that had begun to dash from the town in a vain but late dash for the hills.

'How much warning did they have in Dassaria?' Athan wondered? Did they have a quarter hour? Certainly they did not have enough time to get an adequate head start. It was a long way up the hills to the safety of the crests.

There is something about a running man in the open that is as irresistible to a mounted warrior as a fleeing cat is to a dog. Athan and his men watched as several groups of people, almost certainly townspeople, were overtaken and cut down. It was too far to see the victims clearly, but they could easily determine that some of the fleeing civilians being murdered out there were women. A portion of the fleeing groups made it over the hills; there were too many of them scattered about for their pursuers to take them all. Even so, there were far too many mournful little mounds out there each of which represented a dead subject of King Athan.

"They look like bandits; they act like bandits. Why would King Bardhyllus use bandits? If he wanted to conquer us he could just send an army. Why share the goods with bandits?" Rodas wondered aloud.

"I had word not five days ago that Illyria was quiet," Athan said. He did not tell them how he knew; Mouse was beginning to develop nice little relationships with merchants and travelers.

"New signal from Watch Hill," announced Prokopios observing a fresh set of flashing from Watch Hill.

The men watched it together. There was a small variation this time. The signal was Epsilon Zeta Gamma – 1 – 4 – 50, not 99 this time. This was a subtle distinction. It did not simply mean there were fifty enemy infantry approaching. A better translation was that there were many coming but less than an army. The men speculated about what this meant for a few moments. Then Athan looked up to the men watching on the Northwest Bastion.

"Make the following signal to Watch Hill," he shouted, cupping his hands. The men peered back at him attentively. "Gamma Omicron – 41," the code signal for 'conduct independent operations'; Athan hoped it would be interpreted by the men on Watch Hill to mean, 'Don't get caught up there. Spread out and do some good, using your own initiative, because you are on your own now.'

The people from the town that had fled up the hill toward the Hold were passing by them clustering briefly at the closed gates and then slipping inside the sally port. "Better get your section out here Yure," Athan called back to the door. "We may need to cover some of the people coming up for shelter."

Needles the tailor and his new wife lived in town, and they were two of those poor unfortunate souls who were trying to escape into the hills. Their home was on the far southwest side of town; this was both fortunate and unfortunate. Needles was too far from the Hold to get to safety there before the horsemen cut him off, on the other hand he was closer to the cover of the low rugged hills that cupped the town of Dassaria. The hills that were to provide him shelter were also exhausting him. This sudden attack was especially bitter because this spring had been the happiest of his life. He was of middle years, over thirty, not wealthy by any means, but of late he had been doing pretty well. His wife of ten years had died the previous year of a wasting disease. They had been childless, and the union had been somewhat unfortunate, his wife being one of those people who is never satisfied and always ready to blame others for her own unhappiness. Then, with him a widower for less than half a year, the Hold was unexpectedly captured by a bunch of strangers. Suddenly, Ratimir and his men, the men he knew, who provided both his livelihood (and a dose of misery as well) were gone. Everything was upset.

Almost as suddenly things picked up again. He established relationships with new clients. These new men from the Hold had money and paid their bills on time. Even better, they did not threaten to kill you if they thought you charged too much. With business picking up and with several new widows in town, it was natural with that he remarried. He had arranged a union with Neeta, a young widow whose husband had died in the fighting. It was a practical match. He needed a woman to keep his home. She needed a husband who could provide for her; one that would not come home drunk and beat her this time, if possible.

These two people who had scarcely known one another before their marriage found that they suited one another very well. He did his work making clothing; she could work a loom to make cloth. They quickly came to enjoy one another's company and soon after discovered they were in love. It is a perilous thing to marry and then fall in love with your spouse, but when it can be done, it forms a very strong union. Adding to their mutual joy, Neeta had just confirmed she was pregnant, an unexpected and delightful surprise to both of them.

Now, Neeta, just barely beginning to show, was having a hard time getting over the hill behind their house. The evening before had been stressful. When the first alarm had come Needles, seeing the men riding out of the Hold and all the activity, bundled up his wife and a few critical supplies and headed up to his hiding place. It was less than half a parasang; just over the far side of the hill. The terrain on that side was steep and brushy with many places to hide. Anyone who lived under the rule of King Ratimir knew that it was a good idea to have a place to hide when things got a little crazy. Needles had a good one. It was on the steep reverse slope, well concealed by dense undergrowth. Needles was a slender man, a bit under average height, so he had little trouble in getting in and around to the little dugout area he had made. It had an overhanging bank that protected it from the rain and a southern exposure that kept it warmer in the winter. He had brought in wooden planks to make a bench/bed and kept a spare blanket there along with an old amphora filled with water. He had been forced to retreat there several times in the past when his old customers had a complaint. In those days, if one of the Bear's men did not like what you made, he was likely to indicate his displeasure with a sword. Once, Needles and his late wife had spent three days and two nights in the hideout when one of the Bear's men decided that the best way to avoid paying a tailor's bill was to kill the tailor.

He and his Neeta had gone to the top of the hill the night before and looked back to see if they could see any enemies. When they did not, they decided to return home and spend the night in comfort. Like many men who have a pregnant wife for the first time, he was overprotective. He worried about the stress of her having to spend the night in a rude hideout. They had overslept the next morning and been awakened by people shouting and running about. It only took a moment to understand that the attack, feared the night before, was coming with the dawn. Stopping only to grab a cloak and a staff, the two were up and away toward their hideaway without delay.

At first they made good progress, but it is hard to leap out of your bed and then have to climb a steep hill as fast as you can. Soon they were out of breath and had slowed to a huffing walk. Then they saw horsemen off to their left chasing other people. That led to a burst of adrenaline and a sudden spurt farther up the hill. Bursts only last a short time and, before they could reach the summit, they were left gasping and stumbling. To Neeta it was like a nightmare. She had been having a vivid dream when her highly agitated husband awakened her, and now it seemed to her that she was back in her dream. Her legs felt as though they were weighed down by stones. She was sick to her stomach, and gasping for breath; the summit of the hill seemed farther away now than it did when she had first fled from the house. She was deeply afraid and more than that frustrated; it was so unfair for it to end like this. She had been given a glimpse of a deeply satisfying life. All she had wanted to do was live with Needles and raise their children. Now, suddenly, through no fault of her own, it was all going to be taken away. She leaned forward and rested with a hand against the rising slope of the hill, gasping for air and trying not to be sick.

"Come on, my flower," urged Needles beside her. He was almost exhausted as well, and he could only stand beside her holding on to his staff, breathing just as hard as she was. He looked back and regretted it. Four horsemen were leaving what had recently been two living men below and just to his left and were now coming up the slope after them. He saw three more horses further to his right and on his same level, coming toward them. They would be upon him soon after the ones below. Seven horsemen; and from two different directions. They would kill him, then rape Neeta, then kill her. It was all over. He briefly considered killing Neeta himself. It was a silly thought - he knew he could not do it under any circumstances. Taking his staff in both hands he turned to face the closer group of riders downhill from them. Needles was not a physically imposing man nor was he trained in the martial arts. But he stood bravely in front of the four raiders holding out his staff in one final act of defiance.

The horses checked on the slope below, as he moved back in forth in front of them, waving the staff in front of their faces. It was noisy and confusing; the horses were screaming and stamping with their riders cursing him and trying to get up to him for a sword stroke. He held them back for a moment, and then the three riders from the right were on him and past him and striking at the four raiders below him. Looking at this new group he recognized one of them as one of his new customers. They were from the Hold! They were attacking the four raiders!

The melee immediately below him was confused. None of the horsemen who were fighting each other had any javelins left – they were armed only with the typical hoplite short swords. A short sword is a deadly tool for a man with both feet on the ground, but it lacks the reach needed to be an effective weapon on horseback. Further, none of these men were trained and experienced cavalrymen; they were foot soldiers mounted without stirrups atop small horses. Even so, one of the raiders was down and the others were in trouble. Needles added to the enemy's problems by stepping down and bringing his staff down on the withers of one of the raider's horses. The animal stumbled and bolted throwing the rider. Quick as a wink one of Needles' rescuers was on the fallen bandit, riding the pony right over him, then jumping off to thrust down with his sword. He grinned at Needles and without a word hopped back on his pony joining his two comrades who were now chasing the two surviving bandits back downhill.

Needles stood there amazed to be alive. He turned joyfully back to his wife and his breath caught.

"Oh, no, oh, no," he moaned looking at a very still heap lying facedown just uphill. When, how did they get to her? He leapt up to where she lay, kneeling beside her. Gently he turned her over on her back. She opened her big brown eyes.

"Are they gone yet?" she asked anxiously.

"You stupid woman!" Needles screamed shaking her with both fists clutched in her collar. "I thought you were dead!"

She seemed nonplussed, "That was the idea. I thought if they believed I was dead they would leave me alone. I didn't know what else to do."

Needles didn't know what else she could have done either; way down deep inside a part of him agreed with her, the part that would admit it later, but at the moment he was rather worked up.

"You didn't have to play dead for me! What was the matter with you?"

"I did not think you were alive!" Now the tears were beginning to flow. "I saw you. You just had a stick and there were four of them…" Her voice trailed off as she saw the two dead men laying just down the slope from them. The horsemen had separated, the two raiders having made good their escape downhill and the three men from the Hold had ridden off to the west. She looked back and forth at the two dead warriors and her husband.

"Some men from the garrison came and helped," he explained.

She threw herself around him in a powerful hug and began weeping and thanking him.

Needles was very tired and still excited; after all he had just faced certain death and yet somehow survived. The feel of his wife's sobbing form against him steadied him.

"Come on," he told her gruffly, "we still have to get over the hill to our hiding place."

Though they were both exhausted, they were able to walk the rest of the way up the hill without real difficulty. Looking back, he could see men running around through the town. Other men on foot were faintly visible marching down the road from the north. He and his wife turned their backs on the carnage below and walked over the top of the hill and out of sight.

Back up on the hill, Athan and Rodas could see a line of armed men coming down over the north pass following behind the initial wave of the mounted raiders. They were in no particular formation, just a long column of men on foot, hundreds of them, with the sun flashing off spear points and other metal bits the men were carrying or wearing. Athan sent Giles back inside to tell Ixon to stop getting the horses ready. He then called his sergeants out in front of the Hold for a conference. He wanted to be outside the walls so those few townspeople still hurrying up toward the Hold could see they would be allowed to enter. There was an element of cool bravado in it as well.

Athan had come up with several plans in the last half hour and scrapped most of them almost as soon as they were made. The plan to send two sections of mounted men to take the raiders in the flank was the latest. Inside he had heard the men trying to get horses ready and formed up. Now he could see all the raiders on foot coming down behind the first wave of horsemen, that most recent plan was dead, too. He could not commit half his outnumbered garrison to attack the mounted raiders below with an even larger force of enemy already coming down on their flank. All they could accomplish would be to perhaps kill a few of the enemy, briefly drive the rest of the horsemen away and then have to dash back to the Hold in the very teeth of the foot soldiers coming down the north road. His enemies might be split in front of him but they were still close enough to support one another. And there was that signal about enemies to the west. Athan still did not know what to do about that. He hated having to give up the offensive, but he could not think of anything else to do.

Neither could anyone else. They stood in front of the gate on a cool humid spring morning and watched the men come down from the north, march into Dassaria, and join in the pillaging. A few enemy horsemen came up as far as the first bend in the road leading up to the Hold, but came no closer. Perhaps another dozen or so people from Dassaria made it up to the safety of the Hold during this time. They came scrambling up from left and right having avoided the horsemen who were looking for easy plunder. When half an hour passed and no more refugees came, Athan decided it was time to go inside. The small front door closed behind them, and the main entrance bar was shoved into place. Smaller bars above and below augmented the floor bolts to keep the big gates from opening. Wedges were hammered in so that a traitor could not quickly lift the bar and open the small door. The Hold was preparing for a siege.

Athan walked through the entrance tunnel noticing how crowded it seemed. When he entered the courtyard he was immediately struck by the noise and confusion. A hundred questions were shouted at him. Men and women surged forward toward him, arms outstretched asking, pleading, demanding. His men pushed them back, and Athan moved to his left up into the northwest bastion. He stopped at the second level and walked out onto the wall, followed by his sergeants. Looking back down into the courtyard, they saw a milling mass of people and animals, all interacting, often at the top of their lungs. Men were standing guard in front of the armory, the treasury, and the kitchen. Apparently most of the civilians had not had their breakfast and wanted to steal some of Cook's vittles.

Once he was above the mass below him, Athan was able to gather his thoughts, which were quickly translated into actions.

"Prokopios, I want you to start to sort out living arrangements for these people. Tenucer, continue preparations for defense. Yure, can you take some of your people and help Prokopios get that mess down there sorted out when he comes up with a plan? Maybe you can start by getting them fed."

"Cook won't like that," grinned Linus.

"Stuff Cook," snapped Athan. He knew Cook would complain but there were other things to worry about. "It looks like we will be here for a while." The council agreed the raiders down in the town were definitely coming to stay. Whether the raiders would besiege the Hold was yet to be seen, but the plans for defense now had to incorporate the people that had come in from the town. "Yure," continued Athan, "Find out if there are any men down there with our new refugees who can be taught to fight. Linus, you and Rodas come up to the top of the bastion with me so we can review our plans to resist an assault on this place."

There were many other orders given on that long day. Whenever possible Athan delegated the details on how to do something to his subordinates, though he always later asked them what they had done. On occasion, he would make changes to their arrangements, though by and large he let his men sort things out. While they did all this Athan, Rodas, and Linus stood on the walls and watched an army of sorts move in and occupy Dassaria. The three men estimated that counting the horsemen and foot soldiers more than three hundred men had come down from the north. Later that morning another three or four score joined them from the west. Those were the men that Watch Hill must have seen walking on the west road. They certainly did not march. It did not take a keen military eye to realize that this so-called army was made up of a loose collection of hill men, bandits, brigands, and assorted mercenaries. They had little order and less discipline. In fact it soon was obvious that there were a number of different groups down there that had assembled with all the intended cooperation of a pack of wolves at the carcass. Whatever they may have lacked in cohesion they made up for in fighting ability. Some of the best pure fighting men on earth were down there. It was obvious they certainly had not assembled just to sack the little town of Dassaria.

They did seem busy down there. Athan's impromptu council of war decided that the raiders were already finished looting for the moment and were now trying to make equipment for use in the assault on the Hold. This group of raiders could never stay together to blockade the fort on the hill for an extended time. They lacked the skills and time to build artillery and siege engines to knock down the walls with flung stones. If they were going to take the place it would be done either with treachery or most likely a simple assault. Guarding against someone opening the gates from the inside was easy, and measures were already in hand. So it would most likely come down to a straight assault. The three men estimated there had to be some men down there among their enemies that had served the Bear. They would know the fortress well. Athan was concerned about a secret tunnel or other private way into the Hold, however he had not heard the slightest rumor that such a covert entry existed. His new fort was too small, too simple for such elaborate additions. No, the men decided their enemies would come up here and try to get over and through the walls using sheer weight of numbers.

"It has to come at the back gate," opined Rodas. "It is much weaker than the front gates, and has the advantage of seeming to be unexpected." The other two grunted assent.

"That means they will either try a night attack or will get into position at night and start the proceedings at dawn," commented Linus.

"It is too obvious," cautioned Athan. "They cannot be that stupid. Yes, they outnumber us, but we have almost a hundred men here not counting the scouts that did not get back in. They have less than five hundred, probably more like four hundred. I do not think they can beat us with only four or five hundred men. There is a good chance they will see how strong we are and think better of an attack. If they do come, our fort is strong, and our plans are good. We just have to keep them out. Once they are on the run, we will ride out and keep them running."

'And kill them like a weasel among chickens,' he thought to himself.

His men picked up on his unusually grim mood. "Where is Delbine?" Rodas thoughtlessly asked. Things had been too busy the night before and once the initial alarm was over, she had returned to her house in town to get out of the way. It was in Rodas' mind that she could often calm the King down when he was tense. Rodas thought that Athan needed the quiet woman now to ease the stress.

"She did not come in," was all Athan said.

No one spoke. 'So that was why we went outside the Hold this morning,' thought Rodas. 'If he had seen her coming up that road, I'll bet he would have sent us out to get her.'

Rodas did not think Athan really loved the prostitute. Rodas was sure Athan did like her very much and he certainly enjoyed her company. Athan also needed her. Perhaps she was the only one he really did need, in that sense. Athan stared at the men in stony silence. The other two could think of nothing to say.

The sounding of the bell that signaled the change of the watch saved them. Athan decided he was hungry and headed to his quarters. Giles was waiting in the bastion at the top of the stairs. He had not intruded on the council of war but had carried several messages from the council to the sergeants. Now he followed Athan along the top of the wall and down to their quarters. By now the scene down in the courtyard was transformed. Yure and the other sergeants had brought order from chaos. Athan caught a glimpse of Celeno speaking with Prokopios and gesturing toward a hastily erected corral where some sheep and goats were penned. People were camped under eves and had set up tents and awnings where they were not already inside the rooms of the Hold. He was pleased to see the center of the courtyard was still open, and areas around the front and rear gates were clear. His reserve needed to be able to move rapidly from entrance to the other. There was a line of men and women getting food from the kitchen. Others seemed to be preparing food over small fires here and there in the courtyard. Things had settled down nicely.

Athan sent Giles down to get some food and wine for them. When Giles returned he found his king in his bedroom laying on his back staring up at nothing.

"She said I was busy and she would go back to town. She said it was safe with all the people going back and forth. She told me she would come up if there was any danger." The king was not addressing Giles directly; he seemed to being speaking to the ceiling.

Giles did not know what to say. He wanted to tell him she was probably all right, but he was afraid he would say something that would be misinterpreted by Athan. Giles had an ugly thought 'She is just a whore. She is probably getting rich down there.'

Discretion ruled his tongue - he didn't say anything at all, and Athan never mentioned the subject to him again.

When Needles and Neeta reached their hide-out they were dismayed to find someone was there before them. Adem the wine merchant, sometimes called Amphora for the containers that held his wine, and his wife Ana were peering out from the thicket as Needles pushed through. After the excitement the night before, being cautious, they decided to spend the night in hiding. They had come to the crest of the hill and saw the initial rush of the raiders heading toward town, a sight that sent them scurrying back to safety. They were not best pleased to have others coming to join them.

"Did anyone see you?" hissed Adem to them. "What do you want? This is our place!"

An immediate argument started as the two men disputed ownership of the little covered overhang; each claiming prior possession. Words became heated. Adem and Ana were older than the other couple; still childless. Ana had lost two children and another was stillborn. Without the cost of raising children they were relatively well off; and without other responsibilities, the older couple was better prepared for the crisis. Adem had managed to carry two amphora of his best wine with him up to their little hide, and they had also brought some bread and dried fruit. Now they were loath to share what was, in fact, a relatively small area with the other couple.

The two women tried to hush the men as their argument grew. Neeta, sick with worry and the ordeal she had been through, suddenly put her hand to her stomach and sank to the ground. Needles immediately stopped and turned to her. Ana and Adem were not close friends with the other two; of course, in a small community everyone knows just about everything about everybody. Ana looked at the younger woman, pregnant with her first child, and took charge.

"There is room enough," she announced in a voice that would brook no argument. "Help her in."

In truth there was enough room under the overhang, though it was crowded. The two men would crawl out past the screening thickets from time to time to see what they could discover, however, most of the time was spent simply waiting. The two amphora of wine came to be deeply appreciated. Ana was grateful for the company of another woman, and Neeta, typically nervous with her first pregnancy, actually enjoyed having the time to speak with an older woman about her condition. The weather was not too bad, and even though they made no fire and it got cool at night, four people huddled together can stay relatively comfortable. They would wait and see what happened.

Late that first afternoon a group of the raiders came up from town to survey the Hold. There were over a dozen of them. They would stop at various places just out of bowshot, talking and gesturing, obviously reviewing the defenses. The men rode right around the Hold, dismounting and climbing the ridge. They stopped on the back side of the Hold well back from the rear gate. Perhaps they had heard about what had happened to the Illyrian cavalrymen that had gotten too close. After some conversation they climbed back down and rode all the way around the entire ridge before returning to the town.

Just before dark two small bands of horsemen rode out and camped at the foot of the ridgeline one on ether side. They were positioned so that they could observe the rear gate and walls. There would be no slipping out the back. In fact, no one in the Hold had even considered trying to escape or send for reinforcements. Where would they go? Who could they ask for help? Linus asked if he could send some men down to attack one of the sentry posts in the night; Athan declined to take the risk. He would need every man he could get when the assault came.

The night passed nervously, but without an alarm. This surprised everyone. The watch was told they did not anticipate an attack that first night; even so everyone expected one of the sentries to hear 'ghosties and ghoulies' in the night. As a sign of confidence, Athan had only doubled the watch. He did not expect to be taken unawares. If they came it should not be hard to hear them long before an attack came out of the dark.

The next day was busy for both sides — there was construction of some sort down in the town and drilling and training up inside the Hold. Yure had conscripted every able-bodied man into his forces. There was no effort to teach them the complicated business of fighting in formations. Some of the young men and boys claimed a familiarity with the bow. These were grouped in the bastions each with stacks of arrows. Older men were set to work carrying stones up to the tops of walls. Their job would be to throw loose stones (or other heavy objects that could be spared) down on any attackers. A few of the strong young men were given shields and spears and integrated into the sections that would defend the walls. Most of the conscripts, men just past their prime, or those who did not appear to be cut out for direct fighting, were given a long spear. They would make up the rear ranks of the shield wall. Young boys were told they would be used as messengers and were given places in each bastion. It gave them something to do and kept them out of the way. Of course, the youngsters were thrilled at the chance to be part of the defense.

Prokopios formed up his reserve section inside the front entrance tunnel early in the afternoon as a test. He had Athan enter in the side door, then stand the entrance end of the tunnel with his back to the main gate so he could see what any attackers that got through the front gate would see. Prokopios ordered his formation forward. All Athan could see was a solid rank of shields, helmets, and spear points. The back spears were longer than usual, more like pikes. These protruded over the shoulders of the front ranks so that Athan was facing a bristling hedge of spikes. He was very impressed.

"It looks like a turtle mated with a hedgehog," he told a satisfied Prokopios. The men liked hearing that. They had broken ranks after the demonstration and were sitting around the entrance grinning. Morale was improving as they prepared for the fight everyone assumed was coming.

It would, Athan knew, be harder if the enemy came in the back gate. Although smaller, it opened directly into the courtyard. The bastions there were much closer in so they could provide more fire support but they were nothing like the confined space of the entrance tunnel. There were arrow slits on the ground level of the bastions within the walls, but Athan doubted they would be of much use against an enemy pouring in like a flood through a broken rear gate. Worse, unlike the two big main gates, the rear door opened inward. That made it vulnerable to being hammered in. There were just not enough men available to form a line of sufficient length and thickness to hold back all their foes once they got into the open courtyard. They reinforced the gate, but Athan forbad them to block it up completely. He wanted to be able to open the gate in case he decided to make a possible sally against an attack elsewhere on the walls.

Athan and his sergeants decided that, if the rear gate were attacked, the reserve would form in a horseshoe so that they would be able to counterattack the intruders left, right, and center. There were only enough real phalangists available to form a single continuous rank in the front. They would have a mixed group of phalangists and the long spearmen behind them, making another rank and a half. If an enemy penetrated past the heavily armored first rank of phalangists, the spearmen behind would be at a terrible disadvantage. They were not trained and experienced warriors, and without shields and real armor they would stand little chance against true warriors; they would probably break and run. Then the slaughter would begin. The line would have to hold at the back gate. Of course, there were certainly not enough men to have even a hope of holding back the enemy if they got in at both the front and rear gates at the same time.

It was not a comfortable situation; yet later that afternoon as the men practiced, Athan stood with the rear door at his back and looked at what the attackers would face. There were shields and spears on all sides of him. In particular, there were lots of spears directly ahead of him. Athan thought that if he were the one coming in through that door he would turn to his right and attack the side wing. That way his shield would protect him from those spears on his flank. They discussed forming only a single wing to the left and extending the line to the northeast bastion wall.

"No," objected Prokopios, "I want them going after the wings. That way they don't test the center. I will put Ixon and Arsene in charge of the wings. If they break on the line on either side, we might be able to refuse that flank and hold them in. We want them to avoid the middle. If the center doesn't hold, we are lost." To further dissuade any attackers from concentrating to the center, Prokopios instructed mighty Eustathios to stand in the center of the line in the best most impressive armor that could be found to fit him.

"Imagine coming in that gate and facing all those spear points with that big fella standing there waiting for you," said Sergeant Yure. "I would think twice about going for him."

It was an hour before sunset on the second day when the enemy delegation approached the gates. There were a score or so of them, mounted on ponies. Most of them stopped well back while a smaller group of five approached with the sign for parlay, an evergreen bough lashed to a spear, displayed. Athan stood on the battlements above the gates looking down at them.

"What do you want?" he shouted before they even brought their animals to a halt.

The men were temporarily nonplussed by this challenge; after a bit of rein pulling and shuffling, the men dismounted. One of them, a big man with a long black beard, stepped forward and bellowed out, "We want that gold you stole."

"What gold would that be?" asked Athan in a calm, carrying voice, very unlike the one he used for the challenge.

"The tribute you stole from Doria. We come to get it back. We had to pay twice because of you. Give us the gold you took from those Achaemendian fellows, and we will let you have your little fort there." There was a pause, then he added, "Which you also stole."

It was not a bad ploy. It made it seem that these men had only come to right an old wrong; to recover stolen property. All Athan had to do was give back what he had stolen himself, and these men would go away.

"How much gold do you claim we took?" responded Athan again with a very reasonable voice.

This led to a long whispered conversation with some disagreement. While this was going on, Athan turned to Giles and told him to find all the men who were assigned as archers. They were to assemble in the long room directly above the gate with their bows and a full quiver each. Giles was to tell him when they were ready.

After a short time the big man walked a bit closer and shouted up to Athan, "You know how much you stole. Give it back. Bring it outside your gates and stack it up for us. We will take it away and return it to its rightful owner, the city of Doria."

The man was actually able to make this claim with a seeming of sincerity. Of course, everyone knew it was hogswallop. These people were a temporary collection of robbers, thieves, and opportunists gathered in the hope of plunder. Of course, there was a chance that if Athan did leave them some gold they would fall to fighting over the spoils and leave. But they would be back, and Athan would have to fight them again and again. Right now he had his enemies in front of him, and he wanted to kill them all. He was feeling harder and harder about the matter; **he wanted them all dead, right now**.

"You claim we have stolen some gold," countered Athan still in a reasonable voice. "If so, how much do you claim?"

"Two hundred talents," responded the man promptly. They had thought this out after all.

Athan laughed. "There is not that sum of gold if you took everything in a hundred parasangs. You know that." Then in a still carrying but lower voice he asked what appeared to be a reasonable tone. "How much for you just to leave?"

Now the negotiations began. While they haggled, Athan instructed Rodas to step over to the alarm gong in the bastion. When Athan looked at him and signaled with a nod he was to bang it.

After a quarter hour the amount demanded was down to twenty-five talents. Athan was acting interested. Then Giles returned with the news the archers were standing by.

"Good," said Athan to Giles in a low voice, "it is about time. Here are your orders. Have the men move to the arrow ports. Tell them to stay out of sight. That is important, no peeking! When they hear the alarm they are to shoot to kill anyone and anything they see outside the Hold. Bring a half dozen or so up here on the wall with me so they have room to shoot. Make sure they stay low and out of sight. Oh, and bring me a bow and quiver, too. Remember, tell everyone to stay low; you too."

Smiling grimly Giles headed down to prepare the trap.

Up on the ramparts, the discussion shifted to how the gold might be delivered, and what assurances would be offered that the raiders would leave once the gold was delivered. The five men below had moved closer during the negotiations. The sun was just above the tops of the far mountains. Suddenly Abacus appeared on the scene coming from along the top of the southern wall. He had apparently come up the ramp over the kitchens when he heard negotiations were underway.

"My lord," he exclaimed excitedly, "you cannot do this!!"

Athan hid his irritation, "And why not? It is my gold." His voice was loud enough for the men below to hear the argument.

"Sire," declaimed a distracted Abacus, "you cannot! How much have you promised them?"

"What are we up to now?" Athan asked the bearded man. They had not even bothered to exchange names.

"Twenty-five talents in gold."

Athan thought Abacus would swoon. Suddenly, Athan was enjoying this; it was a fierce mean-spirited pleasure, but he was in a strange humor.

"My lord," protested Abacus in tone that would clearly carry to the men below, "we don't have that much!'

Athan had seen the movement from the northwest bastion. He knew Giles was bending low beside him, a bow with a nocked arrow ready to hand up to him. Other men were spreading along the parapet crouching low. Abacus looked at them in dismay. The men below must have sensed something for their postures changed.

"Well, you heard him; I guess we don't have that much money," Athan told the bearded man below him. A smiling Athan nodded to Rodas in a friendly way, bent down and took the bow and nocked arrow from Giles. In the same moment he drew the bow, stepped into the embrasure, and released his arrow. Many things happened in the next few moments.

He felt first Giles and then saw the other archers stepping up to loose their arrows all along the wall. He heard the gong ring. He watched his arrow flying to his target. Athan had never used a bow in battle before; yes he had killed a man with an arrow but that was different. For some reason, he did not really think of bows and arrows as real weapons of war. Perhaps this was because he was not a good archer. Since he knew he was not a good shot, he did not aim at the bearded man; instead he launched his arrow at the man's pony, a bigger target. He was pleased to see it hit the animal in the haunch, making it buck and plunge away from the man holding it. Athan was aware of other arrows, a lot of arrows, in flight.

"No gold," he shouted. "No gold but lots of arrows!" Athan bent to get another arrow from the quiver Giles had brought. When he came back up and sighted down his drawn bow, the situation had changed. Two of the five men were legging it down the hill. Black Beard was limping along behind them. Another man was half carrying the last of the five. All of them had arrows sticking in them, whether in vital places or merely in the armor was difficult to tell; still the hit total was impressive. Some of the archers had followed Athan's lead and shot the ponies as well. They were bucking and neighing as they scattered down hill. As he watched, one fell. It lay on its side screaming in agony.

As the five men reached their comrades who were waiting for them at what they thought was out of bowshot, the men got another surprise. Some of Giles' archers had climbed up the top of the bastions. From up there they could loft arrows all the way onto the group of men who had waited behind. It only took a few arrows falling among them to cause them to depart in great haste.

It was then that Athan witnessed the finest bowshot he ever saw. Tenucer (Athan later found out) launched an arrow from the top of the bastion; Athan estimated it was at well over one and a half bowshots. He happened to watch the arrow's flight as it was among the last ones shot. It arced down and took one of the fleeing riders either in the neck or the back of his shoulder. The arrow stuck deeply into him, and he reeled drunkenly for a moment then fell in a heap off the back of his horse, landing bonelessly. The others rode by him without stopping. The defenders up on the Hold's walls cheered. Down below those men who had not been able to mount up were scurrying away, staying behind rocks and out of sight. Black Beard was pulling arrows out of himself. Some had to have reached flesh and reached it deeply. Athan thought he could hear him cursing all the way from his perch up on the wall. The other wounded negotiator was apparently on his back and being tended.

The mood in the Hold was definitely upbeat as the evening meal was served. Those who were concerned about potential repercussions were reminded that these were brigands of the worst sort. Nothing they might do in retaliation would be worse than what they already planed to do to the defenders.

At the council of war that evening, Rodas asked if Athan expected an attack that night.

"Only if we are lucky," he replied. "I do not think they are ready yet. If those men were the leaders and we hurt or killed some of them, they will have to sort out who is in charge before they can put together an attack. Of course, if they are angry enough they will come tonight, but I am not worried about an angry attack, I am worried about a well-considered and coordinated assault."

The men reviewed their plans to repel a night attack, then reviewed dispositions and the planned training for tomorrow.

Athan had one more conference that evening in his office.

"Are you sure you are willing to do this?" he asked Pirro and Mouse.

Pirro gave his a grin to hide is nervousness. "Nothing to it, sire."

Mouse only nodded quietly.

Athan looked at the two men. Pirro was in black; Mouse his normal brown. Pirro had a dagger strapped to his thigh; Mouse only a small knife. They were not going out to fight; they were going out to be undiscovered.

"Find out what you can. Wake me when you come back. Do not let them take you alive."

The two men only nodded. They reviewed again the procedures for leaving and returning including a special pass word. Giles waited behind them, a knotted rope over one shoulder, and a thin cord on the other. The plan was simple: the two would climb over the walls from behind one of the western bastions and then make their way down to where the enemy was camped. They would find out what they could and then return long before daylight. Giles would be waiting at the same place where they had descended with the cord attached to his hand hanging down to the ground. When they returned, they would tug on the cord and give the password. Giles would throw down the rope and they would come up; it was simple. Of course how the two would find out anything out there in the dark was beyond Athan. He reminded them that it was acceptable not to find anything out, but not acceptable to get caught or to lie about what they heard when they got back. Then he went to bed.

He was awakened by no fewer than three alarms in the night, all false. None of them were associated with his two spies. Though Athan was not surprised, he found it disquieting that two men could move around the base of his fort and not be detected.

Giles came in with the two men only an hour before dawn. They looked tired but they were also very self satisfied. They had faced death, and death had not taken them. As he had expected, with so many bands of men down in Dassaria, Pirro was able to strike up conversations with several groups of men sitting around campfires. Mouse just did what he always did, sit in the shadows and listen. They had separated shortly after climbing down and neither had seen the other until they almost bumped into each other, returning at nearly the same time. The mood in town was ugly. The bearded man Athan had negotiated with had been one of the leaders but was now being held in contempt by the other raiders for being tricked. The negotiations were his idea, and most thought it was only fair he had been wounded. One of the other leaders was also badly wounded and was expected to die; one man, presumably the one shot off his horse by Tenucer, was already dead. The raiders were building ladders and battering rams as well as movable shelters to protect the rams. There had been no mention of catapults or other pieces of artillery.

Athan thanked them and gave each a purse for their night's work. Pirro indicated he was going to buy the finest wine and best whore in the Hold and sleep until noon. Giles saw his sovereign flinch slightly at the mention of a good prostitute. Outside a gentle spring rain began falling, causing a small exclamations from those who were sleeping in the open. Athan got up to check the watch. He would want to make sure the straw and ready torches were in a dry place. If they attacked at night the light would be needed. He knew the sergeants would have already checked these details and also that Rodas would have checked the sergeants, but suddenly he did not want to sleep.

The next day the garrison had another good training session. Using the ladders inside the courtyard as a model, Yure showed the men how to push over a ladder that had men upon it, substituting bags of sand for men to give it weight. This continued until two of the ladders were broken. The archers practiced using an extemporized archery range, shooting from the top of one wall across the courtyard, down into straw butts at the base of the other wall. This added an element of excitement to a walk in the courtyard. Athan developed a plan with his men to quickly mount up two sections on horses to pursue the enemy after they were repulsed. Ixon persuaded some of the women to take shelter in the stables during the fighting. That way, if the Hold fell, they could release the horses and use the animals as a diversion to escape out the gates. Few of the women could ride; the idea was that they could run alongside the animals in the middle of the herd of horses stampeding out of the gate. It would be very dangerous, but less so than remaining inside a Hold while it was sacked by bloodthirsty brigands. If the attack was repulsed, the women could help get horses out to the counterattacking sections of horsemen.

Athan was very insistent about getting horsemen out to harass the brigands after they were repulsed. "Kill as many of them as you can while they run," he told the men assigned to form the mounted rides. "Take plenty of javelins. You can also stab them in their backs with a spear while the run." He gave them lessons. His men looked at one another. They had not seen Athan in a mood like this before. He almost seemed bloodthirsty.

That night, the two spies were let down once again. There was a difference this time. Pirro returned alone after only two hours.

"The attack is tonight," he told Athan. Giles had brought him straight to the King upon his return. "I almost got caught. I could see something was up, and when I talked to two men in town they wanted to know why I wasn't getting ready. I think they are moving ladders and a battering ram to the back gate. They are going to attack tonight."

Pirro was still breathing hard. Athan could not tell whether this was from his exertions in running back up the hill and climbing the rope or from excitement. Pirro did not know much beyond that. Athan had him sit, and Giles brought him a cup of wine. Athan talked calmly with the red-headed man for a while as he regained his composure. It became clear that the attack would not be for a good while yet as they were just beginning to move the ladders and ram. Athan continued to chat with the man calming him down and finding out everything he could about his adventure. The two had been associated for years, Pirro joining and then departing from Athan's old band of hill bandits several times before he joined him permanently for the theft of the Satrap's gold.

"It seems like so long ago," Pirro recalled amiably. "We have come a long way, you and I. Yes, sir, I mean sire, I hardly knew what living was before I met you. I mean the adventure, the high life in Pella, now, this, a kingdom; well, it has been more than I ever dreamed of seeing."

They were still chatting amiably as though they were old comrades sitting over a bowl of wine after a hard day (which was actually true) when the first report came in from the sentries on the south wall that men were moving out in the night down at the foot of the foot of the ridge.

"That would be those poor fools starting to move their heavy gear around to the back. Pirro, would you find the sergeants and summon them to an immediate council of war here? Don't give away your story. I want them to all hear it at the same time."

After the little red-head departed, smiling, Giles spoke up. "I know what Pirro means."

Athan gave him a questioning look.

Giles continued, "Sometimes I feel like my life did not begin until I joined you. Where would I be if you had not left Pella? I would be dead, probably, fighting a stupid war against the Achaemendians. Instead, I am the shield-bearer to a King." There was a pause as Giles hesitated, struggling with his emotions. He started to speak and then changed his mind about what he was going to say. Finally he choked out, "Thank you, sir," and fled to the anteroom. Athan did not know what to say. After a few moments, Giles called out from the anteroom that he was going back to wait for Mouse.

The council was short. The men took the news of the impending attack calmly. They reviewed their plans for repelling an assault on the back gate. Athan assured his men that the attack could not come for a while yet, to use the time to get ready, and then rest. Athan asked the sergeants to remain available and dismissed them.

After they were gone he laid out the battle armor that he had selected from the stock of gear in the armory. It was not necessarily the heaviest armor, but it was in Athan's mind the best. First he put on a winter tunic that had been modified for fighting. It had half sleeves down to his elbows, the outside of the sleeves reinforced with strips of linen and leather. It also had a thick collar of the same material that could be fastened at the throat, protecting his neck. There was a cuirass with bronze plates over boiled leather. It fit him well; of course he wore it over his own red leather vest. Athan wore the vest almost all the time now, though often he wore it under his tunic so that men would not know he had it on. He did not want others to know just how often he wore it or this would become a topic of gossip. After donning his cuirass, Athan put on his fighting boots. He had them made during those wild days in Pella. They were soft leather, coming up over his ankles, with enclosed toes, covered with a thin sheet of bronze. Athan then put on bracers over each of his forearms. They were of boiled leather reinforced with strips of bronze.

He looked at the rest of his gear, prepared and polished by Giles two days before. There was a fine set of greaves for his shins, bronze over leather like his cuirass. Athan suspected they had been made as a matched set. Next to them was a pleated knee-length skirt of heavy linen with vertical bronze-studded strips of leather on the outer pleats. When this was tied around his waist just below the cuirass and above his greaves, he was protected from shoulder to foot. His head would be inside a superb bronze hoplite helmet, complete with a long horsehide crest. It was a magnificent piece. This helmet made Athan feel that he truly was rich. No one, not even the richest oligarch back in Epiria, had a better helmet. It was an excellent piece of armor, the best, and he would wear it tonight, even though he felt a bit of a fraud wearing it. He would put this heavy armor on later in the night, when he was sure they were coming.

Athan belted on his sword belt, feeling the weight of the kopis around his waist. He loosened the cord that held the sheath of his dagger, Bear's Claw, to his thigh, letting it flop freely. He would pull the armored skirt under those two scabbards when the time came. A pair of bronze-headed spears and two shields were in the corner. One was a classic round wooden phalangist hoplon with a painting of a gorgon. That was Giles' He had had it repainted to his own design and was terribly proud of it. The other was a simple black rectangular hypastas shield with an equally simple rhombus design. No one, not even Mouse, knew that the double pyramid shape mirrored the talisman Athan wore inside the leather pouch around his neck. Athan had fought best as a hypastas, and he liked the shape and feel of the lighter shield. This one was well-made, heavier than most, with strips of bronze on the top, sides, and center protecting his left arm. It had a round boss in the middle of that center strip; Athan fully understood how a defensive weapon like a shield could be used offensively. Athan stopped briefly to touch the slick hard leather that covered the layered plywood beneath. There was a feeling in the pit of his stomach, a deep recognition that he would be fighting and killing behind that shield before the sun rose.

He went out, climbing up to the battlements and circling the perimeter starting on the south wall. In addition to the two men on watch, Tenucer was there along with most of his section and a few spectators as well. The night was dark. The moon, only a sliver as it waned down toward a new moon, had set and there was a high overcast that partially obscured the stars.

"They're moving up something," Tenucer told Athan pointing south down into the darkness at the foot of the east-west running ridge.

Athan could hear men moving down there and moving things as well. Some faint curses could be heard floating up from the darkness.

"They really aren't making much of an effort to be quiet," continued Tenucer. "Maybe this is a feint." Athan only shrugged. "Well," Tenucer finished, "I think if we fired some arrows down there maybe we could hit some of them."

"No," responded Athan immediately. "Tell everyone not to do anything to alert them that we know they are there. We will pretend that we don't know they are there. I want them to come at us tonight; let's get this over with."

He moved on down the wall, quietly cautioning the men not to say or do anything that acknowledged the activity going on below them. Pirro's warning had been welcome, however, with these elephantine movements going on in the dark there would have been no surprise. Athan hoped they fought as poorly as they maneuvered.

At the end of the southwest wall was Giles, next to the coil of knotted rope, leaning back against the battlement, with the thin line leading from his hand over the battlement, looking for all the world like a fisherman.

"Any bites?" asked Athan with amusement.

"Just the one I brought to you already." Giles stood upright as he spoke; he might jest with his beloved King, but he did so with some seriousness. "I should have helped you with that cuirass," he said as he noticed Athan was armored.

"I have been putting on my own armor since before you were born. Everything is laid out and prepared just as you left it. We can be ready in an instant." As Athan peered down into the darkness, there was a crash from below as something heavy was dropped. More curses could be heard.

"Can you hear those louts down there?" Giles commented in a low voice. "Do they really think to catch us by surprise?"

"Never assume your enemy is competent," quoted Athan. Then he changed the subject. "Do you think Mouse will be able to make it past them to get up here?"

"I suspect he will have to wait until the battle is over," opined Giles.

"I would," agreed Athan, "stay here for a while longer, though. We can't just abandon him. You know how valuable he is." Athan turned to enter the door into the southwest bastion to continue his rounds.

He walked the walls, speaking to the men, joking with them, reassuring them, giving them confidence. Everyone seemed to be awake and ready for the battle to start. Once Athan had completed the circuit of the top of the walls, he went down to the second level where most of the barracks and individual rooms were located. It was eerily quiet here, especially after the crowding of the past few days. He heard low conversations, men sharpening their blades, and once, snoring. Looking in he saw the huge figure of Eustathios stretched out, his gear next to him, sleeping peacefully. Shaking his head, Athan continued on, reflecting that there were times when a certain lack of imagination was a definite advantage.

After completing this round Athan climbed down to the ground level and continued his cycle. There were more people down here. Athan noticed the privies were being used far more than usual, especially considering the hour. Abacus was up; he had on one of the new helms that Tito had made and was wearing a cuirass that was too big for his skinny frame. There was a long spear on the wall next to the open door of his room. Abacus was attempting to sharpen a short sword by the light of a lamp. He looked up at Athan but did not speak. Heavy planks had been spiked in place over the door to the treasury. That was probably Abacus' work. It would not stop victorious brigands, but it would stop anyone from trying to loot the treasury before the fighting was finished.

Cook and Cook's Wife were up making pastries of all things. The kitchen was full of the permanent staff of the Hold.

"What are you doing, Cook," asked Athan good-naturedly. The walk had eased his own tension as well as that of those with whom he had spoken.

"We are making delicacies for the victors, oh, King," was the reply.

"Which victors?" Athan came back, still smiling.

"Which ever ones come to claim them," replied Cook seriously.

"How do you intend to avoid being slaughtered if we lose?" asked Athan genuinely curious.

"Same way we survived when you took this place," shot back Cook. "Same way we lived here with the Bear. Everybody appreciates good cookin'. I imagine some of those down there," here Cook jerked his head toward the town, "remember our cookin'. If they don't, these will remind 'em."

Athan remembered how, immediately after he had captured the Hold, Cook had been ready to feed him and his men.

"What about the others?" Athan gestured to the dozen or so other people he saw in the kitchen. He saw Titania, Phila, Celeno and her daughters, and others who would normally never be allowed into the cooking area, now huddled together in the back. Even Celeno, a virago if ever there was one, seemed subdued. "Can you keep them safe?"

"Yes, sir, I think so," Cook said. "We will divert 'em with these," and Cook gestured toward the pastries that were in preparation.

Athan smiled a tight smile, "save one of those for me," he said as he left.

Behind him he overheard Cook say to his wife, "Never had any of the Bear's lot claim to worry about the likes of us."

Athan saw that Ixon had already staked out the horses Athan had wanted ready for his counter attack. They were in a neat picket line between the two granaries. Athan thought there were even more horses than he had expected out here. Two of the stable hands were walking up and down the line, talking to the little horses softly. Athan could see the animals were already saddled; javelins were stacked against the walls of the rough round sides of the granaries ready for quick use.

When he entered the stables he found out why extra horses were outside: the women and children had already moved into the stables. Some of the animals were even double-stabled to make room. Under the circumstances it was surprisingly calm. Some children were asleep; others were playing a game in a corner that seemed to involve climbing over the sides of two of the stalls. In one stable an older woman was telling a story to a clump of children. Women huddled together talking quietly. The mothers were worried, but to the children it was all an adventure.

Athan met with Yure who was responsible for the main gate. With him was an old man who had to be at least sixty, though he still seemed reasonably hale. The three men talked about what to do if the Hold fell.

"If things go badly you must wait until the last possible moment before you make your break," Athan instructed the old man, Hesiod by name. "If you go too soon you may disrupt us. You want as many of the raiders inside as you can so that when the women get past the gates they will not have to dodge too many of them outside the walls."

The old man seemed a steady sort. Athan was slightly reassured that if it all went wrong, at least these people had a chance to escape what would go on inside the walls.

Athan had not seen Ixon in the stables which puzzled him, for Ixon was an active and conscientious Master of the Horse. He found him in the little tack room next to the stables where Adara and he had begun their married life. She was helping him into his armor. It almost seemed a domestic sight, the two talking quietly as she tightened a strap and fussed with his tunic. Then Athan saw that, despite her untroubled voice and calm demeanor, her cheeks were wet with tears.

He made certain that Adara knew the plan for flight in the event of a disaster. She assured him she did; Athan noticed she had a long dagger thrust into the sash around her waist. 'No, he thought, 'if the Hold falls, that one won't be leaving.'

Athan continued on past the smithy where Tito and his assistant were still hard at work turning out helmets. The smith nodded to him and continued on with his labors. The baths were open. Athan stuck his head in to see Hypnos, Iason, and two boys arranging couches and preparing bandages. This would be their hospital after the battle. Iason was in his armor, his sword at his side. Athan talked with them briefly; they were ready. Eventually Athan came to the rear gate, where everyone now expected the main assault to fall. Prokopios was there with most of his men already under arms. When Athan told him that Eustathios was snoozing sweetly, sergeant made to send a man after him.

"Let him sleep," countermanded Athan. "Why not? We are ready. We might as well get some rest."

Satisfied with his preparations for the coming assault, Athan climbed the stairs up to his room, pleasantly tired from his triple circuit.

When he got to his rooms Giles and Mouse were waiting for him.

"I have news," said the Mouse.

It was the carcass of a deer that had died and been covered in snow sometime during the winter. Now, as the drifts receded, such winter deaths were being revealed. He knew that bears, emerging from their winter sleep, often found and feasted on such windfalls. Right now he was about as close to a bear coming out of hibernation as a man could get. His hunger, ignored for so many days, suddenly awoke at the sight of potential food with an intensity that overwhelmed him. He dropped his staff and began pulling at the exposed portion of the carcass. The birds had opened the body cavity but with the cold air the remains had not begun to decay yet. Getting a grip, he tugged and heaved until with a sudden release the carcass twisted and the section of hide he was holding tore. He fell to the ground on his butt, legs sticking out in front of him. He was briefly struck with the ridiculousness of the situation. He took up his temporary staff and used it to hoist himself onto his feet again.

This time he was more careful in extracting the carcass from the snow bank; he was delighted to find that the doe had apparently died early in the winter for she was not winter thin.

He had managed to pull most of the doe's hindquarters out of the snow and was chipping her back out from the ice with his kopis when he became aware that he was being watched; that prickling between the shoulders caused by a direct stare. He stopped for a moment then twisted around to see who was looking at him. Not 30 feet away a wolf stood in the open watching him intently. For a moment he was relieved; he had been afraid that a horseman had come upon him. He knew wolves were not normally a threat to men. Then he noticed another wolf coming out of the brush below him, then another. These were not normal circumstances. He was very weak, and the wolves were very thin. He and the wolves all needed the meat that the doe at his feet offered.

"You are not the first ones who wanted to take what is mine," he said aloud to the wolves. He suddenly remembered how a pack of human wolves had once tried to take the Hold.

Chapter Nine – Pushing Back

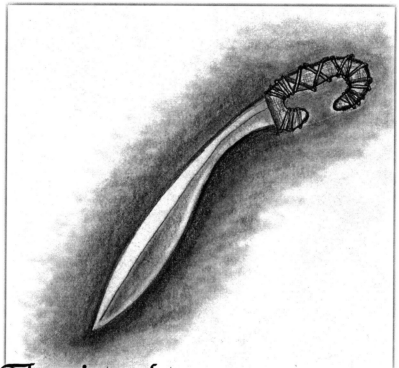

"**They intend to** attack tonight starting at the back gate when Orion's Belt is two fingers above the hills," Mouse began confidently. Athan thought for moment considering where the stars were. It would be at least three or three and half hours before this constellation would be that low. Times were, of course imprecise; that didn't really matter. It told him that the attack would start in complete darkness, not at first light. The Mouse had been doing what he did best, listening to others without them being aware of it. Athan guessed that this time he had been close enough to have heard the actual discussion of the enemy captains. Mouse was able to provide too many specifics with too much confidence – he had to have heard their plans directly.

"They are moving something called a 'house' around the south side of the ridge and then up behind us. I also heard them call it a 'roof'. I think it is a covering for a battering ram."

"It is," confirmed Athan grimly. "I wish them luck getting one up that hill."

"They have it in pieces," continued Mouse. "They are going to assemble this house after they get it up on the ridge and then drag the thing up the back gate. Why do they need to put wet hides on the roof or the house?"

"To keep us from setting it on fire," Athan said. Then he explained to the other two men how a 'house' was used to assault a gate. A stout framework of vertical beams was used to hold up a covering or 'roof' to protect the men from stones and arrows from above. A battering ram was hung on ropes from the framework so that men could shelter beneath the 'roof' and swing the ram against a door or weak section of the wall. Typically a house was mounted on wheels and had side protection as well. The top would have a steep pitch to either side to deflect stones (or anything else) dropped from above off to one side or the other. Slabs of wet leather would cover the structure to prevent it from being torched. This was what Athan had feared would come up to the main gate. He had not thought they could get such a heavy structure up the steep slopes of the ridge.

Mouse had more bad news. "They intend to use ladders to climb the back wall while they beat down the door. Once the attack on the rear is underway, another 'house' is going to be pushed up the road to the main gates, and they will attack the front at the same time. They have some ladders there too, but I think the man in charge of attacking the front doesn't want to use them if there is anyone up there on the walls. He said there were not enough of ladders, and they were too long and heavy."

Athan reviewed the intelligence aloud with Mouse and Giles. The enemy's plan was a good one. They would try to rush the back wall using numbers to overwhelm the defenders. While men were fighting on the ramparts the 'house' would be pushed or carried up to the back gate and it would be beaten in. Then the attacking party would flood into the compound. Meanwhile, a smaller group would see if they could get through the front. That would pin down the defenders on the front gate and prevent them from reinforcing the back. If Athan thinned the men at the front too much, the raiders might get through there as well. The attack at night was not intended to be a complete surprise. The surprise would be in the sudden appearance of a 'house' and the size of the assault. Athan imagined how it might have been if he had not been warned. A major assault, a battering ram on the rear door, and another force attacking the front; yes, it was a good plan; fortunately, forewarned is forearmed.

"Giles," Athan asked after he thought for a bit, "please call Rodas and the sergeants for an immediate council of war here in the office."

Mouse had slipped away as soon as Giles left, tucking a fat purse from Athan in his belt as he left.

The sergeants were both pleased to have specific information about the enemy's battle plan and suspicious as to its source. All seemed both relieved they knew when and where the attacks were coming. Of course, they were also anxious about the upcoming battle. They were outnumbered at least four to one. Their enemies were fierce fighting men who would show no mercy. The men took turns reassuring each other that they had a strong fort, fierce fighters of their own, and nowhere to run. They must win or die. Athan agreed to some changes suggested by his men, then told them to try to get some rest. He told Giles to have Cook stop making pastries and bake some bread, then to have his people share it out with some cheese and well-watered wine to anyone who wanted to eat.

Just as they prepared to leave he told them one more thing. "I will be in charge of the defense. I will stay by the rear gate where we expect the main attack. If I fall, or if anything should happen to me, Rodas is in charge. He will remain in charge even after the battle. Is that clear?"

The men looked at one another and then glanced at Rodas. They surprised Athan and each other by all going to one knee and making an obeisance to Athan.

Rodas alone remained upright. "I told you I don't want to be a king. So take care out there, all right?" Athan only grinned at him.

The men quickly departed for their posts. Athan was left alone. He sat there for a few moments thinking about getting some sleep. Instead, he took out his oilstone and began to sharpen the blade of his kopis. After a time, he put away his sword taking out the dagger, Bear's Claw, and began to sharpen it. Giles entered sitting down to watch and then, drawing out his own short sword, he reached for another whetstone and began sharpening his own weapon. When Athan was finished with the dagger, he took down one of the spears following the same action. The room was quiet with only the rasp of whetstones breaking the silence. Eventually, all the weapons in the room were honed to a find edge. Only then did Athan get up and approach the entrance to observe the night sky. When he returned, Giles had finished with his weapon and was watching him expectantly.

"I estimate it is about two hours or so before the attack is scheduled to begin. I am going to lie down. We are ready, try to get some rest," Athan told him.

The young man and started to get up and go.

"Giles," Athan said, "thank you for waiting with me."

Giles gave him a broad smile, "My pleasure, sire."

"Sir, sir, I think they are coming!"

Athan jerked upright. He had been dreaming of a battle—the one he had lost. He shook himself and went unsteadily over to a basin where he splashed some water on his face. Coming in to the center office, he could see Giles hastily putting on his own armor. Athan had taken off his armor when he lay down and was wearing only his tunic and his red vest. Giles jumped up to help him into his gear. For once Athan did not object. As Giles knelt to help him into his boots and greaves, the men could hear shouting outside. Athan pulled on his bracers as Giles finished attaching his sword belt around his waist over the armored skirt. Athan put his helmet under one arm and his arm through his shield strap taking up a spear with this other hand.

Just then a man began hammering at the entrance door, "Sire, sire, Linus says the attack is beginning and asks you to come.

Athan opened the door in his full armor, startling the man.

"Tell him I'll come," was all he said. Athan turned back to Giles who was frantically trying to get into his armor. "Dress slowly, I will not need you for a while yet; when I do need you I will want to you to be absolutely ready. Take your time and make sure everything is correct before you come."

Athan found Linus on the center of the east wall, directly above the back gate. Athan made his way past a half dozen or so men standing on the battlements until he came to the large figure of Linus, looming up in the darkness. Everyone standing on the wall was looking out into the darkness. In the middle distance, dim lights could be seen. Men were shouting and taunting them from the night. Perhaps they were trying to obscure the sounds of banging and thumps that could be heard coming from the vicinity of the lights. Perhaps they were trying to terrify the defenders. Perhaps they were simply frightened themselves and were trying to work themselves up to an attack.

"They are trying to reassemble the 'house' and finding it is harder than they anticipated," Athan observed.

The men talked about this for a while, speculating on the number of ladders that would be thrown against the wall in the assault. Giles arrived holding his helmet like Athan under his right arm; he had taken time to arrange his hair.

"Here, sire," he said without trying to sound self-satisfied and offered Athan Bear's Claw.

Athan slapped his hand down over his helmet to his empty dagger sheath with an oath. The men all laughed as though it was the funniest joke in the world. Every man on the wall was as tight as a strung bow; laughter helped ease the tension. A messenger called up from the courtyard. It was one of the boys from town. There were a half dozen of them; too young to fight but too old to be considered children. Much to their delight they had been designated as messengers. Now one of these messengers called up from below, "Message for the King from Yure."

Athan stepped to the railing at the back of the rampart and looked down. There were men down there, armed and quiet, waiting in case the rear door was broken down. If the enemy got through the door, these men would either win or lose the battle.

"What is it?" Athan called down.

"Sergeant Yure reports men approaching the front gates. He says some of them are pushing a large wheeled object up the road." The young voice cracked while delivering his message. The silent men beside him roared with laughter, and the boy fled, deeply embarrassed.

Athan was very glad that he knew what the enemy was planning. It would be pretty obvious in any case; still he was glad he didn't have to figure it out. He just had to keep his mind open in case there were any last minute changes in his enemy's plans or, more likely, they did not execute them as planned.

The assembly out in the dark continued. Athan looked at the stars. Orion's Belt had almost set; the attack was late. Athan moved up and down the wall, speaking quietly to the men, trying to steady them. He climbed up each of the battlements and reminded the archers to hold their fire until they could see something. He could feel the pile of stones men had ready to rain down on the enemy. All the while he could feel his deep rage slowly burning. These men were coming to attack his home. They wanted to kill the people he felt responsible to protect—the people he loved. They had already killed some of them; one in particular. It was not a flaring fire type of anger; it was more like the forge in Tito's smith; banked, glowing, and white hot. He wanted to open the gate, charge out into the dark and begin killing. He had never felt this way before a fight. This was strange.

Athan had been a successful fighting man most of his life, and yet he could not remember ever besting a single enemy in a straight-on fight. He was sure he must have killed men in some of the battles he had fought as a young soldier; that was different. Those blows had been a spear thrusts over the front rank's shields that might or might not have inflicted a mortal wound. He had killed Azziz in battle, but his first blow had come when the man had his back turned. Thinking back Athan could not really recall even one case where he had faced an equal opponent on even footing like Achilles and Hector before the Walls of Troy. This did not bother him, in part because he knew that was not a special talent of his; he was not one of those men who could turn a battle with personal strength of arms. Though he knew how to handle his weapons well enough, he was no champion. Athan felt different than he had before any of the other times he had waited for combat to start. In the past he had been nervous before a fight, even apprehensive, confident, any number of strong emotions. Tonight, for the first time in his life, he was eager for battle.

When he returned from prowling the short length of the back wall, he found Giles waiting for him in the southeast corner of the bastion. He had contrived to heat water over a neat little lamp he had found after they had captured the Hold, the previous owner having no further use of it. Now, Giles used it to heat his lord a cup of tea.

Athan gulped it gratefully. "You are amazing," he told his shield bearer. Giles glowed with the praise. "I have changed my mind," Athan then informed him. "We are not going to stay in the bastion; we are going to wait for them on the wall. Let's see how determined they are to come over the top."

Giles did not react. The plan had been for Athan to stay in the top of the southeast battlement and observe how the battle was going. Rodas would be in the northwest tower by the main gate watching things from his side of the fight. They each had a man with torches who could signal any thing important back and forth. Prokopios down in the courtyard could see the signals as well. This would allow the two battle leaders to shift reserves to the critical part of the battle. Athan now did not think he would need to make changes. Mostly he was itching for a fight.

He walked out onto the parapet at the southeast end with his right shoulder against the wall of the bastion that rose up another level. Athan could see the dark shapes of his men to his left along the length of the wall. From the darkness the taunts and threats were getting louder, angrier, closer. The voices were promising certain death to the defenders, detailing intended mutilations, and promising shameful degradations to any survivors. It was a bit unnerving, knowing that just out there in the darkness there were so many people who were looking forward to killing you. Athan had been in situations like this before; all the shouting did was irritate him. He almost never prayed. Suddenly he found himself now praying to a god that he was not even sure existed: Ares, the god of war.

"Oh, Ares," Athan murmured, "make me your instrument. Let me kill those miserable bastards out there."

The shouts continued. No one on the wall spoke. Then, in a lull, one voice was heard in a high-pitched tone apparently designed to be frightening calling out, "We are coming, we are coming, we are coming..." followed by an attempt at a scary wail.

As the wail died out there was a moment of silence. Athan filled it.

"THEN COME!" he roared, and a moment later there was an echo from the hills.

His challenge was not sophisticated, or a well-considered response to the taunts coming from the dark. In fact, he did not think at all before he bellowed his response. But it had a powerful effect. Men about to go into battle, especially hand to hand combat, almost always shift to a very elemental level. They do not engage the higher cognitive functions of the brain; they reach way back to the fundamentals. Athan's challenge, the tone, the pitch, the volume, and murderous intent reached right down into their core. It resonated unconsciously to the men in the dark like the roar of a lion, the howl of a wolf, the bellow of some unknown monster hungry for their blood. And just like that, all the raiders out there in the dark, working themselves up to assault the wall, lost their confidence. The men inside could feel it, too. Now they began to shout back at their tormenters in the dark. But even the responses that were more elaborate, well thought out, and seemly more frightening such as Linus' eerie "Come, death awaits you here!" delivered in his weird accent, did not have the effect of that first challenge by the King. Later, men would remember that call as the beginning of the battle. Many would try to repeat what he said, but no one could quite capture the feeling Athan had transmitted. Everyone did remember the fact that it sent a very elemental message to everyone who heard it: 'Come to me so that I can kill you.'

Even though Athan's bellowed counter-challenge was considered the start of the fighting, actually it was almost a quarter of an hour before there was a yell and a wild rush out of the darkness, and men charged the wall out of the night with their ladders, coming to do murder.

There were far more men and ladders than anyone in the Hold had expected. The raiders seemed like some dark, animated flood. Attacking at night limited the effectiveness of the bowmen on the walls. It was also terrifying. The meager light created by the torches and piles of oil-splashed straw that the men threw over the walls to illuminate the attackers threw weird shadows heightening the defenders' fears. When the ladders hit the wall with thumps, the men had another surprise: the attackers had tied pairs of the ladders together. This made them much more difficult to push over. The ladders had been made long enough so that they were leaning at a less acute angle to the top of the wall. Worse, there were so many ladders up against the wall, at least a dozen, that they would only slide sideways a short way before wedging against another ladder. Finally, the weight of the men frantically scrambling up the rungs made it impossible to push them back from the walls. Within a few hammering heartbeats the men on the top rungs were up to the top of the wall. A few heartbeats after that, many of them were dying of spear thrusts from the defenders who were standing on the wall at the head of each of the ladders.

It was all terribly confusing; the darkness, men shouting and screaming in rage and pain, intense activity, and the narrow focus of men engaged in close combat gave the scene on top of the wall a surreal feeling. At first, the men on the wall held. The ladders were in two groups, one on either side of the back gate with the ladders tending up and off to the side, leaning against the jutting bastion walls. Their plan was simple: get to the top of the wall, work to the center, allow the battering ram to come up and knock open the gate, then pour into the courtyard and overwhelm the defenders with numbers. Their plan worked, sort of. Their leaders had promised a talent of gold and their pick of the women to the first men to reach the top of the wall. None of the first men up the ladders survived, but the men swarming up behind them were able to get up onto the wall, grabbing the shafts of stabbing spears, pushing between defenders, stabbing and hacking up and over. They were hard to kill; almost all had helmets, some had body armor, and most wore shields on their backs. They held onto the ladders tenuously, fighting and waiting to climb up as the men ahead of them were killed or reached the parapet. Stones from above bounced some off the ladders. The archers kept up a steady fire on the men climbing up and hit more than a few, but there were only a few arrow slits, and the men on the ladders did not seem to notice. All too soon, the defenders were forced back toward the bastions. Those who survived in the middle of the wall were caught by men coming at them from both sides. Those who could jumped down to the courtyard below; the rest died. Now the enemy had possession of the center of the wall over the back gate.

While the battle of the ladders raged, the battering ram beneath its 'house' came trundling up. Oxcart wheels where attached to the front. The rear was held up by men both inside the frame and others holding on and pushing on the outside. The archers on the bastions immediately shifted their aim to this more important target. Even though the side screens were only sheets of leather, they did slow the arrows and prevented the archers from taking a direct aim at the men concealed under the little rectangular shed. Men outside the covering began to drop back from the house to avoid the projectiles being shot and hurled at them. Those under cover were still able to push the house up to the rear door with a resounding thud. Then the men inside began to swing the log within against the door. This ram was capped with a bronze head and was hung low at the end of ropes attached to the frame so the men could get a good swing. They set up a rhythm, smashing against the door. It was a lunatic environment inside the house; men were screaming and dying all around them, stones were thumping off the steeply pitched roof of wood and leather, arrows partially punched through the leather screen here and there. The two metal lamps inside the house had gone out but there was enough light from torches and bits of blazing straw to let them see they were beating down the back door. Soon the real battle would begin.

Even as the raiders began to hammer on the door, things began to go wrong for them. There were two reasons for this. One was Linus at the north end of the wall. He was wearing a bronze half helm with long cheek pieces, carried a beautiful round wooden shield, and he had his ax. Linus was a big man and athletic. Men cowered before him, ducking trying to dodge or block his heavy ax. None were successful. His shield covered his left side and his ax his front. All who faced him died.

The other reason the attack faltered was at the other end of the short wall. Athan had gone into a battle rage. Every human has a "flight or fight" mechanism that gives extra energy. Athan was harnessing every bit of this energy, and it was all going to the fight side. He killed two men on their ladders with his spear before it lodged in a man's body and was pulled from his hand as the corpse fell. Athan let it go and drew his kopis with deep satisfaction. The blade was made for this type of battle. Athan used it perfectly, hacking over upraised shields and shearing right through helmets and skulls. He would rock the blade free and then kill anther man. He kept his shield to the front and pushed forward, killing men on the parapet and driving them off the tops of their ladders. His exposed right side was covered by Giles. The shield bearer moved in concert with Athan back and forth, facing out toward the wall, blocking thrust after thrust, stroke after stroke. His heavy shield was dented, splintered and gouged, but it held. The King and his shield bearer appeared to onlookers to be performing elaborate steps in a complicated dance. Giles did a superb job of protecting his lord, but Athan was in the very thick of the fighting, and he could not deflect all the blows aimed at the King. Yet somehow, the blows struck at the King seemed to be turned by his armor or miss him altogether as he stepped back and forth, ducking weaving and striking with his edge and even thrusting with his sword's point. Giles was so concerned with covering Athan he neglected to watch himself and got stabbed in the right thigh by a man coming up a ladder behind him. One of the other defenders came up to deal with the man and fill in the gap. Then, Athan struck a man such a cunning blow his victim's helmet flew off his head and high into the air. The men waiting below in the courtyard cheered. Giles glanced up at the flight of the bronze helmet and got stabbed in the biceps. Shortly afterward, a man down on the parapet revived long enough to stab Giles in his left calf with a dagger. They were painful wounds, but Giles held his place, guarding his king's exposed side.

Now it was the turn of the attackers over the center of the wall to be caught by men coming at them from either side. Some tried to retreat down the ladders. This exposed their backs, a fatal mistake. Some jumped or were pushed to the courtyard below, but unlike the defenders who had jumped down in the first onslaught and were helped up and put into line by comrades, the attackers were promptly speared to death before they could get to their feet.

Linus and Athan each killed the enemy before them and suddenly were facing one another with no enemy left on the wall to kill; the top of the wall was cleared. There was no time to rest. Other men were trying to get up the ladders.

Then with a final splintering crash, the door below split, and the enemy began to charge through the gap into the courtyard. Athan was vaguely aware of this on some level but most of his attention was directed toward finding more enemies to kill.

During this time that was a brief threat to the south wall. Tenucer had already released most of his men from the south wall to reinforce the threatened west wall. Few were aware that two ladders had been placed along that wall by a small group of men hoping to find an unguarded stretch they could reach without going into the hard fight over the back gate. Tenucer had his bow with him. A torch gave him enough light to begin shooting the men off their ladders. He shot so quickly and so well that the splinter group of attackers was driven off; they scurried back into the night, leaving their ladders behind, never realizing that there were only four men left to defend that whole length of the long south wall.

Over the back gate, Athan began prowling up and down the wall, looking out over the wall and daring the men below him to come up and face him. They waited there just below his striking range, enduring the stones and arrows for a time and then began to slip down their ladders to dart through the 'house' which was pushed up against the shattered back gate. Once through they joined the fight going on in the courtyard.

On his side of the wall Linus began swinging his ax down on the top rungs of the ladders, smashing them and making the ascent that much harder. He did not see one desperate man crouching at the top of his ladder. When Linus swung his ax at the ladder next to him, the man leapt up and grabbed Linus's big round shield with both hands and tried to pull him off the wall. As he yanked on Linus' shield, he lost his footing on his own ladder and hung, swinging from Linus's shield. Linus for his part was pulled down flat, his shoulder hanging down over the edge of the wall. In considerable pain, Linus tried to let go of the shield but it was held fast by the leather strap across his forearm; as his opponent fell and hung from the shield, it had twisted tight. Neither could he let go of the shield grip which was pinching his hand just above thumb. He lay their for a long moment, stretched out on the wall, his arm dangling down over the edge, unable to lift the weight of his shield and man holding on to it, and unable to let release the shield either. He was a perfect target for any arrow or javelin launched from below. Linus let go of his ax and pulled his dagger from the sheath on his right side. He reached down and cut the shield strap off his forearm. He had apparently been sharpening his weapons too, the keen blade parted the leather strap effortlessly. The man and shield had a short drop before the entire weight of his shield and an armored man was transferred to Linus' hand, still caught in the shield grip. The man hung there for a moment, then still holding the shield, fell down into the night. Linus' shield, his left thumb, and a big part of the rest of his hand went with him. Linus howled in agony and jammed his ruined hand under his right armpit; then with a deliberate move, he bent down and picked up his ax. He went back to chopping the ladders.

While all this was going on, the attack on the front gate started. This assault did not go well from the beginning. The wall was higher here which meant the ladders were longer and heavier. The defenders on the front of the wall did a better job of lighting fires on the ground to provide light for the archers. Yure had been given mostly either townsmen or new recruits; he had only a few real fighting men. It did not matter; with only half a dozen ladders it was relatively easy to keep the attackers from getting more than halfway up the ladders. One does not need to be a trained warrior to throw rocks down on a man climbing a ladder. Since there was little pressure on the men above the gate, when the battering ram under its house was pushed up to the gate, the men above were able to bombard it with heavy stones and logs. The attackers tried to provide cover from the ground with archers, but that would have been difficult even with expert archers in broad daylight, and the effort was half-hearted. Having rocks weighing as much or more than a grown man crashing down on their roof of their little house sort of broke their concentration on swinging the battering ram against the gate. A log, as big around as a man's thigh and five cubits long went right on through the top of the shed and crushed one of the men underneath. He lay underfoot, screaming in agony. That just about did it for the assault on the main gate. They had managed only two blows against the doors. The solid rebound those heavy doors transmitted to the ram let the men know they would have to be there for a long time before this obstacle could be removed. They thought better of it and fled, leaving behind their siege house with its battering ram in place. The assault on the front gate had been thwarted. Yure sent Pirro down with half a dozen men to reinforce Prokopios' reserve that was suddenly fighting in the courtyard at the back gate.

When the back gate splintered open, and the enemy started coming through, Prokopios and his men had every advantage. He had well over a score of the best fighters, all fully armed, and armored drawn up in formation. There were even more spearmen behind them, most without proper swords and shields but all with long spears, their sharp points pushed out over and ahead of the front ranks. Even so, the invaders did not hesitate; they charged in at once. So fierce and frenzied were the attackers that despite the best efforts of the men in ranks their thin line was pushed back. At first, as the line began to stretch it worked to the defenders advantage. Men had more room to fight and the spears behind them could reach in and strike without interfering or interference. But as more and more enemy came through the back gate and men in the line began to fall, the formation began to falter. Mighty Eustathios was seen to go down in the center of the fighting. The line trembled but held. This all took time, though no one could later tell just how long. Then, just as the line was reaching a breaking point, several things happened all at once. No one understood what really happened until days later, when the various survivors had a chance to compare their experiences.

First, and least important, Tenucer and other archers on the wall began shooting from the wall down into the courtyard. The line of battle was far enough out from the door that they had a clear aim at the shattered entrance. Arrow after arrow went into that gap. Seeing this, Rodas had Yure send two of his best archers from the over the main gates back down the wall to the rear and shift their fire to the shattered back gate. The first thing an attacker had to do when he entered the courtyard was step over dead and dying men. If he did not clear that area instantly he was the target of arrows from two different sides. It was not a decisive advantage, but it helped.

Second, the men on the parapet over the back wall started making themselves useful. Some daring souls down below the wall were still trying to see if they could get up the ladders, but the real threat to the top of the wall had passed. At first no one thought to do anything about the battle going on behind and beneath their feet. Athan muttered something about 'clearing these things away,' referring to the numbers of dead and dying men on the catwalk. Someone, no one was sure just who, decided to dump the bodies over the side. The first body went over the wall to the outside. Then the men noticed they could start dropping things on the 'house' where the enemy was coming in through the gate. Before even the first corpse went onto the house someone, (several men later claimed the idea), noticed the desperate struggle going on down in the courtyard and decided to drop things down on the enemy in the courtyard. In short order, men began throwing bodies onto their enemies below. Others began throwing stones and javelins down onto the backs of the attackers in the courtyard. It is hard enough to fight against an enemy on three sides; fighting on three sides and being attacked from above is even worse. It is extremely disconcerting to have the body of a former comrade land on top of you while you were trying to close with opponents. No one could tell if any of the corpses killed anyone they landed upon, however, a man is a heavy thing, and it is no joke to have a body dropped down on you from two stories up. The enemy in the rear ranks began holding their shields over their heads and cowering down instead of attacking the line. Other defenders began raining heavy stones and logs down on the other side of the wall onto the 'house' leading up to the rear door.

Finally, and most importantly, the men in the courtyard were being reinforced. Pirro and his little group were only part of the men who left their assigned posts to rush into the battle. There was a moment after Eustathios fell when the line wavered, but it held. Then it strengthened. Men who are winning hold fast and keep fighting, and the defenders were winning.

The attackers were losing and they began to know it. Men coming up had to endure being shot at by bowmen as they approached the wall, admittedly not too many, still it was a nervous thing. They could see broken ladders and piles of bodies in the dim light as they ducked into the battered house that led to the shattered back gate. Rocks were making a pounding racket on the roof as they shuffled slowly up to the door, hesitating at the entrance because they could see arrow studded men, some moaning in pain some dead. They could sense other arrows whipping around the opening. Holding up their shields, against the threat of this lethal hail, they stumbled over more bodies. The men hurried to get close to the line of fighting where they felt safe from missiles that were seemingly coming at them from all sides. Once there they faced an unbroken shield wall that fronted by spears and pikes poking over the shields at them. This was hot, hard work. More and more of them began to decide that this was not what they had been promised. Then the raiders fighting in the courtyard began to consider how hard it would be to get out of this place with just that one narrow entrance. A few men broke and ran clawing their way past the men coming in, shouting that the battle was lost. The men coming in hesitated. It looked to them like the courtyard was nothing but a killing field, and they were the ones being killed. They drew back from the door. Seeing an opening, a few more men in the rear ranks of the attackers gave it up as a bad job and bolted for the exit. In ten more heartbeats the attacker's line began to collapse, and a true bloodbath began as the former attackers tried to flee, jamming the door with their bodies, fighting each other, and relentlessly being cut down by the victorious defenders. Some tried to surrender. A few were actually successful.

It was starting to get light as the enemy began to stream out of the 'house' at the back gate and flee down the spine of the ridge or tumble down its steep sides. Tenucer left his post on the south wall and, racing through the bastion, shot his last two remaining arrows at men fleeing the Hold. He was satisfied to hit a man with each arrow. Both dropped where they were shot. Prokopios held his men back at the entrance, preventing them from becoming scattered in pursuit. Instead, he had them push shut the shattered door and reformed them, ready for a second assault.

Athan watched his enemies fleeing from the Hold with a dull expression. He did not think he had ever been so totally exhausted. Still, he willed himself to move to the steps inside the bastion, Giles limping slowly behind him. Athan stopped for a moment to sheath his kopis. He made a half hearted attempt to wipe off the blood and gore, noticing the blade was chipped and dull now. When he tried to put down his shield, he winced in unexpected pain. Giles tried to spring forward to help, though it was more like a stumble. With a grimace Athan carefully slid the remains of the rectangular shield off his arm. Giles had a heavy shield meant to take this sort of fighting, and it was damaged beyond repair. Athan's lighter shield was a wreck, battered out of shape, crushed in, and pierced with many holes. Athan realized that his left forearm that had held the shield was broken. He could not remember when he had taken the blow, but he was not likely to forget the effect. Looking down he saw that he was bloody, that was to be expected, and his armor was badly damaged with bright cuts and dents all over his greaves. His armored skirt had been slashed almost in two above his thigh, again he could not remember when that had happened. His cuirass was hacked and battered. He was unable to see the damage he had received on his helmet but suddenly he had a raging headache, letting him know that he had taken blows there as well. Later he would find the crest partially sheered off and at least a dozen scars and dents on his once fine helmet. But he himself, though bruised and battered, had not suffered so much as a scratch. Every bit of blood on him was, just like in his last battle, someone else's.

The two men took off their helmets, and leaving them on the ramparts with the remains of their shields, limped down to the courtyard. By the time he had gotten there, Prokopios had reestablished the formation and was sending out a strong party of scouts to clear the area around the rear wall. There was a pale gray light now, showing the horror of the battle in the courtyard. Rodas was there looking tired but unhurt.

"We have to get the men mounted up and pursue them before they get away," ordered Athan.

"Sire, we are in no shape to do that," responded Rodas.

Athan cursed him and demanded that the men go to their assigned places.

"Where are the horses? Where is Ixon? Tell him to get those horsemen out after them before they reform! We can kill them easily now. Ixon!"

"He took a spear in the fighting, sire" Stamitos informed him.

"Then you lead them. Get out there and kill our enemies. Hurry!"

It was not to be. The directions became muddled, someone thought that the horses were to be freed, and they were all let loose. Some of the women and children panicked and started running out with them, screaming and adding to the disruption. Tragically, a little girl was run down in the confusion and killed. Of the men who had been detailed to ride out with Ixon, half were dead, wounded, or missing. In the end Athan gave up and settled for sending men out to kill any of the wounded enemy that could not get away, then demolish the siege equipment that had been left against the walls.

"Are you hurt, Athan," Rodas eventually asked, looking at his king and his shield bearer.

"It's his arm," blurted Giles. "I think it is broken."

"It's nothing," mumbled Athan.

"Well look at Giles then," Rodas told him. Giles would have been in the running for the 'most obviously walking wounded' prize even in that bloody place. He had bloody wounds on both legs, on his right arm where blood ran down to drip off his hand. He also had a long slash on his right cheek that had soaked his right side in blood.

"You need to take him to let Hypos and his people take care of him," prompted Rodas.

Giles did not even object. That was when Athan realized how badly he must be hurting. Avoiding the score of horses that had been released in the panic and were moving around in the courtyard, the two comrades made their way over to the baths. Others were moving in the same direction, either slowly on their own feet, or being carried by others. Hypnos took time from tending to the others to see his lord.

"Keep the bracer on it," he advised Athan. "I will come up and see if it needs setting after I get done with these." He made Athan and Giles strip naked and wash for an examination. Even though Athan's tunic had been slashed, but there was not a cut upon him.

The old physician shook his head in amazement. "I will need to tend to Giles," he told the king. I will come and see you when the others are cared for."

"When you come, tell me how many," Athan said tiredly. Then he embraced Giles who was still standing nearby and turned to leave. Before he did so, he stopped and put on his red leather vest and picked up his sword and dagger.

Rodas was waiting for him. He gave his lord a strange look. Perhaps it was his unconventional attire. The King was naked except for his leather vest and a small leather bag around his neck.

"Can you handle things here?" Athan asked him.

Rodas tried to smile a reassuring smile, "Leave it to me. You get some rest."

Athan made it to the door of the bastion before he stopped, looking up at the stairs that led up to his rooms. Why had he taken rooms on the second level? Then he was struck by an inspiration. He turned and walked slowly over to his right to the apartment next to the treasury where Abacus had taken residence. The treasurer was in there, changing to a fresh tunic. Abacus was still on his battle high, as animated as Athan had ever seen him.

"A great victory, Sire! I saw you on the ramparts! You were magnificent! We had some hard fighting down here, too! See, my helmet saved my life! Look!" Abacus thrust his helmet into Athan's face. Sure enough his helmet had a gash on the copper strips that banded the helmet. Athan ignored his steward who continued to babble about how the battle had gone, how he had killed a man with his spear, well, only wounded him, perhaps, but it was a good blow, and how the line had been pushed back, he had no idea that men fighting pushed each other like that, and how when they hesitated he had pushed in, and speared another man, and gotten whacked over the head for his troubles, and how Yure the Younger had told him to not be so eager, and then how young Yure himself had stepped in and gotten killed himself, and how before Abacus could react, Pontus had killed the man, and how the enemy had suddenly turned and run away, and now they were all lying dead out there, what a great victory!

While this discourse was going on Athan wandered around the room looking for where Abacus slept. Finally he caught sight of a low pallet in the corner.

"I am going to rest here for a while," he said and lay down pulling a blanket over him.

Abacus nodded, and rattled on. "Yes, of course, sire, I will stand guard. You must be tired after the battle. Is Giles wounded? Of course, he must be, otherwise he would be here. Can I get you something? Some water perhaps or some wine? Do I need to tell anyone where you are? No, of course not, you need some peace and quiet so you can rest. Do you think I should get some men so we can see if there is any plunder on the men we killed? We will need some money to repair the back gate that they smashed. There is probably other damage as well. They are sure to have ruined, just ruined the town. Are we going to have to pay for the repairs those houses? Surely not; after all the houses belonged to them. If we pay to rebuild them, the houses would be ours."

'It is a bit like the cicadas I used to hear when I was a child', thought Athan as he drifted off. 'A distant, droning background noise.' Abacus continued talking for some time, scarcely taking a breath. He only stopped when Athan began to snore. Then he decided his king needed some rest. He took his helmet and looked at it again. When a man faces death in battle it can change him. It did not change Abacus much. Yet he was immensely proud that he had stood in line to defend this place, and that did change him a little. From that day forward the Hold was his home, his only home. His damaged helmet occupied a place of honor in his rooms for the rest of his life. He would later bore entire generations of his assistants with stories of the battle; stories that grew with time as such stories always do.

If Athan won the battle, it was Rodas who secured the victory. While the wounded were tended and Athan slept, he took over the direction of the immense amount of work that needed to be done. It was Rodas who reset a makeshift new watch, replacing men who were killed, wounded, or obviously exhausted with others more fit. He used townspeople on the walls to let the raiders know there was still plenty of fight left in the Hold. He set other men under the direction of Tito to erect a solid barricade to close off the back gate. Other men disassembled the siege house that was up against the front gate and brought the pieces inside. Rodas made sure people were fed, the livestock herded back in their stalls or picket lines, and arranged for the bodies of friends and foes to be separated. Foes were stripped and thrown out the front gate, friends were cleaned and prepared for a proper funeral pyre. The list of dead was grievous; Jason, killed the first day and Arsene who was the first to die on the wall over the back gate. Both were men who had ridden up to the gate with Rodas when they captured the Hold. Eustathios, the mighty hero who had fallen at the peak of battle; Aorastus, husband of Amara, who had come over the lake with Athan; Yure the younger, killed beside Abacus in the moment of victory; and Pirro, poor red-headed Pirro, who rushed from a place of safety into battle and was slain almost immediately. There were others, almost a dozen dead, and more who would die of their wounds. There were over a score of men wounded badly enough to require treatment from Hypnos and Iason and their two helpers. Giles limped out their hospital and up to his room looking for his king. Missing him, he hobbled about frantically until he discovered where Athan had gone to ground. Linus had his left thumb ripped entirely off, and Hypnos feared he would have to amputate the rest of that hand. The big man had taken many wounds and almost looked like a ghost with his already pale complexion now bone white. Hypnos was cautiously confident he had a good chance to survive. Stamitos was one of the men who shifted over to help with the fight at a critical moment. He had taken a slash on the left side of his face that destroyed that eye. He, too, was expected to survive.

It was another of the wounded that captured Rodas' attention when he visited the bath house where the wounded too badly hurt to move were being tended. Rodas had trouble seeing him at first, obscured as he was by the woman bending over him. It was Adara, hovering over her new husband, Ixon. The Master of Horse was a hoplite first, and had stood in the front rank where the fighting was fiercest. Now he lay unconscious on a couch with a sheet covering him to the neck. Adara looked up at Rodas with the expression of a woman clinging to a log in a cataract and hearing the roar of a falls just ahead. Rodas could not hold that gaze of desperate despair.

Seeking Hypnos he quietly asked about the prospects of Ixon surviving.

"There is a chance," the old healer told him, "if he does not die from loss of blood tonight. He has several wounds. Most are not too bad but he took a spear in the gut." Hypnos went on to say that he would keep him where he was until he was well enough for soup.

"Soup?" asked Rodas

"Garlic and onion soup," confirmed Hypnos. "Then in an hour we smell the wound. If we smell the garlic and onions, he will certainly die. If not, he has a chance, although there is always the chance he will get blood poisoning. Time will tell."

"What about the woman?" inquired Rodas. "Is she in the way?"

"Oh, no," said the old physician shaking his head with a distant expression. "She is quiet. I will tell you, I think having someone there seems to help patients, particularly if that person loves them. Patients that have something to live for seem to recover more often. At the very least it comforts them in their last hours."

Rodas stood thinking for a while after Hypnos went to look at another patient. Rodas had been a fighting man and a brigand for most of his adult life, but that did not mean he did not have an unusually good understanding of people. That was why he was a good leader of a band. That was why he was becoming a good magistrate. Now, he used his empathy to try to help an old comrade and the woman he had rescued.

Adara watched him warily as he approached, waiting for him to tell her something she did not want to hear. She was crouched on the far side of the couch by her husband's head. Rodas squatted down across for her.

"I just spoke with Hypnos," he began.

"Is he going to die," she blurted.

'This is a brave woman, to ask right out about what she must fear more than anything else,' thought Rodas.

"Perhaps not," he told her. A desperate light flared in her eyes. 'Do not give false hope,' he thought, 'give her something to do. Let her have a bit of control.'

"Hypnos said you can help."

"Tell me," she said urgently, "I will do anything."

"Get a stool and make your self comfortable," Rodas began. She looked at him strangely. "You will be here for a while. You must be strong for him. If you exhaust yourself now, you may not be there for him when he needs you." She nodded. Rodas saw she was as pale as Linus. You have some good fresh water there. If he wakes up he will be thirsty. Hypnos says he should drink if he is thirsty."

"That will be a good sign," confirmed Iason who came over to stand by the unconscious Ixon.

Adara looked back and forth between the two men not daring to hope.

"When he wakes they will give him some soup," Rodas told her. "You need to feed that to him." She just looked at him wide eyed and nodded. "It will make him better," lied Rodas.

"He may live or he may die," Iason said gently, "it is too soon to tell."

"Stay beside him and give him water," repeated Adara doggedly. "What else can I do?"

"Well," said Iason, "if he gets a fever, bathe his forehead with water mixed with a tenth part of vinegar. Try to keep him quiet if you can." And after that final bit of advice, the healer moved off.

Adara got up and brought a stool, and sat down next to her man.

"That," added Rodas remembering Hypnos' comment, "and love him."

"I can do that," said Adara, reaching under the cover to take the unconscious man's hand.

Rodas left her to her vigil.

It was past noon when the mounted patrol Athan had so wanted to pursue the retreated enemy finally left the Hold. Over a dozen men, led by Sergeant Tenucer, emerged from the front gates, now completely cleared of the abandoned siege gear. The men swept past the mound of corpses and turned right to circle around the north side of the ridge. Men down in the town began running and shouting an alarm, but by the time armed men could be seen down in the town the patrol had disappeared around the shoulder of the hill. The horsemen trotted by numbers of dead and dying raiders. Those who were still hale and attempted to flee, were ridden down and killed with javelins. Only one small group even tried to make an effort at defending themselves. These, too, died. The patrol completed its circle of the ridge and confirmed that there were not watchers anywhere behind or to either side of the Hold, and then completed the circle, staying well clear of Dassaria. There was no attempt by the raiders to interfere with them during their brief sortie. Even though it lasted only about half an hour, it sent a clear message to the men who had been beaten that morning; we are still here and ready to fight.

Athan was up, dressed, and eating when the patrol returned. He felt terrible. It was as though he had been beaten all over with sticks, which was approximately true. He slowly limped over to where Tenucer had dismounted. He had apparently already delivered his initial report of his little sortie. Nodding to Rodas he stopped the young sergeant. "Council of war in my office in a quarter hour; bring Talos." Then he walked slowly and gingerly back toward his quarters at far end of the compound. He reflected to himself that the time was necessary not just to assemble the sergeants; it also gave him time to get up those stairs. He was relieved to find that as he walked, his body loosened up, and by the time he reached the stairs in the bastion he could climb them with only a moderate difficulty.

He immediately regretted his decision to hold the meeting in his spaces when he saw Giles lying on his pallet. The young man was really hurting. Instantly, Athan called to the watch over the back gate to come to him.

"Take Giles down and have Hypnos or Iason look at him again. See if they have any draughts that will help him sleep." He overrode Giles' protestations by telling him in blunt terms that he did not need him right then but would definitely require him on the morrow. Giles was ordered to rest and heal as quickly as possible so he could return to full duty.

"What is the tally," Athan asked to open the meeting.

"We have a dozen dead and about twice that many too badly wounded to fight," Rodas announced immediately.

Athan wondered if he was considered one of those men.

"As to the enemy," continued Rodas, "based on what we can see and what Tenucer saw, I think we must have killed or badly wounded at least a hundred of them, probably more."

The men thought about what that meant. They had lost about a quarter of their fighting men. The attackers and defenders had each lost about the same proportion of their strength. That was not critical. What mattered was the contrasting morale of the two groups. Although the mood in the Hold was far from ebullient, there was a sense of confidence tinged with satisfaction. It was harder to gage the enemy's mood. 'Until Mouse goes out tonight', thought Athan, then had a pang when he realized Pirro would not be scouting for him ever again. It did not take an expert spy to know the raiders were disheartened. Already, the men watching from the bastions reported a small group quietly moving out from the town heading west. The general consensus was that this group of bandits would not hold together much longer. The chance of another assault was considered low.

Still the men took no chances. They reviewed Rodas' revised watch and battle assignments. Yure promised to hold some light training that afternoon to make sure everyone was ready in case they did try another attack. Athan told the men to start thinking about how they were going to drive this pack of jackals from Dassaria. They would meet in the morning to come up with some plans.

Just before sunset, the scheduled drill was held to check equipment and let the men see the modified assignments. Everyone was pleased to see that Prokopios' reserve seemed actually stronger than they were before the fight. When they had been attacked that morning, there had only been one solid line of men armed as phalangists augmented by a thin second line backed up with spearmen around the rear entrance. Now, thanks to the equipment recovered from the fallen and looted from their dead enemies, there were two solid lines of armed and armored hoplites backed by spearmen. And after the battle that morning, these men were now all experienced veterans. The change showed. There were fewer men on the walls but Athan and his lieutenants were confident that if an attack came, the men could repel the assault. The general feeling inside the Hold was that their enemies had no fight left in them. Too many of the raiders had died beating their heads against the Hold.

Events proved them correct. There were a few alarms in the night, but they were minor. Mouse returned before dawn, reporting that there was much arguing and a few fights down in the town. The leaders who had been the driving force behind the raid were mostly dead. There was no talk among the raiders of a renewed assault. Some suggested going to the King of Illyria and asking for men. Athan was confident the king would simply hang the requesters and go on about his business. Mouse predicted some of the raiders would begin leaving that day. Sure enough, as the morning progressed, bands of men could be seen moving out of Dassaria, not moving like an invading army, but dispersing, like the bands of brigands they were.

The day passed quietly, if somewhat impatiently, as the people of Dassaria gathered up on the western wall to watch what was going on down in town. Two patrols went out during the day, this time getting much closer to town and menacing one of the departing bands, though no blows were struck.

Shortly after noon on the following day, things changed more dramatically. Even more bands had left by then, and time was up for those who remained. A strong contingent of hoplites came out of the Hold and formed up just outside the front gate in full view of the town. They moved down in good order to the foot of the hill where they formed three lines, protected by horsemen on the flanks with young men acting as peltasts in the front. Rodas was in charge of the operation; Athan watched him from the bastion, his broken left arm in a sling. While they were moving down, Athan could see intense activity in the town. Men began to leave the town, singly and in groups, mostly headed west. A few made as if to fight. A group of the enemy horsemen rode out menacingly, but could do nothing to hinder the formation. After a look, the horsemen withdrew first to, then through the town, scarcely stopping on their way west. Rodas' hoplites took their time, methodically surrounding and entering each building in town. Only when some of the buildings were set on fire by some of the retreating bands did Rodas allow his men to begin to disperse and move more rapidly through the town. An alarm was given when a dozen riders were seen coming up from the south on the road; they were soon identified as the riders from Thereon's patrol that had escaped when the attackers first arrived. They had been doing good service by hindering the smaller bands of mounted raiders from plundering too far and by warning the outlying hamlets and farmsteads. Now they joined their comrades in clearing the town of the remaining enemy raiders.

This action took them until almost dark. There was some serious fighting from time to time as some of the raiders tried to make a defense or were caught before they could make their escape. A few of the raiders were found insensible from drink. Rodas and his men had the few prisoners they chose to capture dig a pit at the foot of the hill to cover the rotting mound of enemy dead that had been left halfway down the slope. The vultures and crows were so full they could not fly. Pigs and feral dogs waited just out of range for the men to leave them to their meals. The Hold's own dead had been given a proper group funeral, with the shattered remains of the siege equipment acting as their pyre. All fourteen of the soldiers from the garrison who had fallen, the initial twelve dead and two who had succumbed to their wounds, and the three townsmen who fought and died with them were each covered in one of the garrison's gray cloaks and lined up side by side on the pyre. In the center of all those warriors was one more body, a very small one; the little girl, trampled to death in the accidental release of the horses. Athan had them put her close to his old friend Pirro, the red-headed scout, who had in a sense started them all on the trail that led here when he brought Athan news of the Satrap's gold almost a year ago.

"She will have many good men with her for protection," Athan told her weeping mother. Even though all mothers knew that they would probably lose one or more children in their lifetime, it was always very hard. She was not the only one weeping at that funeral. The garrison was small, the men close, and the losses were keenly felt.

At the military council meeting that evening Rodas reported three more wounded with no additional men killed in the fighting in the town that day. Of the enemy, another dozen or so had been killed, perhaps as many more were found seriously wounded (their fate was not discussed), and the rest were scattered. With the return of Thereon and his men, and the rear gate secured, the Hold was at least as strong as it had been before the attack. This perceived strength was not so much the numbers of men defending the Hold as their attitude. The people of Dassaria had beaten an enemy back from the walls of their citadel and now driven them from their town.

The townspeople who had not escaped into the Hold or the hills had paid a heavy price. Murder had been common. Those who chose to hide in local hidey holes had to come out after the second day of occupation, and these appearances were not well received. Even those who had stayed to openly greet the invaders had their persons mistreated and possessions stolen.

Athan would not ask, and Rodas did not want to bring up the subject, but eventually he had to answer his king's unspoken question.

"There were many killed down there, sire," Rodas began quietly. "We buried them in the graveyard. Delbine was among those killed. I had them put her in separate grave. We can put up a proper stele for her, for all of them, tomorrow." He did not tell Athan how they had found the bodies. Some had been killed in terrible ways. Some, like Delbine, had just been left where they had been murdered. Apparently the last man who finished raping her had decided cut her throat.

Athan felt hollow inside. He had not loved Delbine, had he? She certainly had been good to him. There were, had been, two people in the Hold in whom he could confide—Giles and Delbine. Rodas was a confidant, yes, but he could not be allowed to see Athan's weaknesses. He could be open with his woman and his shield bearer because they each loved him in their own way. Why did they have to kill her? Delbine had been a good person; a prostitute, yes, but a sweet, harmless, and loving spirit. Now that she was gone. Athan had never guessed he would miss her so terribly.

Inside the Hold, Ixon decided he felt strong enough to drink his onion and garlic soup. After a time Hypos made a careful, sniffing examination, Adara attended the examination closely holding her breath. The healer was satisfied that the bowel had not been perforated and pronounced the injured hoplite well enough to be moved back to his little tack room where Adara could tend him. Four men lifted Ixon's couch and carried him there where he began his recovery. Ixon condition improved slowly but his survival was never in doubt; his wife simply refused to let him die. It was a month before Ixon could stand and three before he could resume his duties. There was one amusing artifact from his convalescence; no one ever explained to Adara just why they gave Ixon onion and garlic soup. So, believing the soup to be of a healing nature, Adara made him eat it every day. Soon, he was begging her for something else to eat. She was relentless. So he asked her to at least add some meat to his soup. She was able to afford some chicken, so for a time he had onion, garlic, chicken soup. Then he asked her to add some noodles as well. By this time she was tired of soup, too, for she ate it not just for convenience, but to provide immunity from his breath. As he began to get around and talk with others, there was an almost universal request from people who were not eating a diet that included so much garlic that she cut down on the garlic and onions. So by the time he was ready to walk around they were eating soup that consisted mostly of chicken and noodles. For the rest of her life, Adara would serve her loved ones chicken noodle soup whenever they were ill.

If Ixon made a steady recovery, Giles did not. He was feverish the day after the battle, and his wounds were red and hot. The day after that he was burning up with fever and tell-tale red streaks were visible from three of his wounds. Hypnos told Athan there was little he could do. Amputation was not an option with three such inflamed wounds, the shock alone would probably kill him. All they could do was try to keep him quiet and hope he could overcome the infection. Two other men in the baths also had badly inflamed wounds, and Hypnos was equally discouraged about their prospects.

Athan spent a lot of time sitting with Giles beside his sickbed. Even though his shield bearer slept most of the time and was often not lucid when he was awake, Athan felt compelled to remain by his side. On the morning of the third day, the first of the three men who had become infected died; the other had lapsed into a coma. Athan prepared himself for the inevitable.

He was staring at nothing when he heard a weak voice call him. "Sire."

Athan saw that Giles was awake and giving him a weak smile.

"Hello, brother," said Athan, his eyes welling up as he looked into the pale and drawn face of the young man who had followed him with such single-minded devotion. "Would you like some water?"

"I'll get it, sire," Giles replied automatically, trying to rise.

"Not this time," said Athan smiling into the young man's face. "It is my turn." He gave the man a drink from the cup he had waiting by the couch. Giles drank it eagerly, some slopping down either side of his mouth.

"That was good," he said as his head fell back weakly to the cushions. Then, "I am so cold."

Athan looked at the man's flushed face; he could feel the heat coming from him. But he only smiled again and pulled up another blanket. Raising his voice he called for Hypnos.

It was Iason who came over. "Hypnos is sleeping. I see our patient is awake." There was a false hearty tone that made Athan want to strike this man who was once his band's healer.

"Get him up," Athan told Iason gruffly, "I want Hypnos here now!"

The hoplite/healer hurried away. Athan did not even notice Iason was limping from his own wound he received in the fighting.

"Am I dying?" asked Giles.

Athan had never lied to Giles and did not exactly start now. "I don't know. You are very sick, but Hypnos says you are young and strong. You should think about getting better. Your wounds are not so bad. You are just sick."

Giles said nothing for a time then asked for more water. After he had sipped a little he asked Athan another question. "Do you love me, lord?"

"You know that I do."

That seemed to satisfy Giles for a moment. Then he raised his head up slightly and asked, "Was I a good shield bearer?"

"Oh, yes, the best I ever had," replied Athan at once.

There was a brief pause and then Giles looked at Athan with a question, "Did you have a shield bearer before me?"

Athan was nonplussed for a moment before admitting, "No, you were the first."

Giles smiled faintly and said, "So I was the only one."

"Umm, yes," said Athan cursing himself inwardly for his clumsy responses.

Giles smiled again and made a sound that might have been a chuckle. "That was a good joke." There was a pause before he spoke again. "I am going to sleep for a time. Will you wait here for me?"

"You know I will."

"Good," said Giles faintly and he drifted off just before Hypnos hustled up.

There was nothing anyone could do. Later in the afternoon he became delirious, thrashing around and shouting. Just before dusk his uneasy sleep became a coma. He died shortly thereafter, just as the first stars were coming out.

The final three casualties of the battle, all of whom died of their wounds within hours of one another, were given a fine Prothesis in the courtyard. The bodies were properly prepared and covered in their gray cloaks. The Ekphora was not professional but was heartfelt. Although Giles had not been popular with the men, he was considered too much of Athan's creature for that, out of respect for Athan the entire garrison turned out. The three men were buried side by side. All the spare wood had been consumed, and Athan was sick of the smells of funeral pyres. There was no funeral feast nor were there funeral games. Too many had died in the past six days. Athan did put up a fine stone stele. It read, "Giles, First Shield Bearer of Athan the King."

Neither Needles nor Amphora heard the sounds of the battle at the Hold, but the morning after the fight the men could tell something had happened in the night. Most obvious were the remains of the siege house still leaning against the front gate. The two men watched from just below the crest of the hill, lying down side by side with just their heads up trying to decide what had happened. It did not take long to see that the Hold had not fallen. Soon they could see bodies being dragged out and flung into a pile outside the Hold while the siege house as dismantled. By peeking up a little higher, they could look into town and see a defeated force milling about. The sounds of disputation and screams of wounded men reached them. They eased back down over the hill and brought the good news back to their women. They had little food left and all that day they waited somewhat anxiously for something to happen. When the next morning dawned, all four went to the top of the hill only to be disappointed at the lack of any obvious activity. It was an overcast day, and so they all remained up there together lying side by side at the top of the hill, first watching bands of the raiders begin leaving, then with growing excitement, the progress of King Athan's men as they marched out of the Hold, down the hill, and into the town, ridding it of the invaders.

The sun was trending well down in the west before Adem decided that it was safe enough to return home. They expected to find their residences looted and befouled, and they were; on the positive side, Adem had successfully hidden some of his better stock of wine, and Neeta's loom had not been wrecked beyond repair. They were alive, their homes had not been burned, and they could recover.

"I hear the New King is going to give us some money to help us rebuild," Needles told his wife the next night.

"Do you think so?" asked his wife, as she continued trying to put her house to rights again.

"No, not really," replied her husband, "but it is a nice rumor. I think things are going to be better from now on. Yes, I think I am going to like this New King."

Needles was correct about the New King not giving money to the people of Dassaria to rebuild, although he did provide tax relief, reducing the required tax by half to help them rebuild. His other two predictions turned out to be accurate, as well.

The Old King was frantic with hunger, probably even hungrier than the wolves in the pack that stood looking at him. He was not about to give up this gift that possibly represented his only chance to regain enough strength to walk out of here. On the other hand, he was not about to try to fight what were now six very hungry-looking wolves. With a sudden decision he turned and brought his kopis up and down on the haunch of the doe. The heavy blade cut deeply but he lacked the strength to cut through the hip joint with a single blow. Again he cut, aiming more carefully this time, still he missed. Glancing at the wolves that were slowly advancing one careful step at a time, heads down, eyes intent on him, he turned and hacked down again trying not to look desperate for he knew that would only incite the animals to attack. This time the joint parted. He pulled at the leg; it was still attached by hide and some bits of muscle.

"I get this much," he told the wolves who stopped at the sound of his voice, "you get the rest, but this much is mine." His voice sounded strange to him. The Old King was not in the habit of talking to himself, and so his vocal cords gave a rusty croak rather than a normal human voice. He sawed away at the last bits until his haunch came free. "HAH!" he cried turning suddenly back to the wolves. They stared back from him. Looking right into their eyes, holding them, he bent down, picked up his stick and slung the stiff leg over his shoulder. Holding his kopis and stick in the same hand, he stumbled and almost fell. The wolves were now very close in a loose semi circle around him. The old man had a sudden certainty that had he fallen just then the wolves would have been all over him.

"I have no intention of ending up as wolf shit," he informed the pack regally, holding himself as straight as he could. Then he moved up the hill away from the wolves and their meal, walking carefully, using the staff. He gave the pack every indication that he was still healthy and a dangerous foe.

"Go on," he said the closest wolves. "That is your share. No danger of it fighting back; take the easy meat." He took two more sideways steps, as first one then all the wolves moved in and began to feed. He walked across the little valley toward his stream before he stopped to sheath his kopis and get a better grip on his soon to be dinner. Back behind him were sounds of growling and bones snapping as the pack devoured the carcass.

"Better her than me," he said to no one in particular as he continued his departure.

Chapter Ten – A Time to Build

The remainder of the first year of Athan's reign seemed to go by in a blur. Once the Hold had withstood the attack of the raiders, things began to settle back down and life resumed. Plowing and planting continued. Shepherds tended their flocks. Tradesmen made their products. Merchants bought, sold and traded goods. Women raised families. Guards kept the peace. The Magistrate administered justice. The King ruled.

Athan lost himself in the business of his new kingdom. Even though he continued to assign others the routine recurring day-to-day work, his workload remained heavy. Things were more difficult without Giles there to help him. Even though the other hoplites had not particularly liked Giles, they began to appreciate how helpful it had been to have someone acting as an intermediary. Now the King was prone to show up almost anywhere, wandering around the Hold instead of waiting in his offices like a good monarch should. The people of the Hold were still not quite sure how to treat him, especially when he might just be on some routine errand such as having his clothes cleaned or getting a bite to eat. Both Celeno and Prokopios tried assigning servants to tend to his needs, but they did not seem to work out. Athan looked over the young men in the garrison for a replacement shield bearer. Tenucer was one possible candidate; however, he had his own section now and was happily setting in as a leader of his men. Besides, he had known Athan too long to be his shield bearer.

Privately, Athan also missed Delbine. He engaged other women, but he needed more than sex from them. Being with these women left him unsatisfied; he felt as if he were drowning and dying of thirst at the same time.

Once his broken arm healed (leaving him a small bump he would carry for the rest of his life) he took to leading men out after the scattered bands of bandits. These patrols were bigger than normal, because there were still many large bands of brigands. Leading out so many men on patrols had an unintended result. Athan became the defacto trainer of the troopers that would roam these hills for decades to come. Young men learned the basics of how to move in the hills, how to live, how to signal, how to locate bandits, how to trap them, how to fight them and how to kill them. Even more importantly they learned how their King expected them to relate to the people who lived in the hills of Dassaria. They were taught it was not acceptable to take food from locals without payment. That they should be careful not to scatter their flocks or ride over the melon fields. Soldiers were taught to be polite to the men folk when they visited a hamlet or farmstead and to leave the women alone. In fact, the troops were strictly enjoined against any relations with women at all while on patrol.

"Lovin' is for when you are back home," the sergeants would tell the men. "Patrolling is serious business, and we expect you to keep your mind on your business when we are outside the walls."

A normal patrol in that time consisted of Athan leading two or even three rides of about seven men each, with each ride led by either a sergeant or a chosen man, the rough equivalent of a corporal. The fifteen to twenty men were mounted on the region's small horses or ponies with a few additional pack animals. At first the patrols were more in the nature of explorations than anything else. Not only did the men need to learn the lay of the land, they also needed to find out about the people who lived on the land. The borders of Athan's kingdom were more than merely hazy. People define the need for borders and since the area was so thinly populated, there were large sections of land, especially undesirable land, which no one claimed. There were people out there; families and extended families, sometimes living together or near one another, often bound by tribal loyalties. Though they had a strong independent streak, many years of living with the Bear's men had taught them to treat mounted warriors with at least an outward show of respect.

The soldiers who were not from the region, and initially most were not, found the locals to be figures of fun. Some lived against hills so steep that one level of a house would be entered from the ground on one side and the upper level from the ground on the other side. In some of these steeply sloped farmsteads, the people had their barns literally below their living spaces or, in a few cases, vise versa. The men wondered why anyone would live under a stable, but it seemed to work for the people who lived there.

Many new kings would have felt insecure about being away from the center of their power, their primary fortresses, so soon after establishing control. This was not the case with the New King. Athan knew and trusted the men he had left in charge of the Hold in his absence. Further, the responsibilities were spread among several different men so no one man was totally in charge of everything in Athan's absences. Though he was often gone from the Hold, he was never gone for long — only a few days at a time. Most importantly, he had the unstinting respect of all the fighting men in his little kingdom. He had fought on the top of the east wall during the attack in full view of most the garrison. Men will follow a successful leader, especially a leader they respect as a great warrior. After the battle against the raiders, Athan was held in near veneration by his men. His prestige with the soldiers that summer was such that no one even considered challenging his rule. So there was peace and prosperity both within the Hold and throughout the little kingdom of Dassaria as a whole.

Athan's absences had another unintended consequence; the people he left behind began running things on their own. Decisions were made without having to consult the King because he was out on a patrol. He always reviewed major decisions, such as the award of a large contract, or a restructuring of the sleeping arrangements to better align the quarters with the sections, but even when he overruled or modified those decisions, there were no recriminations. After a while, his people began to anticipate what he wanted, and he began to accept their way of getting things done.

His people understood their areas of responsibilities. Cook bought, prepared, and served the food in the Hold. Abacus managed the money and paid the bills. Yure trained the soldiers, especially the new recruits. Prokopios was the Provost Marshall of the Hold. He was involved with setting watches and managing the everyday issues within the Hold including housing, cleaning, and duty assignments. More and more often the old sergeant worked with Celeno, though it often seemed to be a contentious relationship. People who did not know them would assume from their bickering that they were an old married couple which was not true. Prokopios remained able to deflect the old woman's charms, or perhaps she did not feel it was fair to use magic to capture one's own husband. Ixon was Master of the Horse, which included those stabled in the Hold and in town. Rodas was Magistrate. He acted as a justice of the peace, squire, mayor, and judge.

Acting as a magistrate was a lucrative position, and Rodas prospered. Bribes did not change his position on any issue brought to him for judgment, on the other hand, if he ruled in your favor, he was not averse to accepting a gift. These gifts were in addition, of course, to any fees or fines that he also might impose. This was the accepted way justice was administered in that time and place, and his constituents considered him to be fair, generally accepting his verdicts, and that was what really mattered.

As was common in that time and place, people would bring appeals directly to the King on many issues both great and small. Athan always tried to delegate these petitions to the applicable member of his defacto staff. Soon everyone came to understand the system – if you did not get want you wanted from the person in charge you could appeal to the King and try to get the decision overruled. At first Athan was nearly overwhelmed by the constant flow of petitioners. He learned that overturning decisions undermined the authority of his people and dramatically increased the number of people coming to him. Even confirming the decisions of his subordinates ate into his time. So he began taking measures to discourage those who were simply trying to get around the procedures in place. If Athan did not think the appeal was justified, he would scold the petitioner. He was surprised how often that worked. In other cases, where the petition was too obviously self-serving or unsubstantiated, he might impose a fine. He desperately needed a man to filter these petitioners; yet no one in his service quite met his needs as Giles had. So he continued to spend days listening to complaints about the Magistrates ruling about spoiled wine, complaints about housing, pleas for tax relief, requests to allow a son who had been conscripted to return home, and attempts to renegotiate contracted agreements for building and repairs.

There was a lot of building in this time. The three watchtowers— North Watch, Watch Hill and South Watch—were completed that summer. They were simple one-room stone structures with tarpaulin-covered platforms over the roof so that men could stand watch on the roof and signal from a height with a secure place to spend the night below.

The rear gate to the Hold had an addition as well. A latticed stone enclosure now stretched from the back gate about seven cubits into the courtyard. Any invaders that got past the repaired and strengthened back gate would have to move down this little tunnel exposed by the gaps in the masonry to arrows or spear thrusts from both sides. A second door was installed at entrance to the courtyard. Though this second internal door was usually left open, it could be closed and securely barred at need. Other less dramatic modifications were also made that generally strengthened the defenses of an already strong fortress.

Athan had always considered himself to be a fortunate man, and he and his kingdom were certainly fortunate that first year. The rains came on time and in good measure. The flocks increased, and the harvest was bountiful. Even his patrols were lucky. They scoured the hills of brigands without loosing a single fight.

The fact that they never engaged in a fight when they did not have a decisive advantage was not luck. Athan knew his trade from both sides of the fold, as shepherds put it. Despite the fact there were frequent armed encounters on the patrols, he only had three men die in all that year. One was killed by a javelin in a pitched exchange, one was killed by his own horse when he managed to fall off and then get kicked in the head as his horse rolled around on the ground. The third was murdered one hot night on the edges of what Athan thought might be the borders of his kingdom. The man, actually a teenager, disappeared one night from the camp. His naked body was found some distance away the next morning. The boy's head had been bashed in. Why he left, or more probably was lured, from camp was never known; everyone suspected he had gone out to meet a girl. His fate was held up as an example of the dangers of chasing women while on patrol. 'Some people's lives serve only as a bad example for others,' thought Athan sadly. The aggressive patrols had a positive effect, his men killed dozens of bandits and scattered more, and the roads and hills became safer for travelers than they had been in many years.

Dassaria was not an unpleasant place to live in the warm weather. Summers were warm if not to say hot. Most of the people slept on rooftops under awnings to take advantage of the cooler breezes. In the Hold, almost everyone lived on top of the walls under a variety of cloth awnings. People rose as soon as it was light and did as much of the hard physical labor as possible before the heat of the day. After the afternoon meal (for those who could afford to eat one) everyone who could do so tended to take a siesta. If they did not actually sleep, they would take their ease for a couple of hours, resting out of the sun during the worst of the heat, becoming active again as the shadows lengthened. The scarcity and expense of lamps and candles meant that many people (especially those who could not afford candles) retired relatively soon after full dark.

Athan spent most of that first long summer outside the Hold. Perhaps it was because the structure was so warm and the walls were so crowded in the evening with people trying to escape the heat. Perhaps it was because the work he did when he was back home was so onerous, especially with almost daily discussions, that is to say disagreements, with Abacus. Perhaps Athan was out and about because he wanted to come to know his territory. Some thought he loved the idea of driving the bandits out his country. The real reason was one that Athan kept secret inside himself. He did not know exactly what a king was supposed to do. His past had not prepared him for such an extravagant position. He had grown up in the city state of Epiria which had no king, and he had not even had much contact with the oligarchs of the city when he was a guardsman. So, not being sure of what else to do, he fell back into old habits, mixing his experiences as a city guardsman and a hill bandit, roving the hills with a band of mounted warriors, trading the important and sedentary work of a king for the active and straightforward demands of the leader of a band of men out in the hills. Athan was aware of his utter lack of qualifications as the ruler of a kingdom, no matter how small. He was not completely at peace, even when he was out with his patrols, because he also knew there were more important things he should be doing back at the Hold. These conflicting realizations kept him uneasy all that first summer.

He was not the only one who was adapting to a new set of roles. Sergeant Linus had fully recovered from the amputation of his ruined left hand. At first he had been depressed at the loss, staring at the stump at the end of his wrist. Then his strong personality began to express itself. Linus came to understand his days as a warrior were not yet over. Athan paid for a shield specially made to accommodate his missing left hand. It had a normal strap near the center of the shield but instead of the usual grip near the edge, a long leather cup was attached to the shield. A buckle and straps were also attached to leather cup so that Linus could shove the stump of his left hand into the cup and buckle his arm firmly to the shield. The shield was of the same heavy construction as a regular phalangist hoplon even to the bronze strap around the outside rim but was smaller and oval in shape. With practice Linus was able to wield his custom-made shield with confidence, using it for both defense and offense. He would never stand in a shield wall again or be able to fight from horseback. On the other hand (so to speak) with his ax and new shield, he was a fearsome individual warrior.

Even though everything was different in the first year of the New King, somehow all the necessary tasks were accomplished and with autumn came the harvest. Shepherds brought their flocks to market; orchards yielded their fruit; and farmers brought in their crops. Athan harvested, too. Autumn was the time for taxes. Despite, or perhaps because of, Abacus' concerns about the state of finances, the treasury remained at a satisfying level, even with reduced taxes for those in town who had lost their houses in the 'Bandits' Raid' as it was being called.

Athan's advisors strongly recommended that he tax his all subjects at least to some degree. And so it was done.

In that time and place the job of tax collector was often sold to one or more contractors who were tasked to deliver a certain amount of money back to the state; anything else collected above that amount went to the tax collector. That first year, however, Athan and his advisors took care of collecting revenues from their subjects themselves. Following the harvest, strongly armed groups of men were sent out, never less than a half dozen men, to bring in the taxes.

In addition to the hoplites who provided security (and muscle), two or more men would visit each household or homestead to assess the tax owed. At first Abacus would always be one of the men. Abacus had recruited several men who claimed to be former tax collectors to accompany him on these visits. After a time, he selected two of these men as his regular tax collection assistants, chosen because of their keen eye and experience in smoking out hidden wealth and other schemes to reduce the tax burden, and their relative honesty. No one in that time and place expected tax collectors to be completely honest, but these two did not extort outrageously, or demand sex from the women of the house. They took the little gifts offered them quietly but did their best to accurately assess how much a household could afford to pay. These two men became well known in the community. One was commonly called Crow, perhaps for his prominent nose, lanky black hair, and dark complexion, but most likely because of his sharp black eyes and his way of turning his head alertly back and forth like an inquisitive bird. The other was from Thrace, a solid man with little hair and a ragged beard who answered to the name of Polynices.

In those early years, there was considerable disputation about the expected levels of taxation. The tax collectors usually had a very canny idea of how much a taxpayer expected to pay and could actually afford to pay. They usually tried to set the expected sum somewhere in the middle of those two marks. This was done after a formal examination of the property. The inspection was a bit of a farce since the property owners would do everything in their power to show a poor face to the examiners, hiding wealth and disguising prosperity. This was expected, the entire process was very similar to any negotiation in the marketplace. Crow and Polynices actually seemed to enjoy the game. After the examination, they would confer together and announce the expected tax to the waiting property owners who would then wail, or curse, or plead depending on their personality and mood of the moment. Then arrangements were agreed upon for how the tax would be paid, often in goods such as food, merchandise, or animals. Sometimes arrangements would be made for delivery of the required payment at a later date.

It was unusually easy to collect the tax that first year because, after the tax collectors announced the expected amount of tax to be paid, Abacus got to play an unexpectedly charitable role. He would hear the assessment from Polynices and Crow and then pronounce that King Athan had decreed the tax should only be half that amount that year. In some cases where there had been severe losses in the raid, such as a burned house or smashed pottery wheels and looms, the tax was forgiven altogether. This left the residents of Dassaria with mixed feelings; no one likes to have to pay any taxes but to have the taxes reduced to all-time lows was a relief. There was still muttering about the tax collectors; this was more out of habit and ingrained suspicion than anything else.

With the good harvests and low taxes, no one in Athan's little kingdom was actually afraid they would starve to death that winter. This was a big improvement; some young children and older people in that region died of malnutrition almost every winter. This year, however, people had food stored away and some even had a bit of hard money remaining to them. It had been a good and prosperous year.

The prosperity brought another benefit to Athan's subjects: for the first time since anyone could remember, a fair was to be held in Dassaria. There had been market days in the past, of course, but when your produce can be seized at the whim of armed men, it makes the entire proposition too chancy for many people to attend. Whatever goods that had been offered in past market days had been expensive and of poor quality. Food and goods had been traded out of sight, privately, and with those you trusted. There was some of that feeling still in the air, but as smaller markets were successfully held without disruptions, more and more of the local farmers began to bring their goods into Dassaria.

The idea of a fair slowly grew in the minds of the people as the summer progressed. A fair in that time and place was essentially a market day. Farmers would bring in more of their crops, more animals would be available for sale or trade, wines would be for sale, more products such as cloth, finished clothing, pottery, wood carvings, and other trade goods would be offered. No one was exactly sure who finally decided to have a fair. It certainly wasn't the King. Nor did anyone ever come forward that first year claiming they were the first one to propose the idea. In later years, yes, but that first year the notion of holding a fair just sort of became generally accepted. The timing for major events was usually set to the phases of the moon; somehow, everyone just decided that Dassaria's fair was to be held on the day after the full harvest moon. In small rural communities like Dassaria, news of a big fair spread far and wide.

Rodas found himself to be in charge of coordinating the arrangements for the fair. He had help with this, of course: in addition to Stamitos and his new wife Alesin, Spiros came to live with him as well. Spiros had lost his eye to a sword stroke in the fight with the raiders, and the wound was painful and slow to heal. When it did, his appearance was considerably altered and not for the better. Spiros left Athan's guard though Athan continued to pay him his salary until his wound had healed. The former soldier did not feel he could fulfill his duties with only one eye, and he knew his ruined visage made some of the men uneasy. He feared they mocked him behind his back. So when offered a chance to assist with the Magistrate, he moved into the house of justice helping Stamitos and generally making himself useful.

It was Yure the elder who unexpectedly provided the best advice about how to make the arrangements required for a successful fair. The old sergeant had rural antecedents, as might be expected from his name which meant 'Farmer'. It turned out that Yure's father had assisted in putting on the same type of country fairs that was envisioned for Dassaria. There really wasn't much to it; all that was needed was recognition that there would be extra people in town, which meant a greater need for pasturage and places for people to stay. People did not expect much in the way of support since they were used to taking care of themselves. Expenses would be minimal. The King just needed to make sure that all his men were available to provide security, both from external threats and from the people attending the fair.

That first fair, though a small thing, was an undoubted success. There were enough strangers in town to provide a welcome influx of cash, and there were few actual fights. Though no one actually died as a result of the many contentions, Rodas had to work late into the night trying to adjudicate the many arguments and disagreements that arose from strangers doing business with each other for the first time. Aside from the concept that there would be a future annual harvest fair in Dassaria, two innovations sprang from that first fair; there would be a board of judges to handle disputes involving products and sales at the fair, and the King would judge the best products and award prizes.

The idea of a board of judges came some time after the fair ended. Rodas swore he would never again be put in a situation where he had to adjudicate the inevitable disputes that arose such as deciding if a basket of millet was mealy or not, or if the kid delivered was indeed the one promised at the original sale, or if scales were measuring fairly. In the future, a small group of elders would be empanelled to resolve these sorts of petty disagreements /misunderstandings/ frauds. The system was not original, but it worked well.

The other innovation was a product of sheer ennui on the part of Athan. Late one morning he decided to follow Cook down to the fair to observe purchases for the Hold's kitchen. Athan was looking very impressive that day, a proper King. A boy of about 15 had been engaged to help him. Athan did not care for the lad and refused to learn his name, calling him only 'Boy'. The youngster did know how to dress a gentleman to best effect. King Athan, wearing his diadem, clad in a fine tunic, his kopis on his hip, and Bear's Claw strapped to his right leg, looked like a monarch was expected to look. The royal party effortlessly parted the crowd. Rodas and Yure accompanied the King for companionship, Cook moved just ahead of them providing professional comments on the food over his shoulder and two bodyguards, or comrades, or attendants, (depending on how you viewed such things) brought up the rear.

Athan was there to watch Cook buy food; that was all. But Athan's old military leadership came into play. When a commander inspects his troops, he engages the men as he passes through the ranks. He found himself stopping and inquiring at each of the booths that offered food grown in his kingdom. Even Cook, normally so forceful and domineering, waited patiently as his new king spoke to the farmers in their booths. It was quite natural that they would proudly display the products of their fields, even offering Athan a sample of their fruits and vegetables. He would comment conversationally to Cook and the others about the quality of the produce. Boy, who could read and write, started taking notes. Farmers noticed this. As he moved around visiting the stalls set up outside the little town square of Dassaria, a ripple began to form just ahead of him. Farmers and their wives began to frantically titivate their stalls and rearrange their wares to the best advantage. Those selling other merchandise did likewise in hope of a similar review, just for the prestige of the thing, even though Athan was only looking at the comestibles.

Eventually Athan noticed the bustle of activity that was moving ahead of him. Again his military background guided him; this was turning into an inspection. His first impulse was to call a halt to the farce that he had inadvertently started. Then before he could act on that impulse, he reconsidered. It was not such a bad thing for these people to be displaying their goods for him. So he continued, becoming even more formal as he stopped at every stall that offered produce, spoke with the vendors, and examined the fruits of their labor. He dictated comments to Boy who was now openly taking assiduous notes.

When he had completed his little inspection of the foods being offered he withdrew a little way from the square.

"Well," he said to Cook, Yure, and Rodas, "what do you think? Who had the best crops this year?" The three men looked at him, then at each other, then at the Boy with his notes; then all five looked back at the square where seemingly every single face was turned to watch them.

"This is going to take some time. I think we need to sit down in a house where we can review what we saw," suggested Rodas.

It took them over an hour. When they came out and approached the booths again not only did everyone stop to watch them, everyone stopped talking as well. An expectant silence descended upon the fair. No one was really certain just what would happen next. What had this new king been doing? Would he seize their goods? Would there be an award of some kind?

Rodas, who had a certain flair for the dramatic stepped up and made the declaration they had all been waiting for.

"His majesty, King Athan, has decreed that Jorgr, the farmer, has the finest produce booth at this fair!" There was a buzz of conversation with smiles from the booth of Jorgr and scowls from the others. Rodas then added sugar for Jorgr and salt to the wounds of his competitors; he was awarded a prize equal to a month's pay for a soldier. There were some mixed cheers. Then Rodas surprised them. "Furthermore," he continued, "we award the prize for the best fruit offered to the Widow Myra and her sons for their apples!" This prize was a fourth part of a soldier's monthly salary. Not a lot of money; still it was a nice little bonus. An award was also made for the best vegetables, specifically for some large, full artichokes. Three prizes had been given out. It took a while to make everyone understand that one prize was for vegetables, one for fruits and Jorgr's prize was for the best overall offerings including the presentation of his booth. There continued to be a buzz among the people who were selling things.

"What about my sheep?" asked a man loudly. "I have the finest flock in all Dassaria. Come and judge our flock and you will see!"

"And my wine!" called another. "You must judge the wines! Try mine, it is the best."

At that moment Athan realized he just might have started something a bit larger than what he had intended. In fact, he had no idea of what he had done and how it would grow. Athan merely thought that at least he should judge the animals. After all, shepherding was a major source of income to his little kingdom. Unlike looking at fruits and vegetables, everybody could recognize a good-looking animal. Little did he know how little he **did** know.

After some internal debate, the rules were established. The King and his three companions would look at one animal, and only one animal, from each flock. They would decide the best lamb and best kid and award a prize of half a month's salary to the winner. The contest would begin immediately. The four men did not realize how quickly the gamesmanship, chicanery, and outright cheating would begin. What they thought would take an hour or so took the rest of the day. The two winners were proudly acclaimed, and the losers grumbled about the unfairness of it all. With all the arguments and disputation, Athan worried that he might have caused more dissention than goodwill with his simple gesture.

He did create a considerable controversy; what he did not really understand was that the people (though some would not admit it) loved the whole thing. The judgments were a source of discussion, disagreements, and wonderful arguments for the rest of the year. People who worked incredibly hard to generate just enough to live on were absolutely thrilled to receive any form of recognition. The money was more than welcome, but in truth, the knowledge that their work was considered the best, was publicly acknowledged as the best, in front of all their friends (and enemies) and neighbors by the King himself, well, that was the sweetest thing of all. By the end of the fair, it was obvious there would have to be a judging at next year's fair since it was also obvious there would be another fair next autumn.

Rodas, always one to pick up on a good thing, graciously offered to judge the various offering of wines that very first year. This important task was limited to just him and the King. They had a fine time sampling the various vintages. There were dry white Zitsas and semisweet Debinas. Sometimes these were blended with the red Bekari and Vlachiko varietals to create an interesting rose wine. There were Xynomavro reds that Athan found very smooth with a fine nose. Some of the more robust reds had been aged in oak casks producing a harsh wine with a strong tannic flavor. Rodas seemed to favor this style; Athan could scarcely drink them. In the end they compromised on a Xynomavro that had been brought in from Illyria, in part because the two men wanted to encourage trade. They awarded the merchant a half month's pay.

Of course this, too, generated controversy. Local vintners and wine merchants, such as Amphora, complained bitterly. In fact the whole fair seemed to Athan to have ended in bickering and disputation. The days following the fair, he swore he would never allow such a ridiculous contest again. But long before the next fair, people began asking about the rules for the judging, making elaborate preparations for the competition and jawing with one another about who had the best new lambs, the finest olives, the most desirable wines, best melons, largest cucumbers, and so on. In the end the King felt compelled to continue the competition. Thus, in a very small way in an obscure corner of the world, an annual competition sprang up and thrived. It was not exactly the Olympic Games, but to the shepherds, vintners, and farmers in the little kingdom of Dassaria, the Autumn Fair became the event of the year. Eventually judging was expanded to include baked goods, indigenous pottery, locally woven cloth, wood carving and a wider diversion of the produce and other growing things. Raising food became more than just a way to make a living; it had become a competition with your neighbors. To some it seemed this competition become much more important than merely surviving.

The winter following the first Autumn Fair was unusual in Dassaria; very few people died, and no one died of hunger at all. When the spring came, Athan resumed his aggressive patrolling to discourage any bandits from doing their business in his kingdom. In addition to the three permanent lookouts which were called South Watch, Watch Hill, and North Watch, the King established three more signal towers. These new towers were initially constructed of timber, not stone, and were not manned in the winter. They were placed with clear sight lines to one of the three permanent towers and where they could also see down the roads that led into the kingdom from the south, west, and north. The watchers on these new wooden towers: Plum Hill to the south, West Road, and Rocky Knob to the north, could see anyone approaching town long before they reached Dassaria. Now the Hold and town would have many hours before any large group of enemies could reach them. Patrols that ranged farther out and in between the main three arteries could also signal up to any of the six towers and expect that their message would be received by the Hold within a fraction of an hour. Never again would the people of Dassaria be surprised by raiders.

There continued to be resistance to the forced conscription of young men. To ease the complaints, the press gangs waited to bring in the young men until after the spring planting was done. The families were assured the men would be released to help gather the harvest. Since the young men in question were actually being paid (though a pittance, they were paid monthly just as the regular men were) the conscription did not engender any serious armed resistance. Some of the boys did try to run away after being taken in and were flogged as a consequence, though this was uncommon. Yure seemed to know how to take young men and make them part of a larger group. His training did not emphasize individual fighting skills; instead he taught the men how to fight as a team. By midsummer he would take his recruits out and march them on patrols in the surrounding hills. At first he had scarcely a dozen young men supplemented by five or six regulars, but as time went by and the population of the little kingdom increased the numbers began to grow. Since they were patrolling on foot the new recruits seldom were able to find any bandits. Still, it was exciting for the youngsters to be out, armed and protecting their homelands with other young comrades. On the first full moon after midsummer, Yure and Athan would hold a full set of maneuvers with all the kingdom's soldiers save for a small watch who remain to garrison the Hold. The little Dassarian army would spend three days and two nights on these maneuvers. During the day they would march, form battle lines, advance, change formations, and practice assaulting pretend enemies. At night they would camp together in comfortable male companionship.

As the seasons passed, the members of Athan's little band who had conquered the Hold settled in as rulers of Dassaria. It was a time of relative peace and prosperity, that is, there were no more actual invasions, and there was almost enough for everyone to eat. The people of the Hold settled into their roles comfortably. That is, everyone except Athan. He spent less time out patrolling and moved into his apartments. He went through a series of shield bearers during this time. Some, like Boy, were good at handling writing and lists, but lacked the presence to keep unwanted visitors from interrupting him, and were too weak to act as a shield bearer in war. Others could act as effective secretaries, but could not keep up with Athan's active physical schedule; they were unable to ride or were worthless in the field. Still others where reliable warriors but could not manage the administrative requirements being functionally illiterate. There were some who met all the requirements that Athan simply disliked. Eventually it took no less than three men to fill the job that Giles left: Balasi, Amycus, and Nomiki. Balasi was a young man from Lychnites who acted as the King's secretary and scribe. When not needed by the King, he assisted Abacus. Amycus acted as Athan's personal assistant and valet, sleeping in the reception room where Giles had slept, taking care of the King's personal needs such as dressing the King, taking care of laundry and announcing the King's appointments as well as keeping out those who would intrude on the king's privacy. Though he was not yet thirty, he had the appearance of an older man, with a bit of a paunch and a high forehead. He claimed to have been an oligarch's personal servant; Athan suspected he was a runaway slave from the south. He was faithful and diligent, and he did not remind Athan of Giles, and so was tolerated. Nomiki became the new official shield bearer. He had joined the band just before the theft of the Satrap's gold, had participated in the mad dash away from the Achaemendian cavalry, shared the wild times in Pella, and fought beside Athan when they had taken the Hold. He was not particularly bright nor was he well-educated, but he was brave, a good fighting man, and utterly loyal. He came to serve as Athan's shield bearer and personal body guard. After a time he began to accompany Athan anytime he left the Hold. Nomiki knew he would never become a sergeant and so was more than content to attach himself to Athan. In time the arrangement became permanent. He never failed to give Athan faithful service. None of them did. But none of them were Giles, either.

Without the help of his walking stick, the Old King doubted if he could have made the climb up the slope to his little crevice. In the end he was forced to put the deer haunch down and drag it the final few feet. As soon as he was inside the niche, he took his now dried and bedraggled pine tree and blocked the entrance behind him. It would at the very least let him know if any scavengers had followed him. Dropping the deer's leg, he unfastened his sword belt letting it fall to the earth and moved to the fire which was burning low. It only took him a few moments to get a strong flame going again. Pouring some water from his bag into his cup, he set it over the fire on the two rocks he kept positioned there just for that purpose.

"No tea today," he exalted aloud, "Stew!" The old man realized that not talking aloud had been a mistake. Now that he had a real chance to get out of this predicament alive, he needed to start preparing himself to meet other people.

With the water set to boil, he dragged the haunch up to the fire. Using his dagger he first cut the skin away from a portion near the joint, revealing the meat. He had to work to cut off a thin strip. He had let his weapons lose their edge; he had been lazy, that was inexcusable. Taking the first bit of meat, cold to the touch, he spitted it on a sliver of wood that had been waiting to become kindling. A spit was a much more noble fate for the wood then mere kindling. The old man put the meat over the flames and braced one end with a stone. Then he cut another piece. It took a bit longer to find a proper spit of wood among the kindling for this one. As he put it over the fire, he turned his first piece over. The smell of roasting meat filled the space, and he began to salivate so profusely that he had to swallow repeatedly just to keep the slobber from drooling over his chin. After he set the third piece over the fire, he could no longer restrain himself; he took his first piece of meat and brought it to his mouth. It was tough meat, old and unseasoned, and, of course, it tasted wonderful. He sat there roasting and eating strips of meat for over an hour. After a while he started putting strips of meat into the boiling water in his cup to make a soup. It took all his self-discipline not to overeat. Even so, he consumed almost a third of the haunch in that single sitting.

Finally, he sat back, satiated for the first time in a very long while. He thought back to feasts he had enjoyed. Feasts led his thoughts to interesting dining companions. This led him to think about all the intriguing people he had known as king. Some of them had met him in unusual circumstances. Certainly the man with the half beard had been one. Then there was that girl that nearly drove Rodas crazy. It was strange how they arrived on the very same day. Athan leaned back and smiled, remembering.

Chapter Eleven– Strange Strangers

℘**It was in** the fourth full year of King Athan's reign when two strangers arrived in Dassaria on the same day; strangers who would both become important to Athan and his kingdom in very different ways. They could not have been more different. One was inconspicuous and arrived quietly; the other immediately became the talk of the town.

The obvious stranger would have been noticed for a number of reasons. First, he was an armed hoplite, complete with spear, helmet, and hoplon all loaded on the back of the single donkey he was leading. Second, this warrior, and he was every inch a warrior—tall, lean, and moving confidently—arrived alone. It was a dangerous thing to walk alone through the hills surrounding Dassaria. This man had not only walked alone, he did so out of preference. Apparently he had come up alone all the way from the Peloponnese. His unusual arrival was nothing at all compared to the man's weird appearance. He was handsome enough, but all anyone noticed was his beard. Or rather half his beard, for he wore a full black curly beard on the left side of his face and shaved the right side as cleanly as the New King. It made a distinctly odd impression. The stranger was not exactly unfriendly, but he did not talk much either. He came up the south road in the early afternoon. He had been noticed, and signals about him from the Far South tower had been relayed to South Tower and on to the Hold. A single fighting man on the road was so unusual that a patrol rode out to investigate him. He remained unperturbed when accosted by seven armed men on horseback and responded to their inquiries about his business without hesitation.

He made such an impression that the patrol turned right around and returned to tell the King about the novel warrior who had just arrived in town.

"He says he is considering taking service with the King of Dassaria," reported Sergeant Tenucer who had led the patrol.

"Did he say why?" asked Athan, a bit puzzled.

"He said he heard we were good fighters," responded Tenucer. "And then he told us we were also just beyond the edge of civilization. He said if we were not at the end of the world, we could at least see it from here."

Athan was seated with Amycus and Nomiki in a pavilion pitched on the ridge behind the Hold. Now that summer was beginning, Athan preferred sleeping outside in the cooling breezes to remaining in the stuffy confines of his rooms in the Hold. Others might sleep on the ramparts underneath the awnings that had spread over them; the King did not. Athan had learned a few things about being a monarch in the last four years. One of those things was keeping a distance from his subjects. He still rode on patrol and trained with the garrison, but he now conducted his day-to-day business apart from his subjects. King Athan did expect to be informed of unusual events in Dassaria; this one sounded different from most of the rather dull fare he was usually served. Things had been quiet for the last month or so, and for a wonder he had nothing scheduled for the rest of the afternoon.

"Let's go meet this half-bearded fellow," decided Athan impulsively. Amycus, you stay here. Come on Nomiki, let's go into town."

He headed out of the tent then hesitated and returned long enough to pick up his kopis and sword belt. Nomiki was wearing his short sword but, considering they were going to meet a man described as a warrior, asked if they needed to put on their armor.

"No, it is too hot for that," Athan told him, explaining his weapon. "I just don't want this strange man to think I am some merchant coming to sell him something."

Athan was wearing a tunic, a pilleus against the sun, sandals, and his red leather vest. He really did not expect any trouble; if it came, he had confidence in the powers of that vest. The two men walked through the Hold where Prokopios was drilling the new recruits. Prokopios was now both the Provost and Drilling Sergeant, the title for the man responsible for training the troops, especially the new conscripts. He had assumed the extra duties after Yure had died that winter. Yure had been getting on in years, past forty, and when he caught a winter cold he could not shake it off. Eventually it became pneumonia which did for him what so many enemies had failed to do. Prokopios did not want Yure's old job but he was the most qualified man to train the recruits. There were others who had worked with Yure and knew his methods, but none of them had actually been a guardsman in a city, and none had stood in a real battle line. Further, in Athan's opinion, the candidates still lacked the force of will to effectively manage the recruits. Athan had promised to find a new Drilling Sergeant to relieve Prokopios just as soon as he could. That would not be soon enough for the overworked Provost.

"We are going into town to talk to the new man who just arrived and says he wants to join the guard," Athan told Prokopios casually. The big Provost was watching one of his veterans who was trying to get the new conscripts to move forward together while keeping their hoplons touching.

"No, No, **No**!!!" the frustrated corporal screamed. "You! Farm boy!" this appellation was nowhere near specific enough since most of them **were** farm boys; even so, the offending man seemed to know who he was addressing since he ducked his head in shame. "Yes! You! Why are you sideling right?"

The youngster made an inaudible reply.

"The phalanx always seems to go that way," commented Athan conversationally, "even when they are just learning in the yard. Everybody wants to tuck in next to their neighbor's hoplon."

"Yes, and if you don't try to put a stop to it when they are just learning, when slings and arrows are coming down, the line will move sideways instead of forward," replied Prokopios. "Oh Ares, how I hate this!" he gestured down to the troops who had stumbled into one another, displacing the line. "When are you going to get a replacement for Yure?"

"When I find the right man," Athan responded unconcerned. "If we decide to stay down in town after dark, I will let you know."

"Let the Sergeant of the Guard know where we are," Athan told him and with Nomiki at his side, strode out the open door of the Hold and down the hill to the town.

They found the stranger they were seeking seated at a table under an awning in front of one of the tavern houses in town. His donkey with its burden of warlike tools, a high quality hoplon, helmet, cuirass, and long spear, was tied to a post nearby. The stranger was eating some crumbly white feta cheese and olives rolled into a piece of circular flat bread. A cup was in front of him with a bowl of wine on one side and water on the other. He was wearing sandals and a short sleeveless tunic; there was a straw hat was on the table next to him. The man wore a short sword on his hip in a well-worn scabbard. He looked like a man who was very comfortable bearing arms. The proprietor was watching him anxiously from the doorway.

"May we join you?" asked Athan politely.

The man gestured to the bench on the other side of the table.

Athan and Nomiki sat down on either side of the bench half facing away from each other so that they could quickly get to their feet without entangling themselves. Athan and the stranger studied one another. Athan tried to look beyond the strange appearance of a man who wore a beard on only the left side of his face. The newcomer was no so much dark as deeply tanned. He was taller than most, lean, and very fit. Perhaps there was some fat on him somewhere, but it was not visible. He wore his curly black hair short, just like his strange half beard. His eyes were different as well; instead being a normal black or brown they were a startling blue gray. He had a prominent narrow nose that, with his piercing gaze, brought to mind a bird of prey. There was an intensity to the man that came off him like heat from coals. Yet, he gave no outward indication of hostility. It was more in his posture and the way he held Athan's gaze that made it abundantly clear that this man would make an implacable enemy. Would he also make a good friend?

The stranger spoke first, "My name is Leotychides. I come from Lacedaemonia. I am seeking service with a master of arms somewhere. I am told this place will take men into service."

"What can you do?" asked Athan diffidently.

"I have been taught to fight," he responded mildly. This was a strange answer from this strange man. Most men looking for a place as a soldier would give a bold answer such as 'I am a mighty warrior,' or describe their valor and victories. Some might have even simply said 'I fight'. But this hard case, who had a fine set of weapons of war openly displayed and who had apparently traveled all the way from Lacedaemonia by himself, only said he had been 'taught' to fight. It was inconceivable that he could have come through the hills to the south alone and with valuable weapons displayed and not had to fight off bandits.

"Did you walk all the way here by yourself?" asked Athan curiously.

"A short sea trip across to Aetol on the mainland; then from there I headed north on foot."

"Alone?"

"I had my donkey." Here the man smiled. He had a good smile though the half beard gave it an odd look. "Sometimes I traveled with others."

"Why did you choose to come here?" Athan was frankly curious.

"I just wanted to go north. What I wanted was to go somewhere far away, remote, isolated, to the ends of the world."

"Did you have any trouble on the way?"

"I ran a little short of money at times. Some of the houses where I spent the night had fleas." The man smiled again. Athan waited for him to continue. "What you mean is how did I escape being robbed on the road, right?"

Athan nodded.

"Mostly I paid attention. If you keep your eyes open, you can avoid bad situations. Sometimes I traveled by night and laid up in quiet places by day. When I slept the donkey was there. She woke me up twice when men tried to creep up on me while I was sleeping. I traveled with others sometimes when we were traveling the same way." The man stopped talking. Athan waited; after a time Leotychides told him what he wanted to hear. "I was attacked three times. Once I was with others. We stood them off with no trouble. Once a band of a dozen or so charged me before I knew they were there."

"A dozen," interjected Nomiki, "what did you do?"

Leotychides smiled again. "I ran."

"Why didn't they take your donkey and goods?" asked the young shield bearer.

"Oh, they did. I followed them back to their camp and took it all back that night."

"Didn't they have sentries?'

The man shrugged. This could have meant he walked past a sleeping guard, or slipped past alert one, or that he killed several sentinels quietly; his manner only indicated they were no problem.

"And the third time?" ask Nomiki.

Nomiki was normally somewhat shy and would not talk like this to a stranger, especially one so strange, and most especially with his King right next to him. But even Athan could feel the pull of the stranger. He had a way about him that was not the typical boastful, self-aggrandizing bluster of a fighter. The man carried it off, in part because of his pure charisma. Athan recognized a leader of men when he saw one. The man was already working his magic on Nomiki.

The half-bearded man made a self-deprecating gesture. "I was alone, but there were only three. I do not think they were real bandits; they were just desperate men."

His two listeners waited for a moment, the Nomiki asked, "You fought three men?"

"These bandits were not very good." Leotychides smiled distantly. "I saw one hiding in the brush. I stopped and looked at him. The other two were hiding a little way ahead. When they saw me stop, the two in front came out and tried to talk to me." At Nomiki's look Leotychides explained, "They said they only wanted to talk to me."

It was Athan's turn to smile. He had done the same kind thing himself, years before in his bandit days, though with more people involved on both sides. It was a standard ploy; outnumber the victims, get your men in front of and behind your intended victims, and get them talking. Men who talk are less likely to fight. A clever bandit can get a payday without having to fight; fighting was dangerous, even when the odds were three to one. This man sitting in front of him had not fallen into that trap.

"I killed the one who was trying to get behind me with my dorry. Then I took up my hoplon and charged the other two. Their arms were poor, and they really did not want to fight. One of them ran away. I had to chase him a long way before I caught him. Fortunately no one came along and took my donkey while I was gone."

Athan thought about what he had just heard. Two enemies casually killed, the third man running in terror for his life. He could imagine the chase, he could put himself in the position of the bandit, pursued up and down hills by an implacable foe until, gasping and exhausted, he was overtaken. Athan understood what it must have taken to run down a terrified man while carrying a hoplon and sword. He also understood what kind of a man he was facing; one who would not be satisfied in killing two men and setting the third to flight, but on who would risk loss of all he owned to destroy an opposing foe. His reference to his spear as a 'dorry' was also telling. This was a man who had been trained by the finest soldiers on earth.

Athan thought about the cold courage it would take to walk on and on through wild country alone. This Leotychides told a good story, and Athan had a strong suspicion the story he told was true.

"You say you were taught to fight," Athan interjected, changing the subject. "Fight how? Have you ever fought a battle against an enemy phalanx?"

"Fight every way; and yes, I fought in a phalanx." There was a pause, "Once."

"Do you know how to order men in a line? Make a fighting formation maneuver? Get men to fight together as a cohesive unit?"

The man nodded as each question was asked.

"If your king needs an instructor in the art of war, I am his man. Can you introduce me to him?"

"No," smiled Athan, "but Nomiki here can."

The stranger suddenly understood who the man sitting opposite him must be.

"I apologize, your majesty," Leotychides said rising with a bow, "for any disrespect I may have shown. I did not know who you were."

Leotychides looked at the ordinary-looking man sitting across from him who must be the King of Dassaria. He was plainly dressed, of indeterminate age, clean shaven with a full head of hair, and an apparently complete set of white teeth. Leotychides had known this man was a soldier from the way he moved and by that big sword on his hip. Leotychides had made the mistake of thinking the man was just an officer sent down to inquire about him. That had happened in most of the places he had passed through. He had never expected the King himself to come down here and present himself like this. What kind of a place was this Dassaria?

"That big sword of yours should have given you away," said Leotychides "Is it any use in a real battle?"

"Oh, yes, sir," answered Nomiki for his King. "I have seen him use it. He cut a man's head right off with it!"

"Nomiki," said Athan as a reproach to the younger man. Then to change the subject asked the stranger, "Leotychides, what kind of name is that?"

"A king's name where I come from; I am not related to him, well perhaps distantly, at any rate, that is how my mother came to name me so."

"It is said that you want to take service here," Athan began, "I have need of a man who can teach untrained youths how to fight; I mean fight properly, in line and as a unit."

"I can do that," responded Leotychides confidently.

"Let us take a walk up to my fort and see," said Athan rising to his feet. The other two men rose, Leotychides recovered his donkey and brought it along behind following the other two men up to the Hold to continue the job interview.

They entered the Hold, passed the guard in the passageway and turned left so they could stable Leotychides' donkey; that side of the stables was empty but for them. They put the stranger's animal in an open stall. The three men looked down toward the far end of the courtyard where Prokopios was bellowing at a ragged line of trainees, still trying to get the men to advance without sidling to their right.

Leotychides gave a grin. Athan, looking at him from the side, noted that the newcomer looked like anyone else when viewed that way; it was only when you faced him full on that you noticed his unique beard.

"A common problem," gestured Athan, referring to the tendency of men in line to advance obliquely.

"I know," said Leotychides. "We had some tricks to reduce the amount a line does shift when it moves forward. May I make a suggestion to your sergeant?"

Athan did some quick thinking. He did not want to expose this man's strange-looking face to a bunch of recruits until he had a more conventional appearance; first impressions can be lasting. He looked back at the donkey, still loaded with Leotychides' gear. He did not just have the proper gear for a hoplite, it was of the finest quality. His big round hoplon, loaded on the right side of the donkey, was red, with a black head of a gorgon. A fine bronze helmet with a magnificent crest and wide cheek pieces leaving a Gamma or Y shape for the eyes was atop the pack. A man wearing a helmet like that had his face almost completely obscured. A linen and leather cuirass, reinforced with bronze was on the left side of the animal's load. A heavy spear, his dorry as he called it, rested down the length of the donkey, the butt protruding three feet past the rear of the animal.

"By all means," said Athan with another gesture. "I suggest you put on your armor and carry your hoplon so they will know what a warrior is supposed to look like."

Leotychides donned his armor as easily as some men put on their tunics, speaking of a lifelong familiarity with the gear of war. Leaving his spear leaning against the slats of his donkey's stall, he strode across the courtyard between Athan and Nomiki like the very image of Ares. Athan was always impressed how some men seem to grow larger when they put on armor. Leotychides was by no means small, and the armor bulked him out. The crest of his helmet added inches to his apparent height. He was suddenly a very imposing figure. Even obscured by his gear, the stranger was obviously a warrior in his prime, full of blood and power.

"Sergeant Prokopios!" called Athan as they came up, "Would you be so kind as to allow this soldier to try his hand at maneuvering the men?"

Prokopios looked at the warlike figure walking beside the King and, nodding his ascent, moved to one side. Leotychides grasped the nettle firmly.

Stepping forward he ordered the men back in a loud confident voice. The line of conscripts obeyed; even in the short time they had been in training, Prokopios had made considerable progress in getting them to work together. After some additional orders and pushing of the recruits into what he decided was a proper line, Leotychides moved to the front of the line and addressed the men.

"Men!" he began, his voice strong and carrying with a slight metallic sound from under the helmet. "You must have confidence in your comrades next to you in line. I will put a stopper on the end of the line. Sergeant, can I use one of your veterans?"

Athan offered up his own shield bearer, Nomiki, to act as stopper. The young soldier hastened to take up a hoplon and spear and was positioned at the far right side of the line.

"The steadiest soldier will always be on the right side. He will act as the guideon for the line. Often he will carry a banner on his spear; we will just have to pretend he has a little flag there right below the spear head. Now, Nomiki here is a brave man, a seasoned warrior. He is the King's own shield bearer. You are not going to embarrass him under the very eyes of his King are you?"

The men looked left and right at one another, uncertain.

"Well are you?"

"No Sir!" Now they understood what he wanted.

"**I asked you a question**! Are you miserable would-be soldiers going to push against the King's own Shield Bearer?"

"**NO SIR!**"

"Good; because he will push back. Nomiki will not let you push him to the right, and I will remind you to walk straight like a proper soldier!"

Leotychides was pacing up and down in front of the line as he gave these instructions. Athan noticed that the new man had cleverly told Nomiki what was expected of him without directly addressing him.

"When I give the command, and only when I give the command, you will all step out as one man with your left leg; your left leg. Do you know which leg is your left leg?"

By now the men knew to speak loudly and in unison: "**Yes Sir!**"

"Good. From now on you will step out together with the left leg first every single time you advance whether you are in line or not. You will always take your first step with your left foot straight ahead. You will do this every time for the rest of your life. Do you understand?"

"**Yes, Sir!**"

"What leg will you start with?"

"Left, sir" This response was not as universally answered as the previous responses as some said 'left' and some 'left leg' and a couple of men who were confused said nothing at all, but the general reply was still intelligible.

Leotychides ignored the confusion. "Good. Then you will take the second step with your other leg; that would be the right leg. Then left, then right. As you move forward look out of the corner of your eye and try to match the length of your stride with your comrades. Concentrate on walking straight ahead. Can you do that?"

"**Yes, Sir!**"

"Good. Prepare to advance. Company, Forward."

It was a little ragged at first but on the second try the line moved forward as a single thing, and it moved forward with only a little sidling to the right.

Prokopios and Athan looked at one another. "Can you use him?" asked Athan in a low voice.

"Oh, yes," responded Prokopios. "He knows a thing or two. Even more, he knows how to lead men. What is he like under that helmet?" Apparently the canny Prokopios had already noticed something.

"Don't worry about it," Athan assured him. "If you like his looks will you take him as a Drilling Sergeant?"

"Certainly; I will wager he will be doing all the training here within a half month."

Athan nodded in agreement. "Leotychides!" he called out. "Thank you. That will do. Sergeant Prokopios will take over now. Please attend me; you too, Nomiki."

The three men retired up to Athan's personal chambers where Leotychides removed his helmet and sat down. Amycus was dispatched to bring bowls of wine and water as well as some small snacks.

The negotiations began at once. Athan offered the stranger a position as a sergeant in his guard with initial duties as assistant to Prokopios in training.

"I would not mind doing that, but would you expect me to fight in line?"

That seemed an incredibly strange question from this man. It was not just the stories he told; Athan's immediate judgment of this man was that he was a cool and courageous fighter. Instead of becoming put off at this intimation of cowardice, Athan asked him a question. "Would you be averse to so fighting? A soldier who will not fight is like a bull that will not service the cows."

The stranger smiled faintly and shook his head slightly. "I will fight, but not in the line. I get 'a little shy' in line."

"Leave us Nomiki," ordered Athan abruptly. Nomiki was not eager to leave his master alone with a dangerous stranger but complied.

As he closed the door behind him Leotychides shifted nervously.

"My lord," he said. "Could we walk on the walls to speak of this?"

"There is more privacy here. Come Leotychides, speak frankly."

The man took a breath visibly gathering himself. "I am not afraid of many things, but I do not like being closed up, especially when I am nervous. Please sir, could we go outside?"

Athan looked at him for a moment. The other man sat, tensely waiting. Abruptly Athan got up and walked out the door. Nomiki waiting just outside the door with his hand on the hilt of his sword leapt to his feet. Athan gestured him to remain and walked out of his apartments and up the stairs to the south wall. Leotychides followed him.

It was hot under the sun but there was a breeze. The two men stood side by side looking south over the wall to the hazy hills where Leotychides had come from that morning.

"Is this more to your liking?" Athan asked. Athan was on the stranger's left side. From this angle he looked like any other man; only his bearded side was exposed.

After a time Leotychides began to speak.

"Men of my class were expected to be warriors. That was what we were trained to do from childhood. We were forbidden by the state to engage in trade. After I was taken from my mother at the usual age, I suppose I was about seven years old, I began my education in the 'agoge' with other boys of my age. That is what they called that part of my training, the agoge. The teachers taught me poems; but mostly they taught me to be tough. Or at least that is what they tried to teach me. They didn't give us much to eat; if you wanted to get fed you had to steal food. Of course, if you were clumsy enough to get caught, they punished you. We had a lot of rituals. At thirteen I was put out in the hills with the rest of my 'ageles', which is what we called our companies, where we were taught fighting, gymnastics, and how to endure. As we got a little older we would go out on patrols, just us boys. There were a lot of slaves in our country. If we caught one outside of their assigned huts, we could kill them; we did kill them. I killed my first man one night when I was fifteen."

There was a moment of silence as the two men remained leaning against the parapet, an embrasure between them.

Leotychides began speaking again. "At twenty, I passed my final test, more of an ordeal actually, and became a full fledged soldier. I lived in the barracks with my comrades from our ageles. I suppose I was happy. I had done well in my training, my life was proceeding normally, and I was probably going to get married when a suitable wife was found for me."

There was another quiet time. Athan waited patiently.

"We had a battle. I was actually looking forward to it. I had been in a line before, lots of times, but never in a really big one like the one that day. I have never liked being cooped up; things seem like they are closing in on me. I had always found a way around it until that day. When we formed line I always tried to get in the front rank. If I couldn't I went to the rear rank. But on that day only the veterans were allowed in the front rank, and the older men would not let us 'hide' on the back rank. I was put right in the middle. I wasn't afraid of the enemy. Well, maybe I was a little anxious, it was my first battle, but I was not so much afraid of them as I was of being crushed in the middle of that pack. The longer we waited, the worse it got. When I thought we were going to attack, I was so relieved. Then we stopped and waited. Suddenly I just couldn't stand it anymore. I threw down my dory, then my hoplon, and clawed my way out of that mass of men. Everyone saw me do it. I stopped outside of the press and threw myself down and vomited. When the line moved charged, I picked up my hoplon and spear and tried to follow them. Unfortunately, the enemy fled at our attack. Before I could rejoin my comrades, the battle was over; and so was my life. There is no place in my country for a coward, a man who is 'nervous in the line' as they say. I was not punished; not as such. My family was disgraced. I could never marry. They shaved my beard as you see it; half a beard for half a man. I am bound to wear only half a beard for the rest of my life."

Athan did not know what to say. He suspected this was the first time Leotychides had spoken of this to anyone. Before Athan could think of something to say, the disgraced warrior continued.

"Fortunately, my father was already dead. I cared nothing for my brothers or sisters; I scarcely knew them. I was not supposed to leave the country, but when my mother died there was nothing to hold me there. I just walked away. I thought I might become a brigand, but I did not care for the company of the men I met. If I were to become a caravan guard, I would always be meeting people. Someday I would run into someone who knew what this," here he gestured toward his facial hair, "meant. That would lead to accusations, insults, and murder. Then I heard about a place way up north at the edge of nowhere that was hiring soldiers. So here I am."

"This is about as much of an out-of-the-way a place as I have found myself," admitted Athan.

"So, I can teach others to fight, but do not expect me to stand in line of battle," concluded the foreigner.

"So you will teach my people the proper way of fighting?"

"Yes."

"You will, in fact, fight, just so long as you do not have to be in the middle ranks of a line?"

The man shrugged his assent. "I would not like it if I had to stay inside one of those for too long either," Leotychides said pointing at the bastion. "On top of the wall, yes, but fighting inside would not be to my taste."

"Fighting inside was not exactly to my taste either," said Athan dryly. Then he continued changing to a brisk tone, "Well, good; we almost never form line of battle anyway. If we have to do so, I will give you leave to either remain in front or behind the line, standing alone. Can you do that?"

"So long as you do not expect too much of me."

"If you teach the men well enough, I won't have to worry about your personal battle prowess. You will have to fix your beard."

"I cannot."

"What? Why not? You are in my service now. There is no one who knows or cares about how you wear your beard. But if you keep one side of your face bare and one side covered with hair, people will ask about it. Some of the recruits will probably start wearing it that way."

The prospect of the latter idea seemed to horrify Leotychides. "I am compelled to have only half a beard. I would not be true to myself if I did not."

This was something the stranger was going to be stubborn about. Athan recognized that and did not try to dissuade him. Instead he thought about the problem. There had to be a solution. Athan had already decided he could not bring the man into his service with that strange half-bearded/half clean-shaven look. It would inevitably lead to questions, then ridicule, and in a short time the new man's authority would be completely undermined. He wanted someone to solve, not generate, problems.

"Tell me, Leotychides, what if someone else shaved you? Or, if you shaved your beard off completely, like I do?"

The other man just shook his head.

'Maybe he could wear a mask,' thought Athan. 'No that would be ridiculous. There would still be too much controversy.'

"Why do you shave the right side of your face?" Athan asked, "Does it matter which side is bare?" He could not imagine what good such a question would do. What difference did it make? Athan just knew that when trying to solve a problem sometimes asking irrelevant questions helped.

"No," shrugged Leotychides, "it doesn't matter. Either side will do. That one was just more convenient." From his attitude Athan could tell the other man was losing heart. The two stood on the ramparts looking south. They both wanted the same thing, and that was for Leotychides to serve as the training sergeant in the kingdom of Dassaria. The two men understood without further discussion that the strange half-beard would bar him from Athan's service. It was a stupid reason but it was a sufficiently good 'stupid reason' to ruin an otherwise perfect fit.

Then it hit Athan; there was a possible solution. All he had to do was convince this new man that it was a solution.

"So, you just need wear half a beard? For how long?"

"Until I prove myself, to myself."

Athan did not follow that explanation. Instead he confirmed what he had heard a moment before. "And it does not matter which side you shave?"

The man shook his head no.

"Then shave the bottom side." Leotychides gave Athan a puzzled look. Athan explained: "You have to have half a beard. So shave the bottom half. Keep the top half. Grow sideburns and a moustache like those barbarians do and shave your chin and the bottom half of your cheeks."

"It doesn't work that way," objected Leotychides.

"Why not," countered Athan, "you told me you had to wear half a beard. What I described is half a beard."

There was a thoughtful pause on the other side. Athan's answer was Sophistry of the worst kind. It was a technical loophole to allow Leotychides to circumvent his personal honor. On the other hand, he was a man who had been taught as a boy to use any tricks necessary to defeat your enemy.

"Let me see what it would look like." Leotychides said. "I will go get my shaving gear."

"No need," offered Athan, "you can use my soap and razor. Athan did not want the man wandering about in his strange beard more than necessary. He saw the other man hesitating and so said, "What is the matter Leotychides, are you afraid to use a king's personal things? I thought you said you had a king's name."

This made the warrior smile, and he allowed King Athan to show him where he kept his bronze razor, leather strop, soap, fancy shaving brush, and very expensive silvered mirror. Leotychides carefully shaved the whiskers from his throat and chin on both sides, leaving a set of thick sideburns running down the left side of his face, reaching over to cover the left side of his lip. The fresh shaving highlighted the stubble that was already starting to show on the right side of his face. He looked into the mirror turning his head so he could observe the effect of efforts from the side.

Not bad, not bad," Leotychides decided and then smiled. "I will need to spend a few days to change the side I wear my beard on," he told Athan with a grin that grew increasingly wide. "I can live in the country until it is ready. Then I will come and see you again."

"I look forward to it," replied Athan with an equally broad grin.

Nomiki was detailed to stay with the new Drilling Sergeant and remain discretely out of sight until the stranger's new 'half beard' was complete.

"I suggest you stay down by the lake," Athan suggested, "you can fish there or buy fish if that does not suit you. It is quiet and cooler down there."

As a result, Nomiki spent a fair amount of time at the new man's camp, teaching him about the area, people, and the King. In exchange Leotychides gave him lessons in fighting with spear, sword, and in wrestling. After six days the new man presented himself at the gate and was promptly installed as the new Drilling Sergeant, a role he would fulfill with great skill for years.

Thus, the two men found a way around a 'stupid reason'. In so doing, Athan secured the services a splendid military man who would provide superb military training and profoundly influence an entire generation of young Dassarian men.

The other stranger who would have a significant impact on Dassaria arrived within an hour of Athan's initial meeting with Leotychides. Her arrival was completely unnoticed, in part because she was traveling with her new husband in a large caravan. Her name was Zoe, and she was nineteen years old. Of average height, she had long lustrous black hair, a fresh clear complexion, brown eyes sparking with mischief, and a lush figure; all of which tended to put men off balance. She knew this and used it to full advantage. After all, sometimes a girl needs an edge.

Zoe needed that edge, because although she was both bright and pretty, she had also been born poor. Her father had had the great misfortune of injuring his knee soon after his third daughter was born. Zoe, as the second of those daughters, did not know actual starvation, as some children did, but her father was unable to work his little farm with his damaged knee, and their fortunes slowly declined. Eventually, they moved into Bardhyllus where her father attempted a variety of endeavors to support his family. He tried his hand apprenticing as a potter. Unfortunately, with his bad right knee he could not kick the potter's wheel with his right leg, driving the pottery wheel widdershins like all the others in the shop. At first it did not seem like it would be a serious problem because he could use his good leg. However, his left leg made the wheel turn in the opposite direction than the other apprentice potters making it more difficult for the master to teach him how to create the bowls, cups, and pots that the potter sold. Even worse, after a time his left leg began to bother him, and he had to seek other employment.

One way or another, between the various jobs her father could get and a series of ingenious schemes devised by her mother, Zoe's family was able to survive. Zoe's mother would watch other women's children and help with domestic chores for those without female relations. She also did other things like raise a goat or two and even train dogs; almost anything to provide food, clothing, and shelter for the five of them. But those opportunities were not common and did not generate much for the family. A family with a very small income and three children cannot afford luxuries like dowries. Zoe's elder sister was even prettier than she was, and her parents were able to arrange a suitable match with a carpenter's son. They were aided by the fact that both sets of parents knew and liked one another before the wedding, so the boy's family was willing to accept a token dowry. Even that strained the finances of the family. Then things got worse; Zoe's father died. Zoe knew that now her chances of making a suitable match were small at best.

Being an intelligent person, she knew that, if she expected to have any hope of a decent marriage, she would have to work things out for herself. That was one of the reasons why she decided to fall in love with a handsome young caravan guard. She had had crushes on boys before, but she decided this one had real potential. He was good-looking, a sturdy man of average height with straight light brown hair. His name was Bukchos. Though he was only a caravan guard, he was funny and, to her mind, sophisticated. Part of that belief came from the fact that he was not from her city and had traveled with caravans. He had been to the theater and claimed to have even written plays himself. Zoe first met this Bukchos when he passed through the small city where they were living with a caravan.

There was an immediate connection between the two. That first night she got a chance to speak with him and received a bit of his natural charm. The caravan remained in the town for two additional days doing business and waiting for more merchants to arrive. In that time, though they were never alone together, Bukchos had ample opportunity to talk with the pretty young maiden and fill her head with possibilities. Two months later the caravan passed through the town again and though they only spent one night there before moving on it was a magical night for Zoe. Not only did Bukchos confirm his deep affection to her, he also was able to take advantage of a moment alone to give Zoe her first kiss. When he returned the following spring, he approached her newly widowed mother. Though it was irregular, her mother reluctantly decided that this was as good a match as she was likely to get for her daughter.

The wedding was simple but proper. There was no guest feast, no professional musicians, and no dowry; nevertheless, the occasion was joyous to Zoe. She had the wonderful feeling of having arranged her life to her satisfaction. She was married to a handsome, interesting man. She would travel in the caravans with him cooking and caring for her husband. It would be a life of adventure. Eventually, of course, they would settle down and raise their children, but for now Zoe was in love and in love with life.

Of course, it did not work out quite as she planned. Traveling with a caravan was much harder than she had expected, and she had little time and less money to enjoy the places where they stopped. Her new husband was the biggest problem. Although Bukchos was not a cruel man, Zoe found he was considerably less interesting than she had initially thought. He had a head full of ideas that remained just that—ideas. He was not much for putting ideas into action. He could be jealous of his lively new wife; well, that was far from unusual. He was a philanderer, but that was almost expected of men in that time. He would too often drink too much wine, again a common vice. Unfortunately he was a mean drunk; he would too often come to blows with his drinking companions and return to Zoe battered and bruised and blaming her. He had not actually begun to mistreat her, but the trend made her deeply uneasy. Still, she remained upbeat and cheerful; she was well liked by others in the caravans they accompanied. In fact, she thought things were going reasonably well right up to the time when he left her behind in the remote little town of Dassaria.

"What do you mean I'm to stay here!" she demanded when he told her. Her hands were on her hips, and her brown eyes were flashing dangerously.

"It is the caravan master, my sweet," explained Bukchos. He had not been married long but had enough sense to know when to try to placate an angry wife. "He says it is too dangerous once we leave Dassaria, and that we will have to move fast and be prepared for an attack at any time. All the women are being left here. I will be back as soon as I can, and we will be together again."

"When?" she asked dangerously.

"As soon as we come back through on the way home," Bukchos told her reassuringly. He was in full placation mode, holding her hands in his, trying to jolly her along as best he could. "I have arranged for you to stay with a nice family that sells wine; Amphora and his wife. I think you know them."

"His name is Adem and his wife's name is Ana and they have a young son, just over a year old, who is said to be sickly," Zoe told him through clenched teeth. The caravan had been here three days, and she already knew the people of the town better than he did. "How long have you known that I was going to have to stay here? And who decided I had to stay here? Was it that miserable mule-headed caravan master or was this your idea?" Now she was getting really hot. Tears of anger were threatening to well up. This made her even madder. "Well? Well?"

Bukchos tried to take the high ground, telling her he was only concerned about her safety. That she would be able to stay here at no cost and perhaps even earn a little money helping Ana with her baby. Even a woman less perspicacious than Zoe would have recognized it as a complete load of manure. The argument escalated from there. Bukchos knew he was wrong and so took refuge in anger. But eventually, as young couples often do, they wore one another out. And since they were both aware they would soon be parted, they did finally make up; passionately so. But afterwards there was a deep hollowness in Zoe's heart, and as she listened to Bukchos snore beside her, she could not help wondering if she would ever see him again.

The next morning Zoe watched her husband leave with his caravan going up the north trail. They would be going through Lychmidas and then over the passes to trade with the cities now under the protection of the Achaemenid Empire. She had quietly talked to others in the caravan and confirmed that they expected to be gone about two or three months. She watched the line of men, mules, and wagons disappear into the hills to the north and wept. She was still upset when later that day she found out that two of the other women who had been traveling with the caravan had continued on with their men, going over the pass. Apparently, it was up to the men to assess the danger. Her husband either valued her more than the other men did their wives, or he just wanted to get rid of her.

She walked around in turmoil all day. The worst part of it was that she had no friends or family to confide in or advise her. She was alone in a strange place in a hostile world. Zoe did not know what to do. She walked all over Dassaria, which did not take long. Zoe avoided going up to the hill where the Hold sat, seeming to stare down over the town. At one point she found herself at the northern end of Dassaria looking at the finest house in town. She knew the Magistrate lived there. She had heard he was second in power only to the king. She considered going to him and throwing herself on his mercy. She rejected the idea at once. Powerful men did not respond to pleas for mercy; they only respected strength and money. She was on her own. Very well, if she was on her own, she would solve her own problems. She did not need that worthless husband of hers; she did not need any man.

Just then she saw a man come out of the Magistrate's house. He was a fine, good-looking man, with reddish hair and a well-trimmed beard. He turned back to the house saying something to those inside and then laughed. 'That's a nice laugh,' she thought, 'he seems kind. Is that the Magistrate? But he has no servants with him, and he seems like an ordinary enough man.' Zoe's limited experience with powerful men had been limited to stories and occasional glimpses of richly dressed oligarchs riding horses or being carried in litters. This man was probably a wealthy merchant who had just visited the Magistrate.

He came walking past her heading into town. He stopped as he reached her and smiled. He had a nice smile to go with his laugh. She could not help smiling back.

"Good morning, miss," he said using the term for a maiden.

"Good morning to you, sir," she replied a bit tartly, "but you are mistaken. I am a married woman, thank you." Her smile widened; she just couldn't help it. "And my husband is a fierce warrior. Of course, he isn't here just now…" she finished with just the perfect hint of invitation.

The man laughed and she joined him.

"Oh, I see," he replied, "and just how long is this missing warrior going to be missing?" From the way he phased the comment, it was not clear whether he was politely inquiring about the status of her husband, or if he were trying to find out whether or not she was available for a dalliance.

Zoe should have been angry with this stranger who was flirting with her, but she found it difficult to kindle any anger at this charming fellow; he was a good-natured sort of man, the kind that everyone seems to like at once. She certainly did. She glanced down and then peeked up at him again with her head slightly tilted to one side.

"Oh, sir," she replied with a mysterious smile, "knowing my husband, it will always be at an inconvenient time."

Somehow it was the most natural thing for her to turn and resume walking with this perfect stranger back toward town. After all that was where she was going, wasn't it? It was broad daylight, and this man had to be respectable since he had just come from the Magistrate's office.

Besides, it would be rude for a girl to decline the offer of an escort back to her place of residence, even if the offer had not been explicitly made.

"How long will you be gracing Dassaria with your presence, madam?" he asked her now using the term for distinguished matron.

"Madam?" She chaffed back at him immediately. "First you are too short then too long. Does it always take you three tries to get things right? I wonder that such a distinguished cavalier has such poor judgment!" The word she used to describe him was more commonly applied to much older men.

He laughed at her sally, "You are not alone in that lady," he replied. "Then tell me, how should I address you? What is your name? Surely that will not offend your delicate sensibilities?"

"Why, sir," she came back, "a respectable married woman such as myself should hardly give her name out to any stranger, no matter how handsome." With this she gave him such a wicked grin, he burst out laughing again.

"My name," he replied, "is Rodas, son of Rodas."

"And what is your trade oh, Rodas, son of Rodas? Are you a first son, or did your father lack the wit to find another name?"

The speed of her responses delighted him. "As to the second question, though my father and mother lacked many things, wit was not one of them. It was my mother who so loved her husband that she named her first born son after him. And as to my trade," and here she saw him stop and consider for an instant, "I have several but the most important is that I am the official Inspector of Dancing Girls for the Kingdom of Dassaria. Now, what is your name? Are you a dancing girl applying for permission to perform here?"

"Oh, la, sir," she replied, and gracefully twirled around with the skirts of her loose chiton spinning around her. It was a borrowed garment and a bit too large, but this gave her a certain freedom of movement and, in that instant, she showed it well. Rodas eyed her appreciatively as she returned to walking by his side. Abruptly she was serious, "My name is Zoe; I am the wife of Bukchos, a caravan guard in the party that left this morning. I am staying in the house of Adem until my husband returns."

He looked at her for a moment with an unreadable expression. "Then you need to retrace your steps," Rodas told her, "we just passed Amphora's house."

"Oh!" she said putting her hand to her mouth and looking back and over one street. "Thank you, sir, I mean Rodas. Good day!" Without another word she darted back to the house where her few possessions were kept.

'People are looking at me like I am some sort of harlot,' she thought to herself as she came into the house. Zoe did not know Ana very well yet, but she could tell the older woman was flustered and irritable when Zoe found her in the women's hall with her fussing infant.

The house was large and imposing, built just the year before in the southern style. The entrance hall and men's rooms were in the very front of the house. At the end of the entrance hall was the men's hall, called the andronitis. It consisted of an open court covered with an awning with colonnaded rooms on either side. This was where the men would gather and socialize in symposiums, where they would drink, eat, and discuss business. In the center of the andronitis was a small stone alter to Zeus the protector. Adem was more religious than most. The rooms on the sides of the courtyard were used as store rooms and sleeping cells for visitors and male employees. Directly behind the andronitis, a short passageway led into the inner house. The second major room was the dining hall or andron. Off to one side was the main bedroom that Adem and Ana shared. At the back of the andron was a single solid wooden door that led into the women's hall, called the gynaeconitis. In really large houses, the gynaeconitis was a courtyard like the andronitis, but in this house it was an enclosed room. There were cells on either side for storage or the sleeping quarters for female servants. This was the women's territory, their special refuge, and men who were not family members were seldom allowed there. At the very back of the house was the kitchen, with its oven, cooking fire, pots, pans, and panty. In one corner was a small round altar sacred to Hestia, the goddess of the hearth. Also in the kitchen was a ladder that led up to a trap door that opened to the flat roof. During the summer months, there was an awning up over the roof as well, giving the house an extra room that was open to the cooling breezes. The decorations within the house were plain, with walls tined with a wash, and interior floors of simple plaster.

The only place the floor was tiled was in the area in the center of the andronitis that was open to the weather. It was a large and imposing house for that quiet part of the world; only the Magistrate's house was finer.

Zoe came to understand that Adem had overextended himself to build such a fine house. He had made a considerable profit for the last two years and was counting heavily on having another couple of good years to set the financial foundation of his business. The house was needed (he said) to impress business associates. It was a mark of how close finances were that Adem did not even employ a full time cook. He only had two servants, an apprentice for his work, and a girl, Agalia, to help Ana with the house. Really they needed more staff, but their finances were temporarily tight. Thus the chance to house a young woman for a few months in exchange for domestic help was welcome.

"He just won't eat," Ana said looking up from her son to Zoe as though it was her fault. "Maybe I shouldn't be trying to get him to eat solid food so soon."

Zoe took the youngster from his mother and soothed him. "I am sure he is just full," she said reassuringly as she patted the baby on his little back. Right on cue he gave a surprisingly loud belch.

"You can certainly tell he is a boy," Zoe laughed. She wondered at her sudden good humor. Her husband had barely disappeared over the hill before she was flirting with some wealthy, good-looking merchant. He probably had a wife and two mistresses; still, her taste in men must be improving. She giggled to herself at the thought.

"Why are you in such a good mood all of a sudden?" asked Ana. She was tired and worried about her young son, and it showed in her face. "Are you so glad to be rid of that husband of yours?"

"I don't know," Zoe replied, "I miss him already, but I just don't know."

"Hmmm," said the older woman, "you will forgive me for saying so, but I think you could have done better; him dragging you along with a caravan and then leaving you all alone like this. He may be handsome, but he isn't treating you handsomely."

The two women then resumed their conversation about Ana's infant. Zoe did not think she had ever seen a woman so worried about a child before. When his nappies had been runny yesterday, the woman had been frantic, certain her baby had the flux, though it was far from a crisis. Zoe thought it was because the child's continuing existence was so unexpected; after all Ana was well past thirty, old for only one child. Ana had told Zoe that 'none of the others had lived this long.' Hearing this had nearly broken Zoe's heart. Children, especially babies, died all the time; no matter what the circumstances, it was always terrible. Zoe's own mother had lost her only son when Zoe was six. She still remembered her mother's grief; a normally cheerful woman, she had mourned for months. How awful it must be to know you would only have one child. No wonder Ana fretted over the young one so.

To change the subject Zoe mentioned she had been walked back from the Magistrate's house by a handsome man with a reddish hair and beard. Before Ana could reply there was a greeting from the door and two women entered. One, carrying her young son Zoe recognized as Neeta, who was among Ana's best friends. The other woman, with a somewhat older child and heavily pregnant, was introduced to Zoe as Neysa. Neysa, it transpired, was married to one of the soldiers in the garrison and had come over the lake with the King. This made no sense at the time to Zoe, though she would later come to understand it meant Neysa felt she had a personal connection to the King.

The women put the children down and chatted politely for a few moments. It was obvious that there was more on their minds than a mere casual visit; they had some hot gossip to discuss.

"So, Zoe," asked Neysa broaching the subject, "What did you think of our Magistrate?"

"What?" asked Zoe, confused by the question.

"The Magistrate," Neysa said, "the man you were flirting with just now."

Zoe jerked her gaze to Ana who nodded and said, "Our Magistrate is a handsome fellow isn't he?"

Zoe felt her cheeks burning as the blood rushed to her face. "I didn't know. I wasn't flirting with him. He just asked me about his husband, I mean my husband..." Zoe lapsed into confused stammering. The three women nodded; their expressions ranged from thoughtful consideration, to a knowing smirk, to simple amusement at the young woman's obvious confusion.

"Well, now that your husband is away," teased Neeta, "you can flirt with the most eligible bachelor in the kingdom, well, not counting the King, of course. Have you met the King yet?"

"She has only been here four days," put in Ana, "give her a little more time."

"Flirting with the Magistrate is a good start, though," Neysa said.

"I was not flirting!" objected Zoe.

"I saw you dancing for him," countered Neysa.

"I was not dancing! I just twirled around once, that's all," said Zoe. "He said he was the official inspector of dancing girls, and I was showing him I was no dancer."

"He **is** the so-called Inspector of Dancing Girls for the Kingdom of Dassaria," Ana told her, taking the baby who had begun to fuss in response to Zoe's agitation. "The story is that the King told him he could have any jobs in the kingdom he wanted. So he took Magistrate and made up the dancing girl inspector job. Not many dancing girls come to Dassaria but when they do our Magistrate certainly takes his job seriously." The three older women all laughed.

Zoe excused herself, claiming that she needed to tend to chores to cover her escape. The arrangement she had made with Adem and Ana was that she would help Ana with young Agamemnon (Zoe thought that was a silly and pretentious name for a baby), help keep the house clean for customers, and assist Ana as required. In return she could eat with the family and would be allowed to stay in a small room in their house. It might have seemed a harsh bargain, but it suited Zoe rather well. Most of her job appeared to be simply calming Ana down; she continued to be nervous about her child, and needed a lot of reassurance. The young servant girl, Agalia, which means 'cheerful', might have been as happy as her name indicated, but she had no experience with infants and was too young and insecure to provide company for her mistress. Ana's friends often came by to visit and provide support, but Zoe could be there all the time, even at night, and that seemed to be a comfort to Ana.

The first night alone in a strange room was more than a little scary for Zoe. The lamp cast weird shadows around the room, and the room had all the strange noises that new places seem to have at night. Zoe had not slept alone very many times. As a girl, she had either slept with one or both of her sisters, and for the last six months with her husband. It was hot in her room, and there was little breeze, since she had closed and barred the shutters. Though the room was free of bed bugs and fleas, some buzzing mosquitoes made their irritating presence known. She was very glad to see the first light of a new day outside her window. Taking up an empty amphora, she headed to the local well to bring in the morning water.

Ana commiserated with her about her sleeping arrangements as they fed little Agamemnon that morning. "Why don't you come up and sleep with us on the roof," she invited her new servant/companion. "We get a lovely breeze up there."

Zoe was embarrassed she had not thought to ask. After a moment's hesitation Zoe accepted the invitation for that evening. She cleaned up the kitchen area and banked the kitchen fire, and played with the baby for a while until he got fussy.

"He needs his nap," his mother advised Zoe. "I won't need you until the afternoon meal. Why don't you look around town? It should be safe."

Zoe wandered the dirt streets, barefoot, kicking up dust and feeling a bit like a girl again. Her situation would be perfectly acceptable, except for the fact that Zoe had very little money of her own. She did not like being so dependant on new acquaintances, no matter how nice they seemed. She needed to find a respectable way to earn some extra cash. Zoe heard a dog give a warning bark and turned to see a bitch with four half-grown puppies trailing after her. Zoe could see from the bitch's teats that she probably was no longer nursing her litter. The young ones were still hopeful. Their mother was having none of it, and barked them off again. Seeing the dogs gave Zoe an idea. She would keep an eye out for a dog.

In that time and place, dogs were not often kept merely as pets. Dogs were more commonly considered as working animals: they were used for hunting, herding, or as watch dogs. Zoe knew that some people did keep them primarily as companions, and that was where she hoped her market was — house dogs. Her mother was good with animals and had trained some dogs. She could teach them to sit, stay, bark at strangers, or not bark so much, walk quietly alongside their masters and any number of other useful behaviors. Zoe had watched her mother training dogs and, even though she doubted she would be as good as her mother, she was confident she could train a dog. Clearly there were dogs here in town. Perhaps she could earn a few coins.

Life soon settled into a routine. Zoe had to fend off a half-hearted attempt at seduction from Adem; it was not difficult to do. It almost seemed that he made the effort because he thought it was expected of him more than from any real interest in his new member of his household.

The other member of the household, Adem's apprentice, was a young man just short of his twentieth year with a bad complexion and a retiring, if not to say timid, disposition. Other than when he brought in the wood for the kitchen fire, she seldom even saw him. Adem was concerned that the apprentice might be conscripted by the King in the fall to act as a soldier. This meant Adem would have to take on a new, untrained man with all the attendant disruption to work, and he could not afford to maintain two apprentices yet, just on the chance that one would be conscripted. Zoe doubted that such a shy little bunny rabbit of a man would make much of a soldier. But she did know that this King often took men into his service whether they wanted to or not once they came of age. It seemed unfair to her. She wondered if Bukchos would be so conscripted if they settled here. Zoe heard the men in the King's service were paid for their time. At least Bukchos would be here, and she could see him. He had been gone so long she worried that she was beginning to forget him.

Zoe's prepared the minor meals, helped Ana with the main meal, brought water, watched the baby, cleaned the house, did the laundry (an all day job) when required, and mostly provided company for Ana. Zoe was not required to do some of the worse jobs, such as emptying the chamber pots, changing and cleaning little Agamemnon's nappies, and scrubbing out the terracotta pots and pans; that was for Agalia. Well, Agalia was younger and a full-time servant. The only time Zoe felt uncomfortable during the first part of the time she spent waiting for her husband to return was when Ana's friends would assemble. The older women could be so blunt they embarrassed her. They always assembled in the gynaeconitis in the back section of the house. It was the women's domain, and the women felt comfortable there, comfortable enough to express themselves with unsettling (to Zoe) bluntness.

"My husband is a man of many parts," Neysa declared one afternoon. "It is a pity they weren't put together properly!"

It was a gathering Zoe would long remember, not because anything dramatic happened, but because it was near the end of a happy time in her life. Little Agamemnon had been toddling around all that morning, chasing after his mother. Though Ana was weaning him, the little boy still trailed behind her looking for a snack. Zoe could not help but remember the dog and her puppies she had seen just after she had arrived here two months before. The recollection made her smile. The women were enjoying the lull they sometimes had in the afternoon. Agamemnon was now down for his nap, and the immediate chores were done. The dog days of summer were on them, and few people were about the town.

The women were lounging in Ana's gynaeconitis as usual. There was a small round altar with a token family hearth, a sacred place for Hestia, the hearth goddess. That afternoon the women, Neysa, Ana, Neeta, Zoe, and Egaria, another newcomer to Dassaria, had made a small sacrifice to the goddess, and then remained to gossip. Agalia had brought them bowls for wine and water. Amphora's wine business had been very good lately, and the prosperity showed. Since the new house had only been completed the year before, Ana was fretting to her friends about what their new taxes would be. The women had had a bit of wine and were feeling relaxed and comfortable. Zoe was aware that Egeria's husband owned the new pottery business that had opened in town last year. His shop produced, among other things, some of the amphorae that Adem used in his business. Why wine merchants like Adem were often nicknamed 'Amphora' and not the potters who made the vessels was a mystery to Zoe. Most of the rooms off the courtyard were filled with the tall containers, leaning against one another and the wall on their pointed bases.

There was one much smaller amphora with a flat ring base, glazed and decorated with figures of dancing women, sitting on the floor. It was a very different vessel from the big plain containers used for commercial transport of wine and olive oil. The small dark amphora held some of the finest of their vintages, a red, aged three years and lightly spiced for the afternoon's libations. Agalia sat on the edge with, but not really part of the group.

"I heard that Jacina's boyfriend told her he'd lost all his money," Egaria told them.

"What did she say to him?" responded Neysa right on cue.

"I'll miss you darling!"

The women all laughed, the older more secure women more uproariously, the younger a little more uncertainly.

Egaria began talking about the order for amphora her husband was trying to fulfill for Adem. They were expecting a return of a caravan within the month. This was of particular interest to both Ana and Zoe. Ana's husband had shipped a large order of wine to the west with the caravan two months before. Zoe's husband, Bukchos, had been one of the guards on that very caravan. There had been no word other than confirmation the group had reached Lychmidas safely, and that had been well over a month ago. They should have completed their business by now and be on their way home. Zoe was not sure how she felt about that now. She was beginning to regret her choice of a husband. Her current situation would be very comfortable, if only she had a little money to give her some security. She recalled her idea of training dogs. She had decided it would be best to have an animal of her own so she could perfect her training. Besides, having her own well-behaved dog would be a living advertisement for her services. Perhaps Bukchos would like a dog as well. It could help him guard the caravan at night.

"I was thinking of getting a dog," Zoe said in a break in the conversation. The women, even Agalia, turned to look at her. "For my husband," she tried to explain.

"I have seen that husband of yours," said Egaria dryly, "I think that would be a fair trade." The women laughed, even Agalia when she got the joke.

"A dog, huh," said Neysa, "well a dog is better than a man in some ways."

"Yes," agreed Neeta, "Dogs are not threatened because you are smarter than they are."

"And," chipped in Ana, "a dog feels guilty when he does something wrong."

"A dog," Zoe was getting into the spirit of the thing, "is easier to housetrain."

"They think you are a culinary genus," Egaria told them. "You feed them anything, and they eat it and are grateful."

Now the comments started coming thick and fast.

"They don't mind if you don't arrange your hair."

"Dogs miss you when you are gone."

"They are always glad to see you."

"Middle-aged dogs don't feel the need to abandon you for a younger owner."

"They mean it when they kiss you,"

The exchanges came to an end when shy Agalia, the only maiden among them and one who was being pursued by a number of ardent suitors, made her only comment in a quiet but firm voice.

"Dogs understand what 'no' means."

This contribution broke up the other women who roared with understanding laughter.

Even though he had food, the next few days were difficult for the Old King. He went down and around the spur at first light to see if the wolves had left him anything. They had not. There were a few bones, but with some stew inside of him that he had prepared and eaten before dawn, he was picky enough to leave it alone. It began raining again so he retreated to his lair where he could stand and look out over the valley watching the rain. By the time the weather had finally cleared, the old man had eaten every bit of the haunch he had scavenged including breaking the bones for marrow and using them for a final soup.

The main difficulty during this time related to the start up of his digestive system. He suffered from ferocious stomach cramps, then diarrhea which left him shaky and uncomfortable. His upset stomach reminded him of the trick Zoe had played on Rodas. Thinking of that made him feel a little better.

Chapter Twelve – Various vintages

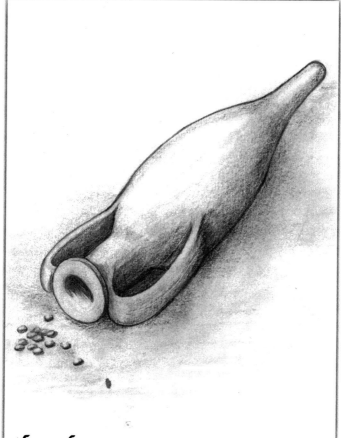

On the day after the gathering in the women's hall, Zoe found her dog. She was never sure just where the little creature came from; perhaps she was one of the puppies Zoe had seen her first day in Adem's house. It was early afternoon; Zoe was coming back from the well, an amphora balanced on her hip. Normally she brought in enough water in the morning to last the day; today they had been cleaning and the supply was low. She decided to refill their little working cistern then rather than wait. It was hot, and there were few people on the dirt streets. She noticed the little animal under a cart. The dog looked at her and whined softly wagging her tail.

"Well, hello," Zoe said with a smile stopping to squat down against a wall in the shade leaning her amphora against the wall as she did. She stretched out her hand to the dog on the far side of the street. "Whose little dog are you?"

The dog watched her for a moment with big dark eyes and then, apparently making up its mind to take a chance, trotted out of its shelter under the cart and over to Zoe with head and tail both down, the tail trying a street-sweeping effort at a wag. The little dog, a bitch Zoe could now see, was not large; her shoulder was well below Zoe's knee. The animal was fawn colored with a white patch on her chest. She had ears that wanted to be erect; they started that way, but gave up and flopped over about half way up. Likewise her tail curled up but did not complete a full circle, ending with an appendage that sort of pointed toward the back of her head. There was a vaguely fox-like look to her. Her hair was moderately long, matted and dirty. After some consideration the dog sniffed Zoe's outstretched hand uncertainly and then allowed Zoe to scratch behind her ears.

"Do you want to come with me?" Zoe asked the little dog. The poor animal was thin and obviously had not been cared for in some time. Even so, she seemed friendly. "What is your name, little one?" Zoe asked thinking about this dog. She looked like she might be trainable. "Come on," Zoe said taking up her heavy amphora again. "Let's go home."

It wasn't that easy of course. The dog followed briefly, then turned back to the safety of the cart's shadow. Zoe was not deterred. She brought the water back to the house and emptied into the house cistern and then left without bothering any of the others in the house who all were apparently napping. Taking a length of twine and a portion of her tiny trove of coins with her, Zoe went to the central square of Dassaria; no great distance. There, under the shade of a cloth fly erected between two buildings, she found the vendor she wanted. He sold bits of meat roasted and stuck on a thin skewer. This type of snack had been popular for many generations. The bits of meat were usually claimed to be goat or lamb but were always of suspect origin. Zoe had far too much sense to eat one of the things herself, on the other hand, she had never heard of anyone actually dying from consuming one either. And people must eat them, they were offered in the square every day.

She surprised the vendor by choosing to bargain for the oldest and least desirable-looking stick. Paying him half a bit, she took the six strips of meat on their thin wooden skewer and hurried back to the cart where she had seen the little dog. Slowing as she rounded the corner, Zoe peered under the cart. The animal was gone. Zoe should have known. Now what was she going to do with a skewer of undefined meat? Zoe wouldn't even bring it into the house; Agamemnon might find it and stuff it into his mouth. Even it he did not get sick, his mother would have a conniption fit. Zoe looked around the corners for the dog. She couldn't have gone far. Zoe thought of calling for the dog, but she did not know what to call it; 'doggie' seemed absurd. She already felt foolish enough standing out in the heat with a skewer in one hand and twine in the other, still, she had to try something.

"Here Lucky," any homeless dog that was being offered a home would be lucky right enough. Zoe called again and again. There was no sign of the little animal. Her shoulders slumping, Zoe turned to go back home. And then, there she was, sitting right in the middle of the street watching Zoe. The dog was on her belly with her front legs straight out ahead of her looking right at her. Zoe had heard of mighty carvings in Egypt of animals sitting like that; she could not remember what they where called. All she knew of Egypt was that there were the names of two places: one was 'Memphis' and the other was 'Luxor'. Well, perhaps she should name the dog after one of those places.

Zoe squatted down in the street, aware of the heat, and pulled off the first piece of meat from the stick. "Come here Luxor." That seemed like too much name for this dog. The as yet unnamed animal looked at the strip of meat in Zoe's hand and licked her lips. "Come here Lux." That sounded better; a small name for a small dog. Obediently Lux got up approached the offering and carefully took the bit of meat from Zoe's hand. She bolted the tidbit and wagged her tail hopefully. Zoe pulled off another piece and placed it flat on her palm. "I hope I am not turning you into a cannibal," Zoe said to Lux. The dog turned her head. Zoe laughed and pulled off anther strip of meat for her. "I have heard the most unsettling rumors about these meat skewers," she explained. "Perhaps it is really just rat."

By the fourth piece Zoe was able to slip a loop of twine around the dog's neck. She explained to Lux that they were going to a nice place where there would be plenty to eat. Zoe picked up the dog and started to carry her back to the house. Lux struggled a bit at first; Zoe kept talking to her in calm tones and let her settle into a comfortable position. Lux may not have been a heavy dog, but Zoe was still glad to put her down when they got to the house. She fed her the last strip of meat and led her into the back of the house on her leash. Ana and Agamemnon were apparently still asleep; Agalia was shelling some peas in the kitchen at the back of the house. The girl looked at Zoe and the dog with interest.

"This is my new dog," said Zoe confidently. Of course, she had no idea if the dog belonged to anyone else, she doubted that, or if it would stay with her. Zoe decided to make sure she did. First she took some scraps of fat and gristle from the bits they were saving for soap and fed a few of them to Lux who was watching everything with rapt attention.

"Mistress will not like it," warned Agalia.

"We have discussed it," Zoe lied confidently. "She is our new watchdog. I am hot and dirty. We are going to the baths. Come along, Lux," she commanded and tugging on the twine still around the dog's neck made an exit. Lux followed dutifully; she knew that the 'Nice Lady' still had food in her hand. Zoe talked confidently to her new friend all the way to the baths. She gave the attendant her fee and brought Lux into the women's side of the baths. The attendant raised his eyebrows but said nothing. Fortunately no one else was in the room, understandable at that time of the day. Zoe slipped out of her chiton and small clothes and eased into the lukewarm water. It took some time, a fair amount of gentle persuasion, and the last of the scraps to convince Lux to join her in the water. The dog put up with being soaped and cleaned and eventually wound up in the big tub curled on Zoe's chest, just above her breasts. They took a long bath soaking comfortably together. Zoe could hear other patrons coming into the baths before she reluctantly put her dog onto the ground and climbed out. She had no oils and so merely scraped herself dry with the common strigil before putting on her clothes. She had just stepped into her sandals when a woman came into the baths. Zoe recognized her as Adara, the wife of the Master of Horse. She had brought her daughter, an inquisitive girl of three, in for a bath with her mother.

"Look Mommy," the girl said excitedly, "a doggy.'

Lux shrank back against Zoe's legs. Zoe picked the wet animal up and smiling and nodding to the other woman, left before Adara could think of something to say; something like, 'Did you bring a dog into the baths with you?' That would be all too likely to lead to other comments and complaints. Zoe had no intention of bringing Lux back to the baths. It was important that when Ana first saw Lux the dog make a good impression. A clean dog is much more likely to do that than a filthy one. Zoe also knew how important it was to bond a dog to a new owner. Their time in the bath seemed to work. Once outside Zoe put her new pet down, and she walked right beside Zoe, all the way back to the house, drying in the remaining heat of the day.

Their reception back at the house was difficult. Ana was not sure what to say. Agamemnon for his part thought it was a great idea. He chased poor Lux around the room until the dog, driven to distraction, huddled at Zoe's feet for protection. Fortunately, Adem was away on business until late that night and did not return until Zoe and her new addition had retired. Zoe chose to sleep in her little chamber that night to remove the temptation from little Agamemnon and also to provide Ana and Adem with fewer reasons to forbid the dog to remain on the premises. It was hot in her room that night, especially since Lux chose to sleep right next to her. Even though the little dog was an extra source of heat, Zoe was glad for the company. She would have reason to be glad for that comfort even more in the immediate future.

The next day the first bit of bad news arrived; the tax collector came early. That was bad for the household; what came with the tax collector was worse. Adem's apprentice was conscripted. Soldiers simply took him up to the Hold to be incorporated into the guard. That meant he would be gone, with some breaks during harvest and planting times, for almost two years. His protests and those of a distracted Adem were politely but firmly ignored. The slender young man left with a guardsman on each elbow, holding a cloth bag with his meager possessions over his shoulder casting back desperate looks at his former and possibly future master. Zoe still thought he would not make a very good soldier.

The departure of the apprentice meant that when Adem was out doing business there were no men in the house. That was unusual, though not unheard of; unlike larger cities, not many people routinely employed doormen in a quiet little place like Dassaria. Most people still relied on relatives or friends of long standing. Hiring a strange man to guard your premises seemed exotic and dangerous. It seemed the double blow of being assessed a new, larger tax coupled with the loss of his apprentice drove Adem nearly to distraction. He knew of no prospects to replace his apprentice, lacked the ready cash to hire a qualified assistant, and had no relatives in town he could call on. His closest and most trusted friends, such as Needles, had their own families to look after and did not want to leave their houses. Amphora had no plans to go out of town and so focused on complaining about the additional taxes he would be paying.

Bad news, really bad news, often comes in waves. Losing his apprentice and having his taxes raised was nothing compared to the news that came in the next day. Zoe returned to the house in the early afternoon from taking Lux out for a little walk. As soon as she walked into the back of the house from the kitchen, she could instantly feel something was wrong. She quickly put Lux into their little cell and returned to find out what had happened. Men were talking together in grave tones in the andronitis, the men's court in the front of the house. This was not an unusual event; Adem always received his visitors there and talked business every day. This time was somehow different, and Zoe knew it. Ana and Agalia were in the andron, the formal dining room that adjoined the andronitis, listening at the door. That was very unusual; the only time Ana would eavesdrop on her husband was when she was expecting to act as hostess for the men, and she wanted to be ready to receive them. She never interfered with her husband's business. Zoe could tell from the two women's tense postures that there was a problem. From the voices that were coming through the door, she knew the business was a lot more serious than just an increase in taxes.

"What is it?" Zoe hissed in Ana's ear.

"That caravan that we were expecting," she replied pulling back from the door and whispering back, "The one Adem had a very big order on. They were bringing back money and some of the eastern wines in trade. It was really too much to risk, but he said the return would be very good. We did it last year, and it was so profitable. Apparently, messengers just arrived from over the lake. It is bad news." In the last few years fishermen had begun to sell their wares at the little cove to the west of the Hold. Not only did they bring in fish, they often could pass on news days before it got to Dassaria by land. This particular news was bad news and, as bad news does, it had traveled fast.

It took a few minutes for the specifics to be delivered from the andronitis to the anxious women waiting in the dining hall. It appeared word had been received that the caravan coming back from Pellas had been ambushed in the mountains. There had been fierce fighting, and the caravan master had been slain. There had been great loss of life and goods. All of Adem's goods were probably lost.

It took Zoe a minute to put things together. She did not want to believe what she was hearing. She knew that Bukchos had been with Adem's outbound caravan. She also knew that guards normally remained with a caravan until it returned home. Zoe recognized the name the caravan master who had been murdered. He was the man who had hired Bukchos. That meant her husband must have been with the ambushed caravan. He was probably dead. She was a widow in a strange place far from home.

Zoe felt the room close in on her, the walls compressing. Her knees were suddenly weak and she staggered back to the wall, her hands covering her face. She was too stunned to cry or even cry out; she just leaned there against the wall then slowly slid down to the floor, her eye looking at nothing at all as the enormity of her disaster sank in.

Ana, staggered by the news of her family's potential ruin did not notice Zoe's condition at first. It was only when Agalia called out Zoe's name that she turned back to see her sitting on the floor just as pale as the whitewashed wall she was leaning against. For a moment Ana was irritated with the young woman. Why was she so concerned? It was not her family that was ruined. Then with a rush she remembered that Zoe's husband had been one of the guards on the ill-fated caravan.

"Her husband," was all she said to Agalia and went to the stunned woman on the floor taking her hands in her own. Agalia now recognized Zoe's loss and also went to her, the two women putting aside their own troubles to comfort and console one whose loss was greater than their own.

By the time Adem had finished talking with the men in that andronitis and come to speak with his wife, Zoe had recovered enough to begin weeping into Agalia's shoulder.

"Bukchos was one of the caravan guards," explained Ana to her husband. He gave her a puzzled look. "Her husband," Ana hissed to him. Comprehension dawned.

"I am very sorry for your loss," he said uncomfortably to the new widow who continued to cling to Agalia. "Wife, we must speak," Adem said drawing Ana to one side. "The King is sending a strong party to investigate. The bandits were operating well outside the borders of his kingdom, but many local people had goods in the caravan. We have prevailed upon him to send men to see if we can recover any of our goods. They will leave tomorrow at first light. I am going with them."

"What! Why! You are no warrior to go off hunting bandits in the hills! What will we do here? Even the apprentice is gone. Will you leave us alone? What are you thinking?!?"

Adem attempted to calm her. He had a cousin, a son of his father's sister. Adem would send for the man to come and manage the business while he was gone. He had to go with the men if he was to have any hope of recovering his goods. He would be gone for less than a month.

Ana refused to accept any of these excuses and alternative plans. Adem bluntly told her he was leaving with the men at dawn the next day. He then left to make the necessary arrangements. He sent a message for his cousin, a man known as Peder, to come to Dassaria at once and manage the business in Adem's absence. That messenger dispatched, Adem went to Ixon, the Master of Horse, to arrange lease of a pony for the ride.

It was a grim dinner that night. Ana was not speaking to her husband who took out his frustrations on Agalia who then fled to her own cell. Zoe remained in her cell not eating. Her faithful Lux stayed right with her and was a great source of comfort to the new widow. Zoe could not stop thinking, the thoughts buzzing around in her head like a trapped bee. How could she support herself? She would have to get married again, but how? She had no family, no dowry, so it would have to be a pallake arrangement. That was not so bad, provided she could find someone to marry her? She wondered about Bukchos. Was he really dead? She had been married to him for less than half a year. She really didn't know him all that well. She did not think she even loved him. That filled her with guilt. Zoe admitted to herself that her marriage had not been happy, and she had been very contented in this house without a man. She wondered what it would have been like if Bukchos had come home. Would she have been better off? When would they know if he were dead for certain?

Things were no better in the morning. The women were up even earlier than usual to prepare breakfast for Adem. Ana was still angry and breakfast was a tense, quiet meal, eaten rapidly.

Adem seemed relieved to hear the cry "Ho, Amphora," from Ixon who was waiting with their horses in the predawn light. "They are already coming out the gate. I don't want to have to gallop just to catch up. We will be moving fast enough today."

Adem hurried to the horse that Ixon was holding. "Needles and Kaj will look in and make sure everything is safe until my cousin Peder arrives to take over. He should be here in five or six days. Just keep to the house and everything will be fine."

Ixon made an impatient sound.

"I must go," Adem said by way of explanation, and he rode away.

Adem was not a graceful rider, and he appeared a faintly ridiculous figure to the three women as he rode away. He rode arms akimbo, his tunic hitched up to mid thigh; his pilleus sitting crookedly on his head, and a short sword flapping at his side.

"Needles," grumbled Zoe, "the tailor is going to be our protector." Her eyes were red and every part of her posture told of her long sleepless night.

"When the raiders came and sacked the town, Needles drove off four armed horsemen," Ana told her somewhat stiffly. "Neeta saw it. She said he saved their lives. Now let's get inside and bar the doors."

That first day was relatively busy. It seemed everyone wanted to see what was going on with Amphora's business. The owners of some of the tavern houses came by to see if they could purchase some wine. The women could not decide if these men wanted to see whether of not they could take advantage of the owner's absence to get wine at a reduced rate or if they were just curious. No sales were made, and no men were allowed entry. Female callers were allowed inside and there were a lot of visitors that first day. It was another testament to the unusual freedom women enjoyed in an out of the way place like Dassaria that women could walk unescorted in town during the daylight hours. Some of the women came for gossip, some to console Ana and Zoe for their different losses, and some out of curiosity. Adem's male friends and neighbors did come by from time to time to make sure everything was fine; Needles was especially conscientious about coming by after dark to make sure the house was safely secured for the night.

Despite all this it was a boring time. Not even her grief and uncertainty could keep Zoe down for long. She occupied herself by working on Lux's training. The little dog was a quick study and in two days would come, sit, stay, lie down and heel during walks. She had learned to bark when visitors called, especially fiercely when they were men and to be still when signaled by Zoe. It was all very gratifying, but Zoe was not sure she was such a good trainer or if Lux was just a smart dog. Unfortunately, she discovered in talking with the women who came by that there was no real market for expert dog trainers. The town was too small, and those people who had dogs either did not need them trained or did so themselves.

This was disappointing to Zoe because she had made up her mind that she was going to have to make her way in the world and do it without a man. She did not imagine that she knew all the unmarried men in Dassaria, though she did know most of them, at least by reputation, and none of them were at all interesting to her. Well, there was the Magistrate. She had heard that he was unmarried, and he was kind of cute, but she might as well try to attract the King; after all, the King was unmarried, and she had heard he was a handsome man. Zoe had no idea; she had never seen a King in her life. No, this was her life now; she was going to have to make it on her own. She had spent way too much time going over what it would be like if she married any number of the single men before she had gotten married. The roles of a wife and mother had always been held out to her as the purpose of her life. Well, if it was not to be, she would just have to make the best of it. If Bukchos came back, then her time would not be wasted. After all, he had left her once; if he survived to return he would probably leave her again. Zoe decided to simplify her life—she decided that her husband was dead and gone. She was going to behave like a widow even if she did not have her husband's body. That meant she would just have to find a way to support herself.

Perhaps she could be an apprentice to Adem? Why couldn't an independent woman help out around the business? She could read a little and could certainly count and write numbers down. If she made herself useful, she might just stay here indefinitely.

All these plans came to a crashing halt when the Adem's cousin arrived to 'manage the business'. Peder, whose name meant 'Rock', arrived seven days after Adem had departed. A man in his twenties, he was of below average height and above average weight, most of which rested around his middle. He had thinning black hair, a patchy beard and deep-set eyes on either side of a narrow red nose. It did not take long for him to make a bad impression. The first thing he did when he walked into the house was call for a cup of wine. Then he openly ogled the women of the household making several pointed suggestions to Ana about his own ability to fulfill Amphora's 'husband's duty' in his absence. He told a blushing Agalia that she would not be troubled by any suitors since he could handle her needs right here on the premises. Then, right there in front of the other two women and with the messenger who had accompanied him still present, offered to console the newly widowed Zoe in the coarsest possible terms.

The other two women were shocked speechless. Zoe rose to meet the crisis. "Perhaps you would like to see your cousin's stock of wines," she said with a wide smile. Zoe guessed that that was the one thing that would always divert Peder. She was not mistaken. Zoe started by showing Peder amphorae of the cheaper red table wines that were a staple for the tavern houses. Zoe opened the top of an amphora of Bekari. "May I bring you a cup?" Peder sat right down on a couch in the andronitis and waited happily for this beautiful young widow to bring him wine. Wines in that time and place were strong; that was part of the reason almost everyone watered their wine. Zoe knew better; she did not even bother with a bowl for the water. Zoe passed him a brimming cup of the strong red wine, lithely avoiding the worst of his groping hands. In an astonishingly short time, he had drained his cup and was asking for more.

The break Zoe gave them allowed Ana to collect herself. Ana did know her husband's business to one extent: she knew drunks. Peder's red nose alone had been a signal to her, and his behavior prompted her to unusual decisiveness. Adem's success had been due in part to his ability to keep his wares secure. She pulled the messenger who had brought Peder aside and spoke urgently to him. Then she slipped away to make sure the hidden trap doors that led down to the two small cellars where Adem kept his most expensive vintages were well secured. Then she, helped by Agalia, she shifted some of their more expensive wines from their store rooms located in the andron rolling the heavy amphorae across the floor on their heavy pointed bases to hiding places behind panels back in their gynaeconitis.

While this was going on Zoe continued to play a game women sometimes play: controlling a dangerous man. Entered into in the right spirit it could be an exhilarating sport. Zoe was aware that the Minoans danced with bulls, tricking them with flimsy cloths, dodging aside from their charges, and even leaping over the enraged animals' backs. Played well, you could handle a dangerous creature using your wits and guile. This was much the same. It was a game not without risk; a woman who blundered or lost her nerve could wind up beaten, raped, and worse. On that afternoon Zoe in a fey mood, undertook the challenge. Peder drunk was more dangerous but also more malleable. She played him off with half promises, mock threats, offers of vague rewards and jokes that he did not seem to quite grasp, just as he was not quite able to grasp this delightful creature who somehow led him on until he was quite unable to stand. Zoe was astonished at the amount of raw uncut wine the man could absorb. Then, just as Peder was about to lapse into snoring insentience, Ana was there with two stout young men accompanied by another woman that Zoe recognized as Adara, the wife of the Master of Horse. Zoe guessed from their attire and odor that the two men were stablemen who worked for her husband. They took the surprised Peder under his arms and steered him into the room off the andronitis that had been prepared for him. Adara watched disapprovingly with her arms crossed under her breasts.

"That one will be trouble," she predicted grimly.

"Oh, I think we can handle him," said Ana uncertainly. "Perhaps it is just the trip. We will see how he is in the morning."

Adara left with her two assistants, the other woman still radiating unfocused disapproval. From Peder's room came the sound of heavy snoring.

"Why is the wife the Master of Horses so angry?" Zoe asked Ana when they had retreated back to the relative sanctity of the gynaeconitis. The three women were sharing some flat bread and cheese, dipping it into spiced olive oil. They also all had a cup of well-watered wine. Both Agalia's and Zoe's hands were unsteady. Agalia's from fear, Zoe's from the after-affects of her adrenaline high. It had taken all her wits and a skill she had not known she had to avoid Peder's attentions while diverting him from the other women and the rest of the house in general.

"She doesn't like men, much," responded Ana. She then related a version of Adara's story and how she came to marry Ixon. "Many of the men are still afraid of her, well maybe not afraid, but they are uneasy around her."

Agalia had not really understood the more unpleasant aspects of what had happened to Adara; she focused instead on her rescue by Ixon. "That is so romantic," she enthused. Ana and Zoe just looked at one another.

"What are we going to do?" asked Zoe. "Did Adem actually know his cousin? Why would he send us someone like that?"

"I don't know," confessed Ana. "I never met him before, and Adem had not talked about him very much. He told me that his aunt had often asked if her younger son could work for him. She had told him Peder was interested in the wine business."

"Well," said Zoe dryly, "that we have seen."

"Let's see what he is like in the morning," Ana temporized. "Perhaps he will be better."

Of course he wasn't. He was hung over and unpleasant. At least his lechery seemed to be under control, although Zoe suspected that had more to do with him being sick than any change in his personality. By midday he had fortified himself with two large cups of wine and headed out to present himself to several of the suppliers and customers recommended to him by Adem. He returned much later that afternoon insisting that Ana put on a dinner for some important clients. It was obvious he had found another source of wine for his tunic had fresh wine stains and his face was flushed. Ana, thinking fast, arranged for one of the tavern houses to provide two serving boys to assist.

The event that night was a form of symposia, held in the men's hall. Bread, fruit, and some simple cheeses were available but most of the guests were primarily there to sample 'Old Amphora's' wines. Ana, peeking into the andronitis, saw that some of the guests were merchants who kept tavern houses or claimed to sell wine. She did not recognize half the men in the room. The hired serving boys were kept busy well into the night. The women took Agamemnon and retreated up to the roof. It was not easy climbing the ladder in the kitchen that led up to the roof, especially with burdens, not the least of which was a toddler. They already had bedding up there; they also brought up food and water. Ana also brought her biggest kitchen pestle. Zoe thought she saw the glint of a knife concealed in Agalia's chiton. For herself, Zoe carried a thick billet of wood almost as long as her arm. Lux was hauled up to the roof with them using the same cloth sling over their shoulder Ana used to carry Agamemnon. The women were glad for the little dog's presence. From up on the roof they could see other people trying to sleep on their own roofs, and the glances (and sometimes glares) being cast their way at the noise from the drunken men carousing down below.

The next morning they found the andronitis was a shambles. Apparently the festivities had even sprawled over into the adjoining andron. Two bodies were found passed out on the floor; Peder, and a man that Ana thought worked at one of the tavern houses, a notorious drunk and layabout of poor reputation. Ana and Zoe managed to half drag half help Peder into his room with only cursory groping on his part. Then the two women, assisted enthusiastically by a barking, growling Lux, drove the other lout into the street.

Zoe needed three trips to the well that morning to get enough water to clean up the mess the men had created. She would rather haul water than clean up the vomit and urine and broken cups left by the gathering. The riotous symposium at Amphora's house the night before was the talk of the women gathered at the well each time she came. It was scandalous, juicy gossip, and Zoe did her bit to assassinate Peder's character to each new audience. Ana was stunned to discover that, not only had the men drunk the amphora of Bekari Zoe had opened that afternoon for Peder, but another of Xynomavro was almost gone as well. Even those dregs did not last until dark, for when Peder awoke sometime after noon he immediately attacked the last of that wine. Then smiling broadly he wandered out to 'seek new business.' This time he returned later and with fewer compatriots; there was no food prepared, but that did not seem to matter. Once again a salute to Dionysus began. And once again the women, child, and dog retreated to the relative safety

316

of the roof. This time the men seem to have brought some women with them, whether common prostitutes or girlfriends, the women on the roof did not try to determine. Instead they did their best to secure the trapdoor to the roof by putting the sleeping couches on top of it. That was not enough for them, and they took turns sleeping while one woman remained on watch. Zoe slept with her dog on one side and her club on the other.

In the morning they found that apparently the revelers had opened an amphora of a fine white wine, a Zitsas. Even though there had been fewer men in the house on the second night of revelry, Zoe was astonished to find they had somehow managed to drink or spill almost the entire amphora. At least this time Peder had managed to go to his own room and no one remained in the house. That did not mean he was acknowledging his responsibilities as head of the household; the doors to the house had been open all night. The combination of strangers in the house and unsecured doors worried the women profoundly.

"He was supposed to run the business and keep up safe," complained Zoe to the women at the well that morning. "We are worse off than we were before he came."

Ana confronted Peder about this when he awakened that afternoon. He was first placating, then truculent, then imperious. "You know nothing about this business," he told her, which was true, but then neither did he. "You need to establish relationships. I am setting up deals with all the places that sell wine here. Of course, I think that the real money will be to open a tavern house." Ana wondered how he could sell wine to the tavern houses and compete with them at the same time. She knew that Adem would never allow strangers to come into his house to pay to drink wine. But what could she do? What she chose to do was retreat to the relative safety of the gynaeconitis and take it out on Agalia and Zoe. At least she was able to persuade Peder not to take a tour of the various tavern houses that afternoon and have a meal with them that evening.

The meal was a disaster. Peder's main interests seemed to be getting his hands on money, wine, and women. Even Zoe's skills were not proof against a man completely taken with himself. He was having the time of his life; this was what he felt he had always deserved. He had a nice place to sleep, lots of new friends, women who would certainly come around soon enough, and plenty of wine. This was his big opportunity, and he was making the most of it. So when men begain dropping by soon after dark to pay a call on their new best friend, Peder was delighted to see them. He ordered another amphora to be opened. "Not that swill we have been drinking, bring the good stuff. We cannot let people think all we sell is that cheap vinegar water."

Ana refused and the scene got ugly. Zoe was only barely able to prevent violence, and even then Ana sported a set of nasty bruises on her arm where Peder had grabbed her. It was necessary to sacrifice another amphora; this one was a rose, a blend of Debinas and Vlachiko varietals. It pained Ana to give it up, but as Zoe pointed out it pained her less than a beating.

That night the three women sat up on the roof, each miserable and each consumed with negative emotions.

Agalia was terrified. Peder frightened her for many reasons. He had been trying to catch her alone. She knew that if he did he would probably rape her. Losing her maidenhead to him would ruin any faint hopes she had of securing a decent marriage.

Ana was frustrated to the point of despair. She could not understand how they had fallen so far so fast. First, they had a tax increase, then their apprentice was taken away, then they had apparently lost all their potential profit from the caravan, now this creature had been foisted upon them by her husband. Adem had chosen to run after lost profits instead of staying to preserve what they had. He had carelessly placed the rest of their fortune in the hands of a drunken wastrel. It would serve him right if she did get raped and beaten. By the time he came back from his hopeless pursuit of the bandits, all his stock would have been drunk up or given away by his feckless cousin. Ana was worried sick about Agamemnon. So far Peder had ignored the infant except to complain when he cried. Ana knew he not only would do little to protect her son, he might in fact be the biggest danger to him.

Zoe was angry. Men! First one goes and leaves her. Then he gets himself killed—probably. Anyway he was not here when she needed him. Because of problems created by another man! All men were good for was getting rid of each other! She could do quite well, thank you, without a man. She would miss the sex, well, it wasn't all that much of a sacrifice. She just had to figure out how first to get rid of that man down there in the andronitis swilling wine that was not his. Then she could sort things out.

They had eaten a melon for their meal, and soon after dark the women decided it was a good time to visit the privy in the back of the house. There were a number of strange men drinking and carrying on in the front of the house but they did not sound especially drunk yet; apparently the men were still in that stage where they were more interested in eating and drinking than fighting, breaking things, and throwing up. While Agamemnon slept the three women crept through the trap door at the back of the roof and down the ladder that let down into the kitchen area. Zoe gave Agalia her club for the climb because she had to carry Lux. The dog needed to be walked if they did not want to step in something she left up on the roof. They did their business quickly and headed back. Zoe held back to let Lux finish her walk. She had Lux's leash in left hand and her club in her right.

"Hurry up," she hissed to the dog. Of course, Lux's training had not advanced that far. She continued to sniff about moving up the side of the house straining at the end of the leash. Zoe was not particularly afraid; Ana, however, was following behind her in the darkness and Zoe could feel the other woman's growing concern. It was emphatically a bad idea to be outside after dark with Peder's friends around. Suddenly Lux began barking and straining at the leash, pulling Zoe toward a window at the side of the house.

"Lux, silence," Zoe commanded; Lux's training had progressed that far, and she stopped barking but she continued a very impressive growl for a dog of her size. Lux kept pulling toward the window. Zoe suddenly saw a figure standing quietly by the window. The man drew back from the window and stepped quietly toward them. There was something in his manner and movements that eased Zoe's fears. He was not a large man, and it seemed he had been looking into the house where all the activity was, not trying to find an empty room to burgle. 'Besides,' Zoe thought, 'this fellow is not one of Peder's friends. If he tries to hurt me there is a whole room of men that can come outside. They won't bother me if they have someone else to chase.'

"Greetings," said the small man in a quiet polite voice. "I mean you no harm."

Zoe believed him. The men inside were singing or they would have heard the noise outside. Now, abruptly, Zoe decided that this man was less of a threat than the men she had been counting on protecting her a moment before. After all, she had Lux, and her club, and Ana was behind her. She pulled Lux back and moved away from the window into the men's hall and back opposite a window in the andron. There was a half moon and the light from the lamps burning in dining hall spilled out from the wide gaps in the window shutters giving light enough for her to see the man she had accosted. He was small, with a large nose, beady eyes, and brown hair. He looked both inoffensive and utterly forgettable. No wonder Lux had barked at him; she probably mistook him for a large rat. Zoe had to smother an internal giggle.

"What are you doing here," Zoe hissed at him trying to appear severe while at the same time not alert the men in the hall who had begun another song.

"I heard the noise," said the man blandly. "I wanted to see what was going on."

"I bet you were looking to see what you could steal!" she accused. Her dog seconded Zoe's suspicions with a fierce low growl.

He quietly protested and began repeating his claim of simple curiosity when Ana leaned over Zoe's shoulder and interrupted him.

"Good evening Mouse," she said in the safe, soft voice they had been using. "We were just retiring for the night. I am sorry to have disturbed you." She pulled a protesting Zoe back, much as Zoe had just pulled Lux away from the man who stood there blinking in the dim light. As they pulled back he did not seem to withdraw from the light as much as fade away.

Zoe's sputtered questions became louder as they retreated from the noise in the front of the house. "Did you know that man? What was he doing? Is he really called Mouse? What was he doing here?"

By the time she had all this out, the two women and one dog had made it up the ladder, through the trap door onto the roof where an anxious Agalia waited for them; they closed the door and moved a couch over it to secure themselves from unwelcome visitors.

The heavy cloth tarpaulin over their heads flapped in a sudden small gust, quieting Zoe. She put the squirming Lux down and turned back to Ana.

"That," Ana said still keeping her voice low, "was the Mouse. He is the King's personal eyes and ears. You are never to mention that to anyone ever again, especially where someone might be able to hear you say it." The other two women looked at her. She pulled them to the center of the roof and squatted down bringing them close. "He skulks around listening to people. And what he hears the King knows. Let me tell you a story. There were some merchants that came here two years back that wanted to know about the treasure up there," Ana gestured up toward the Hold, invisible in the darkness. "Then they started asking questions about how much the men liked the King, and if they knew how to get into the Hold. It was nothing too overt, just asking questions, almost like it was only curiosity, very discreet. And they simply disappeared. The men in the caravan they had been traveling with said their things were still in their tent, but they had not come to appointments they had made the day before with some other men in town. The two men were never seen again. That is the way the Mouse works. He finds out things. And if the King thinks these things are dangerous, the King takes action. Mouse won't hurt you himself, but he knows people who can." Here she paused for a moment; before the others could speak she continued. "It is not such a bad thing. We really don't have much crime. Between the Mouse, the Magistrate and the King, people stay pretty honest. The Mouse finds things out, the Magistrate passes judgment, and the King makes sure that the judgment is carried out." Ana shrugged, "It is simply best not to let the Mouse know that you know too much about him. He likes it better that way."

There was more talk, of course, and by the time the other women drifted off to sleep leaving Zoe to keep watch over the door, an idea had begun to form in her mind. She decided to keep the idea to herself. If she told Ana she might forbid Zoe to go, and she did not want to have to defy her hostess.

Zoe did her chores quickly the following morning. Although the previous night's drinking bout had been smaller and less destructive than the some of the earlier ones, Zoe confirmed that most of the amphora of wine, a good wine, was gone. She finished her duties before the hated Peder arose and was able to escape the house by telling Ana she need to walk Lux. "It's part of her training," she blithely told Ana. Zoe could see how the strain of the past few days had begun to show on the older woman's face. Something had to be done. Maybe if the King had started to take an interest it was time to involve the officials. The sun was well up and the streets were busy. Zoe put on her best chiton and prepared herself as well as she could without giving cause for comment, though Agalia did give her a strange look as she stepped out with Lux. Zoe made a detour to the well to get some help. The only woman there was a serving girl that Zoe did not really know. Even so, Zoe was able to persuade the girl to help her put up her hair in a proper matronly bun. Zoe had brought a set of combs and a small bronze mirror. After the two women had completed their effort to improve her hair, Zoe used the mirror to check her look. The serving girl would never make it as a hair dresser; still, it would have to do. She took her best (she only had two) broach from her pouch and pinned it to her chiton. She was not really ready but it was now or never. Taking a deep breath she took her dog and walked north to the house of the Magistrate of Dassaria.

Standing in front of the imposing house of Rodas, Magistrate of Dassaria, Zoe had a moment of doubt. Bringing Lux was undoubtedly a mistake. Her little friend had given her a reason to be out and about, and she had given Zoe much needed companionship on the walk over. Now it seemed ridiculous to be standing here with a pet dog. Zoe looked around for a place to put her. She could not count on Lux sitting and staying too long, and there was no way to know how long she would be waiting. She whispered a little prayer to Aphrodite for inspiration. The goddess had always been one of Zoe's favorites. Perhaps she was listening, for just as Zoe was losing her nerve, a tough-looking man with an eye patch came out of the door.

"What do you want?" he asked her not unkindly.

Instantly she spoke up before her courage could fail her, "I am here to bring a matter to the attention of the Magistrate."

"Oh, you are, are you?" the man smiled and swung the big door open wide in invitation. 'He has a nice smile,' thought Zoe as she entered. Then she wondered whether he was smiling because he was nice, or because she brought her silly dog in with her. Lux was heeling nicely and behaving herself, but she was far too cute a dog to be taken seriously. Or perhaps he was just smiling at her cleavage. Zoe knew the effect her ample bosom sometimes had on men, and she had artfully arranged her chiton to show quite a bit of décolletage. Sometimes a girl needed an edge.

The man with the patch led them straight to a large room where several men were standing around talking in low tones. She instantly recognized the Magistrate. She was pleasantly surprised to see he was quite as handsome as she had remembered. Seeing her he stopped and turned toward her.

Before he could speak she addressed him, "Sire, I come to you on a matter that requires redress."

"Well, then, I had better hear it properly," and with a broad smile he moved over to an elaborate high backed chair that was positioned on a low dais against the wall. Zoe had never seen anything like it before. She had to admit it was very imposing. She followed him, to stand in front of the Seat of Justice. Lux heeled obediently at her side. Zoe could feel the tension from the little dog right up the leash; or perhaps the tension was going both ways.

Rodas adjusted his tunic, looked down and addressed her, "Now, what is this matter that you wish to bring to my attention?" He used the second person plural in his address to them. After a moment Zoe realized he was referring not to her and Ana, but to Zoe and her dog! The sheer insolence of it! He was making fun of her!

She squared her shoulders (getting the full attention of every man in the room) and in icy tones responded, "Sire, My name is Zoe. I serve in the house of Adem. I had thought that the Magistrate dealt with all people equally. I am probably a respectable widow." She stopped. That had not come out right. The Magistrate smiled faintly but continued to watch her without comment. Zoe restarted, "We recently received word my husband is probably dead." There, that was better. She plowed on, "I come to speak of a matter of some seriousness."

"Yes, I was sorry to hear of Bukchos' death," replied Rodas.

That startled her a little bit. She had no idea that he knew her husband's name or that had been killed. "Thank you, sire," she said to cover her momentary confusion. "Then you must know of our plight, that is, the difficulty Ana and her husband are facing with his business."

"I understand that Amphora went off to try to recover some of his lost profits and put his cousin in charge while he was gone."

"And you must know what has happened since."

"Apparently he is not living up to Amphora's expectations; or yours."

"Or anybody's," said Zoe, her earlier coolness replace by heat. "He is drinking our stock, not selling it. People come by to make purchases, and that worthless layabout sits under the front awning and drinks half the purchase. He calls it 'sampling the merchandise for quality'. Then he gets so drunk he winds up giving it away to his so-called friends. At the rate he is going he will have ruined Adem's business by the time he can get back. That is not all; he is having riotous parties every night. We must crouch on the roof every night in fear of our honor. His behavior is bound to provoke a riot sooner or later. What must the neighbors think of the noise and commotion?"

"They do not like it," said Rodas seriously. Once again Zoe was surprised; he knew about their problem. Why hadn't he done anything about it?

Rodas leaned forward, trying not to be distracted by the lovely cleavage he could see from his elevation; he needed to answer this serious problem seriously. He was a magistrate right now, not the inspector of dancing girls.

Zoe saw him shake his head as if to clear it; then he spoke looking right in her eyes. 'He has nice eyes,' she thought somewhat scatteredly before she realized what he was saying.

"Amphora put the business in the hands of a male relative. That was the correct and appropriate thing to do. I cannot and will not overturn his orders just because his choice for an agent turned out to be a fool."

"Then what good is your justice!" cried out Zoe. Lux growled and gave a low bark in agreement. "What must he do for you to act? Ruin Adem completely? Burn down the house? Rape Agalia?" Zoe was in an intimidating place, surrounded by men some of whom were armed, talking to the second most important man in the kingdom; she did not care. She was angry and frustrated to the point of tears.

"No, Zoe, if he is guilty of arson, or riot, or rape, I can judge him. But I cannot charge a man for being a fool." His eyes that were holding hers shifted to the others in the room, all men. His tone changed, "If that were a crime I would have to charge half the town."

The men in the room chuckled dutifully. That did nothing to assuage Zoe.

"What would you do to him if he did those things?" she challenged him. Lux, sensing her owner's mood, gave low growl. The men were amused, but Rodas responded gravely.

"For rape or murder I can have a man executed. Arson and riot, that depends on the severity. I can give him fine, lashes, or exile him. I could do the same if he were to cheat others. There is no penalty for cheating yourself."

"But it is not himself he is cheating, it is Adem and Ana," protested Zoe.

"I am truly sorry, Zoe, but if Amphora made a mistake in putting his business in the hands of the wrong relative while he was gone, then he shall have to bear the result."

"If you will not protect those who cannot protect themselves, what good are you?"

And with that, she turned and stalked out of the hall, dragging Lux behind her. Lux looked around the room and gave everyone in the place a general departing growl.

Zoe had a fair amount of headway generated by the time she hit the outer door. Spiros was standing beside it, beginning to open the door for someone outside, when Zoe, coming up on his blind side, barged past him, running into a man who was just coming in. Lux yelped and pulled back from the two who briefly tangled.

He was a soldier she thought in the instant she bumped into his hard body. He was wearing riding attire: trousers, tunic, and a red leather vest. Zoe had seen often guardsmen in Dassaria wearing trousers; she still found the look exotic. She noticed he was clean shaven, with wavy russet hair, was in his early middle years, and had the presence of an officer. She was still upset by her unsuccessful interview with the Magistrate. She has been so sure he would help her! The collision had almost knocked her breasts free from the breast wraps Zoe wore under her chiton. Zoe reached up and rearranged herself properly.

"Harrumph!" Zoe snorted. "Is this the way poor widows are treated in Dassaria? Denied justice inside and then accosted as they leave?"

"I beg your pardon," the man said pushing the door open and stepping past her carefully avoiding stepping on Lux who twisted around trying to avoid being stepped on. The man disappeared inside. Lux's leash wrapped around Zoe's legs, momentarily upsetting her. A quick stumbling step saved her from landing ignobly on her bottom in front of a group of guardsmen.

The men were waiting in a group near the door, a bit over a dozen, most still mounted. Apparently the man who had gone inside was the captain of one of the mounted rides that periodically patrolled the realm. The men seemed to think her collision with their leader to be very funny.

Zoe looked back at the Magistrate's one-eyed doorman. "Excuse me," she said, "I did not ask your name when I arrived." She needed a moment to compose herself. Besides there was no harm in being polite and he had been nice to her.

"My name is Spiros," he replied. He was smiling just like the horsemen, "Formerly of King Athan's guard, now in the service of the Magistrate, Rodas."

Suddenly a deep horrible suspicion rose within her. A clean shaven man of early middle years and a red vest; that description sounded familiar. Dreading the answer she still had to ask. "Master Spiros, who was that man whom I just ummm…spoke with?"

"That was Athan, King of Dassaria," replied Spiros now with a huge grin. The men began laughing delightedly.

She could feel the heat of a blush moving up her neck to her cheeks. "Come Lux, heel!" she said trying to make as dignified and rapid retreat as possible under the circumstances.

"It's all right," Spiros called to her as she hurried away, "I think he likes you." The patrol roared with laughter.

"Who was that?" Athan asked his old friend as they sat together on a couch. He did not need to identify who he was referring to. The men in the room were still buzzing about Zoe's visit.

"Oh, her name is Zoe; she's a widow of a guard that got killed in the caravan raid. She is living in Amphora's house."

"A widow, eh?" smiled Athan, "not another one of your dancing girls?"

"No," replied Rodas with a slight smile, "she seems a respectable girl; she was just looking for some help with the agent who came in to help Amphora.

"Ahhh," Athan said understanding, "That idiot who is causing all the trouble. What was Amphora thinking when he made him his agent?"

"We conscripted his apprentice and, before he could find a replacement, he got the news about the caravan. So he chose a family member as his agent instead of hiring somebody he knew. Apparently he did not know the man and took his aunt's recommendation on faith; big mistake. The girl you saw, Zoe, came to see if I could help get rid of him."

"That was a brave thing to do," commented Athan. "I ran into her coming out. She is a bold one. What was she doing with that dog?"

Rodas laughed at the memory, "I have no idea. Let me tell you though, she stood her ground even though she was clearly nervous."

"The girl or the dog?" asked Athan smiling.

"Both. You saw her? Pretty girl, wasn't she?"

Athan looked at his old friend. "Yes she was. A widow you say."

"Yes. Too bad I couldn't do anything to help her."

There was a pause as Athan started to say one thing and then changed his mind.

"Well, keep a eye on that fool Peder. If he presents a problem, get rid of him. I should be back in ten days or so. I will send messages back to let you know what I find out."

"Yes, sire."

Zoe confessed all to Ana back at the house barely able to hold back her tears.

Ana forgave her immediately, "I would have gone myself if I had thought it would do any good. So, you met the King?"

Zoe nodded, "I bumped into him and then told him he was rude and his magistrate didn't help unfortunate women; well I didn't know it was **his** magistrate. Anyway, he apologized to me, to **me**, and went inside. He could have had my head cut off."

"The old Bear, the king we had before this one, might have done something like that or even worse. Did the King seem angry?"

"No, he just smiled at me. Why doesn't he wear a crown, or glorious robes, or have courtiers around him or something? How long has he been king?"

"Oh, he and his men drove out the Bear and took over a few years ago. Things have been better since they did, too. As for crowns and robes and courtiers and bards and such, well, this King Athan isn't that kind of a king. We don't go in for all that expensive king stuff way out here. Make no mistake, he is a king and a rich one, but I don't think he will do anything about you being rude to him. After all, what did you do except tell him the truth?"

"I ran right into him!"

"He might have enjoyed that," said Ana dryly, and the tension in the room eased.

"You are probably right. Why would they worry about an insignificant widow? I bet he don't even know my name."

"Oh, I think they all know your name now," Ana assured her. "And that might not be such a bad thing."

While Zoe had been trying to get the Magistrate to take some action, Peder had crawled out of bed and headed for the baths. From there Ana expected him come back and 'to continue ruining us with stupid business deals with his wine-friends.' Zoe went into her chamber and changed from her finery into her normal chiton. She let down her long black hair and combed it out, the motion calming her down.

"You have a good idea, though," Ana said when Zoe rejoined her. We need someone to help us. I think it is time for one of us to visit Celeno."

"Who is Celeno?" asked Zoe. She had heard the name once or twice, but people seemed reluctant to gossip about her, at least with Zoe. That was unusual.

"She is a witch," responded Ana matter of factly "She lives up in the Hold with Sergeant Prokopios, the Provost of the Hold."

Ana originally wanted to go herself, but in the end, Zoe had to go instead. Ana did not want to leave the house; she was expecting a visit from Adara about temporarily hiring one of her stable hands to 'help around the place'. Actually, the hope was the man could provide some security for the women from the new master of the house. Further Ana did not feel safe leaving the house empty. She did not dare leave Agalia home with little 'Aggie' in case Peder might return and find the girl alone. No, if the thing were to be done, it was best done quickly. That meant Zoe would go alone and soon, as the day was advancing. Ana gave Zoe instructions on what to ask for, some quick advice on dealing with the old woman, and a spending limit for the witch's services. Ana thought the best place to find the old woman was inside the Hold.

The shadows were lengthening when Zoe headed up to the hill to the Hold. It was an eventful little journey. On the way up the hill she passed a large band of warriors, perhaps two score or more, coming down the hill out of the Hold. She recognized the leading sergeant, Prokopios, at the head of the men. She had heard a lot about him; he might or might not be married to Celeno. It was certain that they spent a lot of time together. Like the other men in the line he was wearing a cuirass and had a sword on his hip. Further, he had a hoplon on his back and a helmet was slung from his belt. In addition to the accoutrements of war, each of the men behind Prokopios was carrying a spear over his shoulder with a cloth script bundle hanging over their backs from the shaft of the weapon. This bindle staff apparently contained all the belongings the men would need for the campaign; it was obvious that they were headed out for a long trip. A dozen pack mules followed behind the column of men, loaded with supplies. Zoe wondered why the men were heading out so late in the day. She would later find out that it was common for a band to travel only a short distance on the first day of travel in order to 'settle the men down'. This particular band was headed north following Athan and the mounted band that had left that morning. The king was troubled by the raid on the caravan and intended to make a reconnaissance in force in the hills to the north of Lychmidas. Zoe was thrilled at the sight of so many armed men marching off together. They were apparently thrilled to see her as well for she had many looks, comments, and offers as the young men passed her on her way up. Zoe decided to take all the attention as a compliment.

She arrived at the main gates of the Hold and paused there. The big main gates had been closed and even the smaller door inside the gate was no longer open. Zoe had never had occasion to go up to the fortress on the hill before and was a little intimidated. She thought to knock at the door, though that seemed a little ridiculous with such a big door. No one seemed to be around except for a watchman high on the northwest tower who was watching the column of troops headed north. After a few long moments, she pushed the door open and stepped out of the bright sunlight and into the gloom of the corridor that led into the central courtyard.

"Hello," she called a little uncertainly, stepping inside.

A man wearing a helmet stuck his head out from a door on the right side halfway down the passageway. "What do you want, darling?"

"I am looking for Celeno," replied Zoe uncertainly.

"She is in Prokopios' chambers," the man replied as if that should be common knowledge. Seeing her look he answered her question before she could ask it, "Up on the second level of the south wall, just past the bastion."

Zoe passed through the archway and into the courtyard. She noticed that two metal gates with thick widely spaced bars were opened on either side of the entrance. These had been added three years before. Since this was her first time in the Hold, she did not notice a myriad of small changes that made the place more attractive and a better place to live. The two silos opposite the entrance now had a brick facing which considerably enhanced their appearance. Beyond them she saw a well. She did not know the effort it had taken to get that well down to the water table. Most of the water used by the men and animals was still collected rainwater, stored in the cistern. The cistern had also received a brick facing and now at least gave the impression of being a completed structure. There was a second ramp going up the south wall, matching the one on the north side. No longer did men have to climb up and down ladders to reach that wall without going through the bastions. There were also far more awnings now, both on the walls where many of the garrison slept on hot nights and on the ground level of the courtyard. The back half of the courtyard was kept clear, and that was where all the activity was taking place.

She heard a clack, clack sound and saw some men milling about the open half of the courtyard. Curious, she moved in that direction, looking about her as she moved out from the walls. There were several other women standing beside the well watching the training of the new recruits. Zoe moved up and joined them. A big man who was most obviously in charge was castigating them. Zoe recognized some of the curses but others were new to her. The sergeant had an unusual beard.

It swept down his cheeks as far as his mouth line and then met over his mouth in a magnificent moustache while his chin and cheeks below his mouth line were clean-shaven. Zoe thought it was very handsome. This must be the new Drilling Sergeant who had arrived at about the same time as Zoe. Some people called him 'Half Beard', though never to his face. He had a long foreign name which no one seemed to remember; most people addressed him either as 'Sergeant' or 'Sir'. There were all sorts of rumors about him. Some said he was a king who had lost his kingdom and fled in disgrace. Others said that he was a prince who had been raised by shepherds. The story was that he went back to his parent's city, never knowing that he was the rightful king and killed his father and married his own mother, all unknowing. Zoe thought that was probably not true. Nevertheless, his physical appearance and presence and mysterious background were wildly romantic and a source of fascination to the town. He was also a stern taskmaster, and the men of the garrison had great respect for him.

The recruits, just over a dozen of them, were wearing the leather and bronze helmets Zoe had seen on most of the soldiers here. They also were wearing linen cuirasses and chagrined expressions. Each man held a wooden hoplon; Zoe thought the shields looked very heavy. They also all had a long, thick pole with a padding of heavy cloth at the upright end. She wondered what the poles were for; then as she watched them in two ragged lines facing one another and poking at their opposite numbers with the padded poles, she realized that they must be training spears. This must be battle training. Zoe watched, fascinated.

The big sergeant bellowed something that obviously meant the sweating recruits could stop and take a break. The men relaxed and moved toward the water butts by the well. With a small shock Zoe recognized Adem's apprentice among the trainees. He looked somehow different, still shy, but now he appeared more self-possessed. He saw her and gave her a small smile and smaller wave. His comrades next to him grinned and nudged him making comments she could not hear. Zoe smiled back and waved, then with a flirty backward glance tossed her head and moved away. She realized with a little twinge of guilt that she enjoyed being a widow. It was empowering; she was no longer a maiden looking for a husband. She knew what men and women were all about and had the freedom to flirt with handsome young men without losing her reputation. She felt a pang at how easily she had adapted to the loss of Bukchos. But she had to admit her life was better without him in it, even with all the problems she was facing. Then her thoughts drifted to the Magistrate. Rodas, that was his name, she should think of him as Rodas, not as the Magistrate. He was unmarried. So was the King for that matter and she knew him, now. Zoe giggled at the not quite expressed thought. She was a pretty young widow, and she had met the King. Maybe he was looking for a wife. 'Princess Zoe', no, she would be 'Queen Zoe'. What would her mother think of that!

She climbed the stairs up to the second floor with these daydreams which ended abruptly when she came to the door behind which Celeno awaited.

"Come in," came a woman's voice when she scratched at the door.

There were two women inside the room; one was obviously the witch. The other woman was much younger and shared some of the same unfortunate features as Celeno; she must be her daughter. And indeed, she was so introduced to Zoe. The three women reclined on couches and sipped some tea talking of the weather, the departure of almost half the garrison on an expedition to the north to clear the northern mountains of the bandits that had recently raided the big caravan; apparently Amphora had not been the only merchant to have complained about lost goods. Then the conversation turned to the training of the new recruits.

"I do not envy the poor things," said Celeno, reclining back. "That new sergeant, what is his name? Leo Tied Cheese or some foreign thing; any way he really keeps them hopping. He makes them practice his drills all day and then has them up in the middle of the night to repel pretended attacks. I suppose he knows what he is doing. The recruits are all terrified of him but they also seem to admire him as well. Men are very odd."

The three women nodded together at this obvious truth.

"Now," said Celeno "What can I do for you? Are you looking for a love potion? I warn you they are rather expensive."

"No," answered Zoe confused, "we, that is, Ana and I, well Ana, Agalia, and I; well everybody in the neighborhood really, we all want to get rid of Peder, the new agent that Adem appointed."

Now it was Celeno who was confused. She rallied quickly however. Lowering her voice she leaned in and asked, "So, do you want a death curse on this man. That is a very serious matter."

"No!" protested Zoe, shocked. This whole interview was not going well. "We just want him to leave. He is making ruinous deals, spending all the money on extravagant symposia for his drunken friends, and drinking up what he doesn't waste. We just want him to be removed as agent. Really, we want him out of town entirely. Can you do that?" The last was delivered in a pleading tone.

"Humph," replied Celeno leaning back. "Have him leave, eh? That may not even require anything 'special' if you know what I mean. One way or another we should be able to get it done."

There followed a negotiation as to price. Payment would be in wine, a smaller portion delivered first, the remainder only if the agent departed Dassaria within a ten day period and never returned as agent. Most of the negotiations consisted on agreeing upon the amount and vintage to be delivered. They finally agreed upon the terms and clasped hands to confirm the deal. Celeno would send a man to escort her to a meeting shortly after moonrise. They apparently needed to do whatever it was that Celeno did in a special place. That agreed, they leaned back and each took a sip of the now cool tea. Zoe's peace of mind was disturbed when she recognized the sound of the big bell located on top of the nearby bastion. The bell was rung not as an alarm; it was also rung every day at sunrise and sunset. Soon it would be dark; the doors to the Hold would close. Zoe was far from home; she had to get back.

As she hurried down the stairs heading for the entrance tunnel, Zoe was distracted. Why did Celeno think she was looking for a love potion? Zoe rounded the corner into the tunnel at speed and ran smack into a man coming into the Hold. Zoe was knocked down on her backside. She looked up in dismay to see the man whom she had run into. Of course, it was Rodas. What really surprised her were the expressions she recognized on his face. Surprise, recognition, distress, and pleasure; was he glad he had bumped into her so hard? No, she was suddenly sure he was glad to see her.

"Zoe!" he exclaimed, "Are you all right? Where is Lux?"

'He not only knows my name,' thought Zoe, 'he knows my dog's name.' That might have worried her, but it didn't. In fact it gave her a warm feeling. She instantly made a decision to put this man in his place.

"A fine thing! First you refuse to help me, and now you knock me down!"

She had hesitated a moment too long and he knew she was not really angry with him. "Well," he said trying to rally, "better knocked down than knocked up." It was just the wrong thing to say.

"How would you know?" inquired Zoe icily declining his offered hand and rising as gracefully as she could. She began to dust herself off. Rodas, uncharacteristically flustered, tried ineffectually to help her. She rounded on him slapping his hands away. "Really!" she exclaimed, now she was angry, "Is it not enough that you frustrate me at every turn, knock me to the ground, and then try to paw me in front of all these men."

"I did not mean to frustrate you," Rodas stopped. That was going in the wrong direction. He tried again, "I did not intend to paw you in front of all these men," he continued unfortunately repeating her charges word for word.

"Ah Ha!" Zoe pounced, "so you intended to get me alone and paw me, safe from prying eyes!" Zoe had her opponent off balance now, and this pleased her.

"No!" protested Rodas, "I mean, I am sorry for running into you. Are you all right?"

"I am fine," Zoe responded, "but I think I should leave before you figure out what you are going do to us next." Gathering dignity around her like a cloak, she tossed her head pushed her thick black hair over her shoulder and chin high, swept around the corner and away.

Spiros, who had accompanied Rodas up the hill for the routine council held each night at sunset when Athan was out of the Hold, was working to keep a straight face, but his one eye was shining with amusement.

Rodas gave him a dirty look and headed up to the bastion to his meeting.

Zoe on her part was satisfied. She had turned an embarrassing situation around and put that man right in his place. But part of her thought that being alone with Rodas in a place safe from prying eyes might not be such a bad thing.

The other two women were already preparing for their nightly retreat up the kitchen ladder to the roof when Zoe arrived, coming as she usually did around to the back. The normal revels they had grown to expect had not started yet. The silence, instead of being welcome had put the women on edge. When Peder was loud at least they knew where he was. The unexpected silence was unsettling and somehow ominous. Zoe wanted to wait down in the kitchen for her escort who would be coming at moon rise which was in a bit less than an hour. The other two, Agalia especially, prevailed upon her to wait with them up on the roof. Lux was put into a wooden crate with widely-spaced slats that they had used to secure her when she could not accompany Zoe. She obediently went inside but her whining let Zoe know she was not happy about it.

The three women sat up on the back edge of the roof nibbling bread and cheese, enjoying the last of the sunset and gossiping about Zoe's interesting day. They talked about Rodas and his unwillingness to help them, and of the King, and why he was not married; why Rodas had not married; about the Drill Sergeant and where he might have come from; of the apprentice and how he had waved at her; how Rodas had bumped into Zoe and how she had set him back on his heels; and Celeno and rumors of her love potions; and where Rodas had come from.

"You certainly seem interested in our Magistrate," observed Ana.

"I am not; interested, that is. Well, he should do something to help us. We talk about a lot of people. He is interesting."

"He must be; you brought him up about six times," Ana said amused. Agalia giggled in the darkness.

Zoe was saved from any further embarrassment by the sound of someone at the back of the kitchen. The moon was only just beginning to rise. Apparently her escort was a little early. She lifted the trap and called out that she was coming hurrying down to the kitchen below. It was dark in the kitchen; the shutters let in little of the faint starlight. The kitchen hearth fire was banked to a faint few coals, and of course no lamp was lighted in the empty room. She would light the lamp she had placed beside the hearth from the kitchen fire and then return and collect her club she left by the ladder before checking the door to make sure it was her escort. Zoe knew the layout of the room well and made it almost halfway across the floor before she became aware there was someone else inside the kitchen with her. Perhaps it was the faint sound of breathing, or a glimpse of a shadow, or a scent, or sense of a life force, or a combination of these things, but Zoe suddenly knew there was a man, standing just inside the entrance from the women's room.

Zoe was a physically brave person, yet under these conditions, she lost her nerve. "Who's there?" she called and even to her own ears her voice sounded terrified; and with good reason.

It was a mistake. Now he knew just where she was. The weakness in her voice emboldened the intruder, and he stepped forward in the gloom grabbing her by her upper arms. She knew as soon as he touched her who it had to be: Peder. She could smell his sour body and the wine on his breath.

"You just couldn't stay away from me could you?" he hissed in her face.

Zoe twisted away from his attempt at a kiss. "Get away from me you pig!" she cried out.

He tried to cover her mouth with his hand; Lux, who had been cowering in her crate, went crazy, barking and growling. The women on the roof began calling down in alarm. Peder also had his hands full down in the kitchen. He was drunk and excited and therefore tried to cover Zoe's mouth, fondle her breasts, and hang on to her all at the same time. He failed. Zoe managed to pull away without tearing her chiton, though he did manage to pull it partially off one shoulder. He groped toward her in the dark; she backed away trying to get to the ladder where she hoped she could hold him off with her big stick long enough to get back up to the roof. Or maybe she could get to Lux and let her out. That would complicate things for him. Unfortunately, in their struggle he had gotten between Zoe and both of those things. She did not think she could talk her way out of this situation. Peder was too worked up. She would have to calm him down first and there was no time for that. He made another clumsy grab for her in the dark; she was able to avoid him. They each poised in the darkness, both panting. Anything might have happened then; what did happen was that there was a sudden pounding on the door, and a man called out on the other side of the door, "Is everything all right in there?"

"Go away," shouted Peder.

"Come in," shouted Zoe at the same instant.

"Help!" cried Ana and Agalia from the roof a heart beat behind them. "There is a burglar in the house!"

Peder, forgetting Zoe for the moment, moved to the back door to try to reassure the now agitated man on the other side of the door. Zoe, instead of racing to the ladder, found herself moving at a normal pace back to the hearth and blowing on the coals. A moment later she had the lamp lit. Light changed everything. Peder illuminated was not half so frightening. Ana looking down from the top of the trap saw him and began to rail at him for passing through the women's hall.

"I am master of this house now," he blustered, but his confidence was gone. He moved over to the base of the ladder trying to reason with an outraged Ana, who was letting him have the full benefit of her displeasure. Peder had apparently forgotten all about Zoe, so she walked over to the door with a seeming calmness and lifted the bar. Standing outside with a torch in one hand and a sword in the other was Spiros, the one-eyed man she had seen at the Magistrate's house.

"Are you all right?" he asked looking into the kitchen beyond her. Zoe noticed that even in his concerned state, he did not enter without an invitation.

"Yes," she said briefly. Then she looked at Peder who was now standing silently at the foot of the ladder and added, "Our lord's agent is apparently lost or was sleepwalking or something. He has wandered into places where he should not be." This was a veiled accusation. Peder was not really a family member, and he and everybody else knew it. Still he blustered a bit about his 'rights and duties' but he made no objection when Spiros suggested he go back to the men's hall. He allowed Spiros, who was still holding a torch and sword, to herd him back though the gynaeconitis and into the dark andron beyond. Zoe, who followed, shut the door firmly behind the agent. Then she and Spiros moved several of the couches in the room behind the door, blocking it as well as they could. Adem and Ana had never felt the need to have a bolt on that door before. Now, Zoe was sure one would be added.

They stopped in the kitchen to speak up to Ana and Agalia (and Lux in her crate) to reassure them all was well. The two women firmly closed the top of the trap; Zoe could hear them moving things over on top of it.

"Has he always been like that?" inquired Spiros as they walked toward Celeno's little house.

"I don't know," replied Zoe, "but that is the way he has been since he got here." She hesitated, the added, "This was the first time he came to the back of the house. I guess his friends didn't come by tonight."

"Maybe someone is telling them it is not such a good idea to be seen in your house," suggested the one-eyed door man.

Zoe thought about it. Peder had been having fewer and fewer visitors of late. Maybe the King and/or his Magistrate were trying to help after all. That was little comfort right now. Something was bothering Zoe. "Spiros, why are you escorting me? Aren't you the Magistrate's porter?"

By the light of the moon, his torch, and her lamp, she could see him smile. "Hardly. Well, I guess I can understand why you would think that. Celeno thought you would be more comfortable with someone you recognized. So she asked me."

"How did she know you?"

"Celeno is often at the house, talking to her daughter, Alesin." Seeing Zoe's puzzled expression, he explained further. "Alesin is married to Stamitos. They live with Rodas; they help him out with the house. Alesin acts as the mistress of the house since Rodas can't seem to settle on anyone to marry. He needs a woman. In the meantime, Alesin does the best she can. The role is really beyond her, especially if people need to meet her." Spiros made a face. "She is a good person, and Stamitos says she is a great wife, but brrrr, she is not so pretty to my eye."

They walked along together while Zoe digested this. Celeno was 'often at the house'. Celeno was the mother of the woman who ran Rodas' house. There was much more that a casual relationship there. Likely everything she had talked to Celeno about was now known to the Magistrate. She wanted to be mad at someone, but this was too important. She had to find out more.

"Have you known Rodas long," she asked her escort conversationally.

"I got to know him when he joined his band with ours after we stole the gold from the Satrap," Spiros said. He was normally fairly closed mouthed, but a walk in the moonlight with a pretty girl can loosen the tongue of most men and Spiros was no exception. "I rode up to the gates with him on the day we took the Hold from the Bear. There were only seven of us; together we held the gate until the Chief brought up the rest of the men. You don't forget something like that."

All this was a revelation to Zoe who had heard rumors and innuendos about the King. To hear them so casually discussed by someone who was there was truly amazing. "The Chief?" she asked. To the best of her knowledge that was a term applied to the head of a band of brigands. Hadn't he just said Rodas joined up with his 'band'? Did the Magistrate once associate with brigands?

"The Chief, I mean, King Athan," Spiros explained. "I guess that is what we call him now. It still seems strange. Yeah, Rodas had a tight little band he had been running for a couple of years, and when Athan offered him a chance to share in the spoils he joined his band to ours. It worked out pretty well for him, don't you think?"

Zoe's mind was reeling. Not only had the King been a bandit, which had been hinted at before, but the Magistrate had been a brigand chief as well. Imagine that, a magistrate who was once a bandit!

Just then they arrived at Celeno's little house. Zoe did not know it then but the witch seldom actually slept there. She normally spent the night in Prokopios' quarters in the Hold or stayed with one of her daughters, most usually Alesin. The little house was mainly used for rituals. No one was there yet, so they settled down with their backs to the door and waited. It did not take much for Zoe to get Spiros talking again.

Spiros resumed his discourse while they waited for Celeno. The King had taken about five score men with him to clear the hills north of Lychmidas. That was about half of his available garrison; since was no real threat to the kingdom from any neighbors he felt there was little risk.

"It is not really his territory, but the bandits have been busy up there and are cutting into profits. I think he is going to pick up some men from Lychmidas to help him. He will be the one in charge; nothing like an old bandit to catch another bandit. Besides, he used to be a captain of the guards of the old city of Epiria. Anyway, me and my brother were at loose ends after Father died. There was no work to be had so we took to the hills. There was a certain misunderstanding with the local magistrate, you see. Anyway, when we heard about Chief Athan. He had been running a really successful band for years in the area. He was sort of famous. Anyway we thought we would find him and join up. Of course, we did not find him, he found us. And after he talked with us he let us join."

"Where is your brother now?" Zoe interrupted.

"Oh, he died," replied Spiros matter of factly. "He got a fever about a year later and died. These things happen; still, we had good times while he was alive. So, anyway, we were working what we all thought was a legitimate job for this Satrap fellow, guarding the tribute he was carrying back to their Empire. Then after we finish the job and get paid and all, the Chief tells us that he has stolen some of the gold and we better ride for it. We kept on riding with the Achaemendian cavalry hot on our tails all the way here."

The former bandit's reminisces were cut short by the arrival of three women and two men; Stamitos and another man who was introduced as Iason, a name Zoe recognized as one of the medical men in the Hold. "My son in laws," Celeno explained, then pointed to the two other women, "my daughter Beryl, and Nyx, one of my assistants. Now, let's go inside. These men will keep unwanted ears away."

Zoe was always very reticent about the rituals Celeno practiced that night. If asked by a woman, she would tell her to speak directly with Celeno. If asked by a man she would tell him it was none of his business. A few things did become known, or at least suspected, about what happened that night. First, Celeno agreed to help Zoe. What form that assistance took, whether magical, practical, or just advice was never revealed. And second, Celeno read Zoe's fortune. The details and accuracy of that forecast were never revealed, but there was no denying that Zoe was distracted when she came out of the house. There was another thing people noticed. From that time on, Celeno treated her with marked respect.

Zoe was escorted home by Stamitos and Spiros. Celeno heard about the incident in the kitchen and wanted to make sure Zoe made it safely up to the roof so she got the extra escort. The two men began to talk about their old days together. Zoe interrupted the men twice. Once to ask them to stop for a moment while she went in to a small shrine set aside for Aphrodite. The goddess was Zoe's personal favorite. She was not as high and imperious as Hera, not as scary as Athena, and not so weak and domestic as Hestia whom Zoe dismissed as a mere 'kitchen goddess'. It seemed appropriate for her to worship Aphrodite in the light of the moon, and she left an offering after her silent prayers were done. The second time she interrupted the men it was just before they returned home.

"Spiros, something doesn't seem right. You said the King was once a captain of the guards of Epiria. You have to be pretty old to be a captain, right."

Both her escorts agreed.

"Then you said he was a famous bandit for, what, about ten years?"

They were not sure but that seemed about right to them.

"And he has been King for five years or so?"

Again they confirmed that was about right.

"That can't be right," here she objected, "I met him. Well, I guess really I just ran into him. He is not that old."

Both men smiled knowing smiles. "No one knows just how old the Chief is," Spiros told her, "but he is a lot older than he looks. I bet he is almost fifty."

"Maybe more," confirmed Stamitos.

"That is not possible," protested Zoe, "Rodas looks older than the King. How old is Rodas?"

"Not so old as that. Looks can be deceiving. He is not an ordinary man our King, let me tell you."

And then they were at the house. The two men escorted her home, then checked that Ana and Agalia were safe up on the roof, and also examined the gynaeconitis to make sure it was clear. Then they tapped wooden wedges in the door from the Andron and made sure no one would come through that way again in the night. Zoe barred the back door behind them and took Lux up the ladder. She sat in corner of the roof most of the night, thinking.

Things began to happen fairly soon. The next day shortly before noon Rodas, accompanied by Stamitos, came by and inquired of Peder if he would be willing to sell an amphora of wine to be served at an upcoming symposium for some important visiting merchants. Peder was ecstatic. He had finally made a significant sale. Ana was called in to provide a list of available stock. She admitted the existence of a really fine amphora of Xynomavro red. Peder's joy knew no bounds. Of course, he bungled the bargaining, initially demanding far too much for amphora, then when Rodas made as if to break off the negotiations, caved in completely, and allowed him to purchase the wine for less than his (that is to say, Adem's) cost. Peder's could hardly contain himself when the amphora was brought out to the open courtyard of the andronitis, and the wine sampled. The two men agreed it was a fine vintage. Stamitos loaded the amphora onto a cart and prepared to depart.

All during the negotiations and sampling the women were absent, Ana only coming in to lead Stamitos to where the amphora was kept and then retiring to the women's hall.

Zoe did make a brief appearance and spoke quietly to Stamitos just before he led the donkey-drawn cart away.

"Please inform your master that this particular amphora is best if decanted."

Stamitos only nodded. On the way back to the Magistrate's House, Rodas overtook his old friend. The two men talked and Zoe's recommendation was discussed. Why would she suggest the wine be poured from the amphora into another container? Rodas was glad he had taken the advice, strongly given, that he purchase a high quality vintage from Amphora's new agent. He welcomed the chance to take the measure of the new man that had been the source of so much gossip and even an unofficial investigation by Athan. Clearly this Peder was a drunk and worse a fool. Not only would he ruin Amphora's wine business, he would be a source of unwholesome and infectious behaviors. Overly boisterous parties, drunkenness, thefts, fornication, conspiracies, were all a general irritant to the peace and well-being of the town. The idiot had even talked about setting up Amphora's house as a tavern house with an open temple to Dionysus. Not that Rodas had any problem with the god of wine himself, but he knew that places like that attracted and developed people who were not wanted in Dassaria. Peder had to go. All Rodas needed to do was find something to make a charge against him. It should not be very difficult; he estimated it would take no more than five or six days. Rodas was also satisfied with the wine he had bought. Even though it was expensive, considering its quality, Rodas thought it a bargain. He would have another cup, properly watered of course, when they decanted it. He had two smaller serving amphorae that would probably hold the contents.

After Rodas' departure, Peder was over the moon with joy. He immediately sent a boy out with invitations to his would-be cronies inviting them to a big symposium that night. Celebrating with three cups of wine from the dwindling stores he still had at his disposal, he went out to purchase food and entertainment for the celebration.

He returned two hours later content with the world, that is to say, more or less drunk. He found Stamitos, Spiros, and two other soldiers waiting for him. They did not return his greeting or even answer his questions as they took him by the arms and hustled him straight to the Magistrate's House. It was not a social call.

Court was in session when he arrived, and Peder went to the front of the line. The Magistrate was not in a good mood.

"Do you take me for a fool?" he demanded of the bewildered Peder.

The agent assured the Magistrate he did not and wondered aloud what this was all about.

"Are you the agent of the House of Adem, also commonly known as Amphora?"

Peder assured him he was; and why was he so angry? Hadn't he given him a bargain, a real deal on that amphora of fine Xynomavro that very morning?

Somehow this was exactly the wrong thing to say. "So," thundered a thoroughly irritated Rodas, "you admit that you sold me that amphora and its contents; and for a very substantial price, too."

Peder was drunk and the entire turn of events had him confused. He decided that the Magistrate was going to try to cheat him out of the purchase price of the wine. "Yeah," he exclaimed truculently, "you were there. Don't you remember? We sampled it together. It was my best wine. You said it was a 'magnificent vintage'. You were going to save it for special guests."

This was apparently not the right line to take. Rodas' face became red with his anger. Extending his arm in his best dramatic accusatorial gesture, Rodas pointed to an old blanket on the floor to the right of his chair. The amphora so recently purchased was on its side next to the blanket, its contents apparently emptied into two smaller containers beside it. Stamitos had moved over to stand to one side of the blanket. With a dramatic sweep he removed the blanket from what it had been covering.

There was a wine-stained cloth beneath the blanket, apparently stained by the lees when the larger amphora had been emptied. Sitting on the cloth was a wine darkened oval stone of pumice, just narrow enough to fit down the throat of an amphora. An unscrupulous wine seller did not have to be an Archimedes to know that such a stone would replace some of the expensive wine. It was an old trick; some wine merchants even had amphora with extra thick bottoms to reduce the volume inside. This, however, was a clumsy attempt at fraud, the kind used by men who sold once and moved on the next day. The pumice stone was not the only thing on the bit of cloth. There was also a dead mouse, a dead bird, and a small and very dead snake.

"Is this your idea of a joke?" asked Rodas grimly. Rodas was not a fool. He knew exactly who had put those things in the amphora. He could just imagine her laughing as she did it. She had made a fool of him. He also knew there was nothing he could do about it; not to her, anyway. He did have a very nice surrogate right in front of him.

Peder was not so drunk that he did not know he was in very serious trouble. Perhaps he could have mitigated the oncoming disaster; instead he became angry and made his problems worse.

"It's those women!" he exclaimed angrily. "They did it! They wanted to poison me!"

"Are you not the agent for that house?" Rodas interrupted severely. "Therefore, you are responsible for the actions of the house. It was to me and my household to whom you sold the wine. Was this poison intended for me and mine?"

Peder knew he was caught. He tried to loudly argue his innocence waving his arms in the air. Two guardsmen came up behind him on either side and took his arms. He tried to fight them. The struggle did not last long.

"Enough of this nonsense," decreed the Magistrate. "Peder, I banish you from Dassaria for a period of not less than two years."

Peder should have expected this. It was not so bad; really, all it meant was that he had to go back home. But an angry drunk is not wise. Instead of accepting his sentence he began to rant and threaten revenge. As he struggled his purse fell out onto the floor. Stepping forward, Rodas picked it up. Counting the contents he then fined him the exact amount of the money remaining in his purse. That really ignited the outraged Peder. Even if one is filled with a righteous anger, it is best not to express yourself vigorously at a Magistrate, especially when you are pinned to the floor by two of his soldiers. By the time Peder was dragged away, he had earned an additional sentence of a dozen strokes with a cane for threatening the magistrate and general misbehavior. Following the beating, he was thrown howling down into the underground storage room that was used as a holding cell. On the morrow he was to be escorted not less than two parasangs west of the town and released with nothing except the clothes on his back. He was to continue west, out of the country without delay. Returning to Dassaria within two years would be punishable by death. It was now a harsh sentence. He would have to make his way home on foot, alone, without provisions or money through a thinly inhabited region.

An hour before sunset the Magistrate, accompanied by three men, rode to the house of Amphora, the wine merchant. They were riding horses that short distance to make a point; this was not a simple social call. Word must have reached the house in advance because Ana and Zoe were waiting respectfully wearing their best chitons in front of the house, Lux sitting obediently at Zoe's heel. Of Agalia and the child there was no sign. A small crowd watched as unobtrusively as they could. The story had spread like wildfire. Everyone knew what had happened. Unfortunately, most people thought it was funny. Rodas was not a mean-spirited man but he did not enjoy being made the butt of a joke; the air was tense. He swung down off his horse and approached the women.

"Lady Ana," he began using the formal address, "as you no doubt have heard, I have banished the agent provided by your husband."

"Yes, lord," she replied meekly her head down. Ana was very frightened. She had only agreed to Zoe's plan because she was desperate and had immediately regretted the impulse. She had put in the plug of pumice and so was as guilty as the rest. Agalia had found the dead bird and added it. The snake was from Zoe, of course, and even Lux had contributed: she often caught mice in the kitchen and had one saved for a later snack. Zoe merely confiscated it and popped it into the amphora before they carefully resealed it.

In contrast to Ana, Zoe stood straight, shoulders back, chin high; the little tan dog at her side gave her tail a single tentative wag. Rodas looked at her for a long moment. She really was a very pretty girl, Rodas thought. He turned back to Ana. "It would seem your husband had an amphora of wine that was adulterated and unfit for drinking."

"I am sorry, my lord," she replied in a low voice, her head still down. "I am sure the wine was not so when he departed."

Rodas was watching Zoe. She did not turn her head; she returned his gaze directly for a moment, then dropped her eyes with an enigmatic faint smile. The dog beside her grinned up at him and wagged her tail.

"No," said Rodas still watching Zoe, "I suppose not."

Zoe looked up at him sideways with her head slightly cocked to one side and spoke for the first time. "How was the wine adulterated, sir?"

Rodas ground his teeth. 'You know very well you saucy minx' he thought. He controlled himself and said in a calm-seeming voice. "There was a plug of pumice stone, of the type used by **dishonest wine merchants**," he raised his voice for the last three words so all could hear. Ana winced; Rodas immediately felt guilty; none of this had been of her doing.

"Well, sir," Zoe responded for Ana in a clear voice, "that sounds like something that dishonest scoundrel Peder would do. Everyone knows he was a drunken liar and a thief besides." She was playing to the slowly growing crowd. Everyone had known those things about Peder, and some heads were nodding agreement.

He continued in a lower voice. "There was also a dead mouse, dead bird, and a dead snake in the bottom of the amphora."

"Undoubtedly, that villain must have left the top off. Perhaps the mouse was pursued into the amphora by the snake where they both drowned in that lovely vintage. What a way to go, eh?" She was playing to the crowd; men were smiling at her.

One man was not smiling. "There was a dead bird in there as well," he said ominously.

"Perhaps a spectator or even a suicide, my lord." She made this ridiculous claim with such a bright smile and apparent sincerity that the crowd murmured in amusement.

"I could have gotten a flux from that tainted wine!" Rodas growled. He was losing this battle of wits in front of far too many people.

"Sire, that was a powerful wine, I am sure the animals were well preserved."

He had been moving toward her step by step without realizing it, and now he found he was right before her looking down into a set of brown eyes, sparkling with mischief. It was impossible for a man to be angry with those eyes. There was a long moment, before he could pull himself out of those eyes.

Ana tried to mollify a situation that was somehow taking a strange turn. She had not moved and with her head still bowed she made an offer. "Sire, we will take the wine back and return your money."

"I have already fined the miscreant all the money he had with him. Where is the rest of my money?"

"Gone, my lord," Ana told him. "He spent it all."

"In two hours? On what?"

Ana looked up and gave a hopeless shrug. "Things, sire, just this and that." There was a general muttering in the crowd that confirmed Ana's description about the way Peder could turn money into urine in record time.

"I tried to tell you," Zoe interjected. Her voice was not angry or accusatory but rather almost pleading. "We did not know what to do." She almost said 'what else to do' and he caught the thought. He understood; yet he was not about to let her off so easily.

"So you say I am in no danger from partaking of your wine?"

"No, sire," now Zoe was smiling in a friendly manner. "The wine is safe. I am sorry if those terrible things in your wine distressed you. I assure you, you were in no danger from that wine."

"I am glad to hear it is safe," he continued not acknowledging her apology. He was relieved that the only real danger presented by the tainted wine was to his pride. Why did she have to add that snake? That was just nasty! Trying to compose himself, he continued on, "Because I am not paying for the wine, I thought it best to return it to your house." He made a gesture, and Spiros unslung a large leather wine skin from the saddle of his horse and brought it to them. He could see that for the first time he had surprised her; he decided to press his advantage. Extending the bag to her he decided to do a bit of teasing back. "Since you assure us your wine is safe, Zoe would you be willing to drink some of it for us?" 'Ha!' he thought, 'that will fix her. Let's see if what was good for the gander was good for the goose.'

Zoe hesitated for only an instant. "Sir, drinking from that huge bag is not possible without spilling some on my clothing." She instantly saw that would not answer. She had to have a bold answer if she was going to keep him off balance. Zoe spoke again before he could regain the initiative. "Can someone bring me a wine cup?" she addressed the grinning crowd who had gathered to watch the fun. "Make it a good one, for this is a noble vintage."

There was a stir as people rushed to bring a vessel. Everyone (except Ana who decided her young friend had lost her mind and was about to ruin everything) was interested in seeing how the confrontation between the Magistrate and the saucy widow would play out.

Several cups were offered to Zoe almost at once. She had intended to take one and tip it up, pretending to drink, but when she saw one of the cups, a silver chalice of considerable value, she changed her mind. This man needed to be challenged. The chalice was probably used in wedding ceremonies. In this place and time, it was often the custom after the wedding that the husband would take a cup of wine, drink from it, and formally offer it to his bride.

Taking the chalice she turned to Spiros who was grinning broadly. She did like that Spiros. "Sir Spiros," she announced grandly, giving him a respectful title, "please pour for me."

He carefully filled the cup half full and returned it to her. Zoe saw that Rodas had carefully looked to see the level of wine in the cup. She held it steady and low enough for him to realize she was giving him a good look. Then, giving the crowd a general toast, she tipped the chalice up and took a strong pull of the wine. The crowd cheered. She moved the cup over close to him so he could see she had drained half the contents. He was smiling at her when she sprang her little trap.

"This cup, I offer you. Will you accept it?" In that time and place those were often the words a bridegroom used to his bride in the wedding ceremony. She was turning everything right on his head. Some people in the crowd actually gasped. "What!" she said in mock dismay when he hesitated, "afraid to drink with a woman. I assure you sir, I am clean. I am 'probably a respectable' widow." The last two lines were delivered looking directly in his eyes, and then she winked in a flirtatious challenge. The crowd cheered again.

He was trapped, and he knew it. He took the chalice from her hands. "What you are," he told her in a private, quiet voice, "is a shameless hussy!" And he tipped the chalice high, draining it. The crowd loved it.

Rodas left immediately, with the appreciative audience still buzzing. Stamitos was left behind to provide security until the house could be properly secured for the night.

Rodas rode back to his house in a disturbed state. He was not sure what had just happened; it definitely did not go as he had planned. At least he had more or less solved the problem of the unsatisfactory wine agent. He still could not figure out how Zoe had outmaneuvered him in front of everybody. He had a vivid memory of her offering him the cup, brown eyes shining, her thick dark hair thrown back over her shoulders, smiling up at him.

Spiros moved his horse beside him. Spiros had not been in Rodas' old band, but he had ridden with him all the way from Golibolu. They had shared wine and women in Pella. Spiros was one of the seven that rode up to the gates of the Hold with him that first time. Those things and many others made him a trusted comrade, and there was a certain relationship between two old comrades.

"Did you notice how she stood there so still and unafraid?" Spiros asked his distracted leader.

"Who?" asked Rodas, startled out of his image of Zoe.

"The little brown dog, of course. Didn't you notice her?"

"Oh, yes. Troublesome little thing don't you think?"

"Which one, the girl or the dog?" asked Spiros teasingly.

"The girl."

"You know, Chief, based on the way she smiled at you and wagged her tail I think she liked you?"

"The girl or the dog?"

"Both," grinned Spiros. "Are you going to have her?"

"I haven't decided. She would certainly be a handful."

"More like two handfuls," laughed Spiros. "She certainly is a sweet little peach."

"More like a pair of nice ripe melons," Rodas responded getting into the spirit of the thing. Suddenly he felt better, a lot better. He kicked his little horse into a gallop and rode back to the house in high spirits.

As soon as the Magistrate's party had departed, Agalia reappeared from the safety of a neighbor's house holding little Agamemnon. Stamitos picked up the wine bag and carried it into the house.

"Thank you, Stamitos," Ana said, "but what do you expect us to do with that? We can't sell it. **I** won't drink it. Agalia, throw it out!"

"No!" protested Zoe. "I will think of something."

Ana had been afraid out there in the street facing the Magistrate. Now she was in her own home and all the fear and stress came out in anger. "Thank you Stamitos," she said again. The old campaigner knew when it was time to beat a hasty retreat and retired out the front door.

"Agalia, please bar the door behind him."

Still holding the baby, the girl hastened to obey. Ana went through the door into the familiar territory of the women hall, Zoe following apprehensively behind her.

"**You!**" Ana began rounded on Zoe, "I should have never listened to you. You have ruined everything!" Ana should have been glad to have been rid of the agent, pleased at Zoe's daring ploy, happy that the Magistrate left with no further penalties to their house and business, indeed, with the neighbors cheering. Perhaps it was a reaction to the tension she had been under, whatever the reason just them Ana was angry at the whole world.

"I got rid of Peder," protested Zoe.

"You ruined our reputation!" Ana countered. "Adem may return any day. And what will he find? Our money gone, the wine stock depleted, our merchandise scorned, our credit ruined, and the Magistrate insulted and hostile. I should have never agreed to take you in!"

"It will be all right. I will think of something," Zoe tried in answer to the distraught woman.

"What! What will you do! We cannot sell our wine without a man. Where are we going to find someone we can trust who knows the business? Will some stable boy be able to run the business?" Her voice was scornful. "The money is gone. If Adem doesn't come back soon, we will not even have anything left to eat. If he does come back tomorrow, he will find we are ruined. And the man who did it won't even be here to blame!" As if that were the final straw, Ana went to a couch sat down heavily and began to weep.

Zoe could not help herself from going over to this kind woman who had taken her in and suffered such a terrible reversal of fortune through no fault of her own. "Please," she said to Ana, trying to take both her hands in her own. Ana pulled her hands away and covered her face with them, bent over and still sobbing. Zoe put an arm around her shoulders and tried to console her.

"Ana, I am so sorry I made you do that to the wine. But that wretched Peder is gone. At least we have that. We can think of something to do to get money. People won't think the worse of Adem. They know he had nothing to do with any of this. Adem will come back soon with money. You can recover in no time." Zoe continued in this way for some time. Finally Ana calmed enough to speak.

"Do you really think so," she asked. "Do you think he will come back soon?" Zoe assured her he should be returning any day. "The miserable bastard should never have left me," Ana said grimly. "None of this would have happened if he had stayed home like a proper husband."

Zoe thought that Adem might not receive the welcome he expected when he did return, that is, if he ever did.

Ana looked up at Zoe with a red and puffy face; Zoe still had her arm around the other woman's shoulders. "My courses are late," the older woman said. Zoe did not understand at first. "That bastard husband of mine got me pregnant again and then left me," she explained. "Now we are ruined, and I am going to have another baby. What are we going to do?"

"We will think of something," Zoe said. But at that moment she couldn't think of a single thing to save her life.

The next day the patrol heading out to change the watches on the two western watch towers had an extra, if unwilling member. Peder had spent a bad night in the darkness of the holding cell. He was not allowed to even collect his personal possessions from the house. Instead, he was immediately put on a pony and sent down the road to the west. As was the custom, the patrol went first all the way west to the West Road tower. When they turned off the road to head up the long trail to the top of the hill, Peder was compelled to dismount. He had not been an agreeable companion, and the men were glad to see him go. Peder was enjoined by the patrol leader that should he be found in Dassaria again before the terms of his banishment were completed, he would be put to death. Even though he had made no friends on the short trip by his whining complaints, the men of the patrol felt sorry enough for him that they gave him an old blanket and a water bottle. When the patrol reached the tower, they could see him heading west, down the road. Eventually he moved on and out of sight, finally disappearing altogether. In fact his disappearance was complete for he never returned to the house of his mother where he had lived. No one ever reported seeing him again.

The morning after he finished the last of the deer, the Old King decided it was a nice day for a walk, a long walk. He had rolled his few belongings into his blanket which he placed over his left shoulder and down across his body to his right side. His water bag he wore over his left shoulder. His kopis was on his left hip and dagger on his right. He wrapped himself in his cloak and put his piloi on his head. Taking up his walking stick in his right hand he walked out of the crevice that had sheltered him for months (and had very nearly been his mausoleum) without a backward glance. He headed down the hill toward the stream where he had been getting his water. The old man's load was light and so was he. He estimated he was more than half a medimnos lighter than he had been when he first sought refuge up there. He turned right and headed down the little track, looking for a trail heading down from these hills.

As he walked he was struck by a series of memories. He smiled, recalling all those schemes the 'Widow Zoe' had tried for making money.

Chapter Thirteen – Schemes and Other Plans

"**We can raise** chickens," decided Zoe. It was a brilliant idea. Zoe was sure they were bound to make some money. She knew that people ate chickens from time to time, though not many people raised them. Most people only knew of them as fighting cocks; roosters had the reputation of being very fierce creatures. Zoe had heard that some people raised them down in Delos. They were a rather exotic dish to her, suitable perhaps for a symposia or other big feast. She knew that there was a flock of chickens that lived down by the stables where they fed on spilled grain and other scratching. She was sure she could make a trap for them. She was equally sure she could construct cages to hold them for sale. If people would not meet her price, feeding them would be inexpensive, and she would wait. As to their reputation for fierceness, Zoe reasoned that roosters were like men. Not all men were fierce fighters; almost certainly not all chickens were either. Besides, she wanted to catch nice tasty hens, not some tough old rooster.

Ana was not so sure about all this, but Zoe was able to override her objections and put her project in motion. First, she had to make cages. Agalia turned out to have considerable talent in constructing wicker ware. In one night their combined effort resulted in six cages and one trap. The trap was simplicity itself: a wide oval frame of wood with a high wicker cap. It looked a bit like a wicker pilleus.

"Are you making a hat for a giant," asked a passerby who stopped to watch them prepare their trap in the small garden area behind the kitchen. Zoe ignored her. She propped a long thin stick under the edge of the trap holding one end of it up at an angle. Then she tied a long piece of twine around the stick and backed away.

"See, Agalia," she explained to the doubtful girl, "you put a bit of grain under the trap and wait around a corner. When the chickens come to peck at the grain, you pull the string," and the contraption obligingly flopped down. Agalia looked doubtful.

It didn't work, of course.

First, they had to find a time when the chickens were out scratching around for food. Zoe had seen the chickens many times and heard roosters crow almost every morning, but when Zoe and Agalia went down to the stables carrying their clumsy trap two hours before noon there was not a chicken to be found. So they carried their trap back to the house to regroup. Ana distanced herself from the effort. Zoe decided that she and Agalia would take turns watching until the chickens chose to make an appearance. Apparently the chickens were warier that Zoe remembered because they were not seen all that day. Nor were they found the next. It was not easy hunting for chickens because the two young women had other things to do besides wander around the town trying to find out where a flock of chickens had gone. Early the third morning Zoe saw them by the stables on her way to get the morning water. She stashed her amphora and raced back to the house to get the trap. As soon as they arrived the chickens moved away; that did not daunt Zoe. She set up her ungainly trap and led the trip string back to a hiding place around one of the stable's corners. Agalia was sent to find some grain. She returned empty handed. Zoe continued watching the chickens. They had moved back into the general area of her trap but were showing no interest in coming underneath the upturned edge. Handing the string to Agalia with a whispered injunction to pull it if any chickens came underneath, Zoe dashed around and into the stables. No one was in that corner of the building. She saw a bucket of grain put out to provide for the horses. She snatched up a handful of the grain out of the bucket and darted back to the corner where Agalia waited. Then Zoe sauntered as casually as she could toward the trap. The birds alertly moved away.

'Nothing to see here, birds,' Zoe thought to herself. 'Nothing dangerous here. I am just a little old girl bringing you some easy breakfast; nothing for you to worry about.' As she moved she began to scatter some of the grain on the ground. Then with a strong backhand toss she threw most of the grain under the lid of the trap. Continuing to move slowly and in as non-threatening manner as was possible, Zoe moved directly away from the trap and down an alley until she was out of sight of the trap. Then she hiked up her chiton and dashed like an adolescent back around and came up to the corner of the stables where Agalia was peering around the edge, string in hand.

Zoe came up behind her and leaned her head around the corner; the two women's heads one above the other. The chickens were gone.

"Drat," Zoe said pulling her head back, "I scared them off."

"No," responded Agalia still keeping her watch, "they just moved away. None of them came anywhere near that trap of yours."

After a time the two decided the chickens were not coming back. They carried Zoe's trap back home, and Zoe went back to hauling water.

For the next two days, no matter how they tried, they could not get any of the flock to move under the trap. They were able to locate the normal patterns of the little flock's movements, but nothing they did, changing the bait, using a thinner line, prayers to Aphrodite, nothing would move the birds under that wicker trap.

It was a frustrating time for all. Money was tight, and Ana remained touchy. The only good news they had was word from Adem. He asked a merchant traveling west to come by and relay a message to his wife. It was typical for people to send messages this way. Though writing was not common, or perhaps because it was uncommon, people often had very good oral memories and could accurately repeat messages told to them. So it was with this man.

Adem was very optimistic about recovering at least some of his lost goods. He, with others, had persuaded the people of Lychmidas to send some men to pursue the bandits. He had heard that King Athan was also bringing troops to assist in the expedition. Adem would be going with them to help secure his goods. He expected to be back in less than a month. Love to her and Agamemnon.' The messenger said that Adem had said to ask his agent to give him a beaker of good wine for his trouble.

"A good vintage," the man said.

"Let me get it, mistress," Zoe said, "I know just the wine to use."

The messenger was pleased with the beaker of fine red Xynomavo Zoe brought him and left praising its qualities. As soon as he was gone, Agalia barred the door. Ana gave Zoe a dirty look.

"You were supposed to throw that wine away," challenged Ana. Agalia giggled at Zoe's trick.

"Well, it wasn't exactly good news, now was it," Zoe responded airily. "We might as well use it for something. Besides, I drank some of it. It really is good."

Grumbling to herself about her insolent staff, her tardy husband, and their straightened circumstances, Ana stalked away.

Finally, Zoe gave up on her trap. If they were going to get some chickens, they would have to be more active. She started weaving a basket net attached to a long pole.

"We have been fairly close to them some mornings," Zoe explained. "You wait behind a corner, and I will chase them to you. If they are too slow, I will catch them." Here she whipped her wicker basket over her head and brought it down to the ground, pretending to catch a slow-footed chicken. "You will be waiting around the corner and use your net. Agalia liked the idea but she thought Zoe's basket net with its long pole would never work.

"I don't know if you could get close enough to them to use that thing. I like my idea better." Agalia had woven a large wicker circle, about as wide as her arms could reach. She was in the process of tying bits of string, strips of used up cloth, old yarn, and thin leather straps together to from a sort of net. Her idea was even simpler than Zoe's. She would just throw her makeshift net over the chickens much like some of the fishermen she had seen at the lake. This was like a game of ring toss, though her hoop was many times larger than the ones they had played with as girls.

Zoe liked her more active basket net on its pole, Agalia remained confident in her hoop net. In the end they compromised. Agalia would position herself behind a corner with her net, and Zoe would move in from the other side with her basket driving the flock toward Agalia's position, hopefully catching a chicken or two as she did so.

It was a brilliant idea. Of course it didn't work.

They knew where the chickens would be at dawn, over by the stables. They had a good plan; Agalia was ready behind one corner of the stables, Zoe behind the next. The flock of perhaps a dozen chickens was scratching the ground between them. It was a quiet, peaceful time, just before dawn. Most people were up, of course, but most were still in their homes, dressing, preparing or enjoying breakfast, and getting ready for the day. All was still and cool with the baby blue sky still tinged with high pink clouds. The women stuck their heads out around the corner and nodded to each other. Agalia pulled her head back into cover, and Zoe stepped out and began moving toward the birds as casually as she could. Chickens might not be the brightest of all fowls, but they know a suspicious character when they see one. They immediately recognized that Zoe, carrying a long pole topped with a woven basket net, was obviously up to no good. They began to move away from her. Worse, they were avoiding the corner where Agalia lurked with her hoop net. Zoe tried to move wide in an attempt to herd the chickens toward Agalia's corner. It didn't work. Some of the flock continued down the dirt street between the widely spaced buildings, moving faster now, and others doubled back heading past Zoe. Things got even worse; Zoe tried to cut off the ones heading back, and there was a flutter and a scurrying as the chickens dramatically increased speed. Zoe made a lunge at the nearest bird. That was when things really fell apart.

For reasons she could never justify, Zoe had brought Lux. Lux had done so well minding her that Zoe thought nothing of telling her to lie down and stay while she went off to stalk some chickens. But no matter how well trained a young dog may be, there are limits! Once the chicken hunt was on in earnest, Lux leapt up to join the fray. The quiet little street erupted into frantic clucks, barks, and frustrated cries as the women tried to corral the chickens. Agalia threw her hoop only to have it land at an angle, and the two chickens under the hoop escaped. Zoe began a fruitless effort to slap her basket over a wildly darting bird. Lux had the most fun darting this way and that until she discovered one of the smaller birds was not a chicken at all. It was a rooster. There were those that said a rooster could daunt a lion. This one certainly was able to master Lux who fled yelping from the feathered assault, the bird's spurs drawing blood. Zoe moved to help her dog, and the rooster turned on her causing her to forget any idea of catching one of these birds. Suddenly she was working very hard to keep one of them from getting to her. She backed away from the enraged rooster trying to keep him back with wide sweeps of her net.

She was closely pursued by the rooster who was screaming insults in 'Roosterese', best translated as: "You want some of this! Huh, you want some more! I'll get you my pretty, and your little dog, too!"

Agalia for her part was on her hand and knees holding the rim of her hoop and trying to flop it over the various panic-stricken birds that were flashing past her, heads out and wings helping them move at a deceptively fast pace.

"What are you doing?!"

It was a woman's voice, filled with anger and dismay. "Leave my chickens alone!"

That brought the women to a stop. Even the rooster seemed cowed, or perhaps sensing reinforcements, he simply no longer felt the need to press his attack. Strutting as only a victorious rooster can, he made as if to cease his assault only to feint a rush at Zoe's bare feet once she started to lower her basket. Zoe shrieked and backed rapidly away from the little monster.

"Your chickens?" asked Agalia who, still on her knees was looking up in dismay at Adara, wife of the Master of the Horse. "We thought they were wild."

"They stay in our barn," the older woman said icily. "We take their eggs. When my husband left I thought we might have to deal with thieves, but I never thought the servant girls of the man my husband rode off with would stoop to such a thing." Behind the outraged Adara were four men, holding rakes, pitchforks, and other hastily grabbed implements of defense. Unlike their mistress, the stable hands were smiling.

There followed a most embarrassing scene of profuse apologies, attempted explanations of what they were trying to do and weak excuses, all resisted firmly by an angry Adara. Perhaps they might have been successful in mollifying her but just as she was beginning to show a slight sign of bending, Lux trotted around the corner. Of the three chicken hunters, one at least had been successful. Lux proudly came up to Zoe, a dead chicken in her jaws.

Throw lamp oil on a bed of embers; watch it suddenly flare into open flame. So it was with Adara. The women (and men) quailed from her rage. In vain did Zoe try to mollify the enraged woman by offering to prepare the bird for dinner ("See, Lux hardly chewed on it at all.") Nor would she accept restitution in the form of a jug of a fine red Xynomavro (Agalia strongly suspected which vintage Zoe would use). They were only saved by the sound of Adara's children crying. This recalled her to her motherly duties; she departed breathing threats and directing the stable hands to expel the two young women and 'that animal' from the vicinity.

One of the lads persuaded Lux to release her prize. It would at least be consumed by the house that claimed ownership of the bird. Two of the men remained to shoo the women off, really more to prevent Adara from coming back and resuming her chastisement than from any real need to get the two women to depart.

"You certainly set her off," confided one of the men. "I wouldn't worry too much. She gets tense whenever Ixon is gone. Things will be fine again when he gets back. Just be glad you weren't a man. You know what she does with the men she gets mad at?" And, grinning he made a snipping gesture.

Agalia and Zoe collected their various chicken-catching tools and returned, defeated, to the house where their chores waited them. Ana could see from their demeanor that, not only had their venture been unsuccessful, it had been abandoned completely. She smiled to herself but said nothing to either of them.

If they thought that was the end of the 'Chicken Incident', they were mistaken. That afternoon Spiros presented himself at the front door and asked to speak to Zoe.

"You have been summoned to the Magistrate," he told her. He declined to elaborate until she made her departures from the house and was walking with him to the Magistrate's.

"So, Spiros, tell," she cajoled. Zoe suspected the tough warrior with the patch over his ruined eye had a soft spot for her.

"Adara has brought a complaint against you," said Spiros out of the side of his mouth. "Her husband and Ixon are good friends, so he has to hear the case. Don't worry, it shouldn't be too bad."

Zoe had her doubts. She was not sure if he had gotten over her little stunt with the wine. Well, she had to be sure he would banish Peder. A simple plug in the wine might not have done the trick; it wasn't personal.

Even though Zoe had been in the House of Justice before, and she was becoming quite familiar with Rodas himself, it was a bit daunting to stand before him. If she was not quite quaking in her sandals, she was at least nervous.

Adara made her case first: this Zoe person and an accomplice had tried to steal the chickens she kept in her yard. Her dog had killed one, and the others were so upset there was no telling when they would start laying again.

To his credit, Rodas treated the matter with the same care he did for weightier matters. He asked Adara many questions: how did she get the chickens, where did they stay, how much did she think they were worth, how old was the chicken that was killed, what became of it? It transpired that the chickens were not actually Adara's, they merely had come to commonly roost there. Adara's people had never purchased them, did not feed them, and only got the eggs when they could find them. The chicken killed was not young and was being prepared for dinner.

Rodas listened gravely and treated Adara with respect, even though it was obvious she knew her case was weak.

"What would you have as restitution?" asked the Magistrate.

Adara asked for a sum that would exceed the value of all the eggs of all the chickens for a month. This was for the dead chicken, potential loss of eggs, and disturbance of the peace. Zoe was shocked; there was no way they could come up with that much money. Rodas considered this gravely; he granted that the bird was dead, however, since Adara was going to eat it, that was not really a serious loss. As to the potential loss of eggs, well that was a potential loss. Here he thought and stroked his chin. The real issue, he told the court was the disruption, not just to the flock of chickens, but to the peace of Ixon's household. Adara nodded. In order to prevent such outrages in the future this Zoe person must apologize to the offended party, make restitution in wine, here Rodas indicated a quantity equal to two beakers. Zoe breathed a silent sigh of relief. Ana would not be pleased, but they could tolerate that amount of a fine.

"Make it a white," Adara said, accepting the judgment. Apparently she knew about that skin of Xynomavro. Still, Zoe was vastly relieved; she was afraid it would be much worse.

"And," continued Rodas, "the miscreant will provide one day's work in service to the kingdom as restitution for her breach of the peace."

"What!" exclaimed Zoe. "Just what do you have in mind?" She could see Adara looking mollified.

"You will assist my staff in the house tomorrow evening. I am putting on a symposium for the merchants and envoys that arrived yesterday. Oh, don't look at me that way; there will be two hetaira to take care of those types of things. I need for you to greet the men and help Alysin as mistress of the house, then assist in cleaning up after the event. You are not expected to do anything that would reflect upon your honor."

Zoe was conflicted. On one hand Rodas was well within his rights to demand service to the state. Assigning a few days labor for the state was not an uncommon sentence for misdemeanors, though serving in his house was a new one to her. She thought the whole thing was unfair. Rodas was just getting back at her for the wine trick. After fuming for a moment, she finally accepted she would have to drink this particular potion, no matter how vile it might taste. She formally apologized to Adara, promised to never disturb her or the flock of chickens again, and to deliver the required portion of wine before sunset.

Zoe was right about Ana not being happy about the wine, but in the end there was nothing she could do about it either. Technically she was responsible for the members of her household and so for their wrongdoing as well. Ana was much more concerned about Zoe's service at the Magistrate's house. This concern was wholly different. She was concerned about a woman in her house being put into a compromising position. Eventually, Alysin came by, to brief Zoe on her expected duties, and to reassure Ana as to the legitimacy of the assignment.

Even though it was only a serving assignment ordered by the Magistrate, the three women of the House of Amphora somehow found themselves getting caught up preparing Zoe as though she were to be the guest of honor at a major festival. Perhaps the situation did not call for it, but getting really dressed up could be a lot of fun. Ana took her to the baths. Henna was applied to Zoe's long black hair to give a hint of red warmth. After the bath, Zoe applied almond oil with a hint of rose and sandalwood all over her body; just enough to cause her skin to glow and give a subtle fragrance. Agalia spent an hour doing Zoe's long hair. The hair was brought up high above her neck with just a few curled strands allowed to dangle loose around her face to soften the look. Then Agalia took half an hour in putting on Zoe's makeup, advised by Ana. There was kohl to line her eyes, powdered iron oxide rouge for her cheeks, and berry juice applied to the lips and then covered lightly with bee's wax. Finally, Ana added some rose water for scent behind Zoe's ears and, shocking Zoe, dabbing some between her breasts. Zoe took off her robe and carefully dressed herself in the fine chiton that Ana loaned her. The chiton was of unusual style; it had fine flax embroidered into small star violet flower designs in the neckline area. Once the chiton was on, the star violets were positioned to embrace Zoe's breasts. Ana placed a necklace of small effervescent blue beads with another star violet that fell into place at the hollow just below her neck. They drew back and admired their work, then showed Zoe her reflection in the best, the only actually, mirror in the house. Zoe was astonished to see the self-assured woman looking back at her. She had always been a pretty girl; now she had to start thinking of herself as a lovely woman. After all she was a respectable widow now. The thought of being a widow brought unexpected tears to her eyes. Ana and Agalia fussed in dismay at the sudden threat to their work. Finally, Ana loaned Zoe a pair of gilded sandals for her feet. Zoe carried them in her hands, unwilling to get them dusty, as she walked over to the Magistrate's house, escorted by Ana.

They were early; this gave Ana a chance to look at the things and be satisfied that the situation was, in fact, a respectable one. She spoke briefly in private to Rodas and left reassured before the sun had touched the horizon.

By then Zoe was busy. Alysin was not all that much older than Zoe, but she had been running an important household for over two years and knew what she was about. Fortunately, the two women hit it off almost immediately; Zoe became Alysin's willing adjutant, carrying messages to other staff members, checking details, listening to what she should and should not do, and becoming very impressed with Alysin as she did so. Zoe was checking to ensure that the serving boys were clean, walking toward the main entrance when she suddenly encountered Rodas. Although taken aback, she regained her composure before he noticed her and so, when he stopped suddenly to stare at her, she was able to give him a cool mysterious smile and move gracefully over to the boys and check them carefully, playfully reminding them to keep clean until after the banquet. Zoe was well aware that Rodas had continued to stare at her while she did this.

It was a revelation to Rodas. He had wanted Zoe, of course; she was a pretty and lively young widow. But watching her move serenely in his house, decorously dressed, giving confident instructions to his staff, Rodas became suddenly aware of something every matron in Dassaria already knew—it was time for him to get a wife. That was all, just a realization that it was time for him to complete his settling down. He watched Zoe gliding out of sight considering how nice it would be to have a real wife to manage his home. It was also time for him to start thinking of an heir. This magistrate job was looking like it was going to last. Rodas was still bemused when his guests started arriving.

It was the custom in this time and place that, on the occasion of formal events in the homes of the wealthy, the mistress of the house would greet the guests as they arrived. In the past this custom had often not been observed in the House of the Magistrate; when it had, Alysin had performed that duty. Though she was a good woman, Alysin was too aware of her humble upbringing and plain, if not to say unattractive appearance, to be completely at ease welcoming the Magistrate's wealthy and powerful guests. It was not a job she enjoyed. So on this night, after repeated, strong requests by Alysin, Zoe agreed to perform the duty of acting as welcoming mistress of the house.

As the first of the men came up the short walk to the main entrance, Zoe stood inside the door to one side wondering just how she managed to get herself into these situations. She had been coached in the proper etiquette for greeting guests; it was quite simple really, welcome them in the House of Rodas, Magistrate of Dassaria. They would give her their names, a servant behind her would be there to recall them to Rodas when needed. She would then direct them to the andronitis on the left. The Magistrate's house was laid out in a slightly unusual manner. To the right was a large room, once used as the men's room and now the hall of justice where Rodas heard his cases. To the left was what had once been the andron. It was now used as both the andronitis for the men to gather and as the dining hall. There was a central courtyard behind these two large rooms. In the back portion of the house were the kitchen pantries, and numerous small cells and sleeping rooms. There were larger quarters upstairs in the back of the house. A stairway in the courtyard led all the way up to the flat roof where, like many others in Dassaria, people often slept in summer.

Though Zoe was a confident woman, this social responsibility had her thoroughly unsettled. Although she knew she was pretty, she recognized that she was not really a classic beauty. She took heart in the confidence that at least she was appropriately dressed and and made up. Hadn't she made Rodas stop and look at her? Zoe shyly welcomed the first two men, wealthy by their clothes and manner, and directed them correctly without stumbling over her words. As they moved into the andronitis where Rodas waited, she returned to her post, head down, heart pounding. Fortunately, her shyness was taken for demure deference, qualities not often associated with Zoe. She managed to fulfill her duties without embarrassing herself. Indeed, Rodas received a number of favorable comments about her. Most of the men assumed she was his wife. Rodas usually informed them that she was 'a young widow from the town who has been helping me manage my home.' He let them interpret that comment as they may. He certainly did not even hint that she was, in fact, serving a sentence for misdemeanor breach of the peace.

Just as Zoe thought the last guests had arrived and was preparing to withdraw from her post a small, elegant cart with a cloth covering against the sun pulled up to the front. Zoe's curiosity, always close to the surface, stirred. Two men accompanied by two elegantly dressed women descended and came up to the door. Zoe was able to properly greet the men but the women flummoxed her. These women were so exotic, so utterly goregeous that they seemed to be another gender altogether. They were calm, confident, and self prossessed. They seemed taller and more slender than they actually were. The two were perfectly turned out with a skill that made Zoe suddenly feel dowdy. For the first time in her life Zoe understood what men meant when they described 'beauty'.

She had not been briefed on how to deal with a situation like this, Zoe fumbled something to say. Should she just ignore them? Would the men be angry if she greeted them the same way she had the males?

As she stood by the door fumbling for something to say, the oldest of the women, smiling, took matters confidently in hand.

"Thank you for your welcome," she said giving Zoe an embrace. "I am Damali and this is Eleni."

With a start Zoe realized that these women must be hetaira. Zoe had met prostitutes before, of course, but she had never moved in social strata where hetaira would be encountered. She did not know whether to be impressed or scandalized. She fell back on courtesy, after all this was not her house, and the moment passed smoothly, the women following the two men into the men's hall as though they belonged there; in fact, they did.

The evening turned out to be easy. The cooks and hired serving boys did all the real work. The rest of the staff remained available to assist as needed which meant they just sat around nibbling the delicious leftovers and gossiping, mostly about the guests, and especially about the two women who were allowed, no paid, to remain with the men. The idea that men would pay women for social services other than sex was foreign to them. The conversations were abruptly stopped when the two women under discussion appeared together asking to use the privies. There was a brief uncomfortable silence before Zoe rose and offered to show them the way. The women seemed quietly amused that there was only one outhouse; apparently they were used to inside facilities. Zoe did not tell them that this was the master's personal outhouse and that the rest of the staff used much more basic facilities at the back of the garden.

"So," asked Damali while she waited for Eleni to do her business, "I understand you are a widow. Are you Rodas' mistress?"

Zoe, a bit intimidated, shook her head no.

"Pity," said Damali casually, "he seems a good man. I understand he is quite important out here."

Zoe nodded yes. She was angry at herself for being such a muggle. This woman was just trying to be polite.

"Why are you a," Zoe hesitated for a moment feeling like a clumsy girl, "I mean why did you become a hetaira? You are one aren't you?"

"The woman laughed not unkindly. "Just good fortune," she told Zoe. Eleni exited from the small outhouse and Damali left to attend to her needs.

"Was Damali telling you her story?" asked Eleni. "She was the mistress of a wealthy oligarch. After he died, she began to associate with some of his friends and then got some assignments of her own. I guess one thing led to another."

"Is that what happened to you?" asked Zoe with innocent curiosity.

"Oh, no, I was more or less merely an expensive prostitute. I was fortunate to make some good connections and receive training. You can make more money doing this and do it longer. I was trained by some of the better houses and have worked steadily. Aesculus and I have been together for over a year. I think he would marry me but then I would have to behave like a proper matron and wouldn't be able to go on trips with him and meet his business associates."

Damali came out, and the three women began making their way back to the symposia. "You might consider the profession," Eleni told Zoe, "It is an exciting way to earn your living, much better than being a mistress."

"I was telling Zoe, here, that you can work as a hetaira for years and years. Darien is 40 if she is a day, and Persis has got to be over 50! Mind you they take care of themselves and are still attractive, but really!"

Eleni laughed at Denali's comments.

"Come talk to us, Zoe, if you want to find out more."

She never got the chance. She had just begun to help with some of the cleaning up after the men finished eating when was called in to where the men were drinking. Rodas told the story of her clever way of getting rid of Peder. The men and the hetaira roared with laughter as Rodas told the story on himself in an amusing way.

Did you really put in a snake?" one of the men asked her.

"It had been dead for some little time," Rodas expanded.

Taking heart from the two women in the room, Zoe gave them an enigmatic smile and said, "They say that some older men feel the need to add such things to their wine for medicinal effects. It supposedly helps their," here Zoe put in a perfectly timed hesitation, "personal problems."

Everyone, even Rodas laughed.

"No, Zoe," Rodas protested after the laughter died down, "no problems there."

With a frankly saucy smile, Zoe looked right at him and said, "I am sure I will never know, my lord."

She made her courtesies and withdrew before the laughter died, and Rodas had a chance to riposte.

Zoe had anticipated a long night cleaning up in the kitchen after the men had left and was prepared to remove her jewelry and don an apron to help in the kitchen. Instead, soon after her appearance in the men's hall a smiling Spiros arrived to escort her home. At first Zoe was confused; she was being treated like a guest. Then she was afraid she had offended Rodas. Spiros assured her that to the contrary, Rodas was most satisfied with her and considered her service complete. Alysin also went out of her way to thank Zoe for her help.

"You have no idea how much I dread those formal greetings," she confided to Zoe as she walked her to the door. "You have got to do something to get the Magistrate to sentence you to service again next time we have a symposium like this."

Ana and Agalia were waiting up for her when she arrived. Ana was pleased to see her back so early and in such good spirits. "Half the time when a girl leaves with makeup on she comes back with it smeared with tears," she said giving her comment the weight of a folk saying.

Zoe had a hard time going to sleep again that night. What was she doing with her life? Where was she going? Should she try to be a hetaira? Zoe didn't think she would like to sleep with men for money, even a lot of money; besides she would have to go somewhere where there was a call for that sort of service. She doubted if there were ten symposia a year in all of Dassaria that would justify the expense of even one she-companion. Besides, didn't they talk about philosophy and high-minded ideas? Zoe had not been educated in those sorts of things. It sounded adventurous, but Zoe decided that was not the life for her. She was still wondering just what was 'the life for her' when she fell asleep.

Zoe still didn't know what she was going to do with her life when she woke up but she did have another brilliant idea. She did her morning chores as quickly as she could and rushed over to the small shrine of Aphrodite. She prayed briefly and fervently, then left a small libation of wine. Once her chores were done, she hurried to the house where she knew Damali and Eleni were staying. It was easy for another woman to gain entrance to their sitting room.

The two women were lounging around in loose robes, being served tea by a very plain-looking female slave. Zoe was shocked to realize they had just gotten out of bed. She also immediately understood why these women would never allow a pretty younger woman to be in daily contact with their protectors. 'So there was a place for ugly girls, too, thought Zoe uncharitably.

"Oh, so you are thinking about becoming a hetaira are you?" began Damali, offering Zoe a cup of tea. "Well, we would not be able to take you in training while we are traveling."

"Oh, no," Zoe demurred, "I am quite happy here as a widow. I was just wondering if your, ummm, associate Aesculus might be interested in investing in some very fine wines. We have some of the best vintages available for many days' travel and at favorable rates."

"I thought your mistress had just gotten rid of her agent? Has she gotten a new one already?"

"Oh, his heir is in charge now. He is inexperienced, but he will be the master of the business for the short time until Amphora returns," Zoe told them airily not even hinting that the reason the heir was so inexperienced was because he was not quite two years old.

The two women were sophisticated and knowledgeable about a wide range of subjects including wine. In her time with Ana and Adem, Zoe had learned a great deal, though not enough to answer all their questions. After half an hour of discussion, the two hetaira agreed they would recommend to Aesculus that he pay a visit to the house of Amphora to discuss the purchase of some wines.

Zoe thanked them politely and soon departed, moving casually away from the house until she was out of sight, then she hiked up her skirts and ran. Sometimes plans had to be made step by step, like crossing a swift mountain stream by moving from one rock to the next. And you had to make leaps sometimes.

She was headed for the house of Needles, preparing all her arguments and persuasions, when she got lucky. She did not actually run into Linus, but that only because she saw him just before they made contact. She knew who he was, of course, being from Bardhyllus. Linus was the mighty hero who brought the gold tribute to her old hometown and told stories of his amazing adventures. Zoe had never seen him in person before she came to Dassaria and was more that a little impressed when he was pointed out to her. She had certainly never been introduced to him, but the instant she saw him her quick wit went into action. He had no real regular employment beyond delivering the tribute, the King having provided the one-handed warrior a pension. He was big, imposing, and visiting merchants would not know him. He was perfect.

Zoe skidded to a stop in front of him.

"Sir," she began, "my name is Zoe. I live in the house of Amphora, and I request a boon of you."

Linus took her abrupt appearance as though pretty girls came running up to him pleading for help every day. Well, in fact, it had happened more than a few times. The big man eyed Zoe and smiled. "So you are the little bit that has been giving my old chief such a hard time." His eyes sparkled. "I can see why. So what can I do for you, other than the usual?" He gave Zoe such a confident leer that she felt herself blushing.

"It is for Amphora," and she quickly explained what she wanted. Linus seemed to think the whole thing was a great joke and agreed to not only help Zoe but to follow her back to the house right then and there.

It was a good thing he did; the third part of Zoe's plan turned out to be the hardest.

"NO!" Exclaimed Ana. "I will not do this. It is illegal for a woman to conduct business. Adem did not in any way appoint or approve of him," she looked at the grinning Linus who was leaning against one of the pillars in the andronitis, "as his agent."

"He is not the agent. He is just a man who will help us out," Zoe protested.

"We cannot sell anything. A woman is forbidden to do business. It is the law."

"We have a male—the sole male heir of Adem is right here."

"He is not a man, Zoe!"

"Oh, yes, he is, I have seen inside his nappies. He has what it takes."

"He is just a baby."

"Ana, the law does not say the male has to be of age; just that a woman can't do business by herself. Which is a stupid law: you know a lot about the business."

"Zoe, I might know something about wine and how much it costs," admitted Ana, "but I cannot negotiate with men. They wouldn't take me seriously even if I could bargain with them, which I can't"

"That is why we have this big strong man here," responded Zoe moving over to place a hand on Linus who continued to smile indulgently at the women. 'He really is big and strong,' Zoe thought. She had heard whispered giggling gossip by older girls about some of the women he had taken as lovers. There were supposed to be a lot of them. He really did have splendid shoulders. Linus smiled indulgently down at her as though he know exactly what she was thinking. Zoe pulled her thoughts back with a jerk to the matter at hand. "He can bargain; you signal to him when a deal is satisfactory. We have a man negotiating, what could go wrong?"

"Everything," Ana cast a wary eye at Linus. "What is in this for you?"

"I am always happy to help maidens in distress," he responded good naturedly.

"We are not maidens" snapped Ana.

"Amphora is a good sort," shrugged Linus. "I am really glad to help his house. Besides, I don't have anything else to do, and this looks like fun."

"The future of my house is not fun," said Ana with tight lips. Then she abruptly excused herself and hurried from the room.

"It is the morning sickness," explained Zoe as she moved a step away from Linus.

"Really," said Linus who quit leaning against his pillar and followed her slowly looking deeply into her eyes.

'Oh, he really is handsome and so overwhelmingly male.' Zoe stood looking up at him, a bird gazing into the beautiful eyes of a smiling python.

There was no way to tell what might have happened next if Agalia had not popped in with a cup of wine for their famous guest. The distraction allowed Zoe to catch her breath and move away from the tall, blonde temptation in front of her. Both women were embarrassed; Linus was not and immediately began flirting with Agalia in the same lighthearted and devastatingly effective way.

Zoe had always considered herself lucky, and her luck was running strongly that day. Before Ana could return to put her foot down about this wild scheme of Zoe's, their first customers arrived. Aesculus and Eleni arrived with two servants. They were made welcome, and Agalia was sent to bring Ana into the hall. Ana made an appearance pale and obviously ill. She looked at the situation and realized that events had overtaken her, and she could now do nothing to oppose Zoe's plan. Pleading her obvious sickness, she excused herself.

Fortunately, Aesculus had not come to make a major purchase, merely to obtain some additional wines for their journey, so Zoe's relative ignorance of wines and their prices was not exposed. Zoe was able to perform an assumptive introduction, implying the big blonde man was the agent without actually saying so. In fact, Linus seemed to have a solid grasp of various vintages and understood the expected prices as a tippler of long standing. After agreeing on the sale of some small quantities of wine at prices Zoe thought were rather expensive, the party prepared to depart.

Then, with a casualness that was obviously feigned, Aesculus asked Zoe a question in an offhanded manner. "That special wine, the one you prepared for the Magistrate. Is it true?"

"Is what true?" asked a bewildered Zoe.

"That is has 'special properties' as you say." This was spoken with a slight wink and nod.

This time Linus was quicker than Zoe. He nudged the other man with an elbow, and in a conspiratorial tone said, "Oh, he told you about that stuff, did he. Let me tell you, it is something! It is like you are a teenager again."

"Not that I need it," objected Aesculus.

"Oh, no, it is just for fun. Let us sell you a beaker and try it out. I am sure you will be pleased."

The big northerner had Zoe bring out the skin and pour him off a beaker of the wine. Then he charged Aesculus more than twice what the wine was worth.

The party left in high spirits. Eleni seemed particularly amused. Before they left, she gave Zoe a private little wink. Agalia skipped out to give Ana the good news. Zoe's head was spinning; they had pulled it off! Linus took her elbow with his right hand and spoke confidently and confidingly to her.

"So, pretty Zoe, you did it. How shall we celebrate? He began steering her gently but firmly in the direction of one of the sleeping chambers. 'He is so big and strong, and he smells so good,' thought Zoe distractedly, 'I wonder what it would be like to be with someone other than Baruch?'

This time it was Ana who 'saved' Zoe.

"I understand you were successful," came Ana's voice. Zoe stepped away from what was nearly an embrace with Linus.

Linus laughed. "Yes, and best of all was the special vintage that Zoe prepared."

He stepped up to Ana and poured the coins from a small purse into her hands. She stared at it amazed. "But," she stammered out, "Agalia said you only sold a little."

Zoe looked at the young serving girl and saw Agalia looking at her with thinly veiled jealousy. 'Oh,' thought Zoe, 'Linus had been flirting with Agalia, too. This could be real trouble.'

Linus explained how he had driven a merely good bargain with the first purchases but had made the real killing with the wine thought to be ruined.

Ana seemed unamused. "What happens when nothing happens?" she asked him.

Linus laughed uproariously, "What will he do? Come here and announce to everyone that he can't perform. Don't worry, I bet he will be so inspired by that wine he will outdo himself!"

"What do I owe you for your help?" Ana asked. She seemed determined not to get the joke.

"Nothing!" Linus said, "This is the most fun I have had in months." He stopped for a moment and then changed his mind. "I would like a beaker of that Vlachiko varietal. And maybe some of Zoe's special wine as well." The women gaped at him. Linus shrugged. "Well, you never can tell. I might try it out."

The caravan that Aesculus and his companions were traveling with departed early the next morning. Aesculus made a special point to come by the House of Amphora in his wagon. Fortunately Zoe had returned from bringing water and could greet them. Ana was wretchedly ill and so was unable or unwilling to leave the basin to which she was clinging.

"Oh I hate this part of making babies," she moaned.

Linus was, of course, nowhere to be found. Zoe made her apologies at the door saying that the mistress was ill and the master of the house was still abed, which technically was true.

"I only came for a small boon," Aesculus explained. "Could I purchase six more beakers of that 'special' wine?" He gave her a slightly embarrassed smile and held up a purse.

Zoe looked behind him at the covered wagon where Eleni lay recumbent on some cushions, apparently exhausted.

"Not too much, my love, have some pity on me!" and she waved to him weakly.

Zoe looked at her customer who smiled at her, then around at Eleni who smiled behind her patron's back and gave Zoe a broad wink.

"Right away, Sire," said Zoe.

The word about the special wine spread rapidly, whether from rumors at the symposium, from Aesculus, or from Linus who showed up later that day looking like a pleased tomcat. Fortunately, Linus was there to take care of the sudden influx of business. They were able to resume some sales of wines to their old customers, not at the same level as when Adem was there, but enough to allow sufficient cash flow so that payments could be made on their debts. Much of their business was from men who were eager to try the 'special vintage'. They doubled the price of the wine, then doubled it again, and even so, emptied Zoe's famous wine skin to a customer early on the third day, just before Zoe was arrested again.

The old man took a break and leaned up against a tree basking in the weak sun. He had been walking for a bit over an hour; it was disheartening how quickly he had become tired. On the other hand, for the first time in a long time he was taking action to resolve his situation. The time of waiting was over. The old man smiled at the memory of how Zoe had come up with all those crazy schemes back then. Zoe was certainly resourceful. And she was even more determined than resourceful.

It was time for him to be determined; he had to get up and get moving again. The old man levered himself to his feet and, staff in hand, headed down the trail.

Chapter Fourteen – A
Royal Resolution

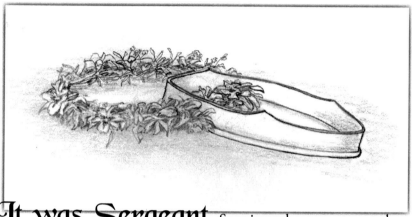

It was Sergeant Stamitos who came to get them. This time both Zoe and Ana were called before the Magistrate. Ana was, of course, furious. She had been relieved to be able to sell some of their stock for cash. That was one thing; after all they needed the money to pay their creditors. But she had never countenanced the resale of Zoe's 'special vintage'. She was certain that the Magistrate would at the least demand compensation for the tainted wine that they had sold him and then resold again.

Stamitos was closed-mouthed about the case; eventually he admitted that it was to settle a complaint against them by another wine merchant. This would have to be Mulius, the only real competition they had in Dassaria. He sold various cheap vintages and even allowed people to consume wine in his house; Adem considered him no real competition at all but merely an 'overambitious tavern house keeper.' Nevertheless, she decided to bring Agamemnon, and leave Agalia in the house.

"It should be safe, and after all, Linus should be dropping by soon," Agalia assured her.

Zoe was not sure it was all that safe. She had been able to resist the big man's charms so far; the worst thing about it was she was not sure she wanted to resist him. He was never coarse or grasping; he never made an obvious pass at her; he was just there and available and interested in her. He was as innocuous and insinuating as a warm bath; so easy to just relax into and enjoy. Then yesterday his attentions had somehow shifted, and Zoe knew he was no longer pursuing her in his languorous manner. At first she was relieved. His gentle seduction had been working all too well. Now Zoe began to wonder just why he had stopped, and why Agalia had been singing this morning.

She said nothing about this to Ana. Zoe was able to dress quickly; wearing what she began to refer to as her 'court cloths' meaning her second best chiton and sandals. Then the two women and the child departed for the House of the Magistrate. Little Agamemnon was at an awkward age: too heavy to carry comfortably and too young to walk far. They passed him between them; before too long Stamitos was carrying the young man on his shoulders, much to Aggie's delight.

Sure enough, when they arrived in the hall and came before Rodas, there was Mulius standing to one side looking surly.

Ana, with Agamemnon in hand, stopped on the other side, Zoe next to her.

"Hello, Rodas," said Zoe with a smile.

Mulius looked startled.

"Hello, Zoe," replied Rodas who did not return the smile.

The case was simple: Ana and her household had engaged in commerce without a male relative or designated agent present. Zoe noticed that Linus was neither present nor mentioned. She understood that the Magistrate and Linus had been comrades for a long time and that no matter what else happened, Linus was in the clear. It also gave her hope that Rodas might be secretly on their side. She was certain that Linus and Rodas must have discussed what was going on privately.

"We had an agent," began Ana in her defense.

"No agent approved by Amphora," countered Mulius. "He had one, and you ran him out."

"There could be no approved agent if Amphora did not appoint him," agreed the Magistrate. "Did you receive any message or other communication from your husband which would have lawfully approved the appointment of a new agent?"

Ana was about to admit this when Zoe stepped in.

"There was no need for an agent, sire."

Ana gaped at her.

"Do you deny that you have sold wine," said Mulius truculently. "I have witnesses who say you lie."

Zoe could see the man irritated Rodas. A feeling came over her; she was about to win.

"There was no need," she said in her sweetest voice to Mulius "his lawful heir was in the house."

This caused confusion. Mulius was initially baffled, Ana looked scandalized, and Rodas did his best to hide a smile.

Finally Mulius understood, "What? Who? You mean the baby? Don't be ridiculous!" he sputtered.

"The law does not specify the specific age of consent, does it Magistrate?"

In fact the law was more than vague about the matter. In most cases Rodas relied on common sense. Zoe was counting on Rodas doing the 'right thing.' She was a bit dismayed to see he was hesitating. He was aware he might be setting a bad precedent allowing unscrupulous adults to take advantage of minors in all sorts of future deals.

Seeing him hesitate, Zoe began thinking fast. She had been so sure he would just smile and agree with her. Now she might lose. Then she had an idea that might work!

Before Rodas could speak again, Zoe took a half step forward and began to speak, looking at the floor not the Magistrate. "My lord, I understand that we are only women and not fit to run a business. However, the appointed agent was found by you to be unfit. Would it not be appropriate for you, the Magistrate, to appoint a temporary guardian and agent until either Amphora returns or sends a message appointing a new agent?"

"What about all the business these women have been doing since Peder left?" objected Mulius. "They should have come to you first before doing business."

Rodas turned his head to look at Zoe who still had her head down. "Perhaps make it a retroactive appointment," she suggested in a small voice.

"The situation is clear," declared Rodas in the tone he used when he had come to a decision. "These women cannot continue to do business without a lawful agent. Therefore, the court appoints Linus of Frigandia as their agent and protector until such time as the wine merchant

Adem, also known as Amphora, either returns to resume his business or appoints a qualified agent in his place. This appointment is made retroactive to the date when the previous agent was disqualified and banished."

Mulius took a moment to figure out what this meant. Linus had been there when they had done all their deals, he would certainly approve them. The women had gotten away with it. "But, but," he began to object.

Rodas looked right at him, stood up, and walked out of the room.

After that, they did a small but steady business. Ana even allowed them to make a few purchases of wine from one of their regular suppliers, a man who had a small vineyard in the region. Everyone in Dassaria was expecting word back on the results the King's expedition to the north any day. Rodas sent a patrol to the north to see if there was any word. Things were quiet in town; it seemed as though everyone was waiting for something to happen.

It had been two days since Rodas had needed to hear a case. He was a bit surprised when word came up to the Hold that there was a case pending for him. Rodas was going over some matters of finance with Abacus. Although normally he would wait until he had several cases to hear at once, dealing with the treasurer was as much a trial for Rodas as it was for Athan, and he welcomed the interruption. He could hear the case, then take some lunch and a short nap before resuming his conference on tax rates.

He walked into the Magistrate's hall and sat down in his chair without even looking at the plaintiffs. A seedy looking man approached him. Rodas did not recognize him, so he must have arrived with the little caravan that had come in the previous evening. This man was a miserable underfed creature, wearing a smelly tunic. His attempt at a beard was pathetic; it was thin and patchy and had already begun to go gray in places.

"Where is the accused?" asked Rodas off-handedly looking around the room for the first time.

The accused poked her head around from around behind Spiros where she seemed to be taking refuge.

"Hello, sire" she said shamefacedly.

"Zoe!"

"Yes, sire," she replied meekly.

"What is it this time?"

"Goats, sire."

"Goats?"

"My goats," interrupted the seedy man. "She stole my goats."

"I did not!" objected Zoe with some heat. "I bought them."

"You did not!"

"I paid two jugs of a nice white for them!"

Rodas stopped the 'did so, did not' argument decisively as he had done many times before with a shout and slap on the arms of his chair. The two stopped arguing and turned to face the magistrate.

"You," Rodas pointed to the seedy man, "who are you, where did you come from? Tell me your story."

"I am Domas sir. I came here yesterday to sell my goats. This morning three of them were gone, stolen in the night. So I went looking. I found two of them behind her house in a pen in the garden, a new pen, too! She had the kid and a pregnant nanny. There she was, feeding them just as cool as you please. So I got a bailiff to arrest her and bring her here."

"Zoe," Rodas said turning to the young woman.

"I bought them this morning," insisted Zoe. "But not from this man. It was another man, a chubby older man I had never seen before. He said he had arrived with the caravan yesterday and had some goats to sell. Ana is worried that Aggie needs some milk, and we have been looking for some goats. He sold me the two I wanted, a jug for each. It was a good bargain."

"Had you ever seen this man before?" Rodas probed.

"No, he said he had just arrived the day before. He said his name was Jason. He was leading three goats on a string and came by the well where a lot of us were getting water this morning. He said he was selling his goats. We talked, and then he came back with me. Linus saw him; you can ask him. Lots of girls at the fountain saw him and his goats. They heard him trying to sell his goats some other people."

"Those were not his goats," interrupted Domas who was becoming more agitated as Zoe talked.

"Can you prove that," asked Rodas in a calm steady voice.

"Yes," Domas said "I can describe them exactly. They will know me. Everyone in my village knows they are my goats. You can ask the man where I kept my goats last night. I had seven goats last night, this morning there were four. Go and ask him."

"Do you know anyone called Jason?" Rodas pressed feeling himself on the trail.

"No," Domas replied, "but there was a fat man who was sniffing round. He wore a brown tunic and had a thick black beard. He wore a silly little hat."

"That's him!" exclaimed Zoe. "He was wearing the ugliest brown tunic; you can ask anyone at the well."

Rodas had heard enough. "Spiros, go up to the Hold and tell the sergeant of the guard to give you three men. Search the town for a heavy-set fellow in a brown tunic with a full beard." Then the Magistrate turned back to Zoe. "You know you will have to give the goats back to this man."

Zoe started to speak then bit her lip and nodded. 'Good,' Rodas thought, 'she knows when to hold her peace. Aloud he told her the charges would be dropped when Domas received his goats. "You cannot keep stolen property, Zoe," he explained. "When we find this Jason you described, we will try to recover your wine."

She nodded and turned to depart.

"And Zoe," she turned to look at him. "If you don't stop coming before me like this I don't know what I will do with you." And he smiled at her.

She smiled back. "Whatever my lord desires," she said. She exited the room swaying slightly more than normal, just to make sure he watched.

'I think he fancies me,' the widow Zoe thought. A world of possibilities opened before her.

The matter was resolved just the way the Magistrate had ordered. The man Jason, a known rascal, had just been expelled from the caravan by the master. To ease his pain and get a bit of money back for his return home, he had stolen the goats. Spiros and his men found him roaring drunk just outside of town with a sealed jug of wine and a second jug with a small, very small, portion of wine still remaining. The other goat was recovered and returned to its owner. It even turned out well for the

House of Amphora because by the time Domas and Zoe had reached the house, they had agreed on a purchase price for the nanny goat, so the household would have goat's milk after all. Thus, justice was upheld in Dassaria (as it usually was).

All the excitement of the stolen goats was swept away by the news a messenger brought, bursting in just as a now satisfied Domas was leaving with his jug of wine he had traded for one of his goats. It was important news indeed. The King had returned and was already at the Hold. He had come over the lake again. There had been three battles fought, all victories. The bandits were killed or scattered. The army was returning. They should arrive in three or four days.

The news spread like wildfire. The next day, advance messengers from the host began arriving with further news. One of them brought news that the House of Amphora had been waiting for since Adem had departed in such haste—Adem was safe. He was traveling with the army. He reported some success, whatever that meant. It did imply his trip had resulted in the recovery of at least some of the lost goods. The little household was thrown into turmoil as Ana began a wholesale cleaning campaign. Things had been a little tense among the women ever since Agalia stopped sleeping up on the roof with the other two. It quickly became obvious that she was sharing Linus' chambers. A servant girl sleeping with the designated agent and man of the house was not a stable situation. What added grit to the meal was having to listen to her endless prattling about how wonderful Linus was, how wise, caring, strong, et cetera, et cetera, ad nauseum.

So it was with double joy that Adem was welcomed home a few days later just after noon. He had been able to recover some of the lost goods and even persuaded the King to partially reimburse him for some of the other goods he had lost. So even if he had not made any profit on his venture, he at least had not lost his entire stake. He was so overjoyed at the news of Ana's new pregnancy that he was able to overlook some of the unconventionalities that had occurred during his absence. He actually admitted that appointing Peder without better references was a mistake. He had managed to contract a new apprentice in the expectation that when his other apprentice finished his service, the business would need additional help. Even Linus was given an offer to stay on in an unofficial capacity. He could lodge in the house at no charge.

"That would be convenient," he said in his dry way. "I was thinking of asking your servant girl to marry me."

There was a crash as Agalia dropped the dish of olives she was bringing for the men. She stood there pale, her hands covering her mouth.

"Well," continued Linus in the same matter of fact voice, "would you mind? I think she will have me."

Agalia turned her face, now pale as milk, toward Adem, her eyes huge over her hands. Adem was feeling expansive. "Take her," he waved expansively.

Agalia flung herself across the room and into her fiancé's arms, covering his face with kisses and weeping with joy.

It was a wonderful day, the women were relieved at the return of the man of the house, their rescue from bankruptcy and shared Agalia's joy. It remained wonderful until just before sunset when in through the back door of the kitchen strode a smirking Baruch, the Widow Zoe's inconveniently surviving husband.

Zoe stared at him in shock. She and Agalia had been trying to put together the evening meal. The bread had just come out of the oven and a stew was coming along nicely.

"Did you miss me, sweetheart?" he said as pleased as the cat that had just lapped up the cream. He reached around and gave her a hug pinching her bottom as he did so. Zoe jumped. "You don't seem too glad to see me," he leered.

Zoe pulled away. "I thought you were dead," she said staring at him.

"Not me," he said turning away to pluck a piece of bread from the counter. Agalia who had been watching with big eyes slipped away into the women's hall leaving the young couple alone.

"So, have you been good?" he asked moving to try to pin her against a wall. "Do you have a new boyfriend?"

Couples, especially couples who have not been together long, always have a difficult time when they reunite after an extended absence; most especially an extended absence with no communication of any kind between them. It requires delicacy, mutual communication, and a careful reestablishment of relationships. Baruch exhibited none of these qualities. Instead, he treated his long-abandoned wife like some tavern house girl. Apparently Baruch felt that his wife should fall at his feet and immediately open her legs in gratitude for his safe return. Zoe bristled at the treatment. To Baruch this indicated that she had found someone else. Voices were raised, threats made, and in Zoe's case carried out.

The crash of crockery was still echoing from the cup Zoe had thrown when Ana entered, the very image of an affronted matriarch.

"What are you doing in my kitchen!?!"

That stopped them both, Zoe still with another cup in her hand poised for a throw.

"My wife and I were just having a little disagreement," Baruch claimed cheekily.

"Get out," Ana told him coldly.

Baruch started to speak but he did not even get a word out before Ana spoke again. "Get out before I call the men."

This was no hollow threat. Baruch knew that if the men of the house came back and found him uninvited in the kitchen, he would be in very serious trouble indeed, wife or no wife.

He raised his hands and backed out of the kitchen door. "I just came back to get my wife," he began.

"Then come to the front and ask to speak to the man of the house. Don't come skulking around and sneaking in the back." She slammed the door in his face, dropping the bar down to secure it as soon as she did.

Zoe fell apart, weeping inconsolably. Discovering Baruch was unexpectedly alive made her felt exactly like she had when she had first heard that her husband was dead. Ana was too angry to comfort her. Agalia, who had sensibly fetched Ana as soon as she grasped the situation, did her best to provide support for her friend. She did not really understand why Zoe was so upset, but it did not matter right then. All she knew was that the bravest, cleverest woman she knew needed someone to hold her; so that is what she did. Eventually, Zoe was persuaded to retire to her cubical.

The four other members of the house shared a subdued meal together that evening. Ana was deeply satisfied with her husband. He was a changed man; he was darker from living outdoors, physically harder from his exertions; and he also seemed more confident. He told them of the events since his leaving: the negotiations with the Lychmidians to mount an expedition, the trip with Ixon to the site of the caravan's ambush. He told how Lychmidians were finally persuaded to provide support for the expedition. Then there were the fights with bands of brigands. He was not in two of the three encounters, but in the final battle he stood in the line right next to Ixon. If he had not actually killed anyone, it was not for lack of trying. Then the enemy had broken, and the pursuit began. Those bandits that did not throw away everything and run like deer were cut down. Some of the King's horsemen were still back in the hills chasing these unfortunates. It would be a long time before the mountain passes were again troubled by a large band of brigands.

About Zoe's husband, Baruch, Adem was hesitant to speak at first. He said as little as possible in Zoe's hearing. Men on campaign gossip like fishwives, and Baruch's character had not fared well in those campfire discussions. He had shown up on the mountain road with four companions. The five had apparently not realized that an army had come into the mountains after the bandits but, seeing the way the wind was blowing, immediately asked to join the expedition. There was considerable speculation about what the men would have done if they had encountered bandits or perhaps vulnerable travelers first. Baruch did nothing to enhance his reputation by his conduct while with the army. He became know as a schemer, a slacker, and a shirker; he avoided his duties and stood a careless watch. He did, like Adem, stand in line at the final fight of the campaign. Of course he had no choice in the matter. When Zoe was not present Adem confided in Ana that it was widely speculated that the reason Baruch had not been with the caravan was because he remained with a woman in town. It was darkly speculated he might have given information about his caravan to those who were in contact with the brigands that later attacked them.

So on a night when most of Dassaria was rejoicing at the return of a successful foray, Zoe sat miserable and alone in her cell. Ana was reunited with Adem, Agalia had Linus; Zoe had Baruch. Ugh. It was past dark when Zoe bestirred herself to take the evenings slops out to the compost pile in the garden. Agalia was in her own cell preparing herself to accompany Linus to a gathering of his friends. Zoe didn't mind doing the chore, it suited her mood. She wanted to be alone in the dark for a while. She definitely did not want to encounter Baruch in the back garden where he had apparently been waiting for her.

As soon as he spoke, Zoe dropped the pail and whirled around, making a dash for the kitchen door. He called for her to stop. Maybe he just wanted to talk, maybe to apologize, maybe he wanted to patch things up, she could not tell. Zoe could tell from his voice he had been drinking, and she knew what that meant. Besides, she just wasn't up to talking to him. Zoe fled into the kitchen. He followed her as fast as she retreated, banging open the back door before she could bar it.

"Zoe, wait, just listen to me," his tone was becoming irritated. "Stop," he ordered.

Zoe was in no mood to stop, wait, or listen. She fled into the Women's hall, Lux barking furiously from her confinement in her crate. Her flight had been almost instinctive; simple avoidance of an irritant. Now she was becoming alarmed. She could tell Baruch's blood was up; there would be no talking to him now. When Baruch banged open the door to the gynaeconitis and barged in, Zoe went from being alarmed to really frightened. Family members came into the women's hall, male friends and acquaintances might be invited in, but no man was allowed inside like that. She fled through the door out past the dining hall, Baruch in hot pursuit, voices calling out behind her in alarm from the side rooms. She made it into the andronitis and saw to her immense relief Linus and Spiros sitting on stools around a low table, sharing a bowl of wine and apparently waiting to accompany Agalia for the evening's festivities.

The two men stood, Baruch skidded to a stop, and Zoe darted behind them.

"So, your boyfriends," sneered Baruch. "As soon as you thought you were rid of me you probably started screwing every man in town."

Linus and Spiros were fond of Zoe. They did not like having her insulted in front of them. They also knew who Baruch was; his reputation had preceded him. They understood that he was an unwelcome invader in the house. Two dogs guarding their flock might have looked so at an unwary fox trotting up to a lamb. They did not speak, they merely watched him and moved slightly apart; Zoe stayed behind Spiros. A man less truculent than Baruch would have recognized his danger; even a Baruch less drunk and upset would have backed off. But all he chose to see was a man with one hand and another with one eye.

"Are these your pimps?" he asked still sneering, "Your protectors."

At that point most men would have asked Baruch to leave and then escorted him out the front door. But these were two warriors, in no mood to be insulted by an insect like Baruch. Neither was afraid of a fight; in fact fighting was one of Linus' favorite pastimes. They closed on him.

Baruch struck first, hitting at Linus. The big man easily avoided the blow and struck back with a powerful right to Baruch's nose.

"You had better get back to the women's place," advised Spiros casually taking her by an elbow and pushing her past the flailing Baruch. She ran into the andron past Adem who was coming out of his bed chambers where he had been relaxing with his wife. She noticed he was carrying his sword. He looked like he knew how to use it now. Zoe fled into the gynaeconitis where Agalia was wringing her hands. Zoe threw the new bar shut on the door behind her thinking that they now needed a bar on the other door as well. She wondered what Adem would do with that sword.

Adem didn't need to do anything with his sword—it wasn't needed. After being rebuffed twice by Linus, an enraged Baruch turned on Spiros, only to be thrown aside with contemptuous ease. A man makes mistakes all his life; some are greater than others. Baruch now made a very big one. If he had not been drunk, if he had not been so infuriated, if he had thought for just a moment, he would have almost certainly decided that when faced by two large and hardened veterans it was a 'bad idea' to pull a knife and attack them. Unfortunately for him, that is just what Baruch did. He did not even use a particularly good blade. Even worse, he waved the little blade around for his opponents to see before clumsily thrusting at Linus.

Linus blocked the strike with his left stump and pulled his own dagger from its sheath and stabbed Baruch expertly through his ribs. At the same instant Spiros took one of the stools they had been sitting on and slammed it down on Baruch's head with killing force. Baruch dropped to the floor, flopped once, and was still. Adem, watching this from the door of the andron, decided he did not know as much about fighting as he thought.

The three men gathered around the corpse. Despite two ghastly wounds there was relatively little blood.

"Probably dead before he hit the ground," judged Spiros professionally.

"Yeah," agreed Linus, "Let's haul him outside before he makes any more mess and upsets the women."

Adem was not sure if Linus was referring to the corpse upsetting the women or the mess.

The two comrades picked up what had once been Baruch and hauled his corpse outside. They threw it to one side.

"Should be good there for now," decided Linus casually. "I will tell the watch and let them take care of it. Is Agalia ready yet?"

Adem decided there was a lot about killing he didn't know either, and he was not sure he wanted to know.

Of course things were not as easy as Linus supposed. Ana went back to break the news to Zoe. The guard had heard of a disturbance, and two men showed up within a quarter hour. The body was hauled away. A stricken Zoe was comforted, given a strong draft, and put to bed in her cell with Lux. Eventually Agalia did go out with Linus and actually enjoyed herself, being escorted as she was by the center of attention. Nobody seemed to think much of the passing of Baruch; no one, that is except for Zoe who cried herself to sleep.

Baruch was buried the next day. There was no real ceremony. He was a stranger, and not a well-liked one. Adem paid to have his body hauled to the town burial ground and had a proper grave dug. There was no prothesis or real ekphora, but Zoe did promise herself she would put a stele for his grave. It was a grim little group, just Zoe, Agalia, Ana and Adem. In truth the others were only there to support Zoe. After the body had been interred, they all returned for a somber meal at the house. Zoe asked for some time alone. She and Lux went into her little cell and closed the door. Amphora's long delayed business dealings began to intrude, sweeping the rest of the house back into the world of the living.

Zoe was much better the following day. She could not explain her grief; she had not known Baruch for long, and frankly he was not that good of a husband. He had decided to move out of her life; he had in fact become an actual threat to her and the people she had come to care about. Still, she honored how she felt, even if she could not explain it.

She received the expected summons to the Magistrate with dread, not because of any fear of sanctions, but because she was not sure she could face Rodas just yet, and the whole business of becoming a widow, a real widow this time, was still too raw.

Ana made sure Zoe went to the baths and was properly dressed, this time wearing her very best chiton instead of her 'court clothes'. All of them, Zoe, Adem, Ana, Spiros, and Linus assembled in the Magistrate's hall. A somber Rodas came in to hear the case. Ana told how she found Baruch, uninvited, in her kitchen threatening Zoe and how she had ordered him out of the house. Spiros and Linus described how later 'Miss Zoe' came running to them for protection with a raging Baruch close behind. How he had attacked them, first with his hands, then with a knife and the inevitable fatal result. Adem witnessed that Baruch had attacked the other two with a knife and they were only defending themselves. Zoe stood through all this with her head bowed, hands held together in front. She appeared distant from the proceedings. There was the sense of people just going through the motions for the sake of appearances. All that changed when Rodas finally turned and spoke to Zoe.

Rodas was normally a calm and good-natured man. Now, however, he turned red in the face and began to perspire.

"So, Zoe," he began with a patently false good humor. "We meet again."

"Yes, lord," she replied quietly in a very un-Zoe like attitude, head still bowed.

"How many times have you been before me now?"

"Four my lord," Zoe was still addressing the floor.

"Five if you count your first appeal to get rid of Peder," Rodas corrected. "Well, this case is clearly one of self defense."

If he thought to put her mind at ease, she gave no sign. Rodas looked uncomfortable but continued on doggedly with what sounded like a prepared speech. "Well, Zoe, you have been keeping my court so busy that I have had to give the matter some thought. I mean just how can I protect our little community from such a mischief-maker?" This might have gone over better if they had not just been adjudicating the death of her late husband. Zoe looked up from the floor, her head tilted sideways a little, a spark of curiosity showing in her eyes. Seeing this Rodas took heart and continued on, speaking just to her, though everyone in the room was now listening with rapt attention.

"So, Zoe, I am going to have to put you under my personal protection for the rest of your life."

"What?" asked Zoe completely puzzled.

"I want you to come live with me."

Zoe just looked at him.

"Marry me Zoe."

"What!?" The same word had very different meanings; incomprehension, and incredulity.

"I want you to be my pallake," explained Rodas. He seemed more confidence now that the offer was out there.

"I buried my husband yesterday," Zoe said.

"He left you a long time ago, Zoe," Rodas said gently. "You have been a 'probably respectable widow' since the first time I met you."

Zoe's brown eyes were huge in her staring face. At that moment Rodas thought she was the most desirable woman he had ever seen. He was so glad he had acted quickly. A woman like this would not be a widow for long.

Then Zoe spoke, "I," she hesitated for a moment, "I will have to ask my family," and with that she spun around, hitched up the hem of her chiton and withdrew abruptly, nearly running by the time she reached the door. She left complete astonishment in her wake. It was a wonder that the fly buzzing around the room did not fly into any of the open mouths of the observers.

Ana was the first to recover enough to speak. "I am sorry, my lord, she has been through a lot these past few days. Your offer just overwhelmed her. I will talk to her. We will get her answer back to you in just a few moments. She is young, remember, and has been through a great deal. She just didn't understand. I am sure when she comes to her senses she will come to appreciate your generous offer. I will go to her. We will be back soon, I promise you." And continuing to babble on, she led the other members of Amphora's astonished household away from the Magistrate before he fully grasped what had just happened.

Small towns thrive on gossip, and this news was exceptionally juicy. It echoed back and forth in the town moving with astonishing speed. Even before Adem's people had returned to their house, they were being asked questions.

'Was it true that the Magistrate had proposed marriage to Zoe? Had she rejected him?' The wildest stories took flight. Zoe's husband had tried to kill her, and the Magistrate had saved her. No, Rodas had sent his killers to get rid of his lover's inconvenient husband. No, Zoe had murdered the man and then tried to get the Magistrate to marry her. It was a wonderful story. To the credit of the people of that little town, in a short time the truth came to be generally accepted—Zoe's worthless husband had returned and attacked her. Linus and Spiros (two men held in high regard in the community) had been in the house and managed to save her. The Magistrate taking pity on the girl had offered to make her his legal pallake. And she had refused him! That story alone was wonderful enough to suit most.

Ana found Zoe up on the roof, clutching Lux. She had been weeping. Zoe thought she had been doing rather too much of that lately, but then **things** had been rather too much for her lately.

Ana came up and sat down next to her, their backs to the roof's high coping.

"I can't marry him," Zoe began, then stopped.

"Well," said the older woman briskly, "let's see. This man who just asked for your hand has a good reputation, he is unmarried, has a good sense of humor, he's rich, powerful, and to my eyes very good looking. Zoe, don't you think you are setting your standards just a little high?"

It was a joke, of course, and Zoe laughed ruefully. She needed to laugh, or she would start crying again.

"It's all too much," Zoe tried to explain. "Yes, he is a good man. And I like him." Here she stopped hopelessly.

"Well," continued Ana still trying to get Zoe to smile, "the King is still unmarried. I guess you could set your sights on him." It was not the words so much as the tone that made Zoe smile.

"It's just that I don't think I would be a good wife for the Magistrate. I mean, what do I offer him?"

"I can think of one thing," said Ana smiling at the other woman.

"Oh, stop," Zoe swatted at the older woman. "I am serious. I have no family, not here anyway, no dowry, no connections."

"He doesn't need those things," countered Ana. "What he needs is a good wife to run up his home, meet his guests and give him children."

"A pallake would not be the kind of wife a man like the Magistrate deserves," objected Zoe. "After a time he would regret marrying below himself. I would wind up just being like those dancing girls he inspects. I think that is all he wants. Maybe he feels sorry for me, but I don't think he would be happy with me as a real wife. That is want he needs, a real wife. That is what he deserves, a woman of proper station."

The two women talked up on the roof for a long time. Ana made no real headway, though, other than to make Zoe feel better. After a time Agalia come up, and the talk turned to pleasant inconsequential things. Ana, properly relieved of her post, came downstairs. She did not notice a man who was listening at the foot of the wall. People tend not to notice Mouse. After a time he quietly left and went up to talk to the King.

"So, she turned you down," Athan said pouring Rodas a cup of wine. The two men were in Athan's quarters in the Hold. Athan had sent for his friend as soon as he heard the news. They spoke primarily of business matters initially but it was not long before the old friends got around to person business.

"Not actually," responded Rodas to Athan's question about Zoe's response to his proposal, "she said she would have to speak with her family, whatever that means."

"I understand she has a mother in Bardhyllus. Is she going there? Or does she mean Amphora and his wife? After all, they have been her family here."

"This is a woman we are talking about Athan," responded Rodas heavily. "It is impossible to know."

The two men sat for a time. Athan tried again. "Well, I approve of your choice. She seems intelligent and a girl with real spirit."

"She can be a handful," acknowledged Rodas.

"Two handfuls if my memory serves," joked Athan cupping his hands in front of his own flat chest. The men smiled at the old joke but it was an effort on the part of Rodas.

Athan plowed on, "I do think you have chosen wisely. She has an excellent reputation. And I am sure she will give you a houseful of heirs. That body of hers is perfect for making babies."

"The worst thing is that I can't get her out of my mind," confessed Rodas. "I have had scores of women, and forgot most of them by the next day. Zoe is the only one who has really gotten into my head. You should have seen her at the symposium. I keep thinking about how proud I would be for her to be my wife. I don't know why she won't have me. I really thought that she liked me. I just don't understand it."

"And she will be your wife, my friend," said Athan getting to his feet to escort Rodas out. "Never fear; I am sure she will come around. What woman could resist a handsome fellow like you?"

Some time after Rodas left, Athan received another familiar visitor. This time the Mouse had an unusual report, one that left Athan smiling and thinking hard. After a time the King called in Balasi and began asking him technical and legal questions. By the time the King retired for the evening, he was smiling.

The King's guards came for Zoe in the morning. She wasn't at the house when they came for her. She had gotten up early; or rather she had risen as soon as darkness began to lift, for she had slept little that night. She was the first one at the well and had completed all her chores long before.

"Where is she?" asked Nomiki. It was an imposing group of three men including the king's personal shield bearer, all formally dressed and wearing swords and armor.

No one knew. She had asked Ana for some time alone and had left the house not long before.

"She might be at that little temple to Aphrodite," guessed Agalia. "She has been praying there a lot lately."

Agalia offered to show them but the men said they knew were to find it. Agalia and Ana tagged along behind them. Sure enough, they could see Zoe praying before the little shrine. Agalia darted ahead of the others. She knelt down before her friend and spoke in her ear.

"There are some men here to see you," she whispered.

"Please tell them I am not in the mood to see the Magistrate today," she replied without looking up.

"They are not from the Magistrate," Agalia told her nervously. That got Zoe's attention. She looked at Agalia and then tried to peer around her to the men waiting. "They are from the King," Agalia finished.

Zoe closed her eyes. Whatever this was, she was certain it was not a good thing. "You have a strange way of answering my prayers, oh my goddess," she murmured as she rose to her feet.

They did not even give her a chance to change, so the first time Zoe was formally presented to the King she was barefooted and wearing her working clothes, basically an old tunic, worn long, almost to her ankles. Her hair, though clean, was worn simply over her shoulders, reaching halfway down her back. She had on not a speck of makeup and after her long night, she could have used some. She tried to forget that when she was ushered into the King's office. The first thing she thought was that, for a King, he didn't have a very impressive place. She expected something imposing, like Rodas' hall. Instead she was in a rather small set of rooms inside the fort. At a second look she recognized that the carpets were very fine, and there were some excellent hangings on the wall. The furniture was polished wood and of the best quality. The King himself was seated behind a desk waiting for her. Again, Zoe thought he looked more like a sergeant of the watch than a king. He was dressed simply in an armless tunic without headgear or jewelry of any kind except for a chain around this neck that led to something under the front of his tunic. So this was going to be an informal visit. Good. If he had intended to banish her or something, Zoe was pretty sure he would have dressed up for the occasion.

"Sit down Zoe," he said indicating a low couch against the wall. She complied. Three men had accompanied her into the room and sat on couches next to the door. There was Nomiki, and two men introduced to her as Balasi, the King's secretary, and Abacus, the King's treasurer. She had heard of them and even seen them in town; now she was introduced to them. Zoe would normally have been embarrassed at her appearance but the whole interview was so strange that instead of embarrassment or concern she found herself mostly very, very curious.

"I understand that Rodas asked you to be his wife last evening," began Athan looking a bit uncomfortable.

Zoe should have expected this. "Yes, sire."

"And that you indicated you needed to consult your family."

"Yes, sire."

"I see. Is it safe to say that you wished to consider the matter rather than accepting without giving the matter careful thought?"

Zoe looked at the three men sitting against the wall and then back at Athan.

Athan understood. "Gentlemen," he said using a term that indicated respectable men of some position, "please give us some privacy."

As they left and closed the door behind them, Zoe gave the King a grateful look.

Zoe tried to gather her thoughts and express herself to the King. This needed to be just right. But he spoke first.

"This is about Rodas' offer to you," he began. "Let me guess," he started, "Your objection is not about Rodas as a man."

"Oh, no," confirmed Zoe. "He is very nice, and quite handsome. But I am a poor widow, a very recent widow. I have no family here, no dowry, no status." She felt herself getting warm and hated the girlish blush that moved up her cheeks.

Athan smiled. "I assume you have concerns, over and above the turmoil of your late husband's unfortunate death."

'There was a delicate way of putting his murder,' thought Zoe.

"You are concerned that you would not be a suitable wife for such and important man," the King went on.

Zoe tried to interrupt but Athan kept on talking. "The state needs for Rodas to be married; married and with a family. After all, when I should die, Rodas will become king after me." Zoe had not known that. "Oh, yes," confirmed the King. "My son is dead, my daughters have no claim on this little throne of mine, and I do not plan to wed again."

Zoe's mind was whirling. 'The King had had children? They were lost? How old must they be? How did this happen?'

Athan kept on talking. "So it was a great joy to me when Rodas finally told me he had found a potential bride." Zoe's mouth dropped. She had no idea that Rodas had spoken of his intentions to anyone. She had assumed that it had been a spur of the moment whim. The

King kept talking. "Yes, I think he made a wise decision, too, though I suspect wisdom had little to do with it. I believe he was hit by one of the goddess of love's arrows. He seems completely besotted with you."

"Me?" squeaked Zoe. It seemed so surprising to have their relationship described that way. She had spent the majority of her time with him in the role of plaintiff.

"Yes, you. It is time for my magistrate to settle down and start producing some heirs. After all, his son might well become king here some day. So I appreciate your wisdom in hesitating before accepting his proposal. It is a very big decision; a very real matter of state."

Zoe felt a great upheaval. Part of her was glad that someone understood that this could not be just a casual marriage. There were really important matters here she had to consider beyond herself—far more than even she had known. Little Zoe would be completely out of her depth as a possible mother of a king. On the other hand, she would have been so proud to be Rodas' wife. She did like him and thought he was very handsome on top of the fact that he was such a rich and influential man. If she were his wife, she would be one of the leading ladies in the land. According to what the King had just said, someday Rodas might even be King Rodas one day. She had her chance last night. But the world was crashing down on her pleasant daydreams of being Queen Zoe. She was just plain old Zoe, a respectable widow; for real this time.

"I considered arranging a marriage for Rodas with a woman from some of the other rulers in the region; there is no end of marriageable ladies whose fathers are interested.

Zoe managed to murmur something that meant nothing.

"On the other hand, I don't really need any alliances strengthened."

'The King was certainly being long-winded about this,' Zoe thought.

"So I was in a bit of a quandary. I really need one of us, Rodas or me, to get married to a woman of suitable rank and produce eligible heirs. Since Rodas is in the mood, we need to move forward to get him a suitable wife, not a pallake, a proper wife."

'Why was he going into such excruciating detail?' she wondered. 'Zoe the poor widow would not do as a possible queen and mother of kings. She already knew that. Now would the King just shut up and let her go and be alone?'

The King kept on talking. "We need to establish a succession, and Rodas seems to be a safer choice than I. After all, I do seem to be the one who keeps getting into fights." In fact Athan had not even struck a blow in the recent campaign, but still, he had been considering what would happen if an unlucky arrow were to strike him in the throat, or if his horse rolled over on him on some remote hill. Not even his lucky vest would protect him from that. Everything he was telling Zoe had been on his mind for a while. It was not until last night when talking with his advisors that they had somehow come up with this new idea.

"So, Zoe, it comes down to this. We need to arrange for a suitable wife, preferably a rich princess, for Rodas and we need her fast."

Zoe nodded miserably.

"If we can't find a proper princess, we will just have to make one."

'What is he talking about?' wondered Zoe now completely confused.

"I understand your father is dead," commented the King.

"Uhhh, yes," stammered Zoe.

"Good. Then I will adopt you. I am assured it is not only legal but common in some places. As my adopted daughter you would have family here, me, plenty of status, and I can even provide an adequate dowry."

"What?" questioned Zoe not quite understanding, her head spinning.

"I will adopt you," said Athan slowly and patiently. "You will be my daughter which will technically make you a rich princess. Then you can marry Rodas."

Zoe was a brave and resilient young woman; but the events of the past few days where just too much for her. She fainted. Fortunately she was sitting down, so no harm was done.

Everything turned out to be much harder than Athan had presumed. Even the adoption turned out to be more difficult than Athan thought it would be. Iason was summoned to provide medical attention after Zoe's fainting spell. He taught her how to avoid future occurrences by sitting down and putting her head between her knees. Zoe found herself assuming this position on a regular basis over the next few days.

The adoption itself only required a royal fiat. It was written down in proper language, and two copies were made. One was read out in public places around the town. The other was delivered to the Magistrate who upon hearing the word hot-footed it up the hill for a rather intense private audience with his former colleague and present liege lord. The meeting was held behind closed doors and involved a great deal of shouting on Rodas' part. The 'princess' had been relocated to the 'Princess' Room' (hearing this caused Zoe to have to put her head between her knees again) which was just down from the King's chambers. The fact that it had been a room for visiting dignitaries did not help Zoe's feeling like she had just fallen off a cliff and was rushing down to an inevitable impact with the earth. She heard Rodas shouting but she could not make out the words. After he left, slamming the King's outer door, Athan visited her and reassured her that Rodas still intended to marry her and that there were only a few details to work out.

"He'll come around," he assured her with the smile of a man who has just thrown the highest possible throw of the dice. "I think that secretly he was pleased."

These were less reassuring words than Athan intended, and his new adopted daughter once again had to 'kiss her knees' until the blood would go all the way up to her brain again.

Athan proved to be correct. Before nightfall 'negotiations' had begun between the King of Dassaria and the Magistrate.

Athan had thought to wed the two the following day; this flew in the face of logistic complications and unified feminine resistance. This was going to be a Big Wedding, combined with a celebration of the recent victory over the hill brigands. Even with shortcuts and efficient planning it took almost a month to get ready.

Zoe spent the first night as minor royalty in her new chambers, but they were too warm for her comfort, so after a few days she chose to move back in with Adem and Ana. They were not sure how to treat her at first, indeed, she was not sure how to behave herself. After a day or so she decided to just be Zoe. This worked well.

Of course, she no longer did chores; she was not allowed to. Now that she had a 'royal allowance', she could afford to hire a girl as her servant. This also took a longer time than Zoe had expected. The first two were not satisfactory, but by the time she was wed she had engaged an older childless widow called Melitta who worked out very well. Zoe spent most of her days getting ready for the big event. There were clothes to have made, sandals to be fitted; Athan even let her pick out a half dozen pieces of jewelry from the old trove the Bear had maintained.

In another act that was becoming traditional around the Hold, she grew to dislike Abacus intensely. She did agree that the King was spending far too much on her, but Abacus treated her as though the games and feast for the entire town that followed the wedding were her idea—her big, fat, expensive idea.

Finally the big day came midway between the Corn Moon and the Harvest Moon. Zoe's mother and one of her sisters came to the event. They were not quite sure how their little Zoe had become a princess, but they were delighted with the catch she had made in Rodas. It was a great celebration: no fewer than six marriages were performed over the three-day event, including Linus and a radiant Agalia. Zoe overheard Abacus berating Athan many times about the cost; apparently all the festivities cost the kingdom almost a full talent. Zoe's new 'father' reminded the treasurer that he had recently brought back almost that much from his investments in Lychmidas, and he considered this marriage to be a good investment of another kind.

It certainly augured well for the little kingdom. For the next few years, the people of Dassaria were to have almost uninterrupted peace and prosperity. And no one was happier than Zoe. She fell in love first with her new husband and then with their many children.

'It was a good marriage,' thought the old man as he hiked along the little path that was heading down from the hills. 'She did turn out be a good wife and wonderful mother; that body was indeed made for babies. How many children did they have? Eight and all had survived to adulthood. It was hard to keep track because of all the other children Zoe took into her household. None of her children gave her more than the usual problem, with the exception of her last two, the twins. Those two girls had provided more excitement and turmoil than all the others combined. He chuckled to himself remembering some of their exploits. Yes, those girls had been just like the young Zoe.

The plan to let Rodas and Zoe's eldest child become the heir to Athan's throne had been a good one. They had done their part: they had produced four fine sons. Any one of them would have made a good king. There was only one problem: their children grew older, Athan did not. Had Athan died any time in the first ten or fifteen years of his reign, Zoe and Rodas' first son, Zale, would have become king after a period of regency by Rodas. Everyone would have accepted this. The idea of a strict patrilineal succession was not strong in that time and place. As time passed, Zale's claim on the throne became almost moot. Most of the ordinary people of Dassaria didn't give the idea of royal succession a moment's thought. This was because King Athan continued on, seeming to remain just the same as he had been when he first became King.

'Those had been good days,' thought Athan of the first years after Zoe had arrived. He continued on his walk out of the mountains down toward home. That is if he had a home any more. He had been gone a long time, and he had been neglecting his duties for a long time before he left. Athan had been a King long enough to understand that when a leader no longer leads, someone else will step in to act as the leader. If a man acts as leader long enough, then one day he forgets he is acting as leader and becomes that leader. One common characteristic of a strong leader is that he doesn't relinquish power willingly. There were always those considered how they could move up in the world, even it they weren't actively conspiring to seize his throne, they were very interested in increasing their own power. Athan had put that from his mind. His kingdom had had a distracted or absent king for the better part of a year. Even in a place as stable as Dassaria, that was a long time. He might return to his own kingdom and find it was no longer his.

So be it. He had taken his kingdom away from another man once, he could do it again. He doubted any usurper could be as fearsome as the Bear. On the other hand, he was in a vulnerable position he was without friends, food, or family, alone in the wilderness. Should he encounter even a single bandit in his weakened condition Athan doubted his ability to either defend himself or escape the threat. It was far from certain that he would even be able to walk out of these mountains alone without starving or perishing of exposure.

It did not matter. Athan would continue to do what had done his whole long life; he would take care of what needed to be done, one thing at a time. First he would get out of these hills, then he would regain his strength, and then he would return to his kingdom and assume the duties of the King of Dassaria again, no matter who or what tried to stop him.

Glossary

Definitions

Pallake – A kind of wife

Hetaira – A "she-comrade" another kind of wife, another kind of woman

Hoplites – A generic term for any organized infantryman

Hoplon – A heavy round shield typically carried by phalangists

Phalangists – Heavy infantry, normally in a tight formation

Hypaspists – Medium infantry, normally in looser supporting formations

Peltasts – Light infantry, mostly armed with missile weapons

Kopis – A heavy chopping sword with a convex blade

Pilleus –A felt or soft wool cap which rises to a forward curving point at its top

Strigil – a curved metal scraper used in the baths for cleaning skin

Katadesmoi – A lead 'cursing tablet' used by witches

Prothesis & Ekphora – Parts of a funeral similar to a viewing and the burial procession

Stele – A gravestone or memorial tablet

Chiton – A tunic with an over fold at the neck to create a flap. They could be worn by men but were usually favored by women

Himation – a wool blanket or cloak worn over the left shoulder

Andronitis – The men's hall, normally located in the front of a large formal house

Andron – The dining hall in a formal house, constructed in the southern style

Gynaeconitis – The women's hall in a formal house; a place where men must be invited

Weights and Measures –

All are rough approximations and are relative, often varying according to subjective conditions or local variations

Numbers – Counting was more casual with terms such a dozen (12) or a score (20) used instead of exact values. The larger the value, the less exact the number: a hundred may represent 95-105, a thousand anything between 900 to 1200

Medimnos – A measure of weight about 55 pounds

Talent – A measure of wealth, about 6,000 drachmae – a lot of loot

Parasang – A measure of distance. About 5.5 kilometers or 3 ½ miles

Cubit – A measure of distance. A bit less than half a meter or ~19 inches

Foot – The length of a man's foot. Roughly 10-12 inches

Pace – The length of a man's stride. About 2 feet or a bit more

Bowshot – A very rough estimate of length, about 50-75 meters

Time –

All are approximations and are relative, often varying according to subjective conditions

Month – A period of twenty eight days based on the moon

Hour – One twelfth of a day or a night, the length changing with the seasons

Moment – An indefinite but short period of time; less than a few hundred heartbeats

Heartbeat – A very relative measurement indicating an even shorter period of time (depending on how excited you are)

Organizations

Band – A group of armed men of varying size usually with no fixed allegiance

Guards – The soldiers who protect a city or kingdom from threats within and without

Ride - A patrol of about seven mounted warriors

Section – 10-20 Guards including an assigned sergeant

Squadron –Three Troops and a few more men led by a captain - about 100 men

Troop – Four rides plus a leader and sometimes a few more men - about 25-30 total men

Watch – A group of men of widely varying number assigned to work together for a specific task and limited time, usually involving sentinel or patrolling duties

Places

Illyria – A region of kingdoms, tribes, and cities north of Epirus and west of Macedonia consisting in part of the following:

> Dassaria – A kingdom for the taking west of Lake Lychnites
>
> Bardhyllus – A kingdom in Illyria on the western boundary of Dassaria
>
> Paeonia – The territory of loosely organized tribes to the north of Dassaria
>
> Dassaretae – A set of tribes and families south of Dassaria

Achaemenid Empire – A huge political entity in the Far East

Epiria – Athan's original hometown; a city-state, part of the region of Epirus

Epirus – A loosely bound confederation of a cities and towns all to the west of Doria and south of Illyria

Doria – A region of city states and tribes south and east of Epiria

Thrace – A political entity between Macedonia and the Empire

Macedonia – A mountainous kingdom north of Doria and well east of Dassaria

Paeonia – The territory of a roughly organized set of tribes north of Dassaria

Lychmidas – A city on Lake Lychnites; about four day's journey east of Dassaria

Lake Lychnites – A large lake surrounded by not much of anything but mountains

Printed in the United States
128891LV00001B/1/P